"Holy hell your girl can shift." Blair came up beside him. "I may have strained an eye when they popped out of my head, she was in mid-air when she did that."

Jesse grinned, "I can see you trying to jump and shift in mid-air now."

Blair snorted, "of course, I have to try it."

That was an image Jesse didn't need, one of Blair naked jumping into the air trying to shift on the run.

"How did the leopard know and none of us sensed it?" Calum came up to stand with them.

"We were all pretty close to the guns," Blair crossed his arms over his chest and looked down at the man, "no jackals in the Alliance?"

Calum shook his head.

"One of them that took Daisie was a jackal."

"Interesting." Calum looked at Jesse for a moment, "I guess we need to get Devin looking into where they hail from."

A sound from behind them had all three tense and glance. It was Noah dragging back a blanket and a pair of jeans.

Calum went over and picked up the blanket and tossed it at the man. "Get up." He picked up the jeans and looked at them, then threw them at Blair. "I guess you get to drag him back." Blair grinned, in an unpleasant way, "lucky me."

ANIMAL SENSES
1 *Heart*
2 *Scent*
3 *Passion*
4 *Courage*
5 *Solace*
Coming soon:

6 Faith
7 Spirit
8 Fury
9 Pride
10 Torment

MAGIC SEASONS ROMANCE
1 *Beltane Magic*
2 *Solstice Heat*
3 *Harvest Dreams*
4 *Autumn Dance*
5 *Winter Mist*

Dreams
Three steamy stories that started with a dream

Curses
Two tales of curses.

After the Silence

SINGLE TITLES
Solitary Witchling
Salvation
Café Serenity

Coming soon:
Outcasts

<u>**Writing As: J. Risk**</u>

REALMS BOOKS:

THE ALTEREALM SERIES
1 *The Huntress*
2 *The Seer*
3 *The Empath*
4 *The Witch*
5 *The Chronos*
6 *The Warrior*
7 *The Telepath*
8 *The Healer*
9 *The Kinetic*

THE SOLRELM SERIES
Coming soon:

Concealed

GEMINI LEAGUE
Coming soon

Dark Moon

Authors note /trigger warning:

In this book, one of my characters displays aspects of a mental health condition. While I did research and study the topic, and had others more intimately acquainted with this condition read through the book, I am in no way stating that my character is the definitive portrayal of a person with this condition. It is merely my interpretation and understanding of behaviors and traits that would, without being highly specific, suggestive of a person with this particular mental health condition/diagnosis. I attempted to avoid triggering readers with specific details and behaviors, keeping most as general as possible, but I have no way of knowing, for certain, that I was successful.

Please know that I do support those with (and those who care for) mental health issues and can only wish that the world realizes the seriousness of the struggles faced by those who live with these issues on a daily basis and seeks to do more to provide help and support to those dealing with the effects.

Jacqueline

SOLACE

Animal Senses Series Book 5

Jacqueline Paige

Published by Exordium Books (FRP)
Copyright © 2022 Roxane Kerr

Excerpts from *Faith Book 6* in the *Animal Senses Series* by Jacqueline Paige copyright ©2022 Roxane Kerr

ISBN: 978-1-990763-11-3

Chapter One

Jesse pulled the van in and looked at the path that led into the trees. It was so overgrown; he could barely make out the trail. There was no way he was driving on *that*. He groaned, which meant he was going to have to walk it. He was so tired of this back country-middle-of-hell's forest area—

"One more, then I'm hopping back over the border and going home." He mumbled as he put the van in park. It wasn't unusual for him to talk out loud to himself, he spent a lot of time on the road alone. Grabbing the phone, he sighed. If a forty percent complete house and a small trailer could be called home. He'd had every intention of finishing it and enjoying that beautiful space he'd bought near his clan—and the Tomas organization had ramped up their chaos in his world.

Opening his window, he snapped a picture of the unforgiving dense growth and typed out a message to Calum. He hadn't talked to him for a few days, so he figured he'd better get in touch, so the big man didn't send out a search party.

He read the message. *Lost in hell. Your kind of fun. After this one I'm coming back.* Nodding he hit send.

He should probably report to Devin too. Jesse liked that he

was dealing with him most of the time now instead of his father. Devin didn't care how much he swore, he didn't have to be political or be afraid of crossing some hierarchical rule. He had the greatest respect for the king of all shifters—but didn't envy the man's job.

His phone beeped. Opening the message from Calum he grinned. *Be careful not to hurt your delicate pads in the undergrowth.* No reply was needed for that, he decided.

He pulled the van in as far as he dared. Shutting it off, he leaned back and looked at himself in the mirror. He looked rough, and with good reason, he hadn't stopped to rest much in the past week. His hair had taken on a new style of its own, not that it lay down and behaved normally. His eyes were bloodshot, which only made the pale green look even paler. If he found this clan, they were going to take one look at him and pass on any offers of assistance because he looked like a wretch.

Getting out, he stretched. The amount of driving he'd been doing lately couldn't be good for a body. His cat ached to get out and run. Looking up the mountain, he debated on going for a quick run, then changed his mind. The last thing he needed was to run onto another clan's territory. Five years ago, he would have without much thought. Now, with everything he knew about the shifter world, not a chance.

Things were messed up. Really messed up. If he hadn't been with Devin and the others when they'd gone to find Calum, he never would have believed the bizarre events that had been going on. Bizarre was a nicer way of saying 'fucked up shit'. The fact that clans had lost touch with the Alliance over the years wasn't shocking. There hadn't always been internet and cellphones—but after the last few months, of looking for those clans he was ready to admit shit was getting real—and not in a good way. Entire clans were gone, without a trace and the only way that could happen was if Tomas had found them. Jesse thought of it as a failure on several levels, the Alliance and the clans themselves. He knew if it were his clan they would have packed up and gone to find the Alliance or even the next closest clan.

Opening the door, he looked in his cooler and found he only had two energy drinks. Should shifters drink these things? No. Most shifters didn't have to drive the entire length of provinces and states constantly either. Ducking his head, he checked out the 'trail' again. Yeah, he was drinking one of these. Grabbing it, he closed the cooler and took a long drink. Setting the can on top, he brought up his contact list on his phone and hit Devin's name.

"Jesse. Where are you now?"

He grinned, he *really* liked how Devin always got to the point quickly. "I'm at the last location on my list."

"Is anyone there?"

Leaning against the door, he twisted the can back and forth on top of the cooler. "I don't know yet, it's a long walk to get up there."

"Middle of a bush?"

Jesse nodded his head slowly, "yeah, on top of a mountain I'm guessing."

"I'm jealous," Devin said in a quiet tone.

"Don't be. I have to do it on two feet."

"Oh, well, not as envious now." He cleared his throat. "I talked to Dad about the last location."

Jesse gave the bottom of his jaw a vigorous rub. A shave was long overdue. "What was the decision?" His last stop had found a long-lost clan of lynx shifters, unfortunately, due to isolation and no communication the clan had more or less died off. There had been six almost geriatric shifters remaining.

"He's going to offer to move them to live among another lynx clan."

Jesse shrugged, "elder knowledge is always welcome."

"That's his take too."

"You know we need to start getting like clans together more or there's going to be a lot going extinct."

"Easier said than done with that Tomas lunatic lurking around every corner." There was a low growl in his voice.

Jesse understood why, Devin's mate had been engaged to Aiden Tomas, without ever knowing what he was all about. Then again at that point, she hadn't even known about shifters. He didn't know how that was possible when you were one, but this year had been enlightening in so for many, himself included.

"What kind are you looking for now?" Devin mumbled something, "I have so many papers on this desk now I can't find anything."

Jesse swallowed the laugh, not wanting to offend the future leader, who was still adjusting to going from being in hiding to the most active in the Alliance. "*My* kind." He grinned.

"That's good, I saw bears on the list," there were papers rustling, "wherever it is, and was worried if we should send like or at least similar-sized Alliance reps to look."

Jesse took another quick sip. "That's a thought." He'd never actually seen a bear shifter after they'd shifted and was sure he could go without ever having to, never mind walking into their area and saying 'hey, Alliance sent me, sorry we lost you' to a clan of much larger shifters than himself.

"How long do you figure you'll be?"

Picking up the can, he closed the door and walked to the front of the van. "Well, as long as this path leads to their area, and I don't have to go searching I should connect with them."

"Great. Dad wants you at Blair's when they're working on weapons training."

"Do we have definite locations now?" Jesse felt like he was out of the loop and that annoyed him. He'd seen the damage Aiden Tomas was doing to his kind and had vowed he would not stop until that organization was stopped.

"We have several. Including the location of Blair's brother."

"Oh shit," Jesse smirked. "I'll get back as soon as I can so we can start coming up with a plan. Is Calum sticking around Blair's for now?"

"Yeah, he's refusing to go anywhere until they figure out how Tomas' people got on the property and basically walked off."

"What?" He'd missed a lot in a few days. "Put a leash on him and Blair, until I get there."

Devin chuckled, "Blair is newly mated, so he's distracted enough."

"He's one brave SOB. Taking on a whole clan of women." Jesse set the drink on the hood of the van and went over and opened the door, reaching in he grabbed his run pack.

There were voices in the background. "Call me once you've found that clan's area and let me know what you find, and Jesse?"

"Yeah?"

"Try to find some that don't need canes, it will be easier for them to walk down the mountain."

Jesse sighed, "let's hope I do."

Devin hung up without notice. Looking at the phone, he checked for any messages. There was none, that was rare, but he'd take it. Stuffing the phone into his pack, he put it over his head and flipped it to his back so he wouldn't get hung up on any branches as he walked. He debated if he should grab the handgun under his seat and add it to the pack. Shrugging it off, he decided not. That was for moments when he couldn't shift and haul ass.

He realized he hadn't asked if a decision had been made about moving smaller clans. Half of the clan reps were for it though, and he agreed with them. Moving clans that were less than twenty to either another clan of the same likeness or closer to any clan would make security easier seemed like a solid plan. When he'd spoken to Zain earlier, inquiring about how the rest of the clan co-ordinating team were doing, the news hadn't been promising. Clans were disappearing and Jesse was willing to bet Tomas was responsible for all of it.

Downing the rest of the drink, he tossed the can in the van and closed the door. Inhaling slowly, he started up the rough trail. This was going to be a long walk.

Chapter Two

Tightening the cord, she checked the tension of the furs. "We'll be warm this year, Thera." Leah glanced at the leopard laying on the platform. She lifted her head an inch, looked back at her, and then lay back in the sunlight. "At least you don't try to eat them now." Going over, she bent down and rubbed her hand along the animal's soft coat. "Aunt Tillie would be so happy you've settled down." Blowing out a breath, she got back up. Her head was aching, the constant pressure that made it feel like something was squeezing it, but that was nothing new. If she managed to get all the potatoes dug up, maybe she'd go have a short nap. There wasn't much free time in the fall for taking long breaks.

She stopped halfway to the garden and rubbed the center of her forehead. "I'm fine. I need to do this before winter hits." Blowing out a breath, she concentrated on staying focused and here. There was so much to do before the cold weather hit. Leah looked around at the leaves, without Papa Low, she could only guess when that would be, she didn't have his intuition about the weather. Her mouth quirked with a smile, Nana Pearl would have laughed at that and said it wasn't intuition, but arthritis that told him when the cold was moving in.

Pausing beside the shed, she opened it to get out a pail and shovel. The potatoes were the last to come out, she'd gotten the other root vegetables stored for winter in the last few weeks. Brushing her hair back from her face, she watched Thera pace back and forth outside the garden area. If it weren't for her, she would be so lonely, so lost.

As she started down the path along the rows, Thera came bounding after her, cutting in front of her. "We don't have time for a run right now, girl." She smiled at the way the large cat stared at her. "Let me get them dug up first, then we'll go for a run and pick them up later." Thera walked over to the edge of the garden and sat down. Leah chuckled to herself quietly. "I'd ask you to help, but then they'd be all sliced up with those claws." Thera made a deep rasping meow noise. To a person that didn't know better, it may have sounded like a huge bullfrog, but Leah understood as if she'd used actual words. "Of course, you'd get your paws dirty."

Picking up the shovel, she moved over to the row. The garden had been good this year, which surprised her. It was the first year without Papa Low's secret fertilizer. She'd planted more than needed, but Papa Virgil had always said it was better to have too much than not enough.

"I could preserve half of it and make the trek to town and sell it at the market…" Like they used to do. Biting her lip, she shook her head. "I could do it." She nodded, "with a little help, but I could try it again." Sighing, she looked across to the other side of the fence. She missed Papa Low. The others too, but her grandfather and Aunt Tillie had been her absolute favorite people on earth.

Leah inhaled slowly. "Not that we know a lot of people." She murmured and then started to turn the soil carefully, keeping the shovel turned to the right angle to not slice open the fleshy roots under the soil.

"I miss people, Thera." She didn't bother to look at the cat, knowing she would hear her regardless of where she lay down. "I know, I know, I can't *handle* people." She paused and looked at the ground, not really seeing it. "They *are* terrifying, rude, pushy…" Minn didn't like it when people weren't nice to her. Blinking, she concentrated on the plant in front of her, bending down, she pulled it from the soil, shook it, and tossed it beside the row. "I could do it, get some other supplies," she whispered. She was running out of so much including paper and brushes. Aunt Tillie had shown her how to use plants and other items to make paints, but she couldn't find all the colors she'd like to have. Painting helped. Helped her stay grounded, stay present. "We could do it, together, go down the mountain."

Evanna had always protected her. Always kept her safe, even before Minn was around. Her heart accelerated, causing her to catch her breath. Pausing she looked at Thera, "I'll think about it some more." Even though she'd said it aloud, she knew already that there wouldn't be a trip down the mountain, there wouldn't be new brushes and crisp paper. She couldn't even control her panic at the thought of doing it, so there was no way Minn or Evanna would let her load up preserves and trek down there and out of their safe place.

She had to get her emotions back under control or she'd lose it and have one of those moments that left her feeling like she'd failed again. It had been better for the last few months, and she wanted to keep it that way. She didn't like when she receded so far into her mind that when she came back there was no clarity on what had happened. According to her journal, Evanna hadn't had to take over for a month now, at least there were no gaps, so she could only assume she hadn't been here.

Thera got up and came over and rubbed up against her. She offered her a quick look, "I'm fine, we've got this."

Chapter Three

Jesse had to fight the whole way to stay on two legs, the scents around him had his cat stirring and wanting nothing more than to explore the area. Pausing he looked around, how long had he been walking? He hadn't checked the time when he started, but it was beginning to feel like forever. He wasn't out of shape, but normally covering this kind of terrain was done in his cat form. Inhaling again, he checked for any scent that would let him know he was going in the right direction.

If he found another empty, deserted clan space, he wasn't sure what he was going to do. This one felt different, maybe he was feeling torn because this clan was the same as his own, he couldn't be sure. Frowning, he lifted his chin and inhaled again—there was a hint of something that was not made by nature. A metallic taste hit his tongue. Definitely not natural. Blowing out a quick breath, he followed the direction he was facing to see if he could ferret out the source of the processed metal he was picking up. It took him some time to be able to narrow down the smell and keep going in the right direction. He blamed the energy drink, it messed with most of his senses, but he needed the extra boost. If he'd been near a populated area, he wouldn't have bothered, but up here, metal had no place.

Stopping, he looked to his left, then right. *Metal?* Inhaling slowly, he took a few steps to his right and then looked down as he processed to make sure it was getting stronger. There were groves in the ground. Tilting his head, he followed them slowly. He was almost right on top of it before he saw it through the very well-built shelter. Going closer, he looked it over, the branches looked like they were still trees. Moving along the side of it, he pulled one of the larger limbs and the wall of leaves moved. He stood there with his mouth hanging open. Behind it was an old pickup truck. Moving in between the wall and truck, he looked inside it. Judging by the amount of dust in it and on it, this thing hadn't moved in a few years, at least.

Going back out, he pushed the wall back in place. That was an encouraging sign, sort of. The fact there was a truck up here—he looked back down the trail he'd walked up—however insane anyone would have to be to drive *that*, it was the first sign he'd had that someone might still live up here. His stomach churning was because it hadn't been moved in a long time.

Jesse's cat rubbed against him again, he wanted out. "Soon, if we don't find something, we'll speed up the search." He couldn't take the chance of crossing onto another clan's territory and being unable to speak.

Listening he looked around, there was a slight noise that was familiar, but not enough to pinpoint where it was. It sounded like paws hitting the earth. Some sort of metal again was nearby as well, not the same as an automobile, but man-made for certain. He checked the ground often and hadn't found any more signs of old tracks from the truck. Turning, he decided it was because he'd headed into the thicker treed area and there was no car made that could fit through here.

The sound echoed in his sensitive ears again, he picked up

the pace, determined he was getting some answers this time.

He cleared the thick vine growth, and almost walked into it as he examined the scratch along his arm. Stopping abruptly, his face was inches from a tall chain-link fence. Leaning back, he checked to his left, then did the same in the other direction. It went on as far as he could see.

As signs went, this was a damn good one that people had been living up here. It wasn't new fencing by any means, but it was a fence. His muscles tensed, was it to keep people in or out, that was the question. After what they'd found at Shaelan's, his worst nightmare was to find more clans that were living under that sort of condition.

Shaking it off, he started following the fence, leading back in the direction where he'd gone off the old trail. Maybe the fence was to keep people outside the shifter world out of their area. He shrugged; hunters could be an issue. It wouldn't be the first time a clan had that problem. He'd know, his own had to install camera systems to warn them of hunters in the area.

Stopping, he squatted down to give his legs a break and opened his pack to check his phone. Jesse's cat jolted inside of him, alerting him to the fact they weren't alone. Crouching down lower, he checked behind him and scented the air. There was nothing out of place there. Moving closer to the fence, into the vegetation so it would hide him. Inhaling, he checked the odors around him. His cat was right, he was picking up two different signatures that weren't the metal fence or plant life. They were the scents of animals.

Slowing his breathing, he listened. The sound registered at the same time two cats came into sight. Two leopards. He smiled, but it was short-lived when he noticed they were nothing alike. Shades and the blend of rosettes varied, he knew this, no two in his clan were the same, but the body types were always the same. The one was so dark; it was closer to orange than the golden color he knew leopard shifters to be. Its eyes, the glance he got of them were more yellow than grey as well. He frowned and watched as they came up beside each other. The tail was much longer, body smaller—had two clans joined together to further their numbers? It wasn't common, but it had happened before. The paler cat stopped and looked right to where he was. He held his breath. The cat gave a low grunt, and both took off back into the thick of the trees.

Standing up, he blew out a breath. Well, at least there were leopards here, that was encouraging. Touching the fence, he frowned again. Why they were fenced in he still didn't know. Closing his pack, he got up and started jogging along the fence line. There had to be a gate somewhere along here. Hopefully, when he found it, he would be able to see people, talk to them, and let them know that the Alliance was here to help.

A short while later he found the gate. It wasn't bolted shut as he'd imagined it would be. He looked in between the wire links; it also wasn't guarded. Searching the area he could see, he frowned, he didn't see any sign of life.

Rolling his shoulders, he opened the gate slowly and winced as it creaked a high-pitched noise that made the hair on the back of his neck stand up. That would work for announcing his presence as nothing else could. A sound at that pitch would be heard by any shifter in the area. Maybe it was like that on purpose.

As he closed the gate, another thought came to mind, maybe the gate was to keep younger shifters from getting lost. This area was very overgrown, it wouldn't be hard to get turned around. He stood there looking around, listening, he didn't hear a sound that wasn't part of nature. His cat was tense, to say the least as he coiled inside him waiting. Inhaling slowly, Jesse felt a small amount of relief when he picked up the scents of something that had recently been cooked. There was no mistaking that smoky smell from a wood stove.

With slow, silent steps, he moved in the direction of the five buildings he could see. They weren't run down or abandoned from the look of them, also a good sign. Maybe the clan was out on a run or a hunt. Fall was here, so preparing for the winter made sense. Stopping, he looked over to the far side, it was a large garden. Again, another good sign. The scent of freshly turned soil was reassuring, it had been worked in recently.

Chapter Four

Alert was the only way to describe the feelings his cat was conveying right now as he walked along the perimeter of the fence. He didn't want to stand in the middle of the common area in the center, that was leaving him too vulnerable. Opening the gate and coming in without an invitation better not come back to bite him.

If his anxious cat wasn't bad enough, his skin prickled when he walked further along the fence and saw what was on the other side of it. Old half torn-down homes and a graveyard, one that was cared for regularly. *That* was something you didn't see with shifters.

Turning away from the sad sight, he studied the largest building in the middle of four smaller homes and headed for it with quick steps. Hopefully, this would be resolved by simply knocking on the door and having someone answer it.

When he was ten feet from it a woman came around the corner. She had what appeared to be an old tablecloth slung over her shoulder and was wearing it like a toga wrap. Had she been one of the cats he'd seen? She was lovely, despite her manner of dress, dark hair, deep brown eyes, and flawless sun-darkened skin—and to his delight was nowhere close to being geriatric.

His cat was suddenly still. "Hi, I'm..." he trailed off when she raised a large, handcrafted spear and pointed it at him.

The dark-colored cat he'd seen in the bush stepped around her and stood to her side, crouched, ears back and teeth bared. "Uh—my name is Jesse." He tried to keep his voice steady, calm, "I'm, um, with the Shifter Alliance."

She lowered the spear to point more at the ground than him. "You came."

She said it so softly that he barely heard it. He glanced to the cat still waiting to pounce and decided standing here was would be close enough. He inhaled subtly, trying to scent the cat.

"Nana Pearl said you would." Her voice was shaking.

Jesse straightened as the smell processed in his brain. The cat daring him to make one wrong move was not a shifter, but a very real, very wild kind of cat. "Is ah," he glanced at the house, "she here?"

The woman nodded her head briefly, then pointed.

Jesse followed the direction she pointed. It was the graveyard. "I'm so sorry." He turned back to her. "Are you alone here?"

She shook her head, "no—we, I..." She continued to stand there looking at the ground like she was trying to figure out what to say. She closed her eyes and gave her head a slight shake, "I'm sorry," she offered what may have been a smile, then glanced over his shoulder.

Jesse jolted and turned to look behind him. No one was there. He checked the rest of the yard to be sure. Looking back at her, he was surprised the spear was leaning against the wall as she pulled her hair back into a tight ponytail, all while giving him a very thorough appraisal. The cat, the real one was now sitting beside her looking all chill. *What the hell?* His animal was calmer, watchful. What the hell was happening?

"So, you're from the Alliance?"

Gone was her soft tone, he had no problem hearing her now. "Yes. I was sent to check on your clan because there has been no contact for," he shrugged a shoulder, "some time."

She chortled. "Good reason for *that*," she pointed to the wires hanging from a pole that was tilted at a sixty-five-degree angle. "Phones haven't worked in years." She put her hand down to rest on the cat's head, "we haven't had power for over a year now."

"We?" He glanced around quickly but saw no movement anywhere.

"Leah, Thera, Minn, and I."

She'd looked at the cat when she'd said Thera. "Thera is…"

"The real cat, yes she is." She squatted down and rubbed her hand along the cat's shoulder and neck. "Leah *had* to rescue her. She was underfed, her pen was small and filthy…"

They'd stolen a real leopard from some wildlife facility. "I've never seen her species before." His guts were in a knot and he didn't know why. There was something off about this situation. Not dangerous or his cat would sound the alarm, but something wasn't quite right here.

"You wouldn't," she stood up, "she's from Africa or," she motioned in the air, "somewhere near there." She looked down at the cloth covering her and jerked it around as if she was annoyed with it. "Are you here to check up on us or to move us? Why are you here now?" She held his look without hesitation.

"That's up to you, if you want to leave, I can take you somewhere with more of our kind."

She inhaled slowly, then smirked, "I wasn't sure if you were the same as us or not. I knew you weren't a normal man, but I haven't had—what's your name?"

Jesse quirked an eyebrow at her, but kept his thoughts to himself, "Jesse…"

"I'm going to get dressed, Jesse, feel free to hang out with Thera until I come back out." She went up the stairs and, in the door, before he could comment.

Jesse tucked his hands in his pockets and looked at the leopard in front of him, "Thera, huh?" She continued to look at him without blinking. That couldn't be good. "So is Leah around?" Not wanting to startle the animal with any movement, he looked, with just his eyes to see if he could see anyone else. "Or," what was the other name? "Minn, are they around?" The cat didn't move or look around. Jesse wanted to pet her but thought maybe he should wait until the woman came back out. He liked his hands—and all the other parts of his body still *on* his body. "Okay," he nodded to the cat, then motioned to the step, "is it okay if I sit down?" Her ears went back. "Or I could stand, that's works too."

When the animal turned to look at the door the woman had gone in, its whole demeanor changed. She was alert, crouched down again instead of sitting, her ears lay back flat, and then she turned those yellow eyes back to him.

Jesse's cat was tense again, ready to spring. The door of the building opened, Jesse turned to ask the woman her name, but it didn't seem to be her. It looked like her, but the movement was completely different. Why had his cat switched gears again? He had to wonder if Leah and the other one were twins, maybe? "Hi," he offered his best smile.

"Thera, be nice." She said softly and the cat immediately lay down. "I'm sorry about that, she doesn't know what to do with strangers." She smiled at him, still a little timid and frightened, but not like before.

His cat went crazy inside him. Not a bad crazy, just strange like he'd never known him to be, kind of weird. If he could see him, he was pretty sure he'd be rolling around like some kind of kitten.

"I'm Leah." She glanced around, "I'm not sure what to do." She clasped her hands in front of her body, "we've never had company." She cleared her throat softly, "I-I could make tea?"

She looked over her shoulder to the inside, he figured she was looking at someone, but he heard no movement. "Tea would be great." He smiled when she turned to look at him.

A look of relief appeared on her face. "Okay," she nodded, a breathtaking smile on her face now, "I will make us tea and we can," she glanced at Thera, "talk?"

Jesse nodded, worried if he said the wrong thing that one of two things would happen, Thera might take offense or Leah would revert to the woman that he'd first seen and stab him. He didn't know why it bothered him this much that she'd been afraid, close to terrified of him when she stood there shaking and pointing a spear at him, but he didn't want her to feel that way.

Stepping back, she opened the door wider. "Do we sit inside? Or-or out here on the deck?"

"Inside is fine." He grinned and tilted his head to the side, "the walk up here was," he glanced behind him, still feeling like someone might walk up behind him, "a long one."

Her smile widened, "okay, then yes, please come in and sit down."

As he moved by her, he noted the hesitant look in her eyes, she was inviting him in, but still wasn't sure if she should be. Hopefully, the other woman inside would put her at ease, Jesse had a soft spot for timid women. Calum told him it was a weakness, but Jesse had noticed over the past few years that Cal exactly immune to helping them either. Jesse found strong women appealing too, not Aunt Mari kind of strong, but those that had strength they didn't know they had. That made him think Cal was wrong and it was all women and not just vulnerable that were his weakness.

Jesse's cat was alert, but calm, which was weirding him out even more sitting inside the house. It was nicer than he'd thought it would be. At some point, this clan had regular contact with the outside world if the ornaments and décor were any indications.

Twice he'd watched Leah go over and crank a handle on the other side of the room. It took a few moments of contemplation to realize it was a power source of some kind. Which made sense when he realized the lights got a little brighter each time she did it.

Leah brought over a teapot, complete with one of those knitted things over it, and set it on the table. "I don't have milk." She said fearfully.

"That's fine. I drink it black." He assured her. A complete lie, but he didn't like the way she was shaking. It was fear causing it and he didn't know why. She was a shifter; she could just use her sense of smell and know he was no threat to her.

With a look of relief, she went over and took two cups out of the cupboard, pausing, she spun back and opened another door, and pulled out two small saucers.

He didn't know anyone that used saucers and china teacups, not since his grandmother had passed away. Jesse tried to give off vibes of being relaxed, even if he wasn't completely. He glanced at the closed door down the short hall and wondered if the other woman was in there.

Setting the cups down with a clattered, she clasped her hand in front of her. "I have biscuits."

He wasn't sure if it was a question or not. "That would be great." He smiled at her and was rewarded with a smile that made his cat rub against him. Clearing his throat, he pulled one of the cups closer. "That's quite the garden out there."

"Oh," she came over and set a basket on the table, "I love working in the garden." She pushed her thick dark auburn hair back from her face, "it's so satisfying and peaceful."

He watched her look down at the empty chair across from him, a look of indecision appearing on her face. He tried to think of something else to say to keep her at ease. "So, you rescued Thera?"

She gracefully dropped into the chair, her eyes were wide. "Yes. I had to." She said quickly as if she was defending her actions. "The cage they had her in was too small, she was so unhappy." She bit her lip, "we hid in the forest beside that *zoo* until everyone was gone." Clasping her hands in her lap, she sat forward further, not taking her eyes off him. "I don't understand why they'd have her and yet make it so she can't have babies. Why else would they want her?" Her brow furrowed. "Getting in was hard, but once we were in, we talked to her and got her out." Her mouth quirked into a small smirk, "Minn had to catch her and persuade her to follow us and not run off or she would end up right back there." Her shoulders dropped and she sat back, "Aunt Tillie screeched when we brought her back, but I like to think she grew to love her as much as I do before she passed."

Jesse wanted to ask about Minn but was afraid to confirm his suspicions. He couldn't be sure, but his gut told him that Minn was her cat. If not hers then another shifter could be stuck in that form. It was rare but did happen. He'd never given his cat a name because, well, *he* was his cat ,and his cat him.

Leah poured the tea and set the pot back down quickly.

Jesse picked up the cup and took a sip. It wasn't the tea he'd expected, and he'd been too distracted to smell the bitter herbs that made up the hot liquid. It wasn't bad, but it wasn't what he'd call tea. Shae would probably love it, was his next thought. Setting the cup down he watched her, she was holding the cup and staring off, like when you're in deep thought. His cat let him know it wasn't just her staring off into space. Rubbing inside him, his animal half was anxious and seemed to be pacing. "Are you all right?" He asked softly.

Setting the cup down, she rubbed the center of her forehead, then blinked slowly, "sorry, I'm just struggling right now." She offered him a quick smile, "I do want to stay but sometimes…" She closed her eyes and blew out a slow breath.

Jesse's cat went still. He leaned forward, not sure if he should get up and offer help or…

Leah opened her eyes, "I'm sorry about that." She grinned, "having a visitor is a bit much to cope with." Pulling her hair back, she secured it quickly with the thin cord that had been in her pocket.

Quirking one eyebrow up, he tried a shrug and probably failed. "That's fine." Her voice was different, not whispers, but calm and confident.

Looking down at the cup, she made a face and pushed it away. "I think I'll make a coffee." She got up, "Papa Low stocked us with enough beans that we won't run out for ten years." She chuckled.

Leaning back in the chair, feeling like he'd missed something major, he watched her in the kitchen area. There was no cautious movement, no second-guessing at all. She walked over to the crank on the generator and gave it several abrupt turns, not slow and steady like before, but with more power.

"Do you want to drink that?" She looked amused as she motioned to the cup in front of him on her way by. "We're low on sugar, but if you'd prefer a strong coffee, I'll make enough for two."

"Sure." Jesse felt like someone had smacked him, his head was churning out possibilities of what had happened in the last few moments. He sat silently as she ground the beans in a hand grinder and measured them out into an old metal percolator. Clearing his throat, he crossed his arms over his chest and tried to look more relaxed than he was feeling. His cat was driving him crazy shifting gears constantly. The woman in front of him changed almost as frequently. "When I found the fence on my way up, I saw two cats out for a run," she didn't pause as she checked the kettle for water and set it on the small wood stove in the corner. "One was obviously Thera…"

"Thera and Minn." She shrugged, "she's not out as much as she'd like to be, but Leah gives into her still all the time." She leaned back against the counter and crossed her arms over her chest. "If I'm closer I can control Minn more."

Jesse nodded his head slowly, that's what he thought. The cat was Minn. Out? Out from where? His mind churned, now he only had to figure out what she was talking about. Closer?

She looked at the table, then spun back to open one of the cupboards, pulling out a jar, she shrugged and then grabbed a knife from the container on the counter and turned. Moving with long strides, she was at the table and set the jar and knife down. "The biscuits are dry without it."

Jesse looked at the jar and surmised it was some sort of jam.

She rolled her eyes and looked up at the ceiling for a second then held out her hand, "I just realized I didn't introduce myself." She offered him a quick grin, "I'm Evanna."

Getting up, he took her hand, gave it a quick squeeze, then released it. He wasn't sure who was more shocked right now, his mind or his cat.

Chapter Five

"While you're making the coffee, I just need to step outside and send a message to someone, so they know I made it and I'm okay and that you're here." He pulled his phone out of his pack.

"Are there a lot of others? Like us?" Evanna leaned back against the counter and watched him, her head tilted to the side.

Jesse nodded, "yeah, there is a lot like us, different clan types, but there's a lot." He motioned to the door, "I'll be right back, I'm not getting a signal in here."

"That's a phone?" She was across the room and right in front of him before he could reply. Leaning over, she looked down at his phone. "That's," she snorted softly, "a bit amazing." Straightening, she held his look. "I guess we've missed a lot." There was a brief hurt look in her eyes. "It was safer to stay here." She nodded, then went back over to the other side of the table. "I'll make the coffee while you do that." Picking up the teacups, she went over to the counter.

Jesse blinked, then shook his head and went outside. Thera was laying by the door. She lifted her head and looked at him as if to say 'you're still here?' then dropped it back down.

Giving her a wide berth, just in case, he went down the steps and checked his phone.

He had to walk to the edge of the fence to find a signal. Opening his contacts, he stared at them, who was he messaging? Blowing out a breath, he brought up Calum, so far there had never been anything that he hadn't been able to find the answers to. He started typing, then erased it and typed, *Made it to the top. I think the only one here is a woman. And their pet.* That made no sense, but he didn't know how else to word it. He hit send, then looked around while he waited for Calum to reply. Sending a message like that ensured he would reply quickly if he wasn't in cat form.

Whoever had been left in this clan, they'd used wood and parts of the whole village to make this one small area to keep the remaining close and safe. The fence made sense now that he'd met Thera. He looked over at her, she looked like she was relaxed, but he could see her eyes were open and watching his every move.

His phone rang, he couldn't help but smile as he looked to see it was Calum. "Yeah?"

"Do you need a nap or something?"

Jesse rubbed his hand along his rough jaw. A shave soon would be good too. "No, well, probably, but I know what I sent you."

"Okay, and it means what exactly? You found the clan and there's just one woman left?"

"As far as I can tell." He turned back to look at the house he'd come out of.

"What does that mean?" Calum no longer sounded amused.

"I'm not sure, exactly. She talks about others like they're here, but I've only seen her," he blew out a breath, "okay, I first met someone else, but then she wasn't the same…"

"Do I need to talk to Dev about you getting some downtime?"

"No." Not that he wouldn't mind some time off, but they were finally getting closer to Tomas, so he wasn't stopping now. Thera stirred on the porch, "oh and she has a leopard."

"A real leopard?"

Jesse nodded and watched Thera stretch and then lay back down, still where she could see him. "Yes, Leah rescued her from somewhere."

"That's—" he could hear muffled voices; Calum must be telling someone else. "Jesse, Shae wants to speak to you."

"Okay."

"Hi, Jesse, how are you doing?"

Jesse shrugged, "I'm good. A little tired, but fine."

"Okay, Calum just wanted me to check on you." She sounded amused.

Jesse rolled his eyes, "Listen, while I have you on the phone, maybe you can help me make some sense out of this."

"I can try." There was no sound of amusement in her tone.

He didn't want to move around the yard, in case he lost signal. Crossing his arm over his chest, he leaned back against the fence. How did he even go about explaining what was more of just a feeling than anything else? "Okay," he nodded, "when I first introduced myself to her, she was scared and unsure, then," he frowned and looked at the ground, "she's completely different. Confident, kind of harder on the exterior—I don't know if this is making sense. She talks about others, but I've only seen her." He blew out a breath, "it's almost like she keeps changing in front of my eyes." He waited for her to laugh at him. "And she calls her cat Minn, at least I'm pretty sure it's her cat, it could be another shifter, but I don't scent them at all—I don't know any other shifter that has named their animal side."

"I see. I don't know a lot about things like this, but I can find out."

Jesse straightened from the fence, she believed him. "What…"

"You need to find out more about her situation, her past. I'll make a few calls and give you a call back in a few hours, is that okay?"

Jesse nodded his head quickly, "yeah, so find out more

about her or her clan?"

"The more information you can get the easier it will be for me to help."

"I'll do that." He glanced over when Thera stood up, "I want to get her and her leopard down from here."

"We'll talk more about that later, Jesse." She was using her healer voice now.

"Okay. The signal is sketchy here, so if you don't get me right away leave a message and I'll call back."

"All right." There were voices in the background, "Calum says to be careful."

Jesse nodded, "always am. Thanks, Shaelan."

"I'll talk to you soon."

Staring at the phone for a second, he tucked it back into his pack and did it up. Thera lifted her head and looked at him. She turned for a second and looked at the door. Shaking his head, he started back. Was he going to be having coffee with Evanna or tea with Leah when he went back in? As long as he didn't walk in to see Minn, he would be good, at least until he knew who Minn was. If it was another shifter, there had to be a reason they didn't let her out often.

The only thing he knew for certain at this point was he wasn't getting them off the mountain today. He looked at the other houses as he walked, something nagged at him and he knew it meant he probably wasn't going to be able to get Leah or Evanna or whoever to walk down the mountain and leave all this as it was. His cat was alert again, making the hair on the back of Jesse's neck stand on end. The next few days were going to be long ones.

Chapter Six

Evanna paced back over to the window and opened the curtain an inch so she could see him. She'd never been so shocked as she was when she'd opened her eyes to see him standing there in front of her. A man. Here. A real man. Not a bad one, either, she'd sensed that in the first minute of talking to him. There was something in his eyes that let you see to the bottom of his soul and he was good. His eyes were so pale they almost looked like they were looking right through her at first, it was startling, not in a bad way though.

He leaned back against the fence as he talked into the phone. She still couldn't believe that was a phone. When he glanced in her direction, she jumped back from the window.

"This is crazy." She mumbled as she went over to the other window and peeked out it. "Papa Low said if anyone from the Alliance came to trust them." She nodded. She did, but she wasn't sure how Leah was going to handle being around him. The first few attempts hadn't gone well. Men represented everything wrong in her past. She was not aware of all of it, but there was enough of it there that they freaked Leah out when they were around. Biting her lip, she peeked out again. She'd have to stay close and keep watch.

Moving away from the window she went over and quickly poured the water into the percolator. Leah had talked to him, that was something though. It was her job to protect Leah and keep her safe, so she was going to have to wait and see. She still didn't know if he was just checking in or planned to move them. He'd said it was their choice. Could Leah leave the mountain? They'd tried a few times in the last year, even gotten as far as the town once. That hadn't ended well. She frowned, still unhappy that they'd lost the purchases they'd gone down for.

Rubbing her hand over her forehead, she blew out a breath. "Stay close, just see how you feel." Evanna wanted off this mountain, not because of the isolation, she was fine with that part, but their supplies were limited now and the trip was too hard to take. Maybe the Alliance would bring them supplies from time to time if Leah couldn't leave.

She added more water to drip through. Aunt Tillie told her when the Alliance came to give them her journals, the ones she'd saved specifically for them. Evanna glanced at the window and then went over slowly. Should she give them to Jesse? Would that make a difference? Leaning on the ledge, she tapped her fingers on it. Would he be willing to stay for a few days? There was too much left to do before winter, and even more, if they were going down the mountain.

Her heart picked up as she watched him walk back this way. "Okay, Mister Jesse whoever with the intriguing eyes, I'll give you one chance to prove there are good people out there." She straightened away from the window. "One chance."

She opened the door when he reached it. "Coffee's ready." Leaving the door open, she walked back into the kitchen.

Pouring two mugs of the hot black liquid, she went over and set one in front of him. "Did you reach your friends?"

Jesse nodded. "I did. They're going to call back in a few hours, but they're happy I found you."

"Was it hard?" She sat down, "finding this place? Papa Low let the trail grow over on purpose."

"It was touch and go for a little while." He grinned, "Once I found the truck, I knew I was going in the right direction."

The truck. She frowned, she'd have to go down and put fresher growth around it. "There used to be more cars and trucks at the bottom, but Papa Virgil sold them off one by one," she shrugged, "with no one to drive them."

~

"The clan was big once?" He didn't remember the numbers he'd been told when he was sent this way.

"I suppose it was." She looked down at the table for a second, trying to keep the emotions locked up. "I've only been back for five years, so I don't remember what it was like before."

"Where were you before you came back?"

Her dark eyes flicked to the floor, then back to him for a second. "Can you stay for a few days?" She picked up the cup and blew on the liquid in it. "We have to figure out what to do."

He noted her ignoring his question and leaned on the table. "I can." He wasn't going anywhere until he got some answers. Jesse wondered for a second if he was going to like the answers, but that didn't change what he needed to know. He also knew he couldn't just turn around and walk back down that mountain and leave her up here. His cat was stirring again. At some point, Jesse was going to have to shift and go for a hard run, he'd never felt his cat change direction so often.

"Okay." She took a small sip, "you can stay at Aunt Tillie's." She glanced over her shoulder at a cupboard. "I'll find some clean sheets after the coffee and take you over."

It was the first time he'd seen a vulnerable expression in her eyes. "Thank you." He sipped the coffee and ignored how much it burned his mouth. "I've been sleeping in the van or hotels for the last few weeks, so somewhere without traffic noise and bright lights would be great."

Gone was the melancholy look, "you travel a lot?"

He nodded.

"What's that like? You've probably seen some amazing things."

His cat settled again at her tone. "I have, but it gets tiring."

"Are you traveling for the Alliance?" She looked genuinely interested. "Papa Low and Nana Pearl once met the prince, said he was a big man with a bigger heart."

Jesse paused in thought, the prince must be Dev's father before he was King. Jesse didn't know too much about the King before that, other than he was a hard man that didn't allow for excuses. "He's the King now." His mind was still stuck on where she had been if she'd only been back for five years.

"Really?" She smiled and looked up, "Papa Low would be happy with that. He liked the man and Papa Low didn't like too many." She chuckled.

Jesse nodded, "he is a big man, but kind." It was the truth, Shepard Addison was a kind man, just not a man you wanted to cross.

Thera yowled outside the door.

Evanna turned and looked at the door, tilting her head to the side for a second when the animal made another noise. "I'll get that bedding." She smiled, "seems like we're going to have rabbit for dinner today."

Jesse looked toward the door and wondered how she knew that by a few sounds from the animal. He'd never been close to a wild leopard before but wondered if over time it was easy to understand, like when other shifters were in their cat form.

He took a sip of the coffee and had to fight to not choke on it. She'd said strong, it was definitely strong.

She pulled out a sheet and a few blankets. "I keep the other homes stocked with wood, so you won't be cold." Grabbing a blanket, she put it on top of the sheet. "If you want to go out for a run, you'll have to put up with Thera going with you," she shrugged, "She watches over Minn when she runs too."

"That's fine." He cleared his throat and watched her drink down her coffee like it was water.

"Leah will make some food, I'm not very good at cooking…"

Jesse nodded, "I can give her a hand…"

Evanna paused after she picked up the bedding, "I don't know if that's a good idea. Leah isn't good around people."

"I won't invade her space if she doesn't want me there." He stood up.

Evanna eyed him up and down, "okay. Good." She started for the door, then paused and rubbed the center of her forehead, "let's go over to Aunt Tillie's." She opened the door, "we'll bring some water over after."

Chapter Seven

Aunt Tillie's house was small, but reminded Jesse of his grandmother's, with pillows, throw blankets, and porcelain figurines all over the main room. He only had to glance around to know that despite her relatives passing away, Evanna, or Leah still dusted and cleaned the place like they were going to return from a holiday.

"The bedroom is in there." Evanna pointed as she set the bedding down. "I'll be back after I've gotten dinner." She offered a smile, "Leah dug up the potatoes today, so we'll have fresh vegetables to go with it."

Jesse motioned to the door, "do you need a hand with that?" He shrugged, "I could…"

She waved her hand, "we got it." Evanna stood there for a moment longer, just looking at him. "Oh," she hurried past him and went over to a small cabinet on the other side of the room, "these," she pulled out two thick leather-bound books, "are Aunt Tillie's journals." She set them on the small table beside the chair. "She told us to give them to the Alliance when they came."

Jesse wondered if they would explain where the rest of the clan was. "Have you read them?"

Emotions he couldn't read flashed through her eyes, "some." She said quietly, "it's hard to read it, brings back…"

His cat suddenly demanded he put her at ease, "I'll take a look, thanks."

She looked relieved, "yeah, okay. I'll be out with Thera for a bit, but if you need anything just give a shout, we'll hear you." Her expression was haunted as she moved by him and quickly went out the door.

Jesse pulled his pack over his head and opened it. Pulling out his phone, he checked for a signal. One bar. He shrugged, it was better than none. Turning in a circle, he looked around, there were no photos or pictures anywhere. He wondered for a moment if maybe they'd been packed up because it was too painful to see them. He went over and looked into the bedroom. Just a bed and a small dresser were in it. The big building he'd been in before was probably the main gathering spot when there had been more of the clan left. It only made sense that it would have been the Alpha family's home.

Looking back at the thick journals he went over and opened the cover of the one on the top. On the inside of the cover, it had two dates, he could only surmise it was the period the entries were for.

Picking up the first one, he went over and sat in the chair that faced the window. As tired as he was, he doubted he'd get far in it, but he needed to know more about this clan, or more specifically where they went. Flipping the page, he was glad to see Aunt Tillie's handwriting was legible, if not near perfect. That told him the clan had been well educated up here and hadn't always been closed off from the rest of the world.

The first entry's date was almost twenty years ago.

Pearl says I need to write in this to help alleviate my loneliness. It's been a year now since my Sawyer passed and the wound is still too fresh I can barely breathe when I say his name. I don't know if writing in this is going to help anything, but at least once I'm gone there will be a piece of me left behind that people can read about.

Our Alpha came back with the men that went searching and still have no answers about where Bette, Naya and Zuri went to. It's like they vanished into thin air. It's very unnerving and has all of us edgy now. No one is allowed to go anywhere without one of the men with them.

Jesse looked up and out the window. Blowing out a breath he rubbed his eyes. Twenty years ago, women were vanishing. *Fuck.* This story was going to be one that was all too familiar. He watched Thera and—Minn? take off across the yard. Is that where Evanna had been? Had she been taken and found her way back?

Getting up, he grabbed his pack and pulled out the bottle of water and a protein bar, he needed to stay awake and try to get through as much of these journals as he could before Shaelan and Calum called back.

He'd offered to help with dinner when he saw Thera roaming the yard, from this far he wasn't sure if it had been Leah or Evanna that had answered him, but they told him to rest, *they* had it under control. Picking up the second journal, he sat down on the doorstep, where he hoped the fresh air would keep him awake longer.

The first journal had covered a lot of ground, he knew now that the clan had been thriving at one point, close to thirty members and they'd still been going to gatherings of like clans to keep the clan going with new mates brought in. Then, like he knew was coming after that opening paragraph in the start, members started disappearing.

He turned the page and read the next entry. It was short.

They searched the entire mountain and villages below. They are gone without a trace. I don't know how that is possible, but my heart is breaking right now. Belinda's Lyvia is gone and so are her girls, Ashtyn and Leah. Little Leah is only four years old. Two of the boys, I can't even think right now to write their names and three more of the older girls are gone too. It feels like some kind of nightmare.

I have to get back to the common house now, the men went back out to look and we'll be needing some hot meals when they get back. I just snuck over here to cry privately for a few moments.

Please let them all be okay.

He looked up and across the yard. She'd been taken when she was four? How had she made it back? He turned the page. *Now*, if he had to use toothpicks to keep his eyes open, he was going to finish this second one and get some answers.

He was about halfway through when Thera bound over to him. Looking up, he saw that Leah was standing outside the bigger building. He looked at the cat, "dinner I take it?" The cat made no motion telling him either way. Getting up, he closed the journal and set it inside the door on the chair. He wanted to finish it but also needed to eat and go for a run so his cat would stop being so annoying. The tension from his cat as he was reading was making Jesse's muscles ache.

Chapter Eight

He ran across the log and jumped down just as Thera came out of nowhere and cut him off. Damn, real cats were hell to keep up with. She was having a great time while he was working hard to not have her make him look like a fool. Despite that aspect of this run, he was loving it. It had been a long time since he'd been able to run like this, without looking over his shoulder. Tomas' people had no reason to come back looking here, as far as they knew they had all the members. All but the elders that were left behind.

Jesse had messaged Devin giving him a quick rundown after dinner, telling him that was probably what happened to the other clans. He hadn't gotten a reply, but if he knew Devin, he was out running off the frustration of it as well.

Calum had messaged telling him Shaelan would get back to him in the morning, she was still looking into things for him.

He slowed and debated on heading back, Leah looked really tired and said she was going to bed. It wasn't his place to worry, was it? She was clearly an adult and able to look after herself, so why was it bugging him so much?

Thera flew past him again. *Get out of your head and run.* He gave his cat more control and felt his legs moving faster.

Jesse watched the water drip through the metal screen into the pot below. He'd never made coffee this way but was thankful for it. He knew once he started reading that journal, he wouldn't stop until he was finished. Somewhere in there were more answers. Tillie noticed things and had written down what was on her mind. In the first one, she'd noted animals acting up in the bush and may not have seen the connection to when people had disappeared, but it was there. During the hard seasons of rain and snow, no one had gone missing—because Tomas' people couldn't navigate the mountain in that weather.

Pouring the coffee into a mug, he added a small shot of water to dilute it. He wasn't sure what type of beans these were but even the smell of them was a lot stronger than he was used to. Blowing on it, he took a sip and was happy with the result. Picking up the candle, he went over to the chair and set it down. Reading by candlelight was different, but he was determined to get through this journal tonight.

The next entry to read was not dated.

It's been five years now since the remaining clan left to find our missing members, we've given up hope of them coming back now. That was a hard thing to do. I couldn't write in here this past two years, I think my heart was broken. I doubt it will ever heal, but someone needs to record our lives just in case some of them someday find their way back.

We started tearing down the outer homes here, Virgil wants us all to live closer, to keep us safer I imagine. Belinda and I were in charge of going into them and setting aside anything important to store. I had to stop often because I was overwhelmed with the feelings of loss and melancholy for these people I grew up with, their children I watched grow. How did this happen? How did our clan shrink to near invisibility?

I have to stop now. I can't face months of carrying sadness in my heart again.

Blowing out a breath, he paused to take another sip. He couldn't even imagine the homes sitting there empty all that time, a constant reminder of the people that were gone.

Flipping the page, he scowled at it. Again, no date. The

writing had changed a lot since the first journal. It wasn't perfect now, like the hand doing it was shaking with age.

Belinda passed on yesterday. I can't believe there are only four of us left now. Pearl suggested we move elsewhere, find more of our own kind, but most of us have lived here our whole lives and the idea of leaving our mountain doesn't sit well. I didn't say it, but all I could think was what if someone finds their way back to us and we're not here? I just couldn't live with my body in one place and my heart still here. Virgil will never leave where his ancestors and wife are now buried, and I don't blame him. My own passed on or vanished long ago, but the very earth here is part of me and I just can't go somewhere other than here.

With no date, he had no idea how much time had passed. He turned the page and hoped for more information.

I can't believe I'm writing this, I dreamed of it for years and now twelve years later I can put pen to paper and write it for real. Leah came home last night. There was no mistaking it was her, she is the spitting image of her mama, Lyvia. We don't have much information yet, she was dirty, tired and half starved so she's resting. She also brought home a friend with four paws. A real honest to goodness leopard. My heart almost dropped out of my body and onto the ground when this skittish creature followed along behind her. Low and Virgil are making her a temporary pen, until they expand the main compound area, but she won't leave Leah's side so we can put her into it.

Jesus, she had been gone twelve years? She would have been sixteen when she came back. He shook his head and looked back down at it.

Leah brought a letter with her, from her mother, I can't bring myself to talk about it, but I am going to tuck it into the leaf of this here book. Maybe someday I can write my thoughts on it, but for now I cry too hard to see the page when I read it.

Our precious Leah is home. I have hope now.

The next page was dated, he made note of it, so he could try to track the events now.

Leah has been resting a lot, so I only found out some bits and pieces.

She prefers her cat form more than two legs. I think maybe its so she doesn't have to deal with what she saw or maybe it's so she can't talk to us. We've been pretty bad with the questions, especially Virgil. I suspect he's trying to figure out where Lyvia is by her letter and what she told Leah, he studies the map a lot lately.

Leah's mama told her to run Northeast when she got out and to keep going until her cat could find home. From the date on the letter from Lyvia it took that child over a month to get back to us. I don't know if anyone will ever read this, but if someone does and they know where we are and can figure where she ran from, please go find who had our precious Leah and our families and bring them some long over due justice. If any of our folk still live, all their special possessions are in the back room of my house. I sealed them up good, so they wouldn't get damaged much over the years.

Jesse got up so fast, he almost fell over his own feet. Grabbing his pack, he opened it and took out the map. Picking up the candle, he went over to the table and set it down. Opening the map, he located where he was right now and then dragged his finger Southwest down the page. He swore under his breath, right in line with it was Aiden Tomas' city. "Son of a bitch." Picking up the journal, he leaned over the table and read further.

Leah is a wonderment like I could never imagine. She's just barely sixteen and can shift faster than Virgil and that's saying something. I've never heard of one so young shifting this early, but with that haunted look in her eyes, I suppose if that's what she had to do to survive, we should be thankful her cat came out and got her back to us.

She was shifting at sixteen. He'd never heard of that happening, ever. He frowned, he needed to tell Shaelan that.

I watched her climb a tree today, it was like there was an invisible ladder she climbed up. She did this without shifting I should have wrote that first, so that's just incredible. I never was much for climbing trees with or without paws, so the fact she can do it is wonderful. She also made Low look a little silly and anyone that can put that man's pride on hold, has my admiration.

Dated three weeks later.

Pearl and I are taking turns working with Leah on some schooling. She came back to us knowing a few basic things, but that won't do at all. A body needs to know how to read and take in things around them or otherwise they'll just stagnate and go nowhere. Low is going to work on math with her, as both of us women hate working with numbers. There's never been much need for adding and multiplying up here, so he can do that part.

Two months later.

We lost the power today. Lowell went down the mountain to investigate and says logging is responsible for it. Some other industrial thing is the reason why our phone lines are gone. Not that we had anyone to call in the last fifteen years, but it's still a loss. I don't understand why those folks on two legs can't just pause and look around and see the beauty and wonderment that is this earth we share. Why do they have to tear down nature and build over it? I will never understand the inclination for any of that. Between Lowell and Virgil they are working on rigging something for us. It's 'borrowed' power, but Virgil says no one will notice what we use, I hope he's right because I need my sappy romance movies.

A month after the last entry.

Something is very different about Leah. It's like there is another side of her, a harder side. She's still loveable of course, but Pearl and I have been noticing that whenever Leah seems frightened or overwhelmed this other self comes out. I'm not complaining, this other part of her is badass (got that from a movie). I miss movies, been trying to coerce Low and Virgil to make the trek down the mountain and get us a few newer generators so the VHS movie player works again, but they're afraid to leave us women folk unprotected. I don't know how Pearl feels, but with Leah's other side and her real cat, I feel pretty darn safe myself.

He reread that paragraph twice, then gently folded the corner over so he could read it to Shaelan. It lined up with what he'd noticed.

I'm not doing well lately. I couldn't go on the fall trip to the market. Low and Virgil went, I stayed behind to watch over Pearl, she's been quite sickly these past few months.

I've decided I like Leah's leopard, Thera, I feel a closeness to her when things are quiet and we're just sitting.

Leah is spending less time in her cat form, so we're hoping she's doing better. I met her other self the other day, officially, she even has a name of her own, Evanna, I guess it's spelled. It's strange that Leah and Evanna are separate but in the same body, but she sure does look after Leah, so I have to love her for that.

He closed his eyes and blew out a breath slowly. It was what he'd seen. She had two personalities. He'd heard about things like that but never thought much about it before.

The next page was dated a month later.

I miss Pearl something awful, I know Leah does too. But Pearl was hurting a long time missing her girl, and I know there's nothing in this world or any other that can fix the ache of a mother's heart over a lost child. May god hold her tight and keep her in the comfort of his realm forever more. She deserved that.

He turned the page and then froze. There were three small entries, in different handwriting. There was no date.

Aunt Tillie passed. She was a wonderful lady and I am so happy I got back to know her.

Papa Virgil fell today. I wasn't able to help him. Papa Low said he was with his beloved Belinda. I hope they can stay together forever now.

Papa Low died last night. I put him beside Nana Pearl, he would have liked that.

It's just me, Evanna, Minn and Thera now.

Jesse flipped the page and his heart sunk to see it was blank. Straightening, he rubbed his hand across his eyes and then stood there looking at the blank page. Jesus, his heart was aching for Leah now. She'd managed to get back here only to find four elders here. How long had she been alone now? He went to close the book and remember the letter Tillie said she'd tuck into the leaf. Opening the front of the book again, he looked under the edge of the worn flap on the back of the cover. Pulling out the creased paper, he opened it carefully, afraid if he made any wrong moves it might tear.

Mom and Dad
I hope Leah finds her way home to you. It's a big risk, but we had to get her out of here. When we were taken she withdrew inside herself and while Ashtyn and I tried to shelter her as much as we could, we failed. She is shattered inside and I know she would not survive if she stayed here. I would rather live the rest of my days believing she is at home with the rest of the clan. I have to believe she made it or I don't know what I'll do.

A part of me knows that Eduard came looking for us and I pray at night when I'm alone that he made it back whole. Leah is going to need him and everyone else to get through this.

Her first shift is very close, and that's why I'm sending her out there on her own. That's what they want, the people that took us, shifters. I can't go into all the details because I only have a short time to write this, as the others work on a plan to get her out. One of the shifter guards is going to help us. I hope nothing happens to him for doing this because inside he is good.

We've been in the same house since being taken. Because of my age I work with the younger ones, to keep them calm and behaved. There are so many from different clans here, it breaks my heart. Over the years I have been permitted some liberties, which has allowed me to hear or see things. On the back I am writing down three addresses.

Jesse flipped the page over and looked, and there were addresses on it. *Holy shit.* He looked back at the letter.

The first I saw on an invoice when something was delivered here, so that is where Ashtyn and I are, along with a few of our own. I don't know where the boys ended up, but I hope its one of the other addresses.

I have to hope you will find someone that can get to us. Be careful, there are two armed men here, they are shifters themselves. They have collars on and I think that is how they are being controlled.

I have to go. We only have an hour to get her out of here and heading in the right direction.

Please, god willing, let her find her way back to you and if there's any good will left, that I will see home once again in my life.

I love you all.

Lyvia

Jesse frowned at it, then cleared his throat. "It's Tomas, or was his father then..." He turned the page over and looked at the addresses. If he had enough signal here, he was willing to bet he could search those addresses and they'd come up in Chicago, where Aiden Tomas was. Moving over, he picked up his phone and came back. He took two pictures of the addresses and then flipped the letter over and zoomed out to get a picture of that too. Devin needed to see these, hell, Rayne would probably recognize the addresses. Going over to the window, he checked his signal, shaking his head, he went out the door quickly and headed to where he knew there was a signal. He was taking no chances that this message wouldn't send.

When he had three bars, he opened a message to Devin and then attached the letter, then address pictures, and hit send. No explanation was needed. Looking up from the phone, he saw that Thera was coming toward him. She didn't appear to be stalking him, so that was a relief.

"Hey, girl." He smiled, even though he doubted that mattered to the animal.

She came over and bumped his leg with her shoulder, then lay down.

"I guess you can keep me company while I wait for a reply." He sat down beside her on the ground and rubbed his hand along the back of her neck. It was weird and cool to be sitting here petting a real leopard. The fur was a bit coarser than with shifters, but then again, this fur had probably never been bathed and was worn all the time.

His phone buzzing had him stop and look down. *You need to get her off that mountain and bring her back.* Jess nodded; he'd already decided that on his own. *I plan on it.* He looked at

Thera for a second. *Not sure how her leopard is going to like the van ride though. I'll let you know when we're heading back.* He hit send and then stood up. A reply right back. *Call when you're on the road.* Jesse glanced down at the cat, "ever been in a car?" He was regretting not bringing a tranquilizer gun. Hopefully, Leah had a way to keep her calm during the drive. It was going to be a long drive.

Chapter Nine

Leah rubbed her hand across her forehead. She hated waking up feeling like she hadn't slept. Some mornings it felt that way because she actually hadn't physically rested. It hadn't happened in a while though, Evanna being up all night.

Lighting the stove, she placed the kettle on it and then went over to look in the journal they used to communicate.

Sitting down, she flipped to the last used page and scanned it. Okay, she wasn't tired because Evanna had been up. The last entry was from yesterday afternoon. She read it again.

The man from the Alliance is staying in Aunt Tillie's house for the night. It's time to leave the mountain, Leah. I'm going to get some meat for dinner, make enough for Jesse too.

Ev

Closing it, she set it back on the table, then got up and went back over to the kettle. *It's time to leave the mountain.* "And go where?" She grabbed the kettle before it had a chance to whistle loud. Pouring it into the teapot, she took down the mint leaves and put some in.

"I can't just leave the mountain and not know where I'm going." She frowned and went over to the window. "What about everything that's here?" Hugging her waist, she looked around the room. "Everything would have to be packed and stored properly."

Glancing outside, she watched Thera walk across the yard and sit down beside Jesse, who was sitting, leaning back against the fence talking—she assumed, on what was a phone. Something about the phone was vaguely familiar. When that happened, it meant Evanna knew something, and she'd been close enough to pick up on it too.

Leah wondered who he was talking to, and also why Thera was there with him when she usually lay outside the door waiting for her.

She studied the man. He seemed like a nice man. Dinner with him had been okay, meaning she hadn't been a wreck through it and had managed to stay for the whole thing.

Evanna must be all right with him too, to say they were leaving the mountain with him. She'd been so shocked walking around the corner yesterday and seeing him stand there that she'd panicked and been unable to stay. It wasn't surprising, really, the last time she'd seen someone outside the elders was over a year ago, and that had not ended well at all.

Leaning against the window frame she watched as he pet Thera while talking. He was quite a pretty man. Shaking her head, she grinned, that's not the right word. Biting her lip, she tried to think of how Aunt Tillie would describe him. Ruggedly handsome? No, he didn't fit that description. His hair was a dark blond, and very messy. She wondered if it was curly or just naturally all over the place. When he'd smiled at her last night, it made her heart do this little fluttery thing. He really did have a nice, infectious smile. He stopped petting Thera and lifted his hand, making her realize he could see her in the window now.

Feeling her cheeks heat, she lifted her hand in the same way as if to say 'good morning'. Blowing out a breath, she moved away from the window and back to the teapot. Should she go out and say good morning? She had a terrible time facing him.

His eyes were mesmerizing, and she couldn't seem to not stare at them the whole time. They weren't grey or even green, but a pale combination of the two. If beautiful was a word fitting a man's eyes, then that's what they were, not to mention very intriguing the way they seemed to change and reflect what he was saying. She liked that, there were no hiding things in those eyes and that was a very good thing.

Pouring her tea, she picked up the cup and started for the door. "I can do this." She nodded her head slightly, trying to convince herself she could. Stopping before she opened it, she stood there. Leave the mountain? Her heart began to beat faster. Closing her eyes, she tried to focus and breathe through it. A feeling came over her, a steadying that had been her salvation as far back as she could remember. Evanna was close now. The fact that she didn't take over meant that she wanted Leah to try to do this. "Just go out and talk to him." She nodded. "I can do that."

She repeated that over and over in her mind as she walked out the door. *Just talk to him.* "Okay." She whispered and went down the steps. Thera spotted her and came bounding in her direction.

When she reached her, she rubbed against her leg, "Is that an apology?" Leah smiled down at her. Thera bumped her. "I know, he's a pretty man." Thera walked beside her, "I bet he's a pretty man cat too, huh?"

Thera looked up at her and then took off to run back to Jesse. She circled him as he stood up. He was smiling by the time she reached him, and she had no choice but to smile back.

"Good morning." Jesse nodded to her.

"Hello." She huffed out a quick quiet breath, "did you sleep well?"

His haunting eyes widened briefly, "off and on." He motioned to Aunt Tillie's, "your aunt's journals were very informative."

Leah had read those before and hadn't found them that informative, well she'd learned about the clan she'd never know, but the rest wasn't anything she didn't know. "Oh?"

"Yes." He glanced at the cup she held.

"I'm sorry would you like some mint tea?" She felt like she'd failed again.

"No thanks." He gave her one of those grins again, "I wouldn't say no to coffee though."

"Of course." She'd tried coffee once, it was horrible and bitter. It bothered her more than she cared to share when she tasted it in her mouth after Evanna drank it. "I don't have the knack for making it like Evanna, but I can make some."

"As long as it's caffeinated, that works."

Turning to walk back, she glanced over at him. "Of course, it's caffeinated, its coffee, isn't that its' sole purpose?"

Jesse nodded his head slowly, "Yeah, but with all the energy drinks out there now, coffee is struggling to keep its job."

"Energy drinks? Like lemonade and mint?" That's what she drank when she needed more energy.

"No, not quite." His tone was respectful, she appreciated that. "I can't even begin to explain it, you'd have to see it for yourself."

She went up the stairs carefully, "will I? If I leave the mountain," she opened the door, "see for myself?"

"If you'd like." Jesse motioned for her to go in first, "I can take you to see as much or as little as you want."

Studying him for a moment, she wondered what that really meant. "I'll have to think about that." She went over and took down the percolator. "Evanna says it's time to leave the mountain."

"Just now?"

She paused and watched him again, "no, she left it in our journal yesterday." Leah motioned to it. There was something calming about him, she couldn't explain why she felt that just that when she was near him she felt a peace inside.

"Do you agree with her?" He sat slowly in the chair and folded his hands on the table.

She wasn't naive, she knew he was trying not to spook her. "I don't know if I can leave." Turning away, she busied herself getting the coffee ready. "What do you mean Aunt Tillie's journals were informative?" She didn't turn back to look at him. It was easier for her to talk to him if she wasn't looking at him.

"I know where you were, where your clan was taken."

She dropped the cup onto the counter and spun around. "How can you know?" She couldn't even count the many times she'd read through everything there.

"The addresses your mother put on the back of her letter." He held her look. "I know the city."

Her heart accelerated. Placing her hand on her chest, she tried to catch her breath. He knew the city, the one she'd run from. The place where all her nightmares were from.

"Leah…" He stood up slowly, "it's okay, we don't have to talk about it…"

She side-stepped until she was at the end of the counter. The collar of her shirt seemed too tight, she tugged at it. "I-I," she tried to swallow, and her throat felt tight, "we," shaking her head, she backed to the other side of the room. Her skin was crawling, she couldn't stay in here, the walls were confining her.

Turning, she darted out the door and down the steps. She ran to the back of the house, tearing her shirt over her head as she went. She needed to run. Needed to move. Pausing, she kicked her shoes off quickly, not caring where they went, and then pulled her skirt down and stepped out of it. Shifting before her next breath, she let Minn take over and run full speed into the trees.

Chapter Ten

Jesse reached the back of the house just in time to see a cat heading into the trees. "Shit." He stood there for a second wondering if he should go grab his pack or just go after her. Thera came bounding around the corner and slowed long enough to look at him. "Yeah, I screwed up."

She gave him a low moaning sound and took off running.

"I'm coming." He called out to her as he pulled his shirt over his head. Shaelan had said to tread carefully and be wary of triggers. Talking about her mother and Chicago was a trigger for Leah. Pulling his boots off, he winced as he took some skin from his ankle with them. Undoing them would have been helpful. Shucking his jeans, he listened, trying to pick up any sound from the cats charging through the bush. He'd expected Evanna to come out when Leah was triggered, not her cat.

All four paws moved fast as he scented the air to catch up to them. Now he was doubting the fence was for Thera at all. Maybe Leah couldn't control her cat side. Tillie had said she spent a lot of time as her cat. Was it her cat that had brought her back to the clan home? He'd imagined it was Evanna when he'd read the journal. He stumbled and his cat gave a low hiss. Now was not the time to think about everything. Jesse let go and allowed his cat to take the lead, he needed to catch up to them.

He caught a glimpse of a tail through the thick growth and jumped onto the rocks to get a better view. Spotting Thera, he took off in that direction. When he cleared the trees, he put on the brakes. Thera was pacing back and forth, clearly agitated. Leah lay on the ground moaning. Had she been hurt? He rushed over and was blocked by an unimpressed wild cat. Thera's ears were back, her sides heaved, and she stared him down.

He chuffed a quiet apology and hoped it translated that way to her.

"Thera leave him be."

Jesse stopped and looked at her. It was Evanna, there was no way Leah used that tone. She was on her knees now, hunched over hugging her waist.

"Clothes, Thera." Evanna hissed out a breath.

Thera gave him a brief glare and then took off back in the direction they'd come.

Jesse ignored the fact she was naked and went over to her, he crouched down so his head was level with hers.

"I had to take over Minn." She blew out a breath. "Always hurts bad when I do that."

He was shocked, he'd never heard of a shift back hurting unless there was injury. She was shivering and it alarmed him. Dropping his belly onto the ground, he moved closer, so she could use him for some warmth. Minn *was* her cat. A cat she— they couldn't control.

She didn't object to his closeness, simply allowed him to curl around her so her bare skin was against his fur. "Leah can't control her." She said as her teeth chattered. "I don't know what you said to bring out Minn, but we're going to have to talk."

Jesse nudged her back, so she'd lean into him more. Her breathing was alarming him, it was half cat, half-human.

"I've got her," Evanna whispered. "She's fighting me. Leah is so far in the background she can't help me."

He didn't understand any of it and that pissed him off. He'd done this. Shaelan had warned him about triggers, and he'd tried to be careful, watch for the signs she'd told him about but clearly hadn't monitored Leah enough to stop in time. Jesse had to make this right and he had no idea how to.

He realized he was struggling to control his animal now. This was no time to have some sort of conflict with his cat. When he was trying to convey that to his creature, Thera came charging out of the trees. His cat gave a low warning growl, shocking Jesse and the wild cat.

Thera gave him an 'are you serious' kind of look and then dragged the table cloth over and dropped it in front of him.

Tightening his control on his cat, Jesse stretched and pulled the cloth closer. He wished he had something to put on, so he could shift and help her back, but he didn't. Sitting up, he watched as she struggled to get it wrapped around her. The first thing he was doing when he got back to the van was giving her a run pack. He always carried some with him because he never knew who he was going to come across on these trips he was sent on.

Jolting, he went over when she was attempting to stand. She did not look steady at all.

"Damn, damn." She cursed softly. "I might have to rest for a few minutes before heading back." She licked her mouth like it was too dry, "It hasn't been this bad in a long time." She stumbled and would have hit the ground if he hadn't thrown his body under her to stop the fall.

He didn't know if she'd been around enough other shifters to understand, but he issued a few short chirps telling her to just stop and wait. Moving back from her, he shifted without further announcement and then went over and scooped her up into his arms. "Just close your eyes and rest."

So many pieces were clicking together for him. Why she was in her cat form so much, was because Leah couldn't control her and it physically hurt Evanna to force her under control. He had to talk to Shaelan as soon as possible and see if she had any suggestions. How had she lived like this for this long? He could barely handle one disagreement with his cat, never mind having to fight constantly.

Jesse closed the door and stood there looking at it for a second. Evanna said a nap would help. He knew after a shift like that food would have been the first thing he went for. The elders had left some important knowledge out in the few years they'd been teaching her.

Putting his hands on his hips, he looked down and realized he was still naked. Shaking his head, he turned back to go get his clothes.

Thera stood on the step waiting for him.

"She's resting." He said as he jumped down the steps and rounded the corner of the house. He needed to call Cal and fill him in, or Shaelan, maybe both.

Reaching his clothes, he yanked his jeans on and picked up the rest. Spotting her clothes on the ground, he went toward them. Before he called anyone, he needed a moment to digest. Some time to reflect on what he'd learned this morning.

Setting her clothes on the porch, he beelined for Tillie's house to grab a protein bar. Then he was getting some of that coffee and looking around to see what needed to be done here so he could get her off this mountain.

"Watch for triggers." He mumbled between bites. He needed to talk to Evanna about said triggers because he wasn't happy with the events that followed Leah being triggered. Ripping off another bite with his teeth he chewed without tasting it. "No shift should end like that." He went over and sat down to pull his boots back on.

He was so mad right now, his cat had even receded. Well, he'd learned a few things today—none of them he felt good about. Then there was what he found out when he picked her up. Stomping naked through the trees with a shaking woman— that was his mate. "How the fuck does that work?" He scowled at the floor. What if it was just Evanna, was that possible?

He grabbed his phone and headed for the door. Most men had to contend with persuading their mates' animal side to accept them. His mate's animal had a name of her own and from what he could tell had a lot of attitude too.

He walked into the house quietly and went to the stove where she'd been perking the coffee. The pot was still hot, the brew might cause him to have a heart attack, but he needed the strong brew right now. Pouring a cup, he looked around for what might be the sugar she'd mentioned the day before.

The third canister yielded a jackpot. He used one teaspoon because there really wasn't much left. Taking a sip, he winced as it went down. "That'll work." He whispered. Strong was an understatement.

Looking around, he spotted a door at the end of the kitchen area, going over he opened it and looked in. A storage pantry. He checked a few canisters and found all of them very low. Shaking his head, he walked out and quietly went back outside. "She wouldn't have had enough to survive the winter." He mused and then looked down to see Thera was right beside him. "And you," he stopped and looked down at her, "what the hell are we doing with you for the trip?" She looked back at him with a bored expression in her eyes. "I'll figure that out later."

Chapter Eleven

With long strides, he walked to where he knew he had a good enough signal. Hitting Cal's number, he stood and watched the house.

"Jesse?"

He investigated the black liquid in his cup, "yeah."

"I didn't expect to hear from you until later." Calum sounded amused.

"A few new things to discuss."

"I was just filling Blair and Gage in."

Jesse took a small sip and swallowed it down quickly. "Is Shaelan there?"

"Hang on. Okay, you're on speaker now, yes she's here."

Jesse sat down because his legs weren't feeling steady now.

"What's happened, Jesse?" Shaelan's tone was in healer mode.

"I was talking to Leah this morning and I was trying to be careful like you said…"

"Is everything all right?"

He looked at the house, "yes, no, not really. I don't know."

The line was silent for what felt like an eternity. "Was Leah triggered?"

He nodded, "yeah, but it's not like you figured, it wasn't Evanna that came out, it was Minn." He heaved a big sigh, "Minn is her cat and she came out with hardly enough warning and took off into the bush." Jesse glanced at the fence, "I think the fence is for Minn and *not* Thera."

"Oh." That was all Shaelan replied.

"Thera took off after her, so I shifted and followed," He got up because he couldn't sit still, "by the time I caught up to them Evanna was laying on the ground." Jesse paced back and forth, "Evanna had to take over Minn and was struggling to hold her in—she was in so much pain, in shock and shaking…"

"Is she all right now?" Shaelan's concern was coming over the phone loud and clear.

"She's resting now." He took a gulp of the brew and almost choked on it. "I couldn't get her to eat or anything. I had to carry her back." It made him mad to think about what would have happened if he hadn't been here. "I don't know what they've been living on since the elders died, but the pantry is basically empty."

"Okay, so some basic care education is needed." Shaelan sounded so calm and reasonable. "There's not a lot of data to go on with dissociative identity disorder as far as shifters go, Jesse, I've called a few doctors from the Alliance and they're looking into some things for me."

"Dissociative identity disorder?" He frowned, she discussed possible issues with him, but he didn't remember what the tags were that went with them.

"I really believe that's what we might be looking at here, Jesse."

He nodded, "okay, so what do I do?"

"We could send someone…"

He cut off Calum, "No," he shook his head, "I think that would just freak her out more."

"He's right, Cal, too many people after her isolation might put her into a spin that will cause more issues."

"Okay, what do you need Jesse?" Calum was all business now.

"I'm going to try to talk to Evanna after she's rested, Leah isn't going to want to leave this place without knowing what's to become of everything here…"

"I can talk to Devin and get someone sent there after you've cleared out and started packing the place up."

Jesse clenched his jaw and thought about that. "I think the issue is going to be the graveyard."

"There's a graveyard?" That was Blair.

All shifters knew that graves that held shifter bodies were something no clan did. It could bring on a whole new world of issues if unsuspecting one-forms came across the bodies and realized they weren't one hundred percent normal human skeletons.

"Yeah, and she looks after it regularly."

"Shit." That was Calum and now he was understanding part of the mess Jesse was in.

"I'll talk to Devin and see what he and his dad can come up with."

"What were you talking about that triggered her?" Shaelan's voice was contemplative.

Jesse blew out a breath, "That we knew where those addresses were on her mother's letter."

"Oh."

"I'm going to talk to Evanna after she's rested and see if there's a way to steer around that."

"Evanna seems like the protector. Do you know who fronts the most?" Shaelan asked him.

Jesse frowned and looked down at Thera. "Fronts?"

"Who is out the most? Evanna, Leah, or Minn," she paused for a moment, "there could be more, Jesse, you need to be aware of that. You will have to ask both Leah and Evanna because both may not be close enough to the other alters."

His brain felt like it might explode. "I really hope not." And he meant it. "Uh, Shaelan?"

"Yes?"

"How connected are these—alters?" He frowned, having no idea how to ask about something he knew nothing about. "To one another, in likes and dislikes?"

"I really don't know enough about it to say, Jesse, I'm learning as fast as I can so I can help, but I do know you need to get her down from there so she can get the help she needs."

He wasn't going to argue that. "Okay, can you call me later if you find out more?" What he needed to ask, he didn't want to ask in front of the men, he knew they'd get it, but already he was protective of Leah and Evanna and didn't want to take a chance of snapping at something someone said.

"I'll keep checking in with you."

He nodded, then cleared his throat. "I'll know later today how soon we can head down this mountain." Honestly, he had no idea how he was going to know that. Turning, he looked back at the house, he needed to explore the other buildings and find things they could pack stuff into to carry down.

Three hours later, he stood looking down at the list he'd made. That was a long list and this one was just things that needed to be done to close up the place so they could leave. He blew out a breath and found himself wishing for a convenience store so he could stock up on energy drinks. Shifter or no, there was no way he was getting all this done in a day, he'd be lucky if he could in a week. He'd have to call Devin and see if some of it could be done by the team sent after they were gone.

Turning, he glanced at the house Evanna was sleeping in. How much would she want to bring with them? Better question, would Leah want different things? He'd tried to do a quick search on his phone to find out more about this disorder. After reading very dry reports, he was no further ahead. They hadn't told him about the different alters? That was the word Shaelan had used, at least he was pretty sure at this point. The sites hadn't told him if the alters liked the same things or not. All he did find out was this was something that had no miracle cure and no matter what happened going forward it wasn't going to go away. Apparently, it was manageable, but he didn't understand most of what he read from that point on, so he didn't know how it was. Case by case was how they dealt with it, there was no point form list that made all people with it the same. Treatment was different for each one.

None of that was helpful. Rubbing his hand over his face, he tried to shake off the frustration. What he really needed to know was what happened if one of the alters didn't care for a mate like him. What happened then? What if Evanna and Leah were both on team Jesse, but Minn wasn't? It's not like he could call up his father and ask about this either. Hell, he didn't even know where to begin to explain this whole scenario to his family.

He frowned pulled out his phone and checked the day. Okay, it wasn't Sunday, this was good. He'd never missed a Sunday call yet to his family. He had two days to try to figure out how to tell his folks about Evanna, or Leah… he had to find out who was out the most…

Thera came over and bumped against his leg. He looked down at her. She looked over to the house in the middle. Smoke was coming out of the chimney, which meant Evanna was up and had lit the stove. Tucking the paper into his pocket, he hurried to see how she was doing.

Chapter Twelve

Evanna stared at the kettle, wishing it to boil faster. Spotting the basket on the counter, she went over and grabbed a biscuit from last night. She really missed that jerky that Papa Low always had. Since his passing, she'd searched in every book, notebook, and piece of paper trying to figure out how he made it. As far as regrets go, she wished she'd paid more attention to things when he was still alive.

Choking down the dry mouthful, she grabbed the kettle and decided partially boiled water would have to do. Her head was killing her, every muscle was aching and now she had to explain to Jesse what had happened. She had no idea why she felt it was important to tell him everything, but she always followed her instincts when it came to people so she was going to listen again. There was something about him—something she couldn't even put into words, she'd never felt this way with another, that she did know. Of course, that presented more problems. She and Leah hadn't vowed it to each other, or anything while they were running for their lives to find their way back home, how could they, but it had always been a feeling that there would always just be them—it was the only safe way…

The door opened, and she turned to see Jesse standing there looking at her with a careful expression.

"I'm okay now." She blew out a breath and lifted one shoulder in a half shrug. "Just a bad headache, but it will fade."

He reached into his back pocket and held something out. "Eat this, it will help with the shakes."

Going over she took it and looked at it. "A protein bar?" She didn't know what that was exactly.

Jesse nodded, "most shifters keep them on hand to replenish after shifting." He looked at it and then to the biscuit in her other hand, "if you don't eat regularly, it's harder on you when you shift and harder to control it."

Lifting both eyebrows at him, she stepped back and went over to the percolator again. "Aunt Tillie used to chase me around saying that too." She motioned to the pantry, "stores are running a bit low right now unless fresh vegetables work."

"Anything helps, but protein seems to be the key."

Adding more water, she put the kettle down and opened the packaging on the protein bar. She took a small bite. She'd never tasted anything like this before. It had a lot more flavor than a dry biscuit too. "Not bad."

He chortled, "you'll grow to hate them once you've tasted other things."

"Yeah? Like what?" She motioned to the coffee asking if he wanted some.

He nodded and sat down. "Things like chocolate, potato chips, and my personal favorite licorice."

Pouring the coffee, she grabbed the sugar container and set it on the table with a spoon. "I've had chocolate, a long a time ago." She studied him for a second, "I've never had potato chips though and I have no idea what licorice is." Putting the cups on the table, she sat down.

Jesse grinned, "I'm going to peg you as a black licorice fan." He took the cup and added a touch of sugar to it. Stirring it slowly, he watched her, his pale eyes looking right through her. "We need to talk about some things," he frowned, "do you think you can stay at the front for a while?"

She loved his eyes, they were so intriguing. Blowing out a breath, she looked away and down at her cup, trying to sense where Leah was. "If at the front means is Leah coming back soon, then the answer is no. I don't even sense her right now."

"I'm sorry about earlier." His tone was soft and sincere.

Evanna took a drink to avoid looking at him for a moment. "I knew it was bound to happen with you staying."

"I was trying to be careful."

She shrugged and sat back, "I should have stayed closer to monitor what was happening."

"You can do that."

"Sometimes." She picked up the bar and took another bite.

"I thought I was sharing good news…"

Swallowing, she held his look, "about what?"

"The addresses on the back of—the letter in your aunt's journal, I know what city they're in."

Washing the bite down with the bitter liquid helped her pause to assess how she felt about that. Anxious, angry, and spiteful were words to describe it. Carefully locking down her reaction, she looked at the dark liquid in her cup instead of him. "That would set Leah off."

"But not you?"

"I don't feel good when I think about there if that's what you mean." She looked back at him and was surprised by the compassion in his eyes.

Jesse shook his head and leaned on the table, "I don't tell you to make you feel bad, what I was trying to tell Leah was if any of your clan are still there, we'll find them."

"You think they're still there?" She ate the last of the bar before she lost her appetite. It had made her feel less shaky to put something in her stomach.

"There's always a chance they are."

Evanna blew out a breath and then looked at the table, checking again to see if Leah was close. She didn't sense her. She could feel Minn inside her, but so far, she was behaving and just lurking to listen.

"If you're up to it, can I ask some questions?"

She liked how he asked and didn't bombard her with questions that made her feel sick inside. "Now might be the best time with Leah in the background and Minn behaving."

"Do you always have to control Minn?"

Aunt Tillie had told her that many would not understand about Minn, Leah, and her connection, but so far Jesse seemed to be grasping things well enough, and better yet was being very respectful about it. "Not as much as I used to." Pulling a small piece of cord from her pocket, she pulled her hair back and tied it in place. There was something about her hair dragging across her neck that bothered her a lot. She knew why but couldn't dwell on the reason. He wanted answers, so she was going to try her best to give them to him. "It was just Leah and me for years."

"How long have you been there?"

Blowing out a breath, she tried to remember the first time. It wasn't a pleasant memory, but it still might be information he needed. "Leah was five, maybe closer to six." Evanna closed her eyes for a second and tried not to see the state Leah's mother was in when she'd first looked upon her.

"If this is too much," Jesse reached across the table and put his hand on hers, "we don't have to talk about it now."

Her first instinct was to pull her hand away, but she didn't. The feel of him touching her was comforting and she couldn't remember a time she'd felt that. "It's not easy, but I want to try to explain." She glanced at their hands and then he moved his. "I've been looking out for Leah since then." She cupped the mug between her hands so she wouldn't ask him to hold hers again. "Until when her mother sent us away, then Minn appeared and ran us most of the way back here—I don't have a lot of details to share."

"I've never heard of someone so young shifting." His tone was soft like he was afraid to talk in his normal voice.

"Aunt Tillie and Nana Pearl told me that," she shrugged, "Papa Low said it happened, so we'd get home."

"That's possible, but after reading the letter I think it was going to happen whether you were running or not."

"Lyvia didn't want it to happen there." She cleared the lump from her throat, "she, ah, said that the people that took us wanted shifters." He held her look as she spoke; it took focus to not get lost in his eyes. "Why-why would they want shifters?"

Jesse puffed out his cheeks and blew out a long breath, "I can't even explain *that*, exactly, but it's out of control."

"How?" She slid closer to the table.

"They've taken many shifters from different clans," he looked angry for a second, "some clans are completely gone."

Evanna lifted her hand and motioned around the room, "wasn't much left of this one when I got back."

"I know. I honestly hope we'll find some of your clan."

"You're going to go to those addresses?" Her heart beat a little harder in her chest for a second. Lifting her hand, she hoped he just stopped to let her regain her composure. Closing her eyes, she breathed it away, forcing her pulse to slow to a normal speed. Opening her eyes, she found him watching her, an anxious look in his eyes. "I'm okay." She swallowed down the bile in the back of her throat. "It's just, after forcing Minn back today, I'll be a little shaky and have to watch to keep my heart steady or she could burst out again."

His eyes widened. "Just tell me to stop if it gets to be too hard for you."

She nodded.

"One of the first things we're going to do once we're off this mountain is hook you up with some elders that will help you tap into your cat and control her easier."

"Is that possible?"

Jesse nodded, then moved his head from side to side, "most of the time. It's not foolproof but creating a bond with your cat helps a lot." He frowned, "I don't think you had the time for that with how young you were, so she's able to come out whenever *she* wants, which could be dangerous once off this mountain."

"Yeah, I've learned that the hard way a few times."

"You've left here?"

"A few times." She took another sip of the coffee, no longer tasting it. "When they went down for supplies, or Leah and I tried it once on our own—" She sighed, "it didn't go well."

"We can talk details later, but just so you know, we're leaving the mountain—now, what I need to know first, is there just the three of you?"

Evanna nodded her head slowly, she checked constantly for more. "As far as I know. Leah and I messaged each other a few years back and agreed if there were any more that we were aware of and the other wasn't, we'd tell the other." She pointed to the journal on the table beside the chair, "we use that."

Jesse bobbed his head and looked where she pointed. "She mentioned that earlier." His eyes connected with hers again, "okay, so there's the three of you." He bit his lip for a second, "that's good, I've read a bit about your disorder..."

"You know why I'm like this?" She almost jumped onto the table to get closer to him.

"Yes, well, I don't know a lot but Shaelan, my friend's mate is a healer, and she knows much more than I do."

Evanna took a deep breath and blew it out. Keeping her heart steady was getting harder, "okay, so what's this *disorder*?"

"Dissociative identity disorder," he searched her face, watching her carefully, "it used to be called multiple personality disorder..."

"It-it's a normal thing?" She shrugged; it had a name.

"It's more common than I knew of, but as I said I don't know a lot."

She couldn't stop looking at him now. What was wrong with them wasn't *just* them. She was relieved, intrigued, and terrified all at once.

"Once we're back, Shaelan says there are ways of managing it..."

"Managing it how?" She'd tried everything for the last five years, to help Leah, control Minn, and get rid of this constant ache in her head. For this entire conversation, she wanted to rest her head on the table and close her eyes but knew that didn't ease the pain at all.

"I don't have those details, if you like, later when Shaelan calls, you can speak to her."

She smirked, "on your little phone?"

Jesse nodded.

Evanna rubbed her forehead, the ache was not easing at all.

"Are you okay?"

The look of concern on his face she found endearing. "My head, it aches all the time, but after earlier, it's not going to let up any time soon."

Jesse frowned, "I have acetaminophen down in the van," he pulled out his phone and looked at it, "I should check with Shaelan and make sure taking it is okay for you." He looked back at her, "most medication doesn't help shifters much, our metabolism burns through it fast, but if it helps…"

"This a seat-what—" she shook her head, unable to say whatever he just had, "it's a pain killer?"

Jesse nodded.

"I've never had one. Aunt Pearl used herbs and teas," she glanced over at the counter, "but they don't work really."

"I don't have a signal here, but I will message her shortly and ask."

"Message her?" She frowned what that was she didn't know for sure.

"Yeah, you can," he held his phone out and leaned across the table, "type a message to someone in it without having to call them."

She watched as he tapped the screen and brought up a list of names, he hit one and started spelling out words—*on* the phone. "That's crazy." She grinned. "Everyone has one of those phones?"

Jesse leaned back again, "most people do, yes."

"I have a lot to learn." A pain stabbed through her head and made her wince.

"I'll go message Shaelan and check my pack to see if I have

any in it." He got up.

"Hey," she cleared her throat, "if you have another one of those bars, I'd take it."

Jesse grinned, "I have a whole case of them in my van."

"Really?" She stood up slowly. "We could run down and get them."

Jesse held up his hand, "I don't think you should go for any more runs today." He glanced at the door, "I can shift and go down, but I can only bring up what fits in my pack."

"Your pack?"

"Yeah, a small pack we wear to put our clothes in," he shook his head, "I have some in the van, I'll bring you one."

"That would be cool." She nodded, then froze for a second. "I can help with bringing more of those bars back up." She darted into the bedroom. Hurrying, she went in and opened the closet. Digging around in the bottom, she pulled out Papa Low's hauling bag, or that's what he used to call it. Going back out she pulled it from the bag and shook it open.

"What is that?" Jesse came over.

"Papa Low and Grampa Virgil used to use them to haul things up from where the truck is hidden."

He took it and looked at it.

"You put your head through here after you shift," she motioned to the loop, "and the bottom is made to slide along the ground and not get caught up on everything." She put her hand inside, "it's padded on the bottom too, so if you're hauling up eggs or something breakable, they won't get broken."

"This is ingenious." He smiled at her, "I've been trying to figure out how to get things down the mountain when we leave."

"When will that be?" She crossed her arms over her stomach, there were butterflies in it.

"That's up to you and Leah. The Alliance is sending someone after we go to pack up things, but I don't know how Leah is going to feel about leaving."

Evanna looked over at the journal, "I'll write her a message while you go get the bars." She really liked them and wanted to eat about ten of them right now.

"I'll see if I have any jerky as well." He rolled the bag back up, "I have some juice and other snacks too."

"Really? You're like a traveling market." She smiled at him. When was the last time she'd done that? Smiled. There was never anyone to smile at or a reason to smile to yourself up here…

"I travel a lot and need to be prepared for everything." Jesse tucked the bag under his arm. "Let me check with Shaelan while I look in my pack."

"Okay, I'm going to write to Leah now and try to explain things to her." She bit her lip, then gave him a wide-eyed look, "there's a lot to explain."

Jesse cleared his throat, "just, please tell her I'm sorry about this morning and that I will do *anything* to keep the three of you safe."

She searched his face for a moment, not sure why she was feeling emotional from his words. "Will do," she whispered and then turned her back to him. Moving over she sat down in the chair where the journal sat and opened it. She couldn't look at him right now, not when she didn't under this feeling inside her. She heard the door close as he left.

Chapter Thirteen

Jesse walked to where he knew the signal was strong. He wasn't going to bother sending messages and seeing if it was a good time. He didn't like how pale she looked. He'd known she was in pain from the look in her eyes and it bothered him a lot. Was the headache part of the disorder?

Calum's voice came over the phone, "is Shaelan there?"

He heard Cal chuckle, "I'm just walking over to her now."

"Okay, I need to talk to her."

"Is everything okay?" He could hear other voices and hoped Cal had reached his mate.

"No, not really, but I'm starting to think things won't be for a long time."

"Here she is."

"Jesse?"

"Hi. I have about a hundred questions right now, but most importantly will acetaminophen be okay if I give some to Evanna?"

"Headaches?"

He nodded and looked back toward the common house. "Yeah, really bad after earlier."

"She can take some, I'd suggest one to start, she probably

hasn't had a lot of synthetic drugs in her life."

Inhaling slowly, he rubbed his thumb and forefinger across his eyes, "she hasn't had a lot of anything in her life, but bad things."

"You've discussed some things with her?" Shaelan's tone was patient, not pushing.

"A bit. I probably could have talked about more, but I can see how much pain she's in," he scowled at the ground, "but she keeps answering me, not complaining." Blowing out a breath to try to calm the hell down, he continued, "as far as she knows there's just the three of them. She has been around since Leah was six, she thinks." He took another deep breath and forced his mind to slow down, "She doesn't consider Leah's mother to be her own?" How would that even work?

"That's not uncommon, Jesse, my best guess is that Evanna developed to protect Leah, but she has her own personality and often they don't feel like they're related to the host."

Host? He shook his head; he'd learn the labels and terminology later. "Okay," he watched Thera lay down outside the door of the house, it bothered him that she was staying so close to Evanna and not following him or roaming. "Evanna doesn't remember most of the trip from Chicago."

"Minn was out that long?"

"I guess. From the sounds of it she has to control Minn all the time." A week ago, he would have felt strange talking about a person's animal side with a name like it was a different body entirely, but now it didn't feel wrong. "Or should I say she struggles to control her, especially right now after earlier."

"I was talking to Doctor Collins earlier, if you think it's a good idea, she could be here at Blair's when you get here."

"This doctor is a shifter?"

"Yes, we have doctors of all types in the Alliance I'm told."

Jesse turned back and looked at the house, "I don't want to say yes and then have them freak out."

"You'll need to ask them about it."

"Yeah, okay." He rubbed his hand over his jaw, "I'm going

down to the van to grab some snacks and bars with the medkit."

"If her diet has been poor for a while, Jesse, it could be why she's struggling with her cat so much…"

"I thought of that too," he nodded.

"Have you discussed leaving?"

He took a few steps toward the house, then remembered the signal and stopped. "Yeah, well, mostly with Evanna, she's writing to Leah right now telling her we're leaving the mountain…"

"They communicate, that's a good thing, it actually makes it easier for all of them."

Jesse snorted, "I doubt we'll get Minn to write in any journals." His pulse increased, no animal should put their body through that kind of pain and stress. He frowned; his cat had his annoying moments but nothing like that.

"Let me know about the doctor coming here. I've been told some very good things about her."

Jesse rolled his shoulders, trying to keep the stress from getting to him. "I will, and Shaelan, if you could send me your number it would save bugging Cal all the time."

Shaelan laughed, "he likes being bothered, but I'll send it to you."

Jesse could hear Cal's objection in the background. "Okay, I'll talk to you later."

Jesse paused for a second and looked behind him at the bag he was dragged back up. It was an ingenious idea, however a lot of work he'd discovered. He looked down at the path, probably would have been easier when the trail was maintained.

His cat wasn't all that thrilled with the harness around his neck, Jesse had to keep pausing to shift it so most of the weight was pulling across his chest. He'd packed the bars, some water, a few juices, the medkit, and most of the snacks he'd had in the van.

Shaelan had said the painkillers wouldn't hurt, but he was still going to monitor her because if she'd never had anything like that before, there was no telling how it would react in her system.

When he got back up there, he really wanted to talk to Evanna some more. She seemed to cope with anything he told her. He needed to explain about the graveyard. Word had come from Shepard Addison and that word was the bodies would have to be removed, for the safety of the entire shifter world. It didn't matter which one he told, he knew it wasn't going to go over well. Hell, if someone told him they were going to mess with his loved one's graves, he'd probably take a bite out of them.

His cat paused for a few steps and let out a low growl, before picking up the pace. That was his way of telling Jesse to shut up with all the thoughts in his head and to work more to get back to the top of the mountain.

When he picked up the metallic smell, he knew to stay on the path this time and cut a lot of time off the trip up. He couldn't help thinking about things. That was his mate up there and so much was uncertain right now. The first thing that needed to happen after he got her down from here was he needed to get her the help Shaelan was talking about. The fact she'd survived this long out here on her own was miracle enough, he was taking no chances.

It occurred to him when he spotted the fence that his cat had been oddly quiet throughout the whole talk with Evanna before he went down to the van. He wasn't sure why that was. Although knowing now that she was his mate explained the strange behavior of his animal side when around her.

Stopping outside the gate, he dropped his head, so the harness was off his neck and shifted. He'd left his clothes here.

Getting dressed quickly, he opened the gate and carried the bag inside. Securing it, he made quick work heading to the middle house.

Evanna was sitting at the table writing in the journal when

walked in. She glanced up and him, "that was fast."

Jesse shrugged, "it's much shorter with four legs." He motioned to the book in front of her, "you're still writing?"

She rolled her eyes, "it's hard to figure out how to say some things." She glanced down at it, "I'm not much of a writer, Leah could go on for pages."

"I don't think I've ever written more than a few sentences at once," he grimaced, "since I left school."

"Aunt Tillie used to make me write paragraph after paragraph." She grinned, "and there was no cheating and getting Leah to do it because our writing is so different."

"Points for trying I guess." He set the bag on the table and opened it. "I brought a little of everything." He started setting it on the table. "Protein bars, water, juice, some chips, and jerky…"

"You have jerky?" She stood up and leaned over to look at it. "I miss jerky. Papa Low made the best."

"Well, this probably won't taste anything like that, because I bought it in a store." He pulled out the medkit. "Shaelan says try one acetaminophen and see how it goes." He opened the plastic box and got them out, "they might make you feel weird because you've never had anything like that."

"If it helps my head, I'll try it." She looked at the bottle in his hand.

Jesse got one out and held it to her. After she took it, he handed her a bottle of water.

She read the label. "You buy water too?" Popping the pill in her mouth, she opened the bottle and took a drink. "It tastes different."

"It's purified."

Evanna gave him a weird look, then capped the bottle and put it down. She picked up the journal and held it out to him, "can you look at this and see if I should add something else? I really want to get through to her."

He nodded and took the book.

"Can I?" She motioned to the things he'd put on the table.

"Help yourself."

She smiled at him, and it was the first time he'd seen that strained, 'hard life' look leave her face.

"You should smile more often." He said quietly as he sat down and looked in the book. It was hard to take his eyes off her for more than a second as she picked up the things he'd put on the table. She ran her hands over the packaging and read the labels one after the other. "Try whatever you like."

Her eyes widened, then she smiled. "I don't know what to start with first. We need to save some of this for Leah to try too." She nodded and picked up the jerky again. Frowning at it for a second, she figured out how to open it. Taking a bite, she nodded her head and with huge eyes looked back at him while she chewed.

Jesse smiled at her and then forced himself to look down at the book. Watching her was refreshing. Seeing her look at things for the first time made him see them in a different way too. He flipped back a page to where she'd started. The last entry was from her telling Leah it was time to leave the mountain. There was no reply.

Hi

That was quite the run Minn took today, huh? Jesse was there for me once I got her under control. He's sorry for causing it. I believe him. There's something about him that is sincere and I'm trusting him, so you can too. You know I always look out for you. I always have and always will, Leah.

He's gone down to his van to get some painkillers that will help with the headache. I'm excited about that. He is also bringing up some other things like juice and these protein bars. You have to try those. They taste like nothing I've ever had before.

Leah, he knows what's wrong with us and says there's help for us if we go with him. I believe him. I'm going to talk to his healer when he gets back, on his phone. He can even send messages on his phone without talking. Almost everyone carries a phone with them. It's completely crazy.

I need you to think about what you need to take with you when we leave. His friends at the Alliance are going to come back and pack everything else up for us. So please think about it and leave a list. We need to get off this mountain and get some help, for Minn especially.

If you feel like you're going to lose control of Minn when you are with Jesse, just hold his hand. There's something calming about it.

Get to work on the list.

Ev

He was humbled by her belief in him. She didn't know him and yet she was putting her, no, their fate in his hands. Jesse cleared his throat and then looked up to see her eating a protein bar. He couldn't believe she liked them.

She swallowed it. "Does it make sense?"

He nodded. "Do you think she'll listen?"

Evanna shrugged, "I think so. I've never been wrong about a person before, so I think she will."

"Okay." He closed the book and handed it back to her.

She went over and put it on the table beside the chair. "She'll check it."

"Will she be back in the morning?" He didn't understand how it worked really.

Evanna came back over and picked up the bottle of water. "Probably. I'm not out for long periods of time anymore, just usually when she needs to work through something."

"What about Minn?" If he was going to load up the van and leave, he needed an idea of what to expect. Having Thera in there was going to be adventure enough, he was sure.

"I usually take Minn for a run when I'm out, sometimes Leah can if all is calm." She made a face, "if it were up to Leah, she'd let Minn take control all the time. It's just been the last two years she's been able to be herself for longer than an hour."

He stood up, "If you have any suggestions on how I can help, let me know. That includes the trip too, it's going to be a long drive back and the smoother that goes the easier it will be on everyone."

Evanna snorted softly, "I don't even know if we'll get Thera *in* a vehicle."

Jesse blew out a breath, "yeah I was afraid of that." He motioned to the door, "come show me what's what. I looked around earlier, and made a list, but if you can shed some light on things it might make this go a little faster."

"Yeah." She paused and grabbed another bar and her bottle of water. "I really like these things." She grinned and went to the door.

Jesse looked down at the protein bars and then picked up a pack of the jerky instead. "We'll call Shaelan before we start." He told her as he followed her out.

Chapter Fourteen

Leah set the journal on the table and looked at everything set on it. Evanna had left little notes on top of things. She picked up the first one and read it. *The water is bottled.* Setting it down, she picked up a bottle and opened it. Smelling it, she paused to process that. Plastic, that's all she could smell. Taking a small sip, she let it sit on her tongue for a second. It didn't taste like plastic, but it did taste clean.

The next note said *'try this'*. Picking up one of them, she read it. Protein bar. Turning it over, she read the packaging and didn't understand most of what the ingredients were. Opening it, she took a tiny bite, having no idea what to expect. It wasn't bad at all, sweet, but not in a bad way. She took a bigger bite and savored it as she checked the next note.

Potato chips!

With eyebrows raised, she turned the small bag over and looked at the ingredients. The ingredients were at least things she recognized, mostly. She'd have to try those after her tea—and this bar.

Hovering over the rest, she randomly selected the next note. *Juice. So good.* It had been a long time since she'd had juice. Having it would have meant a trip down the mountain.

Taking one of the small boxes, she lifted it closer to try to figure out how to get to the juice. There was a tiny straw in a package on the outside. Glancing at the teapot, she decided a treat of juice at breakfast would be okay. Stabbing the straw into the little foil spot, the juice squirted out all over her hand. She would have to do it slower next time. Taking a sip, she smiled. It was good. Looking at the label again, she decided fruit punch was something she liked.

Taking another bite of the protein bar, she washed it down with the juice. This was probably the best breakfast she'd had in a long time.

Spotting the little box, she picked up the note. *Jesse gave me one of the painkillers in here. The headache didn't leave, but it was much better.* Opening the box, she looked at what was in it. Taking her time to read each thing. The contents of the box impressed her. Her grandparents hadn't had items like this. Some medical supplies, yes, but these were miracle ointments and—she paused and did an internal assessment, her head wasn't aching. There was always a headache of some degree present, but normally after she lost control and Minn burst free, she'd feel the sharp pains in her head for a few days.

Sitting down, she put everything carefully back into the box and closed it. The package beside the box had no note, but it plainly said Beef Jerky on it. She grinned. She'd missed the jerky that Papa Low made. No doubt Evanna was happy with this item as well.

Picking up the journal, she opened it again and found the page from yesterday. Moving just her eyes, she looked at the small box of those protein bars and took another out of it. There were plenty, another wouldn't be missed.

She re-read the first part of what Evanna had written. Could it be true? Was there help for them? For Minn, could they really help her and Evanna with Minn? She closed her eyes and felt for her cat. She was there, calm, watching. She always watched, but calm wasn't a word she'd usually use regarding her. Had the painkiller done that? She would have to ask about that.

Looking back at the journal, she re-read the second part Evanna had written. Honestly, it was the first personal thing she'd ever left her. That alone told her there was something about Jesse and the idea of leaving the mountain that had reached a part of Evanna that Leah had never been able to.

Leah I don't know if it's this painkiller or something else, but I'm relaxed and just sitting here thinking. I know, that's normally your thing and not mine. I walked around and showed Jesse in the houses tonight. I like talking to him. He's interesting and funny, but most of all I believe he really cares about what is happening to us. I know our grandparents did and Aunt Tillie too, but it matters more to me that he does and I can't explain why.

I spoke on his phone! It was so clear. I talked to his friend (I can't even imagine how her name would be spelled) Shaylyn? She's a healer and she sounds super smart and really nice too. She told me there are many people out there that are like us and a lot of places that can help us. I did tell her you weren't good going to places and being around people and she said if need be you could meet these people online and not in person. I'm not sure what that is, but I think we need to do this. Minn is getting harder for me to control and you know it exhausts me more and more each day, so if there is a way to help Minn, it would help us too.

Shaylyn also asked if it was just the three of us. I've listened a lot in the last day and I believe it is just us, do you agree? Let me know.

Tomorrow you need to help Jesse by telling him what absolutely has to leave with us. Everything else he says will be packed up and shipped to us, so this is good, right? It means we will still be in charge of looking after all of it. And if they do go to those addresses from the letter and some of our clan are there we will still have it for them.

I'm tired now. This has been a long day for me.

Please write back and know I will make sure you and Minn are safe on our new journey.
Ev

That was the most emotional thing Evanna had ever left her. It scared her to her core, but her head was telling her they needed to leave the mountain. She glanced at the food things on the table again. So many new things. She closed her eyes and felt for Evanna. Smiling she opened them. She was near, not close enough to influence her, but close enough to watch. "Okay." she whispered, knowing she would hear her, "I'll try to do this." Closing the journal, she left it on the table so she could reply later. Getting up, she looked around. What couldn't she live without? Biting her lip, she turned slowly, this was going to be hard.

Shaking her head, she picked up the box and moved it back over to the corner. This was so hard.

A light tap on the door had her spin around, Jesse stood there. "Oh." She clasped her hands in front of her. "I was just trying to," she looked at the piles set around the room, "sort things."

He smiled, "can I help?" He stepped inside and closed the door. "I can at least move things where you want them."

She loved his smile, so warm and friendly. "I don't know what to take."

Jesse came across the room and then looked around. "All of it will be packed up and shipped to you, so," his eyes locked on hers, "you just need to take what you need until everything else arrives."

Leah nodded slowly, "I-I don't know what I'll need." She hated feeling like she was lacking in any way, "I've never been on a trip."

He shrugged in an easy way, "well, we won't be sightseeing

much, so maybe some notebooks, or something to read, clothes, and small things really," he motioned to the door, "We want Thera to have space to move around."

"Oh," Leah exhaled, "I'd forgotten that." Placing her hand over her mouth she looked at the shelves, "so, maybe just important clan records and things?"

Jesse nodded, "those will be helpful for the Alliance, yes."

Leah glanced at the kitchen area and the potatoes sitting in the basket, "can we take the harvest from the garden?"

Jesse rubbed his hand over his strong jaw, "we can try. How much is there?"

"I can, uh, show you the storeroom." She pointed to the trap door on the floor. "I just think it would be a waste to leave it."

Jesse went over and pulled the latch up, "we'll fit as much as we can." He stood there.

Her heartbeat increased as she looked at the dark hole in the floor, "I," she frowned, "I don't- can't go down there in the dark," she held her hand over her throat and looked away from him, was Evanna close? "Usually-usually Evanna puts things down or brings them up for me."

Jesse gave her a caring look, "I can go down and look, you don't have to do anything you don't want to do." He turned and looked around and then went over to the counter. Grabbing a candle, he went over to the stove opened one of the cover plates on the stove, and lit the candle from the flames inside.

When he disappeared into the dark space, she moved over closer so she could look down into it. He came over and looked up at her. "Packed properly we can probably fit this." He smiled up at her.

Leah nodded, feeling torn between the good news and being so near the dark hole. "Okay." She backed away from it as he came back up. "I'm-I don't do dark spaces well." She rubbed her forehead, focusing and trying to let Evanna know she needed her closer.

"Hey," he closed the door and blew out the candle, "It's

okay," he touched her arm lightly, "it's not a problem." Leaning down he looked her right in the eyes, "you don't have to do *anything* you're not comfortable with, okay?" He gave his head a quick shake, "I don't expect you to. I want you to feel safe around me."

She glanced at his mouth as he spoke, a feeling of ease came over her, Evanna was closer, reassuring her everything was okay. "All right." She answered quietly. With jerky movements, she nodded, "thank you."

Jesse gave her another little smile, "now, can you show me how to make coffee that doesn't choke me?" He looked at the percolator on the counter.

Leah smiled, "yes, I can do that."

She liked how he sat at the table and didn't crowd her space. Clearing her throat, she looked away from the stove over at him. "Evanna said if we go with you, we can get help with Minn."

He didn't rush to answer and for some reason that put her more at ease, that he thought his words through. "Yes. I spoke to my friend, and she's been in touch with a doctor who can help both of you with Minn and anything else."

"Anything like how tired we are?"

Leaning on the table, he studied her for a moment, "I'll be honest with you, I don't know a lot about the disorder, I'm learning about it as much as I can until we get back and can talk to professionals that have experience with it."

"I'm trying to accept leaving the mountain," she motioned around the room, "leave our home because we need help, I know this, it's just hard."

"I imagine it is." He didn't move or fidget when he spoke to her, he looked at her, giving his full attention, which made her feel special somehow.

"I don't know if Evanna is okay with seeing a doctor, but I know it exhausts her to control Minn, and the pain it causes her makes me feel," she looked down at her hands, not sure if she should be saying this, "it makes me feel weak." She glanced back at him, unsure if she wanted to see his reaction.

"You're not weak." He pointed to the kitchen, "Evanna admitted she wasn't a great cook, I doubt that made her feel inadequate in any way." He shrugged, "we all have something we're good at, just as much as things we aren't. It doesn't make us any less or more than the next person."

Leah felt her face flush at his words. "I like that." She admitted, "how you explained that." She smiled, "thank you."

"It is what it is, Leah, I'm not good at some things either." He still gave her his complete attention.

"What aren't you good at?" She checked to see how much water was left to drip through.

Jesse chuckled, "the list is long." He grinned, "cooking is one of them, I often cheat and just shift and go eat something." He shrugged, "or order take out when I'm in the mood for something particular."

"What's take out?" She poured the coffee into a cup and went over and set it on the table for him.

"Thank you." He opened the sugar bowl took out a tiny bit of sugar and put it in. "Take out is," he nodded his, "ordering any food you're in the mood for and having it delivered to your door or going in somewhere and getting it to take out and eat."

"Any food?" She sat down, needing to know more about this.

"Chinese food, pizza…"

"I don't know what those are."

He grinned slowly, "you will get to know, because unless we're taking a stove with us, that's how we'll be eating for the trip home."

The idea of trying new foods she didn't have to hunt, grow and cook was exciting. Biting her lip, she continued to look at him, "I think I want to try them all." The excitement of it made her a little breathless.

Jesse chuckled again, "if you like that idea, you're going to *love* a microwave oven."

Leaning a little closer, she watched the playful look in his eyes. "What is that?"

"That," he smirked, "is a tiny oven you put food in and it's ready in a few minutes."

"No." He smiled at her. "In a few minutes?" She felt a little giddy. "I need to try one of those too." Sitting back, she touched her warm cheeks, "Evanna isn't going to believe all of this."

"The magical thing about a microwave is almost anyone can cook using one." He frowned for a second, "almost, they're not foolproof."

"You must have so much free time to do other things if you can cook in a few minutes." She looked around the room, "if this were a normal home, like where you're from what else would be in it?" She sat back and waited; things couldn't be that different off this mountain.

"Well," he took a small sip, "you know about a stove and fridge." He motioned to the ones that hadn't worked since the power was gone. "But there are dishwashers, you put the dishes in, turn on the water and push a button and walk away."

"It washes the dishes, on its own?"

He nodded, "there's clothes washers, and dryers too."

"That's pretty wonderful." She grinned, "I can't even picture something like that."

Jesse took another drink and then set his cup down, "I'll probably stop at a laundromat and do mine on the way back, so you'll get to see firsthand."

"I can't wait." It may have seemed like a small thing to him, but to her, it was nothing short of a miracle. Cooking and cleaning in so little time, there would be more time to read or paint and draw. The reality came back fast. To experience any of those things, she was going to have to leave here. Standing up, she looked around the room. "I need to go back to sorting things." She nodded, "in the other homes too."

Jesse took one more sip and then stood up, "just tell me where you want things and I'll help."

Leah studied him. He meant it, he was here to help and not try to get her to do anything. "Thank you." She smiled briefly and then went into the bedroom.

Once inside she closed her eyes for a second. Evanna was close, watching, she would come out and do this if Leah was unable to face it, but wanted her to choose what was the most important to her. Nodding, she opened her eyes and went over to the cabinet in the corner that all the clan books were in.

Chapter Fifteen

Jesse read the message again and then checked the time. He'd have to go down to the van for this video call. The signal was the strongest down there. He turned and looked at Leah as she carried a box out of the house that had been Papa Low and Nana Pearl's. She was really struggling with her emotions doing this. An hour wasn't much notice. He should have remembered to check his phone where he knew he had a signal. Rubbing his jaw, he watched her for a moment longer and then text Devin back. *I don't want to miss it. I have to run down the damn mountain to my laptop though, so stall it for 15 minutes.*

Tucking his phone into his pocket, he jogged toward the center house she'd gone in. There was one thing he knew to help when emotions were riding you, a run. Hopefully, she could let Minn out without issue. He didn't have time to chase her down through the bush. Thera came over and ran beside him. He glanced down at her. There was no way there were going to get out of this yard without her too. Having to explain chasing a shifter and her pet leopard around the bush if he was late, was something he didn't relish doing.

"Leah." He poked his head in the door.

"Yes?" She came out of the bedroom.

Jesse stepped inside. "I have to go down to the van," he didn't know how to explain it exactly, "there's a video meeting with the King and several Alpha's from Canada that I really can't miss."

"A video meeting?" She raised both eyebrows and put her hands on her hips.

"Yeah," he motioned to the door, "on my laptop, the signal is stronger down there."

"Oh, I see." Her expression told him she really didn't.

"I was thinking you could come with me. Thera and Minn could use the run."

She bit her lip and continued to look at him, but he could tell by the expression on her face that she wasn't really seeing him at this moment.

"I wouldn't mind seeing your van, or this laptop. Is it like the tv?"

Jesse smirked, "sort of, but—" He blew out a breath, "we could bring it back up and watch a movie, I have some downloaded for when I'm at my place." He cleared his throat, "I don't have the power there yet, so I just watch movies when I take a break."

Her expression was almost amused, she didn't understand that either.

"Okay. Um, I can use that run pack you brought up to put my clothes in?" She blushed, "I want to see this with my eyes and not Minn's."

"Yeah, go grab it and I'll show you how to put it on." He glanced behind him, "will Thera stay with us down there?"

Leah nodded, "Mmhmm, she won't wander too far." She went into the bedroom.

He pulled on his jeans and got his phone out of his pack. Bringing up Devin's number he typed quickly, *at the bottom now, give me a few to boot up the laptop and connect. Leah is also with me. Message if it's a bad idea for her to witness this meeting.* Going over he unlocked the van and then went around the back and opened the back doors. He'd sat here for many calls and video calls in the last few years.

Opening the hard case he used for his laptop, he pulled it out and started it. He traveled with two spare batteries for it, the same as his phone. The amount of time he spent on the road, he never knew when he'd need it.

"Is that a laptop?"

He glanced behind him to see Leah standing there. Nodding, he motioned for her to come closer. "It connects with the signal…"

"The signal like your phone?"

He shrugged, "pretty much."

"So, what is a video call?" She clasped her hands in front of her as she leaned over and looked at the keyboard.

"It's like a phone call, but we can see everyone."

She gave him a surprised look. "See them on the screen?"

"Yeah. They'll be lined up on the screen, when they talk the screen will just be of them…"

A look of shock and delight filled her face. "This is exciting."

Jesse laughed, "the meeting may be upsetting at some parts, but it's all about the shifter community."

Leah sobered and nodded, "is it okay if I just stand off to the side?" She hugged her waist, "I'd like to see others like us."

"Sure. I've already told Devin—the Prince of the Alliance that you're with me." He glanced over to where Thera was laying down.

"The prince?" She blew out a short breath, "will the King be there too?"

Jesse nodded, "As far as I know, he will be."

"Oh, my goodness."

Leah stood back watching over Jesse's shoulder as he set up his laptop. She was completely fascinated with it. He was talking quietly with a man on there. It was like a small television, only Jesse could communicate with them. She stepped a little closer so she could see him clearly.

The man looked right at her and smiled. "Hello, Leah?"

Eyes wide, she looked at Jesse when he glanced over his shoulder.

"He can see you." He said softly. He turned back to the screen. "Devin, this is Leah."

"Hello." She said, feeling her cheeks heat. She hadn't realized he'd be able to see her. "I'm sorry to interrupt."

The man shrugged, "You're not interrupting. Jesse and I are in a private room right now, we'll join the others when everyone is there."

"A room?" She looked around them.

Jesse leaned against the door of the van. "It's what they call them, they're not real rooms."

"Oh, I see."

A beautiful blonde woman looked over Devin's shoulder. "Hello, Leah, I'm Rayne, Devin's mate." She smiled at her.

Leah moved a little closer to Jesse. "Hello." She offered a smile.

"I'm so happy Jesse found you. I can't wait to meet you in person." Rayne smiled at her.

"The others will be ready in a minute, Jesse," Devin told them.

"Okay, I'll go back to the lobby and wait." Jesse reached over and did something with the keys on the machine. He turned and looked at her. "Are you okay with this?"

Leah sucked in a breath and nodded. "It's not scary with them not really here."

He grinned, "Good. If you hear anything that upsets you or that you're not comfortable with, just walk away, okay?"

She studied his pale eyes and could see how concerned he was for her. "Yes. Thank you." She motioned to the machine, "for letting me see this."

He smiled at her again, "I'm happy to show you anything you're interested in."

She glanced away, feeling Evanna closer now. "Evanna's close." She whispered.

"Are you okay?" He straightened and placed his hand lightly on her arm.

Leah looked down at his hand, it didn't bother her at all. That was surprising. "I'm fine, she's just interested too I think."

"Oh, okay." He cleared his throat. "How's Minn doing?"

She didn't understand why it pleased her as much as it did that he was asking about Minn, or that he understood about Evanna. She checked inside briefly. "She seems content." Putting her hand on her throat, she shook her head slowly, "it's so unusual, but I will take it."

Jesse searched her face, "maybe she'll enjoy leaving the mountain."

Leah bit her lip and thought about that. "I don't know about that, but Evanna told me that you would take it slow."

Nodding, Jesse glanced briefly at the screen before looking back to her, "as slow as you need. If I have to stop every hour, we will."

"Thank you." Her heartbeat increased, but not in a panicked way, it was—she wasn't sure, but thought maybe it was excitement. The screen changed, and she started to back up. "I'll stay out of the way."

"No need. You're just as important to this meeting as I am." He touched the small of her back encouraging her to stay beside him. Leaning over, he adjusted the angle of the screen.

"If you're sure." She hugged her waist, feeling nervous. She didn't know why, but she leaned closer to him, there was something that calmed her when she was near him.

Jesse glanced down at her and smiled. "No need to be nervous. You already spoke to the Prince and Princess."

Her eyes felt like they bulged out of her head. "I didn't know."

Jesse chuckled, "there's no bowing with video meetings."

"Okay." She nodded and swallowed the nervous lump in her throat. Her nerves were forgotten as the screen changed into several boxes. She leaned closer, she was in one of the boxes with Jesse. She smiled and then watched him smile and look at her. It was the strangest, but a most interesting thing.

"Hello everyone." The screen changed to a man's face in it. It was a kind, but stern face.

There was a chorus of hello's, Jesse was one of them. Leah didn't feel right about speaking, so she just stood there. There were so many people. She'd seen people on screens before, but these were real people. These were shifters like she was. She sensed Evanna telling her to pay attention.

"This is the first time we've had this many on a call. To make things simpler, the first time we speak, we'll introduce ourselves, where we're located, and our clan type."

The heads in the boxes on the screen all nodded.

"Most of you are here because you represent an area and have been working to help the Alliance with tracking and checking in on clans. Zain, why don't you run the numbers for us."

"Sir," another face appeared, he bowed his head, making Leah wonder if that had been the King speaking. "I've got the numbers so far from the other clan coordinators, this includes yours, Jesse."

Jesse nodded, even though he didn't say anything.

Zain looked down at something and continued. "I'm still waiting for word from Foster and Deva, but so far it's not great." He cleared his throat, "we have twenty-five clans at this point that are no longer." He looked back at the screen, his blue eyes conveying a deep sadness. "We're still looking into more."

"Shep," a woman with grey hair and dark eyes appeared on the screen, "sorry, I'm Effie, Alpha to the Harpy Eagle clan in BC." She nodded her head once, "Shep, I could send some of mine to help with check-ins, as you know we can cover a great distance not having to travel on the roads." Her expression was very serious.

The man appeared again, Leah looked closely, he did have kind eyes, maybe he was the prince her grandparents had met. "I appreciate the offer, Effie, but I'm trying to keep clans close together. It's easier to keep everyone safe that way. I will keep you in mind if we need some of yours to fly out to more remote areas."

Leah was astonished, there were shifters that flew? She looked to the box the Effie woman was in to see her nod.

"Ed, here, tiger clan in Ontario," The man was older, but not old-old, Leah decided, "have the one hundred and seventy-two remaining clans been confirmed then?"

Zain's face came back on the screen. "I would say about seventy percent have been so far, those we can just call up were easy to check, the others either our clan co-ordinators are checking or from other clans that are closer are."

Ed came back on the screen and nodded. "Let us know if you need any done in our area."

"Thanks, Ed." Devin's face came on the screen, "for the most part those around us have been."

It went back to the boxes again. Leah tried to count how many people there were, but each time one of them spoke, the screen would change, and she'd have to start over.

A woman with hair that was close to orange came on the screen, "Maxine, wolverine clan, Northwest Territories," She gave a brief nod, "we still have a lot of ground to cover up here and haven't been able to reach the clans in Nunavut."

"Zain, is any of ours on the way there to help?" Devin's voice came over the speaker, but he didn't change the screen.

"Checking," Zain answered. His face came on the screen, "we do not have anyone that far North. It could take a few weeks before we can get anyone there."

"Lois, are you able to assist and send someone up to check on a few?" Shep spoke clearly.

An older woman with white hair and brown eyes came on the screen. "Uh, Lois, Polar Clan, Northern Manitoba," She paused and gave a brief smile, "I can send two of mine up to take a look, send me the locations."

"Thank you, Lois." Shep said calmly, "In light of that, perhaps Liz, Maxine, and Effie could assist in the area above them." Shep looked away from the screen, "I'm told there's six in the Yukon and Northwest Territories that no one can get in touch with. Zain will have locations for you."

"Happy to." Leah recognized Effie's voice again, even though she didn't put her face on the screen.

A woman with black and white streaked hair came on the screen, "Liz, from the crowned eagle clan in BC, I have a few trackers that would gladly help out, Shep."

Leah looked to see Shep nod when the screen went back to boxes.

"I can send a small team, Shep, send me the details." Maxine disappeared from the big screen before Leah could blink.

A handsome man with black hair and dark green eyes appeared on the screen. "Lloyd, jag clan, Ontario, many of mine are at Shae's clan helping there right now."

Shep didn't put his face on the big screen, "That's fine, Lloyd, we already have your nephew's time monopolized for the Alliance."

The man in the box beside Devin grinned wide. Leah wondered if that was the nephew. This was so fascinating; she forgot her face was on the screen too until she looked along the bottom and saw her there with Jesse.

"Cecil, lynx clan, Quebec, Shep, let us know if you need anyone to check in the Eastern provinces, we have delivery flights in that direction weekly." All Leah noticed was how his pale amber eyes were very cat-like.

"I'll have Zain get in touch with you after this call, Cecil. Thank you." Shep told him.

"Benny, Lion Clan, lower BC, if you need anyone to cross the border, Shep, we're practically sitting on it."

"We've had a few down that way and the clans were gone, Benny, but there's a few more to check in Northern Washington, so we'll coordinate with you once we have those reports," Shep said softly. "As I said I don't want to separate clans right now, but we also need to know if there are more out there needing help." He cleared his throat and then nodded to someone Leah couldn't see, "we've found a few from a couple of clans, so the urgency is there that we look faster." His face disappeared from the big screen. "Jesse located the last member of a leopard clan in Michigan. We're happy to have you, Leah."

Leah jolted and grasped Jesse's hand without warning.

Jesse reached over and tapped a key on the laptop and then their faces were on the screen. "We're packing up here and should be on the road in the next day or so." He said, giving her hand a quick squeeze.

Leah nodded.

Then he made their faces disappear.

"Welcome, Leah, we're happy you're well."

She heard a few more people welcome her but was too busy focusing on keeping her breathing even. Thera got up and moved over closer.

Jesse leaned closer to the screen, with one hand he typed something and hit another button.

Devin's face came on the screen. "If there's nothing else, for now, we need to have a brief meeting with a few of the members here."

There was a short pause where no one spoke.

"Thank you everyone for doing this, we're going to start doing general meetings this way more often." Shep's tone left no room for anyone to wonder if they were dismissed or not.

Leah blinked and found she and Jesse were on another screen, the other boxes were gone. Then a box appeared with Devin, and Rayne was with him.

"Dad and the others will be here in a moment if you want to grab a quick drink or something," Devin said.

"I'm just going to mute us for a second, Devin." Jesse hit another key, then tugged on her hand to pull her away from the screen. He stopped and turned, placing a finger under her chin, and tilted her head up. "Are you okay? You don't have to be in this next part."

His tone was so soft and coaxing. "I just—" Leah blew out a breath and looked down, she saw she was still squeezing his hand. "I'm sorry." She released it.

Jesse stepped closer and took both her hands gently in his. "It's fine. Are you okay?"

"It was all so fascinating and then everyone was looking at me…" She put her hand on her chest and took a deep breath. "How am I ever going to be able to be around people?" There was so much else that worried her about leaving the mountain, but now this was foremost in her mind.

"We'll take it slow." He nodded, his pale eyes reflecting concern and something softer. "You don't have to meet anyone until you're ready."

Leah could feel Minn stirring, she blew out a breath, determined to stay here. Closing her eyes, she concentrated, trying to feel Evanna. "A little help," she said under her breath. Evanna's presence was much closer now. Close enough she felt the urge to get the hair off her neck.

"Leah?" Jesse's voice was so soft now, barely a whisper. "Just take a few breaths and focus on the scents around you. Ground yourself with the soil you're standing on."

She could feel his hands sliding softly down her arms and back up slowly. It was surprisingly soothing. She took a deep breath like he'd said and took the scents into her body. The trees, the soil, she could smell nearby critters and—she opened her eyes and looked at Jesse. She could smell him, and she didn't know why, but she felt an immediate sense of calm, Minn settled too.

"Okay?" He leaned down, his face was so close to hers now, that she could feel his breath brushing over her cheek.

"I've got it." she was breathless, but not panicked. Nodding, she gave him a small smile. "We're good."

The smile he gave her made her feel like she'd done the most spectacular thing. Her cheeks heated. "Okay, we should get back." He cocked his head to the side; a questioning look on his face

"Yes. I'd like to join you and meet your friends."

Chapter Sixteen

Leah stood close to him as he unmuted the laptop. Jesse wasn't going to complain. His cat was ready to freak out when the waves of panic had been pouring off her. He turned the mic back on and stood back.

On the screen were Cal and Shaelan in one box, the same as Devin and Rayne were sharing one. He was happy to see Blair and Kobie there as well. He'd meant to call Blair, but things had taken a turn after he went up that mountain. The last box was Shepard Addison. He bowed his head without even speaking, some things were just ingrained.

"We're back."

"Noah is out on a call, so he's here, but not patched into the video," Rayne told him.

"I'm assuming this meeting is because of the new team?" Jesse crossed his arms over his chest and tried to focus on what was being said. He preferred this, where everyone could speak, and you didn't have to put your face on the screen larger than life.

"Looking a little tired, Jesse," Calum said without any readable expression on his face.

Jesse huffed out a breath, "the past week has been rough, I

covered a lot of miles."

"You should get a few down days when you get back," Devin stated.

"Do you have a timeline on when that will be Jesse?" Shep stared at the screen.

Jesse glanced at Leah to see she had a wide-eyed expression on her face, he turned back to the screen. "I'm not sure how long it will take us to get back to Blair's, it may be slow going." He didn't want the attention on Leah, so he picked up the laptop, "I'll show you why." Turning, he lifted it up, so that the camera could pick up Thera. She was lying in the shade of the trees a few feet from the van. Satisfied they'd all seen, he turned it around and set it back down. "We don't know how Thera is going to take to a ride in the van.

"Oh my, she's gorgeous," Rayne said.

Kobie leaned closer to the screen. "That's a wild leopard?"

"Yes. Well, I don't know how wild she is anymore." Jesse grinned and moved closer to Leah, so their arms were touching. "We may have to stop often until she gets used to it."

"It's probably a good thing the van doesn't have windows," Blair grinned, "I could just see the reaction as you're heading along the highway with a leopard sitting in the back."

"Keep us up-to-date when you leave, Jesse." Shep cut off all humor.

"Will do," Jesse said just as abruptly.

"I'm setting up the weapons training to start at the end of the week for Blair and Kobie," Shep glanced down for a moment, "as much as I'd like to take our time with this we can't afford to." He cleared his throat, "those addresses checked out, Jesse, so they are a top priority right along with Lindon Eldon's location."

Blair's expression changed to one of retribution.

Jesse looked at Leah, she wasn't as steady as she looked now that he looked at her eyes. Hoping he didn't spook her; he wrapped his hand around hers and gave it a gentle squeeze. She gripped it and held onto it. Turning back, he looked at the

King, "do you have any numbers from those addresses?"

"We're working on it."

"I was there." Noah's voice came through the speaker. "At two of them. I can draw out the layouts."

Jesse felt Leah grip his hand harder.

"Is Leah here?" Noah asked.

"She is." Jesse turned to look at her. Her brows were drawn as what he was saying registered.

"I always wondered," Noah said. "I helped Lyvia get her out and I always wondered if she made it."

Leah's hand went over her mouth. The one holding his started shaking. She dropped her hand to her throat. "You knew my mother?"

"I did."

Rayne and Shaelan looked almost as upset as Leah did.

"Do you think she's still there?" Leah's voice was shaking now.

"I don't know." Noah's tone was quiet, "all the men stationed there were moved after you got away, so I-I don't know."

Jesse's cat couldn't stand the way she was shaking. Wrapping his other arm around her, he pulled her closer. She seemed to relax and then stiffened and leaned away from him for a second.

"When was that?"

He didn't need to look to see that Leah was gone and Evanna was now fronting. The harsher tone told him all he needed to know.

"Four and half years ago, maybe, I can't be sure," Noah answered. "I have to go; they're going to drive the rig right off the embankment."

"Thanks, Noah," Calum said quickly.

"We have teams monitoring all motion at those addresses," Devin said while looking down at something.

"Can you see who is inside?" Evanna moved away from Jesse but didn't release his hand.

"I'm sorry, everyone, I need to take a call." Shep interrupted.

"Okay, Dad, I'll check in later."

Shep nodded his head once and then vanished from the screen.

"We're getting as many pictures as we can from those locations." Devin looked back at the screen.

"I want to see them when we get where we're going." Evanna leaned down closer and looked at the people on the screen.

"I'll send them to Calum," Devin told her.

"Evanna? Hi, I'm Shaelan by the way, we spoke on the phone." Shaelan waved at the camera.

"Hi. Wow, you are so pretty." Evanna said with a big smile.

Jesse felt her relax a bit and was thankful for Shaelan intervening and distracting her.

"Thank you," Shaelan glanced at Calum.

"I think you're lovely as well, Evanna. I'm Rayne, Devin's mate." Rayne leaned closer and smiled.

"Nice to meet you," Evanna said nodding. "I love your hair." She shrugged, "I couldn't deal with it, but it's very pretty."

Rayne laughed, "trust me there are days I want to shave it off."

Thera got up and came over, she nudged Evanna and then sniffed the laptop.

"Oh, I think Thera is done with this," Evanna said glancing at Jesse.

"Yeah, I think so too." He leaned down to adjust the laptop so they could see them again, "we're going to have to go. We still have to get back up to the top and finish packing things up."

"Call me when you're on the road," Calum told him.

"I will. Uh, Shaelan? Any ideas on something herbal we could give Thera to keep her chill for the ride?"

Thera sat down and looked at him as if she understood him.

"I have a few ideas, but good luck feeding them to her."

Shaelan grinned.

"Text me them, preferably with pictures if they're plants and I'll try." Shaelan nodded. "Okay, I'll talk to you all soon."

"Bye." Evanna leaned down beside him.

Jesse disconnected from the call and powered the laptop off. Closing it, he put it back in the case and then closed the door. He had promised to take it up top so Leah could watch a movie, but he wasn't quite sure how he was getting it up there.

"That was something." Evanna motioned to the case in his hand, "seeing people like that."

Jesse nodded, "technology is a wonder." If not annoying at times he thought. Going around to the side door, he opened it and pulled one of the duffle bags over. "I need a way to get this up to the top, I told Leah we could watch a movie."

Evanna was right beside him again. "You can watch movies on it too?"

Jesse gave her a quick smile, "no promises you'll like my movie choices, but yeah you can." He studied her for a second. "Is Leah okay?"

Evanna nodded her head slowly, "yeah, she was trying hard to stay, but Minn picked up on her emotions and was getting harder to control," she lifted her arms, "so here I am."

"I didn't know about Noah."

"Do you know him?" She watched as he wrapped some cord around the handle of the case.

"Yeah, I was there when they got him out." Jesse paused and glanced at her, "he was pretty messed up."

She snorted, "anyone that was there would be."

He wanted to ask questions but knew it was too soon to delve into it. He hoped someday they could talk about it, both Evanna and Leah. "Are you going to be able to control Minn for the run back up?"

Nodding, she went over and picked up the run pack. "A good run will help settle her down." She grinned at him, "any more of those bars left?"

Jesse laughed, "we didn't eat the whole box if that's what you're asking."

"I want to get boxes and boxes of them when we leave." She looked in the van and checked it out. "We have money. They sold the vehicles and preserves, hides, a lot of things, but just kept putting the money in a box."

"We'll get you a bank account set up." He tied the case to his run pack, "keeping it in a box once we're off the mountain isn't a good idea." Now he was curious how much money the elders had hoarded away. He'd already been doing the math on his finances and figuring out how much he could afford to help get them whatever they needed.

"Where *are* we going once we're packed up?" She watched as he locked up the van again and put the keys in his pack.

"To be honest, I'm not sure. I have to go back to Blair's-"

"We're sticking with you, so I guess that's where we're going." She nodded her head once and then turned and walked into the trees to strip down and shift.

Jesse rubbed his hand along the bottom of his jaw, it pleased him more than he could express that she wanted to stay with him, but how was she going to get the help she needed if she was with him. He was never in one place long enough to do anything—with all the locations they were found, things were going to get even more hectic than they were. Shaking his head, he stepped back behind the van and took his jeans off. As soon as they were on the road, he needed to talk to Devin about this, and Calum as well, too much had changed.

Chapter Seventeen

Jesse opened the map on the table and smoothed the many creases from it being in his pack most of the time. He needed a route back that would allow for stops if Thera—or Minn decided they needed to go for a run.

He had no idea what to expect from Leah on this trip but was figuring if he could find low traffic, off the beaten path route, she would be more at ease.

Leah came in carrying a crate. "This is the last of it." She set it on the floor with the rest.

They'd decided it would be too wasteful to leave the vegetables here, so somehow Jesse was going to pack them, the eight boxes and three bags into the van with Thera for the long drive back.

They would be adding to it along the way. After he'd seen what little clothing she had, he'd decided one of the first stops would be a small town along the way to buy her some new things. Hopefully, taking her into a store didn't turn out to be a mistake.

As soon as they got back to Blair's he was going to get Kobie and the other women to help her, maybe order some things online. Of course, to do that he'd have to set up an account for her and he was pretty sure she was lacking any identification to do that. Among the boxes was one marked clan paperwork, so he was holding out that it may be in there.

Leah was standing beside him now looking down at the map. "This is nothing like the map Papa Low had."

Jesse blew out a breath, "A lot has changed."

"Where are we right now?" She leaned closer.

Jesse put his finger on the map to show her.

"And where are we going?"

Flipping out the rest of it, he pointed to Blair's, or as near it as he could, half that area wasn't marked on the map.

"That's far." She said breathlessly.

Nodding, he dragged his finger along the map, "I'm going to take a long way back, avoid any big cities and heavily populated areas."

"You can do that?"

"For the most part." He turned and looked at her, "if at any time you're having problems dealing with it let me know, and we'll stop."

"Okay. Thank you." She smiled at him, but he could still see how nervous she was.

"I'm actually more concerned about Thera," he grinned, "I think you're going to handle it just fine." He motioned around him, "you looked after everything here this long, so I think you'll be able to handle a drive."

She didn't answer, just leaned over the map and ran her fingers along it, pausing a few times to look closer at the names of places. "Is it going to matter if I cross this?" She was pointing to the border.

Jesse shook his head, "not really. The Alliance will get some papers for you so no one will question it." He shrugged, "Kobie's whole clan are now Canadian." He winked at her.

"If we weren't shifters…"

"Things would be more complicated." He sat down, leaving the map open for her to look at, "hiding our existence is the only way we've survived this long."

"No," she scrunched up her face, "one-forms? I think that's

what Papa Low called them, none of them know about our kind?"

"Some do. Some can be trusted." He cleared his throat, "but for the most part we try to stick to our own and stay off other people's radar."

"Bad things happen when they know about us." She said quietly and then continued to look at the map.

Jesse didn't need to clarify she was right. They both knew that what Tomas was doing, *had* been doing to their kind was because of what they were. When he was younger, he always pictured a world where everyone knew and it was okay. Now, he knew that wasn't true and would likely never happen.

Leah straightened up and clasped her hands in front of her. "Do we stop to rest or keep going?"

Picking up the map, he began folding it back up, "normally I'd stop and stay in a motel, but I don't think Thera will like that." He gave his head a slight shake, "there will be too many smells in them, it would bother her."

"She's not fond of being inside." She covered a yawn.

Jesse paused and really looked at her. "You could take a nap if you like, I was going to take some of this down today, then we'll finish the rest in the morning."

"I could help you."

He searched her face, she looked exhausted. That worried him, he needed to bring that up next time he spoke to Shaelan. "It's fine. It's going to take a few times of rearranging the van to make the most room for Thera."

"Okay." She yawned again. "Oh," she spun around and went over to the boxes they'd stacked in Aunt Tillie's entranceway. Opening it, she pulled out what looked like an old metal fishing tackle. "I wasn't sure what to do with this, so I put it all in here." She held it up.

Curious, he went over and took it out of her hand. Balancing it on one arm, he popped the rusty latch and opened it. Inside were stacks of money. Giving her a quick look, he lifted a few of the bundles and looked under them. "This is a lot of money."

Leah nodded, "Papa Low sold things, like the cars no one used anymore." She shrugged, "we didn't have much to spend the money on, so it's been sitting here." She touched the stack in his hand, "I bundled it together with five hundred in each," she looked back at him, "there's lose stuff in the bottom." Clasping her hands again, she exhaled slowly, "I want to help pay for the trip." She nodded.

Jesse put the money back in the box and closed it up. "The Alliance pays for the trip, but we will use some of this to get you some new clothes," he looked at her feet and the sandals she had on, they'd been fixed many times, "and shoes."

Leah looked down at the threadbare dress she wore. "I would love a new dress, and we could get Evanna some jeans. She likes jeans and all of hers are so patched up there are no more jeans left." She gave a long sigh, "I think I will go lay down for a little while, then I'll get started on dinner." Giving him a sleepy smile, she bowed her head and walked out the door, closing it quietly behind her.

Jesse looked at the box in his hand. He wasn't taking this down to leave unattended overnight. Putting it on the table, he looked at the other boxes. Hopefully, the flat wagon he found wouldn't be too hard to handle going down. He grimaced, coming back up wasn't going to be fun. The wagon had two harnesses attached to it. The elders must have shifted and pulled it up. "Good thing we're in good shape." He told his cat out loud. Grabbing a box, he went out the door. He needed to call Shaelan before he started down.

"Seeing her shift in front of our eyes was something," Shaelan said with a clinical tone in her voice.

"I probably had my mouth hanging open," Blair admitted.

Jesse grinned, "I didn't notice."

"You're going to have to give us a cheat sheet." Kobie told him, "So we can tell which one is," she paused, "out? Is that the word?"

"Fronting." Shaelan supplied.

Jesse checked the rope holding the boxes on the wagon. "Well, the tone of voice is a big indicator, Leah is very soft-spoken and Evanna isn't rude, but you don't have to listen carefully to hear her."

"And if they're not speaking?" Calum inquired.

"Leah wears her hair down and Evanna pulls it up tight as soon as she's out." He frowned, "it's almost like it bothers her to have it down."

"It could be related to an unpleasant event in the past," Shaelan said softly.

"Should I," Jesse leaned against the wagon and kicked off his boot, "should I be asking about things in the past?"

"I would wait and speak to the doctor about that, Jesse, bringing up some things could cause her to have a bad episode."

Leaning down, he pulled the other boot off and tossed it on the trailer. "Okay, I'll do that, I just," he lifted his hand and then dropped it, "I want to help."

"Letting her know, both of them that you're there and that they're safe is the best way to help them right now, Jesse. Especially if they're still foggy after switching, just reassuring her."

He blew out a breath, "okay."

"How much are you hauling down?" Calum asked him in a tone that said he was getting impatient.

"It's not as bad as I thought." Jesse hissed out a breath, "she handed me a box of money today."

"A box of money?" Blair sounded amused.

"How much money are we talking about?" Calum wondered.

"Five thousand? Roughly. I guess there wasn't much to spend money on here." Picking up his other boot he added it to the trailer.

"It will help her get a good new start," Shaelan suggested.

"Yeah, the first stop is clothes, they're both wearing more patches than dress or jeans."

"They dress differently too?"

He pictured Shaelan making notes. "Yeah, Leah wears dresses and skirts. Evanna prefers jeans." He remembered his earlier thought, "maybe when we get back one of you ladies can help her order some stuff online?" He rubbed the back of his neck, "I still have to call Dev to get some documentation set up for her."

"Send him a picture and he'll take care of the rest," Calum informed him.

"I'll do that in the morning." Jesse looked at the wagon again, "too bad one of you aren't here to help me pull the wagon back up."

Someone snorted.

"Get the real cat to help." Blair offered.

Jesse looked at Thera where she sat watching him, "I'm pretty sure that would be a no-go on that." He grinned at the cat. "I'm going to go, I don't want to leave her up here too long alone, she's looking really tired today."

"Stress will do that, changes in routine. Trauma is a heavy thing to carry, Jesse." Shaelan was back in healer mode.

"Yeah, I guess it is. Hopefully, she'll get lots of rest on the trip back."

"Call us when you're heading out in the morning." Calum's tone told Jesse the call was finished.

"Will do."

"Bye," a few of the others echoed.

Hanging up, he put the phone in his pack and then pulled his shirt off. "This is going to suck." He mumbled as his jeans followed and he stared at the load on the small wagon. He was going to attempt it in cat form for the trip down too and hoped he wasn't going to have to walk it on two legs and hold the wagon back from flying down the rough path.

Chapter Eighteen

Stepping back, Jesse looked in the van. He'd managed to keep most of it to the sides, so there was room for Thera to lounge. He hoped she was going to lounge and not try to pace. Turning he looked to where she lay listening to Leah as she sat beside her talking.

Going around he opened both back doors and hoped Leah had some plan on how to get her *in* the van. She'd spread out a blanket on the floor, so maybe it had some sort of special meaning to the animal.

His phone buzzed and startled him. Pulling it out of his pocket, he grinned when he saw who it was.

"Foster."

"Hey, Jesse." He sighed loudly into the phone, "I'm fading here, so I'm going through my contact list calling *everyone* to keep my eyes open."

Jesse knew that feeling, "glad I rank such an important call. Where are you?"

"I have no idea anymore, it's a blur."

He couldn't remember the last time he'd seen him. Their clans were close together on the map, right along the border of Ontario and Manitoba, so they'd grown up together. "I hear that. How did you do with your list?"

"Struck out, all six I went looking for." He could hear the radio playing quietly in the background, "it's really fucking depressing, man."

"I know what you mean."

"How did you make out?"

Jesse turned back to look at Leah. "Found a few elders and one woman from two of mine."

"Same clan?"

Shaking his head, he walked around to the other side of the van and closed the door. "No, not even in the same state."

"Wow, one woman is all that's left of a clan?"

Jesse leaned on the hood and watched Thera roll onto her back so Leah could rub her belly. "Yeah, but there was information here that's led us to a few houses that Tomas is holding people. Noah even knows of them."

"That's some good news. How is Noah doing? That day we got him, and the others still haunt me."

"He seems to be settling well, adapting to life." Jesse couldn't help smiling as Leah lay down beside Thera and rubbed her face against her. "Gage and the clan have been good for him."

"I told Devin we need to start getting the survivors hooked up with like clans, it does seem to make a difference."

That made Jesse think of Evanna saying she was sticking with him. "Have you heard from any of the others?"

"I just talked to Amari, she found three clans, or what's left of them, so she's up to her ass in relocations right now."

"Three? That's great. The summary numbers Zain gave really hurt."

"Yeah, but the good news is there's still enough of us left to make a strong come back."

Jesse always loved Foster's optimism, even when it was hopeless, he thought of the good side.

"I talked to Webb earlier too, he was growling about something."

"He's a bear, I think that's just his nature." Jesse grinned.

"He's a happy asshole in any form." Foster laughed.

Leah got up and brushed off her dress, she looked over at Jesse and smiled.

"Listen, I know you need someone to talk so you stay awake, but I have to head out shortly."

"You are going home?"

"Not yet. Just spent two days hauling things down a mountain and now we're heading to Blair's—Ed's clan area."

"You're taking one of the survivors there?"

"Something like that."

"At least you have someone to talk to." Jesse could hear the window opening. "I heard about Blair's brother. Give me a shout when you guys are heading that way, I could use a good brawl."

Jesse snorted, "I don't think he'll need help, there's a lot of anger brewing in there."

"Anger is a good motivator," he paused, "shit, I gotta go, our king is calling."

"Drive safe."

"Talk to you later." The line when quiet.

He walked around to the other side of the van.

"Was that one of your friends?"

"Yeah, not one from the video call. I grew up with Foster."

"Oh, is he like us?" She clasped her hands in front of her, giving him her complete attention.

"He's a shifter, not leopard though, a coyote."

She looked excited, "really? Will I get to meet other shifter kinds?"

Jesse shrugged, "I'm sure you will. Blair's clan are tigers, and Cal and Shaelan are there and they're jaguars."

Leah glanced at Thera, "I wonder how she'll be around them."

Jesse watched Thera get up, "Hopefully friendly."

"I think she'll be fine just as long as she doesn't feel I'm threatened."

Jesse went over to the cat and rubbed his hand over the

back of her neck. "I won't let anyone scare or make her feel threatened, girl, you have my word." Thera bumped her head up against him. "Okay," he glanced back to Leah, "I have one facetime call to make to my folks, then we're on the road."

"Facetime call?"

He loved when her eyes went wider when she was interested in something. "Exactly what it sounds like, I'll be able to hear them and see them on my phone and them me."

"Is everything all right? The reason you're calling, I mean."

"Everything is fine. Because I'm on the road so much I call them every Sunday, just to check-in." She gave him one of those looks that made his cat purr, at least that's what he liked to think his cat was doing.

"That's sweet. I think family is important." She glanced up the mountain.

Jesse didn't want her to focus too much on leaving, so he sat down and motioned for her to come to sit. "You can meet them."

"Oh, all right." She came over and sat down gracefully.

"There's my mom, Joanie. My dad Jasper and my little sisters Jaide and Joslin, they're twins and," he closed his eyes for a second trying to remember, "thirteen, I think, almost fourteen."

"All of your names start with J." She grinned. "Do your parents work for the Alliance?"

He shook his head, "No my family is the second family in the clan."

"I never did understand what that is." She pulled up her knees and hugged them.

"Well, my dad helps our Alpha, Deshon, with clan things and basically if something were to happen to the entire Alpha family, my father would become Alpha."

"Oh." Her eyes widened. "That's a very important job then."

Jesse nodded. "It is. Fortunately for us, our Alpha has two sons, and a daughter, so I think we'll be just second family." He grinned, "and I'm very happy about that."

"I read through the clan records, but I didn't understand most of it." She looked at her hands as she spoke, "I guess I don't really have a clan now."

Jesse's cat went nuts inside him, prompting him immediately to fix how sad she was. "Hey, we may find some of your clan at those addresses, so let's not worry about that now."

Leah sucked in a shaky breath. "Okay."

He stood up, "you have Thera and now you have me, that's a good start if you ask me."

A smile slowly appeared on her face, "yes, I think so too."

With his hands on his hips, he looked at the cat, who was watching the both of them. "Now, think we can get her into the van?" he shrugged, "Then I'll call my folks while she's settling."

"We can try." Leah climbed into the van and sat on the blanket. "I was thinking maybe she'd be happier with me back here to start?"

He nodded, "anything that keeps her in the van while it's moving works for me." He glanced back to the animal, "come on, you know what we want you to do." She rolled onto her back.

"Thera, let's go," Leah said in a firm, but quiet voice.

Thera sat up and looked at the van, then Jesse. He wasn't sure what the look meant, but he was thinking she was blaming him entirely.

Chapter Nineteen

Jesse checked on Thera once more before he started the call, she'd finally lay down and stopped sticking her face to every box in the van. Leah was sitting beside her running her hand over her back in a slow soothing manner. His sisters were going to love this.

His mother's face came on the screen. "Hi, honey." She always managed to get her quick motherly assessment of him done before he could see the others.

"Sorry I didn't send a warning text," he held the phone up a bit, so they'd be able to see Thera and Leah, "we had to convince Thera to get her in the van."

"Oh my gosh, is that a real leopard?" Jaide's excited face took over the screen.

He grinned, "yes she is."

"She's beautiful," Joslin grabbed the phone, "I thought you were looking for shifters, not real animals," she smirked.

Nodding, Jesse glanced back at Leah, "I am, I did." He looked back at the phone, "Thera's been keeping Leah company."

"You *have* to bring her here." Jaide looked like she was going to go into one of her hyper spells.

"Let your brother speak." His father's voice was heard, but he didn't have the phone.

"If it weren't for the pretty leopard, I'd be mad you didn't notice." Joslin made an exaggerated pout and then moved the phone back.

Jesse chuckled, she clearly needed his comment on the shorter hairstyle, "notice how great your hair looks?"

She squealed, and patted her hand over her hair, "I like it so much." She glanced away from the phone, "Jaide's isn't as short, but her face isn't as thin as mine..."

"Did you just say I have a fat face?" Jaide scowled and then looked back at the phone, "she's clearly not getting the *identica*l twins' part of our physical bodies." She rolled her eyes.

"You both look great. What have you been up to this week?" He held the phone back so Leah would be able to see them.

"Training." They said in unison.

"For?"

"What do you mean? Have you forgotten what's next month?" Joslin gave him a wide-eyed stare.

"Right, sorry, it's been an exhausting few weeks. What's the competition like this year?" He knew he wasn't going to be able to be there for the yearly tracking event, but couldn't bear to tell them right now.

"They are going to lose so bad; we have found the pelt in record time three times now." Jaide grinned.

"That's right, they're going to be running in circles as we cross the finish line." Joslin nodded.

"You do know it's a solo event, right?"

Jaide rolled her eyes, "not this year it's not, we're going to carry that thing across the finish line *together*."

"And," Joslin grabbed the phone and held it close to her face, "we *will* beat your time, bro, and be the new best trackers in all the clans." She pouted, "when we have co-clan gatherings again."

He didn't have the heart to tell them unless they could beat Calum, they wouldn't be the best, and now with Kobie, according to Devin, the competition was getting scary. "You two are going to be a force to be reckoned with once you shift."

"We are going to rock that like serious champs." Jaide nodded.

"I know you will."

"Okay, stop hogging the phone, girls, your brother has things to do." His mother's voice was close to the phone now.

"Okay, okay." Jaide looked at the phone, "come home soon, I miss you." She made a kiss on the phone.

"Yeah, when you're done saving the shifter world, you better spend a month here before you go hide in your trailer." Joslin nodded and motioned to blow him a kiss.

Jesse chuckled, "I'm hoping to get back soon."

His mother and father's faces appeared on the phone, "you look tired." His mother frowned.

"I'm okay." He smiled, "We're heading to Ed's when I hang up." He held the phone up again so the boxes could be seen, glancing at Leah, he noticed she was looking a little intimidated, so he brought the phone back to show his face.

"Long trip back?" His father asked.

"Yeah, it might be slow with Thera," he smirked, "she's never had a car ride before."

"Be careful." His mother warned as she did every time they spoke.

"Deshon was telling me there would be some more rescues soon." His father looked at the phone with an expression that said he knew more about it than he was going to express.

Jesse nodded, "yeah, things are on the brink of change."

"That's great news." His mother glanced away from the phone, "I wish nothing more than things to return to the way they were."

He knew she was talking about his sisters being able to go places and do normal things again but wasn't sure if it would ever be that way again. "We'll know more in the next few weeks."

"You take it easy." His father's tone was quiet.

"I'm so happy you have someone to travel with for the trip back," his mother smiled, "I worry when you're out there driving for days on your own."

"I know."

"You call if you need us, Jesse." She had that stern look now, the one that he wondered if it would ever change or if he'd see it for the rest of his life.

"You know I will." He checked that Thera was still content. "We better get going before Thera changes her mind."

"Okay, son. Safe travels."

"Take care, honey."

Jesse nodded his head slowly. "Love you guys and the brat pack."

"We heard that," Jaide called loud from near the phone.

"Love you too." The twins echoed in unison.

"Bye." He smiled and then disconnected the call.

Standing up, he turned to see Leah's eyes were glistening. Panic hit him.

"They're lovely, your sisters." she wiped her hand across her eyes.

"They're exhausting." He grinned, "but yeah, they're something else."

"They look so much like you, and you like your father." She inhaled abruptly. "They're in a competition?"

He nodded slowly, "It's something we do with the kids too young to shift, just to help them learn scenting and tracking."

"That's a wonderful idea." She glanced at Thera, "I've never really known family and togetherness," she shrugged then looked back at him, "it seems nice."

He closed the one door and leaned on it, "it is, most of the time."

"I might like to meet your family sometime." She sucked in a breath, "I just don't know if I'll be able to stay if I do."

"We'll take everything as slow as you need, Leah." He looked at Thera, "shall we try this with the vehicle moving now."

Leah grinned, "okay, I'm going to stay here with her for now."

He started closing the door slowly, "hopefully that will keep her settled." He looked at Thera, "it will be an adventure, Thera, with lots of new places to check out." The animal just held his look, giving him no indication, she understood. Blowing out a quick breath he closed the door and walked quickly to get in the van.

Meeting his family was going to have to happen at some point. It's not like his mate was never going to know his family. He just had to figure out how to tell her she was his mate and how to explain her to his family.

None of which, he had the first clue how to do.

Chapter Twenty

Jesse was surprised Thera had lasted three hours in the van before demanding they stop and let her out. At first, he was worried she'd take off, but she didn't. She rolled in the grass, and then lay down and sniff the air.

Something he hadn't considered was how Leah was going to react to the ride. She'd been quiet, only speaking after he said something, and it wasn't until they stopped that he noticed how pale she looked. Now he was sure the cat had only asked to stop because her friend wasn't feeling well. Leah had gone and sat on the grass and rested her head on her knees for several minutes. He wanted to go over and do something to make her feel better but didn't want her to feel bad for having motion sickness either.

He looked through the medkit and found nothing useful. The first town they passed through he was going to have to remedy that. He should have already thought of this and had it in the kit. If things went according to plan, he was going to be transporting a lot more shifters that weren't used to travel. Opening the notes on his phone, he added them to the list of things to talk about with Shaelan and Devin. The kits and supplies the coordinators carried should be updated.

Tucking his phone back into his pocket, he started walking over to Leah, then stopped when he heard her talking.

"Did you hear that? I know you were close. His sisters adore him. The look on his face when he talks about them—I feel like he's good in all ways, don't you?"

He watched her stare off toward the field. Could she actually be listening to Evanna? The first thing he was doing when they got back was talking to whoever Shaelan was getting her information from. He had to know more, everything they could tell him about this. He wanted to understand. He needed to be there to help her and so far, he was completely winging this—his cat was good at picking up vibes and prompting him, but he wanted more than that.

Leah turned and saw him and smiled. "Thera is heading back now."

Jesse stepped out of the shadows, "I didn't want to startle you by walking up on you."

"You probably think I'm crazy."

He shook his head, "I don't." Giving her a shrug, he hoped he looked sincere. "I want to understand, to help when I can."

She laughed softly, "I don't think I'm the one to fill in the blanks for you. I don't understand most of it and it's my own head." Glancing over to where Thera was running full speed toward them, she continued speaking, "if I listen really hard, concentrate inside my head, I can talk to Evanna," she looked to him briefly, "if she's close."

"Can you talk to Minn too?"

Thera went running by them and toward the van. Leah sighed and followed her, "I don't really know how to communicate with Minn, I mean I don't need to speak out loud, but communicating with her internally is hard."

"It can be, most have trouble with it in the beginning."

She looked annoyed, "It's not the beginning for me. It's been over five years."

"I know, but Minn came out about five years before most female cats do, so I think that may have something to do with it."

"Is there a way to help me with that? Can someone help me so I can control and communicate with Minn?"

Jesse nodded, "I'm surprised your grandparents didn't help you."

"Oh, they tried. Minn was having none of it. Evanna stayed quiet for the first bit when we were back, I'm not sure why. It was before we used the journal to talk to one another, but in that time Minn was out almost all the time."

"I know someone will be able to help you." He watched Thera circle the van, he'd left all the doors closed. At least she wasn't complaining about the ride. "My cat is in synch with yours, for the most part, maybe with a bit more time and trust I can help you get through to her."

"Do you think so?"

"I do. I've done it with a few of the younger shifters in my clan before." He shrugged, "we could go for a short run now if you want."

She bit her lip, a look of focus on her face. "I think she'd like that." She frowned, "or that's Evanna telling me to go for it, I can't be sure."

He motioned to the tree line on the other side of the field, "the grass is long enough we won't stand out if anyone is nearby, we'll just have to stay on this side of the trees." He'd purposely stopped where there was no sign of life in all directions but couldn't be sure what was on the other side of the trees.

"Okay." She gave him a hesitant grin. "Maybe if we do, she'll be more content in the van."

He frowned, "Minn's been bugging you this whole time."

Leah nodded, "we don't do good with confined spaces, but maybe if she sees that we're not stuck there she'll settle down."

Jesse sighed, "you should have said something." He pulled his shirt over his head, "a run, something to eat, and then she should be appeased." He stood there with his shirt balled in his hand when he noticed how she was looking at his bare chest.

Clearing his throat, he pointed over his shoulder, "I'll go shift by the van and give you some privacy."

Her cheeks were flushed, but she nodded and watched him back up a few steps.

Spinning on his heel, he went over to the van and walked to the front of it. Now was not the time to notice things, he berated himself. His cat was quiet, telling him he agreed with that. Yes, she was his mate, but things were too complicated for him to act on it. He shook his head as he tossed his shirt on top of his boots, hell, he may not be able to claim her as his for a long time. He paused in taking his jeans off as that thought hit him. What was he going to do if he never could? *Fuck*. The only reason his cat was being so understanding was because of the situation, but he doubted that would last forever. Stepping out of the jeans, he dropped them on the ground and shifted.

As soon as paws were on the dirt, his cat took the lead and bound in the other direction. In the direction of their mate. His cat knew it was more important to bond with Minn than anything and seemed to have his own idea of how to do that. Jesse let him lead the way, but wasn't going to give him total control because he had to monitor too much.

Thera and Minn were pacing when he reached them. Going over, he butt Thera playfully and then moved over closer to Leah's animal. She watched him intently. Stopping a few feet from her, he stretched and lowered his head while he watched her. When Minn did the same it was like they had just bowed to each other.

She bounced back up and looked at the field and then back to him. Jesse didn't wait for her to decide, he turned and took off running across it.

With a soft chuff, Thera followed and had no problems passing him. She was all for more animals to run with. In wild leopards they were pretty solitary creatures, Thera didn't seem to have that preference, making him wonder if she'd been bred in captivity or taken in when she was too young to remember. He'd have to add a vet visit to the list, just to check her over. Minn caught up to them and ran in front of him cutting him off. It was the first playful thing he'd seen her do, in any state.

His cat wanted to breeze past them both, but reigned it in and tried to stay out of their space. Jesse was happy his cat and he were in total synch about making transitions easier, even for Thera. It was going to be a rough couple of months going forward and he needed the wild one on his side as well. Trust was the most important thing between animals, and he had until they reached Blair's to establish that with her. Leah and Evanna's untamed side were going to be a lot more work.

Minn turned and started for the tree line and Jesse's heartbeat increased. He hadn't stopped to think if Leah could control her to keep her on this side of it. Thera was right beside her. Cursing inside his head, he stopped trailing and took off after them.

When he almost reached them, both made abrupt turns and headed back the other way. As they flew by him, he laughed inside his head, they were screwing with him. Releasing his cat, he decided he'd let him settle the score with the two female felines.

Chapter Twenty-One

Jesse glanced in the mirror, he seemed to be looking at it more than the road for the last hour. Adjusting it, he checked to see if Leah was still curled up sleeping. Moving it back, he caught the look Thera was giving him. "We can't stop yet. Can you hold out for another hour? I want to get us past the city." Thera's expression didn't change. A low chuff sounded right behind his head. Before he could figure out what she was doing, her head pushed between his shoulder and the window.

She was lifting her face and sniffing the air that was coming through the open window. She nudged his shoulder, "okay, but if I open it, you have to behave I can't have you hanging your head out the window, that's the last thing we need is to draw attention to ourselves." She bumped his shoulder again. "Fine, three more inches is all you're getting."

Her fur rubbed against his cheek as she shoved closer to the window. He could hear her inhaling and tasting the air. With a huff, that sounded close to a spit, she turned her head and bumped her nose against his jaw.

"Yeah, I smell it. Pollution, cars, waste, I want away from here as much as you do."

Without further drama, she backed up. He thought maybe

she was going to lay down with Leah again, but instead, her head appeared between the seats. Jesse glanced at her, "you are co-piloting now?" She didn't look away from the window. "Okay then, I guess that earns you a snack." Opening the console between the seats, he reached in and pulled out a piece of jerky. Holding it up, he waited while she sniffed it. "I know it's not running from you, but it is tasty."

Thera pulled it out of his hand and then moved backward. Jesse straightened and watched as she lay down, careful not to disturb Leah, and chewed the jerky slowly. Looking back to the road, he nodded to himself. A case of jerky it is. What else would work for cat treats? He smirked, or leopard treats as it were.

They'd made good time today. A good six hours of driving behind them. It was starting to worry him that Leah had been asleep since their run. He glanced at the animal. "How's she doing?"

Thera bumped her head against his arm and then turned back around. Adjusting the mirror, he watched as she lay down and rubbed her face against Leah's shoulder. Leah moaned softly.

The sound hit him, right to his core. Wide-eyed, Jesse looked back at the road. Scowling at it, he noted where they were and then focused on trying to remember the route and where he'd planned on stopping.

"What is it, girl?"

Her soft raspy voice had him glancing in the mirror again, "I think she wants to tell you the city smells." Dragging his eyes back to the road, he blew out a quick breath. Her looking sleepy and comfortable was not helping his concentration.

"Have I been sleeping long?" She sat up and stretched.

Jesse groaned in his head, he needed to get out of the van. "A few hours." He cleared his throat, "I thought once we pass the city, we could stop in one of the smaller towns and get some gas and grab something to eat." He'd considered passing through the city and getting a few burgers, but with her sleeping, he didn't want her to wake up to him in a busy drive thru.

She knelt and leaned up between the seats and looked out the window.

Her scent filled his head causing his cat to go still.

"So many buildings." She said softly.

He frowned and wondered if she remembered going through Chicago at all. "Thera's not happy with the smell."

"I will just take her word for it then." She picked up her half drank bottle of water and opened it. "Smells can sometimes set Minn off and we don't want that."

Jesse shook his head, "no we don't." He looked over his shoulder to see her taking a drink and groaned in his head with her throat exposed like that. Snapping his head around to glare at the road, he blew out a short breath. He needed to get out of this vehicle and put some space between them. His cat did something inside him that Jesse could only interpret as bumping his head against the inside of his ribs, hard. "I'm not sure what will be available in the next town, but most will have either a sub shop or pizza place."

"I don't know what either of those is, but I'm quite hungry." She gave a soft chuckle, "the raw potatoes even have an appeal right now."

Jesse grinned, "we can do better than raw potatoes, that I do know."

"Okay." Her head was beside his shoulder, "Evanna doesn't want me to look at the city, so is it all right if I stay back here until I can't see it?"

That reined in all rouge thoughts immediately. "You do whatever you need to feel comfortable," he remembered what Shaelan had said, "and safe."

She touched his arm softly, "thank you."

Nodding, Jesse looked at the speedometer and accelerated slightly. If Evanna was that close and sending Leah suggestions, then he needed to pay attention and get them away from the city. He gnawed on the inside of his lip, bringing up the route in his head. When they stopped, he was going to have to go over the map and see if he could adjust it, so they weren't close to any cities. "After we eat, I'm going to have to grab a quick nap, do you think we can set Thera in guard mode while I do that?"

Leah laughed quietly, "Thera only has two modes, watching and playing. I'm sure if you're napping, she will keep watch."

Jesse nodded, he hoped so, because if he didn't get a short nap, this trip was going to be slow going with him having to stop and pace around the van trying to stay alert. Thera pushed her head between his shoulder and the window again, startling him. He leaned away from the door giving her space as she checked the air again. With a low rumble, she pulled her head back. "Another half-hour, girl, and the air will be cleaner." His phone lit up with a message. Leaning forward, he tapped it and glanced at it while keeping his eye on the road. It was Devin telling him the guard they knew, one of their own was on duty at the border check in two hours. Sitting back, he did the calculations. Quick stop, some food, and then get across the border before stopping for rest. There was something about being on this side, the side that Aiden Tomas was on that made his skin crawl the whole time.

"After we stop to eat, we're going to drive for another hour or so and cross the border, then we'll rest."

"Is it hard to cross the border?"

He didn't like the worried tone in her voice. "Sometimes, but one of our kind works at the one crossing, so that's where we're heading."

"Oh good. I didn't know how getting Thera across was going to work."

Neither had Jesse which is why he had Devin working on finding which location they could do it at. He grinned as he switched lanes, the chaos it would have caused if they'd pulled up to any checkpoint with any guard when they looked in and were greeted by Thera staring them down. "It's all taken care of," he assured her.

Reaching, he tapped the screen of the phone and hit

Devin's number.

"Jesse."

"Let him know we'll be there in roughly an hour or so."

"All right. Everything going okay?"

Jesse glanced to see Thera giving the back of his head a look. "So far we're good."

"Call me when you stop for the night."

"It will be shortly after we cross."

"You made good time so far."

"Let's hope it continues." Jesse glanced over his shoulder to see Leah looking at his phone. "I'll talk to you soon."

"Sounds good."

The call disconnected.

"I still can't believe you can talk to people anytime you want. "

"It's great most of the time, except when you don't want to talk." He grinned at her in the mirror.

"I still think it's wonderful."

He realized how different her life would have been if she'd been able to talk to someone in the time she'd been alone. "Are you good for a little longer before we stop?" He suddenly wanted to get her back to Blair faster.

She nodded, "we're fine." She leaned into the animal beside her and rested her head on Thera's shoulder.

It was hard for him to focus on the road, he just wanted to look at her. Clearing his throat, he nodded abruptly, "okay, time to put some space between us and the city."

Chapter Twenty-Two

He watched Thera run in a wide circle around where Leah stood. He needed to keep his distance after the thoughts that had been in his head for that last bit of the drive. Jesse leaned back against the van and watched as she ate the sub sandwich with small bites. Each time he could see the amazement on her face. He looked at the last piece of his before he put it in his mouth. To him, it was a sub, one of too many he'd eaten in the last five years, to Leah it was a combination of flavors she'd never experienced.

She glanced over her shoulder and smiled. It was the kind of smile that made his heart thud louder in his chest, all while breaking it slowly. She had no idea how appealing she was, her innocence was refreshing, but distracting at the same time. His cat was prompting him to go over closer to her, all they could smell at this point was the sub he'd just eaten. It was going to be a long trip and even afterward if he had to be able to scent her *all* the time.

Straightening, he denied his cat and opened the door to get the map out. He was hoping there was a route that got them across the border sooner, he just wanted to get across it back into territory he knew and had more backup if he needed it.

There was no way Tomas knew of Leah's existence, but he still had this nagging feeling that something was going to happen. As he spread the map on the warm hood of the van, he glanced over to see Leah making Thera sit for a small offering of her sandwich. Shaking his head, he forced his muscles to move so he looked at the map. There was that too, the way she communicated with a wild animal like it was a house cat. Everything about her drew him to her.

His phone rang, bringing his head back to focus. Going around, he reached in the window and grabbed it out of the holder on the dash. It was Shaelan.

"Hello."

"Hi, Jesse is this a good time to call?"

"Yeah, we're stopped for a quick leopard break." He grinned as Thera bounced around like a small cub.

"Oh good, I wanted to send you some links that Doctor Collins gave me, they have some good information on them. I thought you might want to read them when you have a chance, maybe share them with Leah and Evanna."

He glanced over to see Leah teasing Thera with the last of her sandwich and smiled. "Yeah, please send them."

"Okay then. How's the drive?"

"We're making good time, all things considered."

"Oh good, I know Cal's been checking the time too often today. "

Jesse grinned, "yeah he still likes to think I'm incapable of doing anything without his backup." Leah turned and smiled at him, making his heart slam against his ribs. "Listen, while I've got just you on the phone, I had a question."

"Oh?"

"Yeah." Frowning at the ground, he tried to figure out how to word it. "The doctor you've been talking to, she's one of us, right?"

"Yes, she is."

"Yeah, okay, uh, can you ask her how it works if your mate has this D.I.D?"

"Oh, Jesse."

From the compassion in her tone, he knew he didn't have to explain it later. "It's a bit a cluster—mess in my head right now. I don't know how to, or if I should say something, I don't know how it works with the different personalities, never mind Minn—" he stopped when Leah started walking back this way.

"I will talk to her and see what she knows. I think it's wonderful though."

"What is?" He smiled back at Leah.

"That her mate is someone as patient and understanding as you are."

He snorted, "Yeah, well I don't understand anything right now."

"That's not what I meant. Oh, I have to go, here comes Cal and he has that intense focus look on his face."

Jesse nodded; he knew that look all too well. "Okay."

"I'm assuming you don't want to share this information with anyone just yet?"

"I'd like to know more about everything before I do."

"I understand. "

"Thanks, Shaelan. Go deal with your broody mate."

She chortled, "will do. Bye Jesse."

"Bye." He hung up and checked to see if the links she sent came through. Hopefully, somewhere along the way he'd get a chance to read through them. Turning back, he watched Thera come charging at him. "No, we're not going back for more subs, girl." She slowed just before she reached him and bumped her head against his leg. Reaching down, he rubbed his hand over her head, "next time we'll try chicken nuggets, you'll *love* those."

Leah walked over to him. "That sub sandwich was really good." She put her hand over her stomach. "I'm so full now."

Jesse patted his own stomach. "I could eat three of those before I'm full."

With eyes wide, she shook her head, "you're much bigger than I am." She moved over and leaned on the van beside him. "I suspect Evanna would love to try a sub."

"The way she dug into the snacks I had; I think she'll try just about anything. She has a bigger appetite than you do."

"That's true, but we share the same stomach, thankfully." She grinned up at him.

"Yeah," he frowned, "I can't imagine how that would feel." He grimaced, "coming out and feeling full, but not having eaten anything."

"I'm always full if Evanna's been around. She takes care of me without even realizing most of the time." She shrugged, "at least I think she doesn't do it all on purpose."

"She's always thinking, you can see it."

"Really?" She smirked, "well, she doesn't like writing down thoughts, that I do know." She started to walk around him to open the door, then paused, letting her hand rest on his chest. Jesse froze, not wanting to do anything to frighten her. Leaning closer, her face an inch from his chest, she inhaled slowly. Lifting her chin, she looked up at him. "Is that rude? To smell you?"

He shook his head, unable to say anything.

"You smell so good, I'm not sure what it is about your scent, but I feel calmed, yet excited at the same time." Her cheeks flushed and she gave him a shy smile. "It's not just me either, Evanna said something about you too in our journal." Her eyes went wide and she stepped back. "I'm sorry, you probably think I'm strange."

Jesse's cat panicked inside him. Reaching, he caught her hand gently before she could move away. Holding it, he reached and tipped her chin up. "I don't think you could ever do anything that would make me think you're strange."

A surprised expression filled her eyes.

"I mean it, Leah, to me I only see a brave, unique woman and there's nothing wrong with that."

"Brave? I don't..."

Gently he placed his thumb over her lips so she couldn't finish. "You are, I don't know many that could have survived on that mountain without help this long." He was afraid to breathe as he leaned down and placed a soft kiss on her mouth.

His cat went completely still. Straightening, he released her chin. If he stood here much longer, he'd kiss her again, and he didn't want to frighten her. She stood there, her fingertips on her mouth, a dazed look in her eyes.

Thera bound over and nudged Leah's leg.

"We should get back on the road." He inhaled sharply and forced his feet to move back, letting her hand drop from his.

Still touching her mouth, she nodded and moved by him toward the van.

Jesse watched her for a second and then glanced down at the animal. He wasn't sure what that look was she was giving him, but he hoped there were no plans to take a chunk out of him.

Chapter Twenty-Three

Good sleep and now a run, Jesse would be able to focus now and get some miles between them and the border. He dashed after Thera, trying had to close the distance. He was fast, probably one of the fastest types of shifters, but the real deal he was chasing made him look moderately slower than he would like.

Thera made a short turn and then crouched down. Inhaling, Jesse realized why she had been pouring on the speed. She was hunting. As he slowed, it dawned on him that she really hadn't eaten since their trip began. It wasn't like he could pull up to a drive-thru and order ten pounds of raw meat.

He turned and purposely went in a wide circle away from where she was stalking something. He couldn't get a clear enough scent of what it was. Mostly because all he could smell was Minn. Her scent was making it difficult to keep his cat under control. His animal side knew the risks and issues pertaining to their mate, but that didn't make him any less aware of her.

Thera bound after her prey and shortly after that, the squeal of a caught animal sounded through the quiet valley. Jesse stopped short and stood there, scenting the area again and checking that the sound hadn't alerted natural predators. Although, if there was anything in the area that could compete with leopards, he'd eat his shirt when he got back to it.

Minn paced back and forth a respectful distance from Thera and her breakfast. Leah had filled up on protein bars and a few apples when they'd woke up this morning. Saying she didn't dare let Minn free to hunt.

Jesse hadn't meant to sleep as long as he had, but the relief of getting over the border to a quiet area he recognized had him relax enough to get some real rest. His plans were to drive through, with few stops for the entire day, bringing them close enough to Blair's that they would get there the next day. He just wanted somewhere stable enough to settle for a short while and let Leah adjust to her new life.

Lifting her head, Thera paused in her meal and sat there, alert and watchful. Jesse stopped the internal dialogue and listened. Minn was paused in movement too. Inhaling, he brought the scent around them into his body to process. His cat reacted before it registered what they were smelling. There was no mistaking gun oil. That scent was one every shifter learned early on, for survival. There were hunters in the area.

Crouching, he issued a few soft grunts to let Minn and Thera know he scented them too and that they needed to get back to the van. Keeping low, he looked back in the direction they'd come and cursed himself that they'd gone this far from it. There was a lot of open ground to cover to get back to it.

As quiet as he could, he growled, telling them to get moving. Minn was the first to react and started with a slow pace run, keeping her legs bent and trying to keep as low to the ground as she could. He looked over to Thera to see her looking down at her kill and he was sure she was pissed that it was going to have to be left behind. He'd buy her something from the next store they passed, he promised her silently. When she swung her head around, he knew she was plotting the course to get back.

He waited a few seconds when she went by him to follow. He wasn't taking a chance with anything happening to them. He would run at the back and be the distraction if that was what it took. Calling out a few short commands, telling them to run, he straightened up out of the short growth and started after them.

His head and back would be visible and he knew it. Hopefully, the hunters were looking to the sky and hunting birds and no one would notice an animal that was not normally in this region.

The first crack of a riffle split the silence and in turn spurred both of the other cats to pour on the speed. As they blurred across the open space, Jesse kept his run slow enough that he would catch the attention of anyone looking. His heart was going crazy in his chest, and it wasn't for his own safety that was causing it.

As Thera and Minn hit the area with the longer growth, he decided he could pick up the pace and get moving. The echo of another shot registered around the same time an intense stinging in his side did. The last thing he picked up as he increased his speed to his absolute fastest was blood. His own blood. He'd been shot.

When the van was in sight, he saw Leah, half-dressed opening the door and Thera jumping in. He slid to a stop where he'd left his clothes and shifted fast. His injury didn't take well to the shift and the moan he heard was his own as he staggered to two feet and grabbed his jeans.

Tossing his boots in the direction of the van, he looked down to see a gash in his side and blood running down his side. *Fuck.* Balling up his shirt, he pressed it against his side and stepped out of the trees.

Leah tossed his boots in the van and closed the door. The look on her face told him she could smell the blood before she noticed him holding the shirt against his side. "Get in." He told her as he rounded the front and opened his door.

As he started the van, she pushed the console between the seats out of the way and placed her hands over the shirt. "Is it bad?" Her voice was shaking.

"We'll look at it once we get out of here." He put the van in gear and stomped on the gas. His side was burning and throbbing, as he steered out of the hidden spot they'd found.

"Jesse, it's a lot of blood."

He nodded, not even needing to look to know. "Grab the med kit. It's under your seat." He couldn't look to see if she heard him, there were too many trees to navigate around to get back to the road. The pressure on his side changed, so she must have been holding it with one hand and reaching with the other.

Thera pushed her head between the door and his seat. Rubbing her face against his. "I'll be fine, girl, just lay down and keep out of the way for a bit." He could smell the blood of her kill on fur. "We'll get you a snack in a while." The cat must have understood his words, or tone because she moved back out of the way.

"I'm not sure what to do." Leah's tone was filled with panic.

"We'll be on the road in a second. Just see if you can pack it with some gauze and tape it up or something. I'm not stopping until I know they're nowhere near." Logically the hunters wouldn't associate that their leopards had just driven away in a van, but he wasn't taking any chances.

When the tires grabbed onto the pavement, he reached and quickly tapped the screen of his phone. "Call Calum." He said in a loud tone.

"Calling Calum." His phone repeated.

"Are you calling for help?" Leah was on her knees between the seats now.

"No, just need someone to be aware of what's happening." He didn't say it out loud, but he knew if this turned out to be more serious, he'd need others to know where they were.

"You're up early." Cal's voice came through the speaker.

"I've been shot." Jesse knew not to waste words on Calum

"What? By who?" Cal's tone was lower now.

"Hunters. We were out for a run so Thera could eat before we got back on the road."

"Where? How bad?" That was Shaelan, Cal must have put the call on speaker.

"His right side below his ribs," Leah said in a loud voice that shocked Jesse. "He's driving, I'm trying to stop the bleeding." Now her voice shook.

"Okay, Jesse you focus on the road," Shaelan said in an authoritative tone. "Is this Leah?"

Jesse was pleased she'd thought to ask.

"Yes."

"Okay, Leah, see if you can tell how big and deep it is. Push hard on it for a few seconds before you look and hopefully it will slow a bit so you can see."

"Okay. I have the medical box, there are some big bandages in it."

"You'll need those. Is there some gauze? You're going to have to pack some in it if it's deep."

"Let me get that ready before I look."

Jesse glanced to see her blood-covered hand riffling through the med kit. He blinked and brought his focus back to the road.

"Jesse, start pounding back some liquids, juice if you have it." Cal's tone said it wasn't a request. "As soon as you put enough miles between you find a spot to hole up so you can deal with this."

Before he could speak, Leah held up a bottle of water. "I'll get the juice in a moment." She told him softly. "Okay." She blew out a breath, "I'm going to look." He felt the air hit the site and it stung. "I don't," she made a soft noise as she dabbed against his side, "I don't think it's deep. It's long though."

"Good. Sounds like a graze. Grab the gauze and the big bandages and get that on it. You will have to keep pressure on it until he stops, but it should clot and slow until he's able to shift and heal it."

He watched her grab things out of the box and then she pressed the gauze against his side, it stung like a bitch making him clamp his teeth together.

"How are you doing, Jesse?" Shaelan asked.

"Just dandy." He growled out.

"No dizziness or shakes?"

He looked at his hand on the wheel and shook his head, "no, I'm good."

Leah leaned closer and looked up at him, "he's a little pale."

"Okay, if you have it covered, get him some juice now." Shaelan's voice never changed in tone as she spoke.

Leah moved out of his peripheral vision for a moment and then she was back with a juice box and holding it out to him.

Setting the water, he hadn't drunk between his legs he took the juice and literally sucked it back until the box was indented. With a quick nod, he held out the box to her.

"How's it looking, Leah?"

"The bandage is red, but it's not running out of it." Leah's tone was filled with worry.

"Okay, it should be okay until he stops."

"How much distance have you put between them now?" Calum asked in a less harsh tone.

"If I remember right, we should be to a good spot in fifteen minutes," Jesse told him. He was not stopping until then.

"Don't wait too long," Calum said in a quiet warning tone.

"I won't." Leah still had one hand over his injury as she straightened up so her face was level with his shoulder. Reaching, he cupped the back of her head in a brief awkward hug with his other arm as best as he could manage while driving. He felt her breathing change against his bare arm.

"I don't—I can't stay Jesse." She said in a hushed tone.

"It's okay. I'll be fine now. You do what you need to feel safe." He assured her.

"Okay," she blew out a breath, her head resting completely against his arm for a few seconds.

Jesse had to focus hard on the road and not check to make sure she was okay.

"What the actual hell was that?"

He smirked knowing that Evanna was fronting now. "I'll be fine once I shift."

"I heard. I was right at the front but didn't want to take over." Evanna moved out of his hold and pressed against his side. "It's going to take some work to mop up this mess." She held out one of her blood-coated hands.

"How's the bleeding, Evanna?" Shaelan's voice startled him, he'd forgotten they were on the phone.

"Uh, I think it's slowed down. Should we put some of this antiseptic spray on it?"

Jesse cringed at the thought of spraying it with that.

"If it's going to be a while before he shifts, you could, but otherwise infection shouldn't be an issue."

He could see Evanna nodding out of the corner of his eye.

"Okay. It's a good thing I was close," she moved so she was sitting sideways on the other seat, leaning over and still holding his side, "Leah was close to losing her hold on Minn and Minn wanted to go hunt down the hunters." She grinned at Jesse before lowering her head to look closer at his side.

"I'm glad you were close, chasing after Minn would not have helped things," Jesse said quietly.

She chortled, "when are you stopping? This isn't going to soak up much more."

"A few more minutes."

"Okay, I'll stay out and Thera and I will watch your back while you fix this."

"Jesse, send me a text after you've shifted and are back on the road."

Evanna looked at the phone, "Hey, thanks for the help, Shaelan, Leah was close to freaking out until she heard you."

"Anytime, Evanna. She did great."

Evanna nodded, "yeah, she held it together."

"Stop soon, Jesse," Shaelan said just as the line went quiet.

It was silent for a moment, then Evanna looked away from the road and at him. "You don't look the greatest, you should stop and shift to close this up."

He nodded and motioned with his head to the windshield.

"There's a small roadside rest area up here, I'll stop there and do a quick shift."

Evanna moved her hand off of him and looked down at her hands. She picked up his shirt and wiped them. "You're going to need some food after that."

"I'll look at the map then and see where is the closest, maybe grab some breakfast."

"I could eat." She said with a grin.

Jesse pulled on his jeans and stepped out of the shrubs that surrounded the little area. Thera and Evanna stood looking in opposite directions, watching.

"You good?" She came over as he cleared the scratchy growth.

He nodded, "Yeah." He looked down at his side to see the graze was healed and gone. "I could use a bath now." He mumbled.

She came over and leaned close to him, running her hand over his skin. Glancing up at him, she smirked, "if you could try to not get shot often, I'd appreciate it." Straightening, she dropped her hand away from him. "I'm all for the excitement, but Leah isn't."

"I'll keep that in mind," he smiled at her.

With a nod, she turned back to the van.

Evanna stopped short and spun back to him. "I'm just going to say it. I know it's probably something people just don't say to other people, but I'm not other people." She snorted, "I don't even know other people."

Jesse grinned, "that's not an entirely bad thing—once you meet some people, you're going to wish you didn't. Not all, but some."

"Don't distract me, Jesse, this has been driving me mad."

He sobered, not sure what could have her so wound up. "What is it?"

"Okay," she blew out a breath, something that wasn't really in her character, to be nervous, "okay, I like the way you smell." She waved her hand around, "without the blood scent.

Jesse grinned. He wanted so much to tell her why that was but needed to find out more from that shifter doctor that Shaelan had talked about. "Well, if we're confessing, you smell amazing to me too."

"Really? I'm not weird?"

"No." He brushed back the strands of hair that had fallen out and rested against her jaw. "You're not. It's a perfectly normal thing for our kind."

She looked relieved and smiled, "I was so worried about it, I thought it was an *us* thing," she motioned to herself, "Leah and I—us," she clarified.

His cat was practically pacing inside him, urging him to explain. Jesse clamped down on him, hard, it wasn't the right time. "It's a good thing you're both in agreement. I can't explain why right now, but just know it is."

Evanna nodded slowly, "I believe you. We all trust you."

"Even Minn?" He needed to know. She didn't let him anywhere near her when they went for runs.

"Well, she's coming around, but she hasn't tried to take a bite out of you, so that's good, right?"

Jesse laughed quietly, "yeah, that's good."

Evanna nodded, "we should get Thera loaded up again." She reached up and rubbed her hand over his chest. "Thanks for being so cool with everything, Jesse. It means a lot." Turning she went back to the van and opened the door.

He stood there and watched her get in and close it. He was going to lose his mind being so close to his mate, but not able to be *close* to her. She looked at him as if to say 'are we going or what?' Jolting, he went around to get in.

Lose my mind.

Chapter Twenty-Four

Jesse ran faster, determined he was catching up to her. Minn was using all her reserves now, but had to tire at some point, he thought. He ignored the fact that he knew she'd run all the way to the mountain once Leah had gotten out of that place.

Seeing the rise in the ground on the other side of the trees, he darted between them, so he was literally on the higher ground. Jesse's cat poured on speed he didn't know he had. That was their mate he was chasing and short of interference from the heavens, he was catching her.

Minn was still darting in and out of the trees, it was slowing her down, even if she didn't realize it. Part of him hoped Evanna was working on getting control of her, but after seeing what happened to her when she did, he needed to be able to get through to her. At least they were headed back toward the van now.

Spotting an opening, he pushed harder and then leaped down so he bumped against her, breaking her stride. She slid to a stop and then spun back to look at him.

Her sides were heaving, although he wasn't doing much better in the breathing department. Putting his head down, he kept his legs straight and uttered a low growl. Not a warning really, but enough to get her attention. She stared him down, her tail flicking in annoyance.

Jesse took a few steps closer, keeping his tail still, and gave a breathless yowl, trying to communicate with her. He had to keep his cat in line while trying to get through to his out-of-control mate.

Minn's tail stopped, she hissed at him, ears back, but wasn't belly to the ground, so she was at least considering listening.

Advancing a few more feet closer, Jesse lowered his head down, so she wouldn't feel like he was trying to pick a fight. He sat down, but his cat inside was coiled and ready if she bolted. His cat sounded a soft yowl, more of a 'come on, let's get along'.

The she-cat paused, her ears lifting, eyes wary.

Jesse let his cat take the lead, he knew what was at stake here. His cat shook his head, then made the low rasping meowing noise. Jesse had only ever heard it a few times in the years he'd been shifting and still thought he sounded like a big old bullfrog when he did it.

Minn yowled quietly back to him and took a few hesitant steps toward him.

Jesse got back up and waited for her to reach him. He would have stayed sitting, but his cat took the lead again, letting him know that was asking for a serious nip or swat. When she got closer, he stretched his neck as far as he could and made a show of sniffing at her, as if to say, 'smell me, it's not what you think.' He admitted to himself that neither he nor his cat would ever be considered a lady's man.

The scared she-cat moved closer and sniffed the air in his direction. He could see the surprise in her eyes when the scent registered with her. She had just learned that he was her mate.

Inside he was cheering, thinking, okay all three parts of her now know, on the outside he sat completely still and let her move closer and take his scent into her body.

When she flinched, it startled him and he moved closer, thinking something was out there and he'd missed it. The first priority was to protect his mate, once beside her he turned his head and checked the air. Three was nothing out of the ordinary. Looking back to her, she was laying on the ground, her breathing changing from cat to normal. Evanna had control now and was working on shifting back. He backed up to give her a little space.

"What happened?" Evanna sounded out of breath.

Jesse shifted quickly and sat behind her, "a noise like a gunshot, I think it was a car backfiring."

"Oh. One second everything was fine and then she just took off." She groaned. "How did you get her to settle?"

Jesse frowned, he'd thought it was Evanna that had done it. "I don't know, I guess she realized I was calm and there wasn't a threat." He stood up, "I'm going to grab our clothes, are you good?"

"Yeah, it's not as bad as it usually is. I'll be good in a few minutes."

"Okay, I'll bring your clothes over."

"Thanks."

Jesse hurried over and grabbed his jeans. Pulling them on he, went to behind the van and picked up hers. He looked to see Thera sitting by the van. He was surprised she let him to the chase alone. "Standing guard?" He motioned to the field, "go run, this is the last time we stop for one until we get to Blair's."

Thera eyed him up for a moment and then got up and walked toward Evanna.

Shaking his head, Jesse went over and set her clothes behind her. He couldn't stand here and look at her laying there naked. Nope, not for even a second. "I have to call Calum. Come and grab some jerky when you're steady."

Jesse paced over and looked out across the field. He could see Thera and Minn dashing around, he still couldn't believe Evanna had shifted again so soon. Something about wanting to check on Minn and work on their bond.

"Hello?"

He'd forgotten he was on the phone. "Yeah. Sorry, Cal, I'm just stuck in my head."

"That sounds fun." The sarcasm wasn't hard to hear. "What's going on? I thought you said everything was fine."

"It is." He rubbed his hand across his forehead, "considering I'm hauling a leopard around, it's going much better than I expected."

"Okay—"

Jesse hissed out a breath, "shit, Cal, I don't know which way is up right now."

"What's happened? You have someone following you?"

Jesse turned and looked along the road, he could see for miles in all directions. "No, no tail."

"Then?"

"It's Leah," he snorted, "and Evanna and Minn."

"Minn?"

Jesse watched her race ahead of Thera, "her cat."

"Her cat has a name?"

It wasn't hard to hear how strange Calum thought that was. "Yeah, her cat is a separate personality, like Evanna is."

"All right," Calum cleared his throat, "Is everything okay with her—them?"

"Sure, there's just this one thing that isn't, or mostly it's me I think."

"You used to make more sense than you have been lately."

Jesse laughed quietly, despite it not being that funny, "They're my mate. At first, I thought it was just Evanna, but no, it's Leah and Minn synchs with my cat."

"I—uh, don't know how that works."

Jesse appreciated the honesty, "that makes two of us."

"Does she know?"

Checking the road again, he shook his head, "I don't know. I don't know if her elders explained *any* of that, or if they were even able to, she was in cat form more than two legs—and she shifted so early, so they may not have thought it would be an issue for a while…" He lifted his hand and let it drop, "I don't know."

He could hear Calum exhale loudly, "I can talk to Shae and see if she's gotten anywhere with the shifter doctor she's been talking to."

"I'm just happy one of ours knows about this disassociated," he waved his hand around, "disorder."

"That's what I took it to mean when she was talking about it earlier. Hang on, she's coming this way now."

Jesse nodded, even knowing he couldn't see. "Yup." He added just so Cal would know he wasn't zoned out again. He could hear Cal's deep voice, but nothing from Shaelan.

"Jesse, it's Shaelan."

"Hi." He turned back around to see the cats coming back this way. Going over to the van, he grabbed a few bottles of water, noting they'd have to stop for supplies sooner than later.

"I was just telling Cal some of the statistics the doctor shared with me."

He was surprised, "good kind of statistics?"

"Yes, it's more common than any of us ever imagined."

Stretching, he got the bowl from under the seat and set it on the ground beside the van. "Then she knows about mates with this?" He poured the water into the dish and looked to see Minn veering off so Evanna could shift as Thera came back.

"She does, it's complicated, which I don't know about you, but I expected. Have you figured out if it's just one personality or all?"

He didn't need to clarify. "All."

"I suppose that's easier than if it were just one."

Jesse snorted, then rolled his eyes, "I don't think easy is a word I'd use for any of this." He watched Evanna walk out from behind the small cluster of trees, "so," he cleared his throat, "do you think she knows?"

"You could ask her."

She was pulling her hair up, he watched her, not that his focus could be anywhere else, she was beautiful, graceful, and all parts of her were always graceful. "You don't think that will upset her?"

"I don't think so, she knows what she is and for the most part I believe how everything works."

Jesse nodded slowly and then smiled back at Evanna as she got closer. "Okay, I guess I'll broach the subject and see if she does."

"While I've got you, do you want me to arrange to have someone here when you get here? That doctor has said she'll be happy to come."

Jesse rubbed his hand along his jaw, "hold on, I don't want to make that decision for her. I know Leah agreed, but I just want to clarify."

"Of course."

He lowered the phone and held it against his chest. "Shaelan is asking if you would like to meet with the doctor when we get to Blair's."

Evanna paused and ran her hand along Thera's back. "This doctor knows what's wrong with us?"

Jesse nodded.

Evanna inhaled a slow breath. "Okay," she nodded, "I guess the sooner we talk to them the sooner we'll have help for Minn." She made an exasperating sound, "I had to fight to get back control again just now."

Jesse straightened and really looked at her, he could see it around her eyes, the headache was bad. As he reached for the first aid kit, he put the phone back to his ear. "Shaelan, she said yes, she'd like to talk to them as soon as possible." He opened it and took out the acetaminophen, "she's having a hard time controlling Minn." Opening it, he tipped two into his hand and then turned and held it out to Evanna.

"I spoke to Rayne about that, and she said she knew of someone that can work with her to help with her cat. Someone from Ed's clan may be able to," she paused, "Blair's clan still has a lot going on, so I haven't asked them."

Evanna took them and gave him a small smile, before reaching around him and opening the cooler. "That sounds good, get all the help there for when we arrive."

"Devin is sending a trailer for you to stay in while you're here."

He watched Evanna take the pills and then finish the juice box. Had she looked that tired before the run? He needed to start watching for that better. "I appreciate that. I'll call him later."

"When do you think you'll be here?"

He could hear other voices in the background now. "I'm hoping to drive straight through and be there late tomorrow. If not, then the first thing the next day. It depends if we stop to rest or just take short breaks."

"Make sure you're getting some rest, Jesse, this is going to get more stressful before it improves."

He nodded, "I will. Okay, we're going to get back to it, Shaelan, thank you."

"Any time, Jesse. Take care."

Hanging up, he looked down at Thera, "ready for another drive?" She didn't look thrilled but jumped into the van. He smiled at her, "soon, I promise, you can race around Blair's for days if you must." She huffed and lay down.

Closing the door, he watched Evanna as she opened the passenger's door. "You should try to get some sleep."

"I should be okay once those pills work." She motioned around her, "I just like seeing something different every time I look out the window."

He closed the door when she got in and leaned on the open window, "next few hours are miles of nothing to see, grab some rest while you can." Reaching in, he flipped the handle on the side and reclined the seat.

"Oh," she chuckled as she was suddenly laying back, "that's handy."

Jesse smiled, "I'll wake you if there's anything worth seeing." He patted his hand off the door, "tonight we're going to have to stop at a store, so get some rest while you can."

Chapter Twenty-Five

Leah sat forward in the seat as he pulled in, she'd never been *in a* store. The few times she'd been able to go with her grandfather, she hadn't been able to bring herself to go in with him. Jesse said it was up to her, but thought she should so she could select some snacks of her own. He'd gone in alone the last time for snacks, so she thought maybe she should help. She had no idea what she would like. She could see rows of items on a shelf. Leaning closer to the windshield, she read all the colored signs on the window, not understanding what any of them were for.

"Ready?" He turned off the van.

Blowing out a breath, she undid her seat belt. "I think so." She looked over at him, trying not to panic. "Is it—can I hold your hand?" She felt silly saying it. "It helps me stay here."

Jesse smiled, "absolutely." He got out and quickly went around the front and opened the door. He held out his hand.

She was now more excited to hold his hand than she was to see what all those shelves were full of. Placing her hand in his, she got out. "We have to get more jerky for Evanna, and Thera." She leaned her head back in the door. "Stay, Thera, we'll be right back."

Closing the door, she watched to see Thera's head appear between the seats.

"As long as she stays down, no one will see her." Jesse looked around, "we're the only people here right now."

"Thank you for waiting until it was dark to do this." She glanced up to see her was watching her and listening, "I feel better if there is no one looking at me." It was hard not to squeeze his hand too hard as they walked toward the door. "What if I don't know what I'll like?"

"We're in no hurry, take your time." He opened the door and then motioned for her to lead.

Trying to remember how to breathe, she stepped inside. The first thing she noticed was it was warm, then she picked up all the scents in the store. So many. Too many to know what any of them were.

A young man came out of a door carrying a box. He smiled and then set the box down. She paused to watch him open it and then turn to start putting things on a shelf.

"Drinks first?" Jesse leaned down and spoke softly to her.

She nodded and let him lead her down the aisle. There were so many things on the shelf. Bright colored packages of—she wasn't sure of what. When he stopped, she looked to see colorful bottles behind a window.

"Juice, milk," he motioned to the windows, "pop, water," he pointed to the end one, "and other stuff." Giving her hand a squeeze, he smiled down at her, "I'm just going to grab a basket, I'll be right back." He released her hand slowly.

Leah watched him go back over by the door and then turn to come back to her. Turning, she looked at the bottles. Stepping closer, she read the names on them. How was she ever going to decide?

Jesse went past her to end glass doors and opened one. He reached in a picked up two cans, then two more, putting them in the basket.

Inhaling slowly, she pulled on the door and opened it. "Apple," she said quietly. Picking one up, she noticed how cold it was.

Jesse was beside her. "That one?" He held his hand out and waited until she set the drink in his hand. "What about orange? Or you could try a few others." He reached in and picked up one, "you can try a few."

Leah nodded and reached in for another one. She wasn't sure what the flavor was, she had to consider what Evanna might want to.

"Okay, I'll get a case of water when we're ready to pay." Jesse wrapped his hand around hers and lead her toward another row of items.

She was so appreciative that he was taking his time and letting her look at things, it was a complete overload, the number of things in this store. More than half of the things she looked at; she had no idea what they were. Evanna was going to be happy, there had been several kinds of jerky, so Leah had grabbed a few of each.

The row with chocolate and sweets seemed to be never-ending. She paused and leaned down to read the packages near the bottom.

Jesse bent down, "sugar is great, but too much will make it harder with Minn." He said softly.

Straightening, she looked up to see his pale eyes studying her. "Are cookies okay?" She bit her lip.

"Cookies are always okay." He grinned and lifted her hand and kissed it. "What kind do you think? Chocolate chip? Oatmeal or…"

"Oatmeal?" She hadn't had oatmeal for months. "I like oatmeal."

"Oatmeal it is then." Tugging her hand gently, he walked to the end and went around to the other row. He picked up two packages and put them in the basket.

Leah looked at the basket and was surprised to see it was almost overflowing. "I didn't bring any money in," she said softly.

"Don't worry about it. We're stopping for clothes tomorrow." He led her up the aisle toward the young man standing behind a counter.

"I'll pay for the clothes." Leah raised her eyebrows at him, "I don't know…"

He winked at her. "We'll figure it out then." He turned to the man taking things out of the basket. "Add two cases of water and some washer fluid, please."

The man nodded and continued to make the machine in front of him beep. Leah was fascinated by what he was doing. But the most interesting thing was Jesse paid him with a piece of plastic. She had no idea what it was and couldn't wait until they were outside so she could ask.

She carried one of the bags out to the van and then it hit her, she'd gone inside and helped pick things and hadn't had to fight to stay here. Turning, she watched Jesse come back out with two cases of bottled water. It had to be him, the reason she'd been able to do it. Setting the bag in the van, she rubbed her hand over Thera's head as she checked to see how close Evanna was. She was there, but it took a lot of focus to sense her, so it hadn't been her.

"Are you okay?"

She was startled to find Jesse beside her. "I'm fine. It just hit me that I went inside and I'm still here."

Jesse reached over and brushed the hair back from her face, "I knew you could do it."

"I think you're why I could do it."

He pulled out a package of the jerky and opened it, offering Thera a piece. "Me?" He grinned as Thera took it and moved away from the open door.

Leah nodded, "I'm calmer when I'm near you." She smiled up at him, "you're some kind of magic."

Jesse chuckled, "I don't know about that, but I understand why you're calmer."

She watched him pull the cooler over and start putting the drinks in. "You do?"

He paused and glanced at her for a second, "yeah, it's a normal thing with our kind." Closing the cooler, he reached and set the bag of the other items between the seats. Sitting down, he looked at her again.

She liked that they were closer to the same height, it made it easier to look into those eyes. "We're calmer around our own kind?" Taking her hand in his warm one, he stroked his thumb over it. The movement made her feel excited, but at peace at the same time.

"I don't know how much your grandparents and Aunt Tillie explained to you—but it's because we're mates, Leah."

She knew about mates, obviously, that was something she heard talk of from her grandparents. She'd read about it in some of the journals too. "We are?" Her nerves weren't as steady now, "what does that mean for," she licked her now dry lips, "us?"

"Us? Evanna and Minn too." He squeezed her hand.

"You know that?" She looked down at their hands. It would explain why Evanna was doing things that she'd never done before, like sharing feelings. Minn did seem to be a little better, well, for Minn, it was better.

"I know that." He said softly. Picking up her other hand, he held the two of them. "It doesn't mean anything right now, no pressure." His eyes searched her face, "I'm not going anywhere, so we have lots of time."

She nodded, unable to say anything.

"We'll get back and get you some help with Minn, the headaches, how tired you are then we'll take it from there."

Her heart felt strange in her chest. "I'm…" She blew out a breath, "I don't know if I can talk about this right now."

"Hey," he released one hand and put his hand against her cheek, "we don't have to, I just wanted you to know."

"Okay." She felt shaky.

"You can ask questions or talk about it whenever you're ready, okay?" He stood up, still holding her hand, "we should get going. I want to put another hour in before I rest." Leaning down, he kissed her cheek. "And you, have snacks to try." He smiled down at her as he closed the door with his other hand.

Leah got in when he opened her door.

"Leah, are you okay?"

"Yes," she smiled, "just sorting through that."

He nodded his head slowly. "Okay."

She watched him walk around the front of the van. She had a mate. A kind-hearted, good-looking, mate—and she had no idea what she was expected to do in this situation.

Chapter Twenty-Six

Jesse couldn't help wondering if him telling Leah they were mates was why Evanna had come out when she'd woken and not Leah. It constantly churned around in his head, he needed to know more. Did the doctor have all the answers to his questions? Should he just start asking Evanna and Leah? He didn't know and it was distracting the hell out of him. He looked over to see Evanna was looking out the window. She hadn't said more than ten words since she woke up. Had Leah communicated with her what he'd told her? Could they even do that? Evanna was straightforward, she'd say something if she knew. At least he figured she would. "Are you okay?"

She looked at him, the light from the dash highlighting her eyes. "I'm just thinking about stuff."

"Anything I can help with?" Just blurting out questions was a bad idea he decided.

"That video call, I was close, watching—what were they talking about with the weapons training?"

That caught him off guard for a second, he hadn't expected that at all. "Blair and his mate Kobie are going to be part of the team that goes in to get ours out, for the most part, it's going to be situations that shifting and using our animals aren't possible, so the Alliance makes sure we know how to handle a variety of weapons."

"Our? You're part of this team?"

"I am. I've been doing this for five years now."

"Have you rescued many?"

"Personally? I've only been on a few of the actual ops, I'm usually the one waiting on the sidelines to get those found out and back to safety."

"Where do they go—for safety?"

"That varies. Usually back to their clan or a clan of the same. Those that aren't ready to go back or have nowhere to go are either in safe houses or at Devin and Rayne's campground."

"I meant what I said, I don't want to be dumped off somewhere." She glanced at him, "Leah doesn't do well around strangers and Minn seems to have accepted you, so we're staying with you."

"As much as I'd love that, I don't spend a lot of time at home, I'm on the road a lot and I will be going on the trips to those addresses and a few other locations."

"Give me this weapons training and I can come and help."

He looked at her briefly while he was at the stop sign, "I don't see Leah dealing well with it."

"Obviously I'd be driving the body then, not her." She shrugged, "and if Minn is required, you know she can handle herself."

He wanted to explain why he wasn't comfortable with her going. It wasn't a question of her abilities, he had no doubt she would be able to handle herself, it was more the fact that he didn't want his mate involved, put on a dangerous path. "I know she can, you as well, but we can't know how Leah, you, or Minn are going to react when you're back there." He rubbed his hand along his jaw, "it's going to stir up a lot of memories."

"I didn't think of that." She looked out the window again, "what if I'm part of the team that stays back and helps to get them to safety?"

"And what are you planning to do with Thera during

this?" He turned to see the creature watching them.

Evanna looked at the leopard. "I didn't think of that either."

"We can't have a real leopard running around in the city."

"No, I guess not. Leah isn't going to let her be put in a cage again."

"No one will put her in a cage, we just have to find somewhere she can run free as she did on the mountain." In his mind he was going over the terrain on his property, trying to figure out how hard it would be to fence it in. It was a big chunk of land, with lots of trees, and even a river ran through it. He'd never planned to fence the property, just install a few cameras around the border, but a camera wasn't going to contain Thera—or Minn in her frantic moments. He would have to talk to his father about sending someone out to assess if it could be done.

"There's ah—" she stopped and looked out the window and sighed loudly, "I've never told anyone," She turned back to him.

Jesse made sure she saw him looking at her, that she had his full attention before he turned back to the road. "You can tell me anything, I won't share it with anyone unless you want me to." He hoped that was what she needed to hear.

"Yeah, I get that feeling from you." She made a noise, "this is harder than I thought." Unclipping her seatbelt, she turned in the seat, so she was facing him. "I just—I never told even Aunt Tillie, you know? I don't know if I should…" He could hear the torment in her voice. "I don't know the rules," she waved her hand around, "all the rules on what is allowed and what isn't with the shifter clans."

"Hey," He reached over and rested his hand on hers, "anything. You can trust me."

She nodded her head slowly.

Lifting his hand away, he tried to split his focus between her and on driving. "Do you want me to pull over so we can talk?"

"Uh, no. No, I can talk like this." She sighed again, "I just don't know how to start."

"Take your time." Trying to grip the steering wheel lightly, he flexed his stiff neck. His cat was wide awake inside him now, their mate was struggling with something. The anxiety coming off her was strong.

"Okay, when they got Leah out of there, her mom, right-"

"Right." He agreed so she knew he was right there with her, hearing whatever she had to say.

"I was out before she got far, she was panicking and almost paralyzed by it," she blew out a breath.

"It must have been terrifying." He offered quietly.

"It was." She cleared her throat, "I took off in the direction that a man told us to go. The direction he told Leah to go."

The anxiety in her voice was making it sound hoarse. Without a word, he reached over and took a hold of her hand.

She squeezed his and continued to hold it, "I didn't get as far as I'd hoped." She snorted, "I mean there we were running through the city, looking all young and vulnerable, I guess…" She took a deep breath and then inhaled it slowly, "Minn burst out, to save us. I-I didn't see this creepy man—" Releasing his hand, she adjusted her ponytail. "Minn saved us. I don't know what could have happened." She cleared her throat, "the creepy man didn't survive it."

Jesse looked over at her, he didn't need to see her face clearly, the anxiety and fear pouring off her were almost choking him. Grabbing her hand, he held it firmly. "You and Minn did what you had to do to survive."

"I've never told Leah. She doesn't remember most of the trip back to the mountain."

Her tone was so soft, that he almost thought it was Leah out for a second.

"I won't claim to understand how it works between you, but if you feel this is something she needs to be sheltered from, then I'm behind you in your choice." Her first shift was far too early, and her animal had killed someone. In Chicago. Could Devin research that? No, he couldn't tell anyone, he'd just said he wouldn't.

"I never told the grandparents, because I didn't know if Minn had done something wrong..."

"Hey," he leaned down so he could see her eyes, "you're here now because your cat protected you. Period. There is no wrong in that." His cat was going crazy. She was upset. Jesse could hardly breathe. She could have been killed if not for her cat. He looked back to the road, checked the mirrors, and then slowed and pulled onto the shoulder. Putting the van in park, he unclipped his seat belt and shifted in the seat so he could take both of her hands. "Look at me," he waited until she did, "it shouldn't have been that way. Your first shift should have been fun, an amazing thing in your life." He held her gaze with his own, "the fact that it wasn't, pisses me off in ways I can't even express. Just know those responsible for it are going to pay."

"But he's already dead."

Her quiet tone bothered his cat as much as it did him. "I'm talking about all of them, not just that creep Minn dealt with."

She nodded in a shaky way.

"Is this why you have to fight to keep Minn under control? Are you afraid of it happening again? When Leah loses control of her it's because your cat doesn't know what's safe and what isn't?"

"I-I, we both aren't sure of what Minn will do, anytime she's out." She cleared her throat, "on the mountain, it was safe, right? There weren't a lot of people there, at any time—what do you mean my cat doesn't know? How can she know what's safe and not?"

Jesse squeezed her hands, "we all struggle with our animals at times," he smirked briefly, "like right now, mine is so pissed, but worried at the same time. He's demanding justice for you, but is pushing me to make you feel better, to feel calm," he shrugged, "they're always there, just under the surface monitoring things, that part is normal."

"So how-how do you control him? How do you keep him inside?"

"With a lot of practice. That's another part you were robbed of, the normal bonding that happens with your animal before they emerge. There was no way for your—" He remembered she didn't call her mother. "Lyvia to help you with that and still keep it a secret that your animal was close at your age."

Evanna nodded, her complete focus on his face. "They uh, worked really hard keeping us away from the guards and the men that came there."

Jesse's cat felt like he was taking claws to his insides, he focused so he wouldn't visibly flinch. *What men?* "She did the right thing getting you out of there."

Evanna nodded, "I don't think Leah would have survived there much longer. I-I don't know what happened before I was around, I can't see it," she pulled one hand free and tapped her head, "in here, there are parts of things that are closed off and I can't see them. There's a lot of parts that I keep Leah from too."

Jesse nodded slowly, even though he understood none of it really, "you're all doing what you need to do to survive and be safe." He gave her a gentle smile, "that's all I want, for you to feel safe. I don't care if I have to drive you around the country to see different people from all over, I will make sure you get any help or training you need to feel safe, do you understand?"

"We can stay with you?" She lowered her eyes, "because to be honest, I've been freaking out a bit thinking you were going to dump us off somewhere and go back to your life..."

Jesse gripped her chin as gently as he could manage as his cat raged inside him, "I'm not dumping you off anywhere. If anything, I'd take you to my place," he cringed, "that isn't even completely built yet, and leave you there in peace where you'd be safe—if circumstances made it so I couldn't have you with me, but I'd be coming back. Do you understand what I'm saying?"

She held his look for what felt like hours, "Yeah, you're going to look out for us." Her eyes glistened with unfallen tears, "I'm glad, I am really." She sniffled, then cleared her throat, "it means the world that you will watch after Leah when

I'm not out."

"I'll watch after all of you, and I will help with Minn as much as possible."

"Right, okay." She blew out a quick breath, "that makes me feel a lot better. I've been a little worried about what was going to happen when Minn was around others." She straightened back, so his hand dropped away from her face. "Thanks, Jesse, I can't even find the words to explain how much better that makes me feel. How being with you makes things easier."

His cat was still agitated but settled a little bit when he heard those words. He wanted to tell her, now he felt like he was keeping a secret from her that he and Leah had shared.

Turning in the seat, she lifted her hand toward the windshield, "we should get going." She turned and grinned at him, "I'm hungry and I can't wait to try a burger."

Jesse turned back in his seat, "burger and fries, maybe a milkshake."

"I don't know what a milkshake is, but I'll take it, so far all the foods since you wandered into our village have been off the charts." She smacked her lips together, "a ten on the tasty scale."

Jesse's stomach rumbled as if right on cue, "yeah, some food would be good." He put on his seatbelt and looked in the mirror to see Thera was awake now and looking at him. "Maybe some chicken strip snacks for the kitty in the back."

Evanna turned to look at the cat, "I'd say she's up for it."

Jesse pulled back out onto the road, "twenty minutes and we'll stop for food."

Evanna leaned forward and tapped the clock on the radio, "noted on your fancy clock."

Chapter Twenty-Seven

Jesse pulled up the lane slowly, hoping that Blair had gotten the message, and few would be there when they pulled in. "This is Blair and Kobie's clan."

"And they're tigers?"

"Yeah. Calum and his mate are here, they're jaguars. "

"Everyone's animal gets along when they're out?"

"They do." He grinned, recalling a few instances over the years, "for the most part."

"They probably have better control of theirs than I do of Minn."

"You'll learn, there are many elders and experts that will be able to help you, Leah."

"I look forward to that. I think."

He parked as far from the house as he could.

"How-how many people live here?"

"Uh, I'm not sure now, a few have come back, around fifteen I think, including guards."

"Guards?" Her eyes went huge.

Turning off the van, he closed his eyes, knowing he didn't word that right. Turning, he looked at her, she looked so scared. "Kobie's clan got away from Tomas, and some of them made their way back. One of Tomas' men wants them, so we have Alliance guards here to help keep watch."

"Are all of our kind affected because of that Tomas person?" Her voice was shaking.

"For now." Reaching over, he took her hand in his. "We're getting closer to ending what he's doing."

"I always thought," she squeezed his hand, "I thought we were the few that suffered, my mom," she swallowed and shook her head, "but it's all of our kind, isn't it?"

He nodded slowly, lifting her hand and kissing the back of it. "We're going to end it, Leah, I promise."

Thera stuck her head between the seats and bumped their hands.

Leah looked out the window, "she wants out."

Jesse glanced toward the house, Blair and Calum stood there. Most likely making the others stay inside because of Thera. Turning in his seat, he looked at the leopard. "No biting. You don't want to deal with those two if you hurt one of theirs."

Thera gave her head a shake.

He didn't know if it was a yes or she was shaking him off, but he got out and opened the door. Thera jumped down and lifted her head to scent the air. He heard the other door close and turned to see Leah basically forcing her feet to move. Trusting the cat to behave, he rushed over and took her hand. She squeezed it so hard, he knew she was really struggling. "They're friends." He told her quietly. "They'd never do anything to hurt you." Leaning down, he made sure she looked at him, "you're safe here."

She nodded but didn't look convinced. "I don't know if I can stay." She whispered it, her voice vibrating.

"I'm right here." He glanced over to see Blair and Calum stood where they had been, knowing that it was best they come to them. "Come on, one step at a time." He wrapped his arm around her, still holding her shaking hand.

He didn't want to drag her, but it felt like he was. Thera walked on the other side of her, with cautious steps. Jesse glanced at Calum to see he was watching the leopard as well. He'd know probably before anyone if Thera was going to do something regrettable.

"Jesse, how was the trip?" Blair smiled at him but still made no move to come closer.

"Long." Jesse gave him a quick look and then turned so he could see Leah's face. "Calum, Blair, this is Leah." He didn't like her breathing. She held her hand against her chest. "It's okay." He whispered.

"Hello," she finally rasped out.

Pulling her closer, he wanted her to feel like he was surrounding her, keeping her safe.

"Leah." Calum inclined his head, but his body was still tense.

"And this," Jesse motioned to the leopard that wasn't as relaxed as he'd like her to be. She was hunched down, ready to spring at any moment, "is Thera." Her ears flicked back at the mention of her name.

"I'm sorry."

He glanced at Leah to see she had that glossed-over look in her eyes, she was staring at the ground. "It's okay." He told her and he knew she was too overwhelmed to stay at the front. He looked to Calum, who was watching her carefully now as well. When the woman he held stopped shaking, he knew Leah was where she felt safe.

Evanna leaned over and put her head on his shoulder for a few seconds and then straightened so it was necessary for him to keep his arm around her. "Thera, behave." She said in that deep brisk voice he knew well. With a short huff of air, she turned to look at Calum and Blair, "Sorry about that, Leah has a hard time with strangers."

"Calum, Blair, this is Evanna." Jesse said as if he hadn't just introduced Leah.

"Evanna," Calum said without pause.

"Glad you're here," Blair said. "We put the trailer back there, so you'd have some privacy." He motioned to the back of the yard.

"Thanks." Jesse looked at him. "Does it come equipped with a shower?"

Blair grinned, "yeah it does and two beds with soft mattresses."

Jesse let his shoulders relax. "A shower, coffee, something to eat that doesn't come in a wrapper, and then I will probably sleep for twenty-four hours straight."

He glanced down to see Evanna was looking at the house.

"This is huge." She said with awe

"Doesn't feel big enough sometimes," Blair grinned.

"Your whole clan lives in that?" She reached into her pocket and pulled out a tie for her hair.

"For now." Blair tucked his hands in his pockets, "we're going to be building some smaller homes around the property so some of the couples have their own space."

"I'm pretty good with a hammer, let me know if I can do anything while we're here." Evanna turned and walked toward the back of the house.

Shaelan came out the door.

Jesse was surprised when Thera ran over to her.

"Aren't you gorgeous," She bent down and rubbed her hand along Thera's jaw.

"You must be Shaelan." Evanna turned around and came back over. She held out her hand, "Evanna."

Shaelan took her hand, "I'm so glad you're finally here." She motioned to the other side of the yard, "come on, I'll show you the trailer."

Jesse, Blair, and Calum watched them walk away.

"You look like you haven't slept in a week."

Jesse turned back to Calum, "I don't think I have really." He rubbed his hand over his eyes and blew out a breath. "I was hoping Leah would be able to stay at the front."

Calum clapped him on the shoulder, "it might be easier if she just observes the coming and goings around here for a while, to make her more comfortable."

Blair gave him a surprised look.

Calum shrugged, "who do you think Shae runs every thought by?"

Jesse shook his head, "just going to grab some bags from the van. And someone needs to unload those crates of vegetables." Going back over, he opened the door and pulled out the three bags of clothes and other items Leah had bought. Once Evanna realized she was in that fluffy skirt, she was going to want something more of her style to put on.

"Vegetables?" Blair raised an eyebrow at him.

"She wasn't leaving food behind to spoil."

Blair grinned, "food is good." He looked around the yard, "I'll go grab some help and get that done." He looked in the van, "what about the other boxes?"

"Leave them here for now. At some point, I have to go through the clan paperwork and see what is what."

Blair nodded, "yeah clan paperwork is something I never thought I'd have to care about."

Jesse chuckled, "Alpha looks good on you though."

"Everything looks good on me," Blair smirked and walked away.

Evanna stepped out of the small bathroom, water droplets still rolling down her neck. "*That,*" she motioned behind her, "was pretty amazing." She smiled, "and nothing like getting washed from a basin."

Jesse nodded his head slowly, "a hot shower cures almost anything."

She gave him a blank look, "I don't know about that, but I've never felt this clean." She jerked on the collar of the bathrobe and then looked at the skirt in her hand. "Why did she have to buy fluffy stuff?"

Getting up, Jesse reached past her to pull the bag out of the cupboard. "She picked these for you." He motioned to the bag on the floor, "boots too."

Evanna's eyes went wide, "boots?" Squatting down, she

opened the bag and pulled them out. "These are amazing." She glanced up at him and then looked at the bag, "tell me there are jeans in that bag."

Unable not to grin, he held out the bag, "two pairs and a few different tops." He left out how good they looked on their body. Leah hadn't liked the feel of them, but she knew Evanna would.

Hugging the boots, she stood up and grabbed the bag. "*Now* I'm excited." Squeezing by him, she went to the back of the trailer. "Be right back."

Jesse glanced out the open door to see Thera laying there. Daisie was sitting beside her chattering away. He stepped out.

"She's so pretty and *so* much better than a dog." She nodded, "and she's not afraid of us and our cats."

Going over, he squatted down beside them. "I agree, cats are better than dogs," he winked, "our kind of cats." He rubbed his hand down the back of Thera's neck. "So, how have you been while I was gone?"

"My dad's back, so mom is *much* happier." She looked over at the house, "he still has to get better, but I'm *so* happy he's home."

Jesse still hadn't had time to get caught up on everything he'd missed, he looked at the trailer, he wasn't comfortable leaving Leah, or even Evanna on her own just yet. "I look forward to talking to him."

Daisie's expression changed to serious, "you should talk to Blair too," she lifted her chin, "he's our new Alpha and I'm a princess."

Jesse laughed softly, "I heard, congratulations."

"You're a princess?" Evanna came outside.

Jesse stood slowly, freshly showered in clothes that weren't patched together, she was breathtaking. She'd pulled her hair up, but damp tendrils fell around her face. "Those fit good." He cleared his throat, "the boots, they look like they fit good." He blinked, not even sure where this bumbling twit had come from.

"I *love* them." She put her one foot out and moved it back

and forth.

He forced his eyes to move away from her face and look down at the hiking boots she wore. Unable to think of anything that wasn't stupid to say, he settled for nodding and then smiling at her.

"Yes, I'm a princess, sort of." Daisie stood up.

Evanna glanced at him for clarification.

"Blair selected her family to be the clan's second family."

Evanna looked back at Daisie, "that's an important position. I'm sure you'll do it well."

Daisie glowed with praise. "I have to go. I have my reading class soon." She bounced past them, "I'll see you on my next break."

They both watched her skip away.

"Are there a lot of kids here?" Evanna stood close to him, not touching him, but close enough he could smell the fresh scent of the shampoo she'd used.

"None as young as Daisie, but there are a few teen girls here."

"I'll have to meet everyone that lives here." She crossed her arms over her chest. "If I don't check them out, Leah may never surface again." Her tone was quiet, remorseful.

"We can do that. I tried to have it so she only met two when we got here," he rubbed his hand over his jaw and glanced at the house, "I'm not sure what happened."

Evanna touched his arm, "it's nothing you did. She just can't handle meeting people."

Placing his hand over hers, he held it there, "she did fine in the stores."

"She didn't have to speak to them, did she?"

He shook his head.

"She can see others, just not talk to them." Clearing her throat, she pulled her hand from his. "Is the rest of our stuff in here or the van? I need to check the journal." She grinned, "see what she was up to that she stayed out for two days without incident."

Jesse motioned to the van, "I'll go grab the rest of the stuff." He watched her look around, "you can wander around if you want, just no going for runs alone."

Turning back, she looked at him, "Minn seems okay right now. Why not alone though?"

"There's been a few incidents with trying to take members of this clan." He didn't want to go into too much detail about it.

Her eyebrows raised, "same people that took mine?"

Jesse nodded.

She was quiet for a second, "okay, I'll keep Minn locked down."

Walking backward, so he wouldn't go back over to her, "Just shout if you want to go for a run, there are plenty of women here that do often." There were men too, but none of them would be going for a run with her, not as long as he was around.

"Great. Okay."

Chapter Twenty-Eight

Evanna flipped through the pages. Leah had written about ten of them. She went back to the first page, what could have happened that she needed to write that much? She'd been close for most of it, but there hadn't been any overwhelming emotions, so it was harder for her to pick up on everything that happened. She rolled her eyes, there was no way she was writing a ten-page reply.

The first few pages detailed things that Leah had seen on the drive. She talked about the radio and some of the things said on the radio. Commercials, she didn't know what those were but wanted to hear some now so she could be as entertained as Leah had been.

Leah talked about being in the store and how there were rows of snacks and food things, so many kinds of drinks she hadn't known what to try and what not to try. Evanna made a note to ask where these items were that were bought, so she could try all of them. She bit off another bite of the jerky, made with turkey no less, who knew that was even possible. She definitely needed to see inside one of these stores of snacks.

Tossing the last of the jerky to Thera, she turned the page.

The writing was neater now, meaning Leah wasn't as excited when she was writing.

"Are you doing homework too?"

Evanna turned to see Daisie standing by the corner of the trailer. "No, I'm reading some notes from Leah."

"Is Leah your sister? I don't have a sister."

Evanna closed the journal, using her hand to mark which page she'd been on. "She's not my sister." How did she begin to explain this to a child? When she didn't understand herself. "Leah is—another part of me."

"Like your cat? My mom says my cat is another part of me."

"It's kind of like that."

"I wished there was another part of me. A part that likes math."

Evanna laughed, "I don't think any parts like math."

"My dad does." Daisie looked over her shoulder, "I better go. Say hi to Leah for me."

"I will." She watched her run across the yard. She was a happy child. There were a few creases in her forehead, telling Evanna that things hadn't been good all the time, but she wasn't haunted or fractured, so that said a lot about the adults that were here with her.

Thera got up and wandered after her.

"Don't be a pest," Evanna told her as she walked by. She checked how Minn was doing. Something she'd had to do constantly throughout every day and night. She was quiet just now, so it was a good time to finish the journal."

Opening it, she studied the first line.

I've just found out something that explains everything.

Evanna smirked if only that were true.

Jesse just told me that I, we are his mate. It explains why he smells so good all the time. I believe it's why we are so calm around him. I don't know how that works though, I know what mates are, but most mates don't have three parts to them.

I didn't know what to say when he explained it. He told me it was you and Minn as well, so I suppose that's a good thing. The last thing we need in our life is conflict with each other. He said I could ask questions or talk about it whenever I wanted to. I don't think I want to right now.

What I want is to be able to control Minn. To be able to speak to someone without hiding inside. Do you think that will ever happen?

Evanna hugged the journal to her chest. She had no idea if it ever would. If it was somehow managed though, where did that leave her? They shared the same body, so it's not like they could ever both be out at the same time.

"Am I interrupting?"

She looked up to see Shaelan standing there.

"No. I'm just thinking about things." She held up the journal. "Leah left me some interesting notes."

Shaelan gave her a friendly smile. "Is that how you two communicate?" She sat down on the other chair that sat outside the trailer.

"It makes it easier if we need to know about something or remember something."

"It's a good idea."

Evanna was at ease around her, she gave off a sense of compassion. Which, she thought made sense because she was a healer. "It's good for when we've done something that the other one should know about."

"Did Leah tell you all about the trip?"

"The parts I missed, yeah. I was out a few times." She shrugged, "I control Minn better than she does so if they go for a run most of the time it's me when we shift back."

"Why do you think Leah has trouble controlling Minn?"

Setting the journal down, Evanna studied it as she thought. "I'm not sure."

"Minn came out after Leah escaped, right?"

Evanna nodded, "yeah, up until then it had just been Leah and I."

"And you step in when Leah is emotional?"

"That sounds right." She looked her straight in the eye, she liked her, so it was the respectful thing to do.

"I don't mean to sound nosy; I'm just trying to understand more." She leaned forward in the seat. "There's a doctor that will be here tomorrow."

"The one that knows what's wrong with us?"

"Mmhmm, she has more experience with it than I do."

"Do you think she can fix us?" She watched Shaelan look at her. It was a good thing that she was considering it and not just blurting out an answer.

"I don't know if there's ever a complete cure, Evanna. I want to be honest with you. The goal I believe for now is to help Minn and Leah. To make it more manageable."

"What would more manageable be like?"

"Do you have specific concerns?"

Evanna stood up, not feeling still enough to sit. "Well, I don't want any of us to be all drugged up, I saw that on a movie with Aunt Tillie and I don't want to be like that."

"I'm sure no one will drug you like that."

"Okay," she nodded, "good."

"Is something bothering you, Evanna? You seem agitated."

"Agitated?" Evanna smirked, "I don't know if I'm that, but I was just thinking about things. Leah said Jesse told her that we're his mate." She snorted and then shook her head, "I don't even know how that would work? How would that work?"

Shaelan smiled, one of those soft understanding ones. "I have learned one thing about mates."

Evanna nodded her head slowly, giving her complete focus. "What is that?"

"That when it comes to one's mate, it works out." She smiled again, "I've spoken to a lot of elders in the past few months, and they have so many stories of mates finding one another and overcoming insurmountable obstacles to be together." She clasped her hands in front of her, "I don't think fate would give you a mate that wasn't up to the challenges you face."

Evanna looked over to see Jesse standing talking to a few men. "He's pretty good, he can even talk to Leah without sending her into a panic," she shrugged, "except that one time, but he's been doing really good since then." She motioned to her clothes, "he's had Leah in stores, that's a first."

"I think he'll figure it out, you'll figure it out together." Shaelan smiled again, "now if you'll excuse me, I'm going for a run with my mate."

"Thanks, Shaelan." And she meant it, she decided as she walked away to go over to that tall dark-haired man, Calum. He was a serious man, and she got vibes of danger from him, but not at her, so that made a difference.

Thera came flying over to her and looked at the couple walking hand in hand toward the trees at the back. "Shaelan, Thera wants to come for a run."

Calum and Shaelan stopped, "she's welcome." Calum called back.

"Be good," Evanna warned the leopard. Thera looked at her for a moment more and then took off after them. She watched her for a moment and then turned back to look at Jesse. She knew that the light-haired one was Blair, but she didn't know the other two. One had curly red hair and a smile on his face. She shrugged; happy people were nice to be around. Aunt Tillie for the most part was always a happy person. The other one was tall, not as muscular as the rest and he had something haunting his soul. A phrase Aunt Tillie used to use. He had short, brown hair that looked like it hadn't been brushed, with what she could only describe as golden streaks in it. He was not smiling and even his posture said he was in no way relaxed. She understood that all too well. That was how she felt a lot of her life, tense, waiting for the next thing to go wrong. He crossed his arms over his chest and stood there listening to the other three. He wasn't a leader, so far, he hadn't said a word. She frowned, there was something that seemed familiar about him, which was impossible. Unless—

Evanna started toward them. She didn't get three feet before Jesse turned and looked at her. Later, she'd wonder how he'd known when she was heading over there. He cocked his head to the side like he knew she was on a mission, and she was, she needed to know why that man seemed familiar.

When she was almost to them, the man turned and looked at her. She stopped and stood there. His eyes, the look he was giving her—she'd seen those eyes before, that expression.

"Leah?"

She shook her head. Jesse came over and stood close to her. "Evanna."

The man nodded his head slowly, "Evanna." The heavy expression on his face lightened, "I'm so glad you got home."

"You're Noah."

He nodded, a hesitant look on his face.

"Jesse said you were rescued too." She looked him up and down, he seemed whole—on the outside, "you weren't there by choice?" She frowned, trying to piece together things that she remembered, things she didn't want to remember. "It was you." It had been Leah and all of it was a blur, but the pieces… "You're the one that unlocked the door and let Leah go."

Noah nodded, the pained expression still in his eyes. "I couldn't get your mother and sister to go with you." He took a step, then stopped, "not with your sister's condition."

Evanna looked from him to Jesse, then back to him. "Her condition?" There was something wrong with Leah's sister? She tried to picture her, the memories had faded, she couldn't picture her clearly. She stared at him, not really seeing him.

Jesse and the other man both turned to Noah.

Evanna's heart started racing, she rubbed her hand across her forehead. A faded image of Ashtyn formed in her mind. They both had the same dark hair and eyes, Leah's sister was taller, more exotic looking. She could see her smile, but the smile faded. Taking a step back, she tried to focus. She could feel Minn stir and shook her head, trying to will the cat to stay calm so she could see, really see.

"Evanna?" Jesse was right in front of her now. "It's okay, you're safe."

She looked with a blurred vision at his pale eyes. "It's not okay." Her voice didn't sound like her own. Her throat started to ache. "Minn." She whispered, not sure if it was to the cat or to Jesse.

"Take deep breaths, try to slow your heartbeat." He was leaning down in her face.

"Ashtyn," she blinked, trying to focus. "There was—" The pains in her stomach started, it was always like this when she fought Minn. Shaking her head, she backed away from him, she didn't want to hurt him by mistake. "I'm sorry." She turned and ran for the trailer. She didn't get far before the pains were so bad, that she couldn't move any further. "Leah, help me." She groaned, the slight movement to get her boots off was almost too much to bear.

"Here." Jesse was behind her now, he dropped down and pulled her other boot off. "Just keep breathing, change, but control it."

"Can't." she hissed out a breath and tried to pull the shirt over her head.

"Jesse?" She heard Blair but couldn't see him.

"Watch the drive, so she doesn't go that way," Jesse said in a hurried voice.

She could feel hands on her waist now, the pressure of the material around her hips was eased as he undid her jeans and slid them down her legs. "Can't..." she moaned, and it sounded more like a growl.

"I'll be right behind you."

She could hear him but was unable to concentrate to see him.

"Minn, stop hurting her and let her shift." He growled out low.

Evanna could see again and realized as she moved fast it was through feline eyes. The trees flew by, she felt like a passenger, unable to reach Minn enough to take control of the cat's form.

Chapter Twenty-Nine

Jesse watched Blair, in cat form bound down the drive. He nodded and stripped his shirt over his head. "Keep the others in the house, Cale." He shouted as he ran, "she can't control her cat." He didn't stop to see if he listened. Pausing long enough to kick off his boots and get out of his jeans, he shifted fast. One second he was jogging, barefoot on the damp ground, the next he was four paws in the dirt moving fast.

He slowed long enough to bellow out as loud as his feline vocals allowed, warning Calum and Shaelan that something was happening. Hopefully, Minn would heed the warning as well. He heard a reply and knew it was Thera and she was on the chase for her friend now.

Racing through the trees, he lost her scent for a moment and had to stop and check in all directions. She wasn't heading into the bush but had circled and was heading back to the house. Jerking his body to turn, he increased speed and tried to close the distance to the house.

When the fence at the back came into sight, his heart stuttered in his chest. In the small yard to the side, Daisie was sitting there playing and Minn was heading right for her. He called out a loud roar to warn the child and any adult that was in the area.

Jesse caught sight of a white tiger running through the trees to his left. It was Blair. Relaying to his animal that they *had* to reach the yard first, to protect their mate, his animal responded with more speed. There was no way a tiger could outrun his leopard body.

He leaped over the fence and then slid to a stop. In the middle of the yard, Daisie squatted down in front of Minn. He took cautious steps toward them.

"It's okay to be scared. My mom says everyone is sometimes." The child's soothing tone seemed to be working on Minn. Jesse prayed that Minn understood she was just a child. Whatever had happened to Leah had happened when she was little.

"See, just keep breathing." Daisie placed her hand on Minn's head, "that's what I heard Blair tell Nichelle when she shifted, so it must be good." Daisie nodded.

Thera was coming up behind Daisie, Jesse hissed for her to stop. She did, but her tail flicked a few times showing she wasn't happy with that command.

Jesse walked with slow careful footing toward Minn.

"See," Daisie said quietly, "everyone has come to help you." She nodded, "that's what we do. We help our kind." She stood up slowly and looked at Jesse. "She's calmer now." She stepped back, "I'll go get your clothes."

Jesse went over and placed himself between Minn and the retreating Daisie. He looked at the side of the house to see Blair in cat form waiting there. He called out in a tone that left no room for confusion, telling the other shifters nearby to back off.

Going closer, he held Minn's look and rubbed his face against her neck. Her breathing was erratic, half-human, half-cat. He nudged her again, purring softly, telling her it was okay, she could shift back. He knew Evanna was going to be in a world of hurt once she did.

He stepped back when he heard the first pop, out of the corner of his eye he spotted Cal's jag, standing far enough back to be unseen, but close enough to spring into action if needed.

"Jesse."

He turned to see Kobie standing there, his clothes in one hand and a blanket in the other. He titled his head to show his thanks. She came a bit closer and then set them on the ground. She backed up until she was far enough away to turn and leave the little yard. Blair in cat form was right there to insert his body between them.

Jesse, uncaring of who was watching, shifted and then picked up his jeans and pulled them on.

It was taking a lot longer than it should for Evanna to shift back. Going over, he knelt beside her, his face close to her cat's, "just breath, babe, let go and let it happen." He stroked his hand along her throat, "Minn, let Evanna out." He kept his tone soft, even though he was freaking out inside.

The fur under his hand receded, and he sat back to give her some space.

By the time he grabbed the blanket, Evanna lay on the ground shaking. Going over he covered her and scooped her up into his arms.

"I'm sorry." She said in a quiet voice. "I just—"

"Shh." Tucking her head against his shoulder, he began walking toward the trailer. Kobie and Noah were standing off to the side, he was glad Evanna had her eyes closed and couldn't see him. Something Noah knew had done this, but the expression on the man's face told him no one could berate him more than he was himself.

"Jesse," Evanna whispered.

"I'm here." He walked faster, wanting to get her inside.

"Find out," she licked her lips, "Ashtyn. Don't tell Leah."

"I will, you just close your eyes and rest."

"Minn caught me off guard."

"It's okay," he kissed her forehead, "it happens to all of us sometimes."

She opened her eyes a crack and looked at him, "not like that, but thanks for lying to make me feel better."

He grinned, "it wasn't a complete lie. Sometimes we lose the hold on our animals."

"Yeah?" She closed her eyes, "good, then someone can help me." She moaned when he shifted to open the door, "the pain sucks."

"We'll take care of that in a minute." Turning sideways, he went down the narrow hall and lowered her to one of the beds. He grabbed the cover off the other bed and put it over her. "I'll be right back with some painkillers and something to eat." He straightened and looked down at her, she looked so fragile like this. Evanna wasn't fragile. "Rest, I'll be right back."

"Thanks." She mumbled.

Going back out, he paused and exhaled to keep himself calm.

"What do you need?"

He looked to see Shaelan and Kobie standing at the end of the trailer. "Something for the mother of all headaches she's going to have, some soup or something easy to get down, she's going to be out of it for a bit."

"Does it happen like that every time she shifts?" Shaelan had a pained look on her face.

He shook his head, "no if Minn is under control, it's just like if one of us shifted," he glanced over to see Calum, Blair, and Noah standing across the yard looking this way. "Something set Minn off and Evanna was caught off guard."

Kobie looked back at them, "come in the house and get a coffee and something to eat."

"I'll get the things for Evanna." Shaelan turned and hurried toward the house.

"Blair is asking Noah now," Kobie told him softly and then turned and waited for him to come.

Jesse glanced at the trailer and then spotted Thera laying at the bottom of the step. She'd stop anyone from disturbing Evanna. Nodding, he rubbed the back of his neck and went with Kobie to the house.

He waited until long after dark for Evanna to come to again. After the painkillers and broth, she'd gone to sleep and barely moved for the last four hours. Getting up, he went over to the small fridge and opened it. Studying the few items in it, he closed it again. He needed something but didn't know what exactly that was. Glancing back at the small bedroom, he checked that she was still asleep and went outside to sit and wait.

He had just sat in the chair when Calum came around the corner of the trailer. "She still resting?"

Jesse nodded.

"If you need to go for a run, I'll sit here." Calum leaned against the trailer, crossing his arms over his chest.

Jesse debated on it for a second and then shook his head, "I'll wait until she's awake." She'd asked him to find out about Leah's sister for her and he didn't want anyone else to tell her. Noah said Ashtyn had been six months pregnant when she'd gotten out of there. He knew from the journals that neither of them knew. He felt guilt for reading the oldest one but needed to know.

"Are you okay?" Calum wasn't usually one for concerned questions.

Jesse hissed out a breath and sat back in the chair. "No."

Calum sat down. "Shae is on the phone right now with the doctor."

"I appreciate that." Jesse glanced at the door again wondering if he should go check and see if she was warm enough. He hadn't wanted to disturb her and dress her, so he piled the blankets on her instead.

"From my understanding, the path to controlling this is going to be a rough one." Calum's voice was low.

Jesse nodded, "I figured as much." He'd been reading on his phone every chance he had since they left the mountain and hadn't found anything that led to a quick fix in the whole process. Rubbing his hands over his face, he looked back at his friend. "Whatever she needs, whatever it takes."

Calum nodded slowly, "you know she'll get any help she needs."

Jesse nodded again. He knew that, whether it was the Alliance or friends, he would make sure that she got anything needed.

"The girls saved you some food." Calum glanced at the door, then back to him. "You can go grab it, I'm sure she'll be hungry when she wakes up."

Leaning forward in his chair, Jesse debated on it. He was hungry, had been for the last few hours, the jerky wasn't doing a good job of staving off the growling in his gut. "I don't, uh…"

"Jesse."

He didn't need to see her to know that Leah was standing looking out the door at him. He would know her voice anywhere now. He got up and opened the door. "Hey," he gave her a soft smile, "how are you feeling?" She was dressed in one of the skirts she'd purchased and had a warm sweater to go with it. She looked tired though, he didn't like that.

She blew out an exaggerated breath, "a little shaky," she touched her head, "the ache isn't too bad."

He held out his hand. "There's food in the house, eating will help. Shaelan probably has herbal tea," he glanced to Cal who nodded, "that might take care of the shakes."

Taking his hand lightly, she smiled. "Tea would be lovely." She came out and stood close to him when she saw Calum. "Hello." Her hold on his hand tightened, "I'm sorry for all the commotion we're causing."

Calum grinned, "A little commotion keeps things interesting." He stood up slowly and motioned to the house, "I'll go get Shae to the kitchen so she can rhyme off her very extensive herbal teas."

Leah nodded her head slightly. "Thank you." She watched him walk away. "Your friends are probably wishing we weren't here."

Jesse put his arm around her and held her against his side. "Not at all. They will help you with anything you need, just the same as we do for all our kind."

She tensed, "Minn, there was a little girl…"

"Daisie and she's fine. She talked Minn down."

A surprised look was on her face, "I don't think Minn would hurt a child."

"Neither do I." He nudged her to start toward the house, he didn't like how she was shaking.

"What set her off? It's rare that Minn breaks free when Evanna is out." She leaned into him when they walked.

Jesse didn't want to upset her he didn't know how she'd react. "She met Noah."

Leah stopped, "the man that helped us escape?"

Jesse nodded, "he mentioned your sister and it upset Minn, or that's my take on it."

"I wondered, normally it's not me that's out after that, Evanna usually comes back to keep an eye on Minn." She looked up at him, worry in her eyes, "do you think she's okay?"

"I think so, she was pretty beat though."

"Yes, sudden ones like that take their toll on her."

"On you too." He tightened his arm around her, "you're shaking pretty bad."

"Something to eat and some tea will fix that." She nodded her head slightly, "I'm sorry I was so scared and couldn't stay when I met your friends."

"It was fine, they understand that you do what you need to in order to be safe and survive." Jesse glanced at the door and hoped Cal had cleared out the traffic in the kitchen so it didn't happen again, he honestly wasn't sure if she could physically handle another shift right now and if Evanna was that bad off, he wanted her to recoup before she made another appearance.

They had done well to keep the flow of people out of the kitchen while they were there. At no time was there more than one person in the room with them. Jesse made a note to thank Blair, or it may have been Kobie's doing. Either way, it was easier to get Leah to eat and relax without a parade of others in the room.

She was finally sitting back in the chair; eating had helped her a lot. He needed to talk to Shaelan and ask if improper nutrition was a factor in the management of her condition.

"I really like that tea." She smiled at him, "I'll need to get some honey."

It floored him that simple things like honey she'd never had before.

"We'll work on a grocery trip once you're settled more." The idea of taking her into town bothered him. He wanted to shelter her, protect her, and prevent any moments of upset, no matter how small they were.

Jesse's phone buzzed in his pocket, he pulled it out and looked. It was Gage, wondering if it was too soon to come over.

"Is something wrong?"

He looked up at her.

She smirked, "you get this little crease," she touched her forehead, "right there when something is heavy on your mind."

That surprised him, he had no idea that he had tells. What surprised him further was that she picked up on it in the short time they'd been together. "It's just the clan across the road wondering if it's a good time to come over." He jerked his chin in the direction of the other room, "Blair's clan he grew up with."

With big eyes, she leaned on the table, "they live close? Other clans?"

"Many do." He regretted that none had lived near hers.

"That's nice, being close." She took a deep breath and blew it out slowly, "I can just go sit in the trailer, I want to write in the journal."

Jesse smirked, "pretty sure they were coming to meet you."

"Me?" the shock on her face was genuine. "Why?"

Jesse sat back, "it's just the way things are with our kind, we stick together, support each other."

Her eyes watered, "that's wonderful."

It hit him that she'd never had it. "I'm kind of beat, so I think I'll tell him tomorrow." He quickly typed a message telling him tomorrow might be better.

Leah nodded, "yes, perhaps tomorrow I'll feel brave enough to meet more people."

Daisie came skipping into the kitchen. She stopped, a guilty look on her face, "I forgot I wasn't supposed to come out here." She pointed to the fridge, "I wanted a drink."

"Go ahead and get a drink," Leah said with a friendly smile on her face.

Daisie stood there for a moment and looked at her. "Your Leah, Evanna's other part." She grinned. "I'm Daisie."

"Hello, Daisie. Yes, I'm Leah."

Jesse watched carefully, he didn't need her upset forcing another switch today.

"You were pretty brave today, helping Minn calm down."

"Minn is your cat?" Daisie looked excited, "I need to think of a name for my cat when she comes out."

Leah gave Jesse a quick look, "you have lots of time before that happens."

"Yeah, that's what Mom says, which is boring. I want to go on runs and have all the fun too." Daisie stood there fidgeting with the fridge door handle.

"You can't rush her to come out, she needs to come out when it's time for her to," Leah assured Daisie.

"Yeah. I guess I don't want to make her come out when she doesn't want to."

"Daisie."

Jesse turned to see Cortney standing in the doorway.

"Sorry, I forgot," Daisie said.

"It's fine. She just needed a drink." Leah said.

"Mom, this is Leah, the other part of Evanna," Daisie said excitedly.

"Nice to meet you." Cortney said quietly then turned to her daughter, "get your juice, then upstairs."

"Okay." Daisie opened the fridge and grabbed a juice box.

Closing it she spun back around. "You're very pretty." She smiled. "Evanna is too." She left the room in a rush.

"I'm sorry if she interrupted you."

Jesse hadn't noticed any increase in Leah's breathing, so he shrugged, "she was fine." He grinned, "energetic, but well behaved."

Cortney laughed, "the only time she isn't *energetic* is when she's sleeping."

"She's lovely." Leah nodded, "and very happy."

"Thank you." Cortney inclined her head, "I better go chase her down before she's in someone else's face."

Leah stood up and picked up her cup. She went over to the sink and turned the water on, glancing over her shoulder, she grinned, "I love running water."

Jesse got up and took his cup over. "The smallest things are the best." He reached around her and took her cup. "I've got these," he motioned to the pantry, "Kobie said it was okay if you took some teas or snacks to the trailer."

"Oh." She looked at it, "that's very nice of her."

On the way back to the trailer, Leah was quiet. "Everything, okay?" He watched one of the guards and Cale come back from checking the perimeter. Cale gave him a nod telling him everything was good.

"Yes, just a lot to take in."

"If it gets to you, let me know, we can go somewhere else."

She paused and looked up at him, "what about this training and the team?"

He shrugged, "what you need comes first, they'll understand that."

"I'm fine, really," she started walking, "I have moments, but it's all so new." She glanced at him again, "where would we go?"

Jesse shrugged, "We could go to my property. The house isn't built, but I have a trailer there."

"You have your own property? You don't live with your clan?"

"They're fifteen minutes away, so close enough." He smirked, "I have a big clan, and I like my space."

"I didn't think you were home much."

He chuckled, "I'm not, that's why the house isn't finished."

"Do you have a garden?" She hugged the few items she'd selected from the pantry to her chest.

"I could have if I knew anything about it."

"I could show you."

They reached the trailer. "You might change your mind when you see the land."

"A little work and any ground can grow things."

He grinned, "my sisters are going to love you. They have flower gardens planted all over the clan territory."

"We didn't have many flowers. I'd love to see them." She gave him an excited look, "I've always wanted to plant sunflowers."

Jesse turned to watch Kobie and Blair coming from the back, judging by their bare feet they'd just gone for a run. "You can plant sunflowers, as many as you like." He answered, distracted by the idea of a run.

Leah touched his chest, he looked down at her "if you want to go for a run, I'll be fine, Jesse. I'm going to write in our journal."

Jesse put his hand over hers and held it there. "Are you sure?"

She nodded, "I'm too tired to shift and run, but you look like you need one, you're a bit edgier than I've seen you before."

He wanted to say with good reason, he didn't know how to help his own mate. "Okay, I won't be long." Leaning down, he kissed her mouth softly, lingering for a second, and then stepped back. "Lock the door if you don't feel safe."

She smiled at him, a warm expression on her face. "Thank you, for understanding."

Jesse lifted his hands out from his body, "I don't but I am trying." He backed a few feet before he changed his mind and then turned and jogged toward the back of the treeline.

Calum was leaning against the fence. "No one runs alone."

Jesse stopped, "even you?"

"Even me. Not after they tried to poison Jake."

Jesse raised his eyebrows, "how the..." he shook his head, "I don't want to know," he motioned to the trees, "try to keep up."

Calum grinned, "whatever you say *spot.*"

Chapter Thirty

Jesse checked the house and then went back to the trailer. He was almost to it when Blair came across the yard.

"Other side of the house." He smirked at him.

Jesse gave him a blank look and then changed directions to walk beside him.

"She's with Nichelle and Kobie, they're working with her to communicate and control her cat."

Heaving a sigh, Jesse shook his head, "I'm not normally so distracted." He waved the papers he had in his hand, "I'm supposed to be calling Devin, with this info, but…"

"Your cat is telling you to find her, check on her and see her?"

He glanced at the man beside him. "Yeah."

Blair nodded, "I know all about it. Almost lost my mind doing that."

"Great, something to look forward to."

"Kobie is pretty impressed with your mate," he shrugged "Calum shared that tidbit, so we were all aware."

Jesse nodded. It was a good idea, one less thing to worry about.

"Anyway, Kobie thinks she's pretty amazing for keeping it

together the way she does with everything going on."

"I don't know how she does it."

"I don't know how you're doing it." Blair rubbed his hand over his hair, "it was bad enough with Kobie, you have a hell of a lot more to deal with."

Jesse stopped and watched the three women; he didn't want to interrupt if they were helping her. "I just don't know what to do half the time."

Blair chuckled, "I think that's normal with mates, regardless of the situation."

"You think so?" Leah was smiling and he felt his mouth move to form a grin just seeing her like that.

"Pretty sure." Blair clapped him on the back, "I'm going to kiss my mate, then get over to work. Ask Devin when that weapons guy is coming."

Jesse nodded, but didn't say anything, he had to find out when the doctor was going to be here too. Thera got up and came over to him. She nudged his hand. He rubbed his hand down over her head. "You're adjusting well to everyone." He continued to move his hand, but his mind was on Leah. The sun was shining this morning and her hair looked like it was glowing in the light. He frowned, could dark hair even do that? Shaking his head, he decided he was interrupting, after all, anything was better than standing here thinking weird shit.

Leah turned when he was almost to them. Her face lit up with a big smile, her cheeks flushed, and then she hurried to him. "Nichelle has only been shifting for a few weeks now, so she's in the same position I am." She sounded excited and relieved at the same time.

Jesse couldn't think for a second, the look of delight in her eyes had him momentarily stunned. She was so beautiful. Reaching, he brushed the hair back from her cheek and then cupped the back of her neck, his palm resting against her face. "That's great news." He feigned a frown, "I've been wracking my brain, trying to think back to my first few so I could help you."

"Kobie has told me so many stories about others having

problems with their animals." She smiled again, "it makes me feel so much better, knowing it's not just me." She rested her palms against his chest and looked up at him, "I communicated with Minn, and felt her respond." She bit her lip for a second, "I usually only feel when she's about to come out."

He could have stood here all day and listened to her, no matter what she said, just hearing her talk without hesitation and doubt. "That's great, babe." He leaned forward and kissed her mouth gently, because he just had to, felt like he was going to suffocate if he didn't. Each time he did kiss her, she would touch her lips, making him want to do it again and again.

"Did you need me? I wanted to stay and practice some more with Nichelle."

Did he need her? That was a question he didn't dare answer. "I just wanted to see how you were doing." He lifted the hand full of pages, "I have some calls to make and later there will be a conference call with the king and a few others."

"About rescuing others?" A line appeared between her brows.

He fought the urge to rub that crease away. "Mostly updates, we're still waiting on reports from the teams watching the locations."

She nodded, a serious expression, "do you think we'll be able to go?" Her jaw clenched for a second, "I want to be there, in case my mother or sister," she shrugged one shoulder, "any of my clan are still there." A look of resolve filled her eyes, "I owe it to my clan to help. I left them all there."

Jesse's heart pained, "you were sixteen, Leah, and you couldn't have done anything to help them at that point."

"I know that, mostly, but I just feel like I failed them."

Tightening his hold on the back of her neck, he leaned down so their foreheads touched, "you failed no one." He held her dark eyes with his own, "you had to get out of there to survive. Sometimes you have to put your own survival above others."

Her gaze locked on his, "yeah." She nodded, "Minn will

attack if she thinks I'm threatened. I sense that now." Her smile was gone.

He felt like a heel, for crushing her good mood like that, but he couldn't accept her blaming herself for shit that Tomas and his goons were and had done. "Now," he smiled, "I'm going to take another taste of you with me so I can get through these calls." He kissed her mouth, then kissed it lightly again. "Go make peace with Minn so we're not chasing her all over the country." He straightened up and stepped back.

With her hand over her mouth, she nodded, the expression in her eyes made his heart lighter again. Smiling, she turned back and went over to Kobie and Nichelle.

Blowing out a breath, Jesse spun on his heel and went toward the trailer. Might as well sit and be comfortable while he made these calls. He was almost there when Shaelan came out of the house.

"Jesse."

He stopped.

"The doctor had an emergency at the campground, so she wants to set up a video call with Leah later today."

Jesse nodded, almost relieved that it wouldn't be in person. "Let me know when."

She went back in the door.

Changing directions, he went in the direction of the van. He needed to make sure the batteries were charged so he could set her up with this call. Emergency at the campground? The only one he knew of was Devin's and if it was there, then it was related to one of those rescued. Hopefully, it wasn't too serious.

Jesse heard doors close and footsteps.

"Jesse." Devin sounded winded.

"Did I call at a bad time?"

"No. I just left my phone in the house. Rayne had to track me down."

"Is everything good there? I heard the doctor was called there." He leaned back in the chair and looked around the yard.

"Yeah, we think so." It sounded like he was walking. "Rayne was concerned about some of the children here, so the doctor is coming to check them out."

He leaned forward again, "concerned how?"

"After she learned more about Leah, the doctor told her it happened in cases of repeated trauma when the child was," he paused, "four to seven I think she said."

Jesse nodded, "is that something they can look for early?"

"I have no idea, I just had a mate pacing and worrying, so…"

"Ah, okay." He completely understood that. Frowning he realized a few weeks ago he wouldn't have quite got it, but now he did. "The doctor is going to be doing a video call with Leah later today."

"I'll make sure there's somewhere quiet for her," the call paused, "to do that." He sighed into the phone. "Sorry, let me take this call for a sec or she'll just keep calling."

Jesse didn't get a chance to ask who before the line went silent. He picked up the papers in his lap and looked at the top one, still not sure why Blair had handed them off to him. A month ago he would have taken them and just gone through it, but he had a little more on his mind right now than square footage of as yet unbuilt structures. The Alliance was paying for some of the new buildings Blair wanted for his clan.

"Sorry about that, it was my agent."

"Do you have an exhibit coming up?"

Devin snorted, "when have I had time to paint lately?"

Jesse grinned, "during the lull moments."

Devin laughed, "lull. The only time there's a lull and silence is when Rayne and I are asleep, and even then it's rare."

The sound of two of the girls arguing hit him, he turned to see them on the other side of the yard in each other faces. He had sisters, so he knew to just stay out of it. "I understand that."

"How is Leah doing?"

Jesse couldn't see her from here, and now wished he'd sat where he could. "Managing despite everything."

"If you need to tap out of the retrieval team, I get it."

Jesse shook his head, "it's too soon to say." He looked down at the paper but didn't see it. "Leah and Evanna have both said they want to go with us when we go where she was."

"Is that a good idea?"

"Probably not. I want to talk to the doctor about it and a few things once she has some time." He shrugged, "she wants in on the weapons training."

"That couldn't hurt, even if she never has to use it. They'll be there tomorrow, wait, no day after," Devin sighed, "I'm losing track of days."

Jesse grinned, "I get that." He lifted the papers, "Blair gave me these damn calculations and outlines for the buildings they're going to be putting up..."

"Why do you have them?"

"Damned if I know." He watched the man they were talking about drive in. "Maybe to keep me busy."

"You keeping busy isn't usually an issue."

"Not normally."

"Just send me pictures of them and I'll forward them." He sounded annoyed, "I'm not cut out for this office work."

"Well, once you're king, you have teams that do all that work for you." Jesse knew this because he was one of the teams for the current King.

"That's not a great selling point."

"When is your dad planning to step aside?"

"Don't even think things like that, better not be for another twenty fucking years or more." Devin's tone was rough, "I am not ready for all that, fuck, I don't even know if I will ever be ready."

Jesse chuckled, "I'm pretty sure Rayne will help."

"I'd be lost now without her." He cleared his throat, "I have to run, get in touch with Dad when you get a few minutes, he's been asking about you and Leah."

Jesse nodded, "I will later."

"Take care, Jesse, call if you need anything."

The line went quiet. He did not envy the weight on Devin's shoulders. Setting the pages on his lap, he snapped a picture of them one after the other and then opened his email and sent them to Devin. Getting up, he tucked his phone back into his pocket, only to take it back out again. Going to the end of the trailer, he spotted Leah still with Kobie and one of the other women, Franki he thought her name was. Leah seemed to be quite involved in the talk. Now that he was assured, *again*, she was well, he brought up his call list and tapped his dad's name.

"Hey, son."

What was it about a parent's voice that could either calm you inside or piss you right off, depending on the life situation? "Hi." Although comforting, he doubted anything was going to calm Jesse for a while to come. There was too much unknown.

"How are things?"

That was his father's opening line all the time. "I'm back at Blair's," he couldn't remember if he'd told him where that was, "by Ed's."

"Done on the road for now?"

"Yeah, for at least a few weeks I'm told."

"You should try to carve some time out and come home for a day or so. It's been a while since you were."

Jesse couldn't even remember when the last time was he had been home for more than a day. "That's part of why I was calling."

"Oh?"

"I was wondering if you and the girls could pop over to my place and do a few things for me."

"Like water your plants?" His father chuckled.

"Someday I might have those, once there's a house to put them in." Jesse crossed his arm over his chest and rested his other elbow on top of it, "no I need to get some estimates done and," he wished he could see his father's face for this next part, "some spots marked out for gardens."

"Gardens? Son, you know winter is almost here."

"I didn't say I was planting them, but the girls are great with that and will know the best locations to mark out for light and drainage and all that other stuff they go on about."

There was a long silence and then he heard his mother's voice.

"It's Jesse, he wants gardens marked out at his place. What estimates are you getting done?"

"I need to fence the whole lot in." Jesse waited for the questions he knew were coming.

"Is this about that girl that was with you, Jesse?" It was his mother; he was on speaker now.

"Yeah, it is. I need the fence for Thera, her leopard." He smirked.

"The girl, I'm sorry I forget her name, is she coming with her leopard?" His mother was fishing now.

"Yes, she will be." He cleared his throat, "she's my mate, but there are a few complications before you start planning any celebrations."

"What sort of complications?" His father's humorous tone was gone.

"She was taken by Tomas when she was four," he blew out a breath, "she got away when she was sixteen, but what she went through caused a mental disorder. Dissociated Identity disorder—it hasn't been diagnosed, as yet, but even the doctor is saying that's what it is…"

"Is that where they have more than one personality, honey?" His mother's tone was soft and understanding.

"Yes."

"I'm sure you will be able to help her with this, son."

His father's confidence in him made him feel a little more at ease. "She was the last of her clan, living on top of a mountain alone…"

"She sounds incredibly strong."

He nodded to his mother's comment. "She is. She doesn't think so, but she is." He cleared his throat, "her cat came out when she got away and they ran for a month to find home— she has trouble controlling her cat—" his cat stirred inside him, feeling the emotions Jesse was having.

"We'll get that done for you out at your place." His father said, "do you want the fence started? Are you thinking chain link or something solid?"

"Chain-link."

"Okay, I'll get on that and message you the details, Jesse." His father's take-charge tone had kicked in.

"You call us if you need anything." His mother commanded.

"I will. I really want you to meet her when she's able to, she has trouble meeting people." He watched her with Franki as he spoke. One or two seemed to be her limit, which he thought was better than when he met her.

"You take care, honey, we'll go over to your place tomorrow and do that for you."

"Thanks. I just don't want to drag her around too much. She's meeting with the doctor today and we'll have to follow her suggestions…"

"It's fine. You just take care of her, and you know we'll be here when you get home."

Leah looked around and then nodded to Franki and started walking in his direction. "Okay, I'll let you go."

"Bye." His parents echoed, then the line was quiet.

He looked at his phone and then tucked it in his pocket, that went better than he'd hoped.

It was still nagging at him, them wanting to go when they went in to get others out. How would that even work? Is Evanna fronting with Minn right there watching? Then there was Leah, where was she while this went on?

Rubbing his hands over his face, he dropped them and exhaled a loud breath. He needed to talk to someone about this. Turning, he decided the four standing in the drive were the ones that he needed to speak to right this second.

When he reached Blair and Calum and their mates, he lifted his hands in the air and then just let them drop. "I need to run something past you guys." He scowled, "then I have to run it past the doctor too."

Blair and Calum looked amused. Bastards. The women looked concerned. Concerned he could work with.

"What's happened?" Shaelan asked, her focus solely on him.

"During various conversations, both Evanna and Leah have expressed their desire to go with us on the ops when we go to those addresses." He stopped and gauged the different reactions. Calum, he couldn't read—no surprise there. Blair was looking to Kobie, he had no idea why that was.

"I think in some way it's a good idea," Shaelan said slowly as if she was still processing it in her head.

"How do you figure that?" Calum studied his mate, "I sensed the vibes coming off her cat when she lost control…"

Shaelan held up her hand, silencing her large mate. Jesse made a note to ask about that later. "That's just it, Cal, for most of her life, she hasn't been in control of much of anything." She glanced to Kobie who was nodding right along with her, "I think this will be a huge step in helping her feel like she has control over a situation."

"So you think this would be something that will *help* her?" Jesse didn't see how.

Shaelan nodded, "yes." She made a face, "I don't mean send her in or anything, but her being present and feeling like she has an important role in what's happening." She shrugged, "she can stay back with me."

Calum raised an eyebrow, "we hadn't finished that discussion."

Shaelan smirked, "I am the only trained healer among the collective group, so I decided I'm going." She gave him an even look.

"I won't be on the breach team," Kobie made quote marks in the air, "so I'll be there with her too."

Calum and Blair exchanged a quick look. Neither mate was happy with them going.

Jesse took a deep breath; he didn't have time to help other couples sort *their* couple stuff. He had enough of his own sorting to do. "I'll talk to them about it some more and see." He looked at Shaelan, "I want to ask the doctor about it too." He rubbed his hand across his forehead, "if she thinks it will cause more harm than anything, she can't go."

"That's still her call, Jesse," Shaelan said in a soft tone. "She's been on her own for a long time, you can't expect to issue orders and have pleasant results."

He looked from her to Kobie, who was also nodding. Calum just crossed his arms over his chest and looked at the ground to remove him from any possible comment or suggestion.

"Talk to her—them," Blair shrugged, "and see where it goes."

He noted the pleased look on Kobie's face with that comment. "Yeah," Jesse smirked, "after the gun incident on our trip, she may change her mind completely." He glanced to the end of the house and wondered if she was still there.

"Or she'll embrace it," Kobie said.

Looking back at her, he frowned. "I suppose."

Calum pulled out his phone and looked at it. "Shep will be ready for the call in half an hour."

Jesse nodded, "Are we doing that in the house?"

Blair shook his head, "no we'll use the bunkhouse that was mine." He exchanged another look with Calum.

Jesse didn't know what was going on that he wasn't in the loop with but shrugged. "Okay, I'll be there. I'm just going to check on Leah. She was pretty excited that she's been able to communicate with Minn."

Kobie smiled. "Maybe someday her cat will be a complete part of her."

He nodded, even though he was frowning. He wasn't sure what that meant.

Chapter Thirty-One

Jesse looked at the solemn faces in the small room. He'd thought this call was about the team, but from the hard looks on Blair and Calum's faces and the anxious look on Kobie and Shaelan's faces, he wasn't so sure now.

"He'll be on the line in a second." Zain's voice came over the speaker.

"Thanks, Zain," Jesse answered when no one else looked like they were going to. "What am I missing?" He looked from Blair to Calum.

Calum put his finger over his mouth and shook his head.

Frowning, Jesse didn't say anything, but he knew he wasn't in the loop with something.

"Thank you, Zain. New supplies have just arrived to distribute to your team, can you oversee they're sorted accordingly?"

Jesse could hear Zain respond in the background and then there was silence for a few seconds.

"Devin are you on?"

"I'm here," Devin answered in a quiet tone.

Jesse knew he should wait, let the King explain, but his gut was having none of that. "What have I missed?"

"Sorry about the secrecy, Jesse," the King said in a serious voice, "we've had a few realizations while you were off the grid and there was no way to bring you in until we knew more."

"I understand." He didn't really. "What *realizations*?"

Calum made a low sound of annoyance, "Tomas knows too much. He was here before we were back, he's been to other safe locations that few know about..."

Jesse's mouth dropped open, "you're saying someone is feeding him information?"

Blair nodded.

"That's what it looks like," Devin answered.

"Do we know who?" Jesse wanted to swear and kick something but managed to hold it together.

"No. We don't." Calum crossed his arms over his chest and stared at the phone sitting on the chair.

"How do we find out?"

"I wanted you on this call to discuss your team, Jesse."

"The clan coordinators?" Jesse gave the phone a wide-eyed look.

"Yes." The king answered and then paused. "You know them better than anyone, you have been working with them for five years now."

"I," he threw his hands up and looked around at the others, "there's no way it's one of them. None at all. We've gone into some pretty serious situations putting ourselves at risk..." he trailed off not even knowing how to explain it.

"I understand that. Which is why we're talking to you about it now. If you can verify that it's none of them, I will look in other directions."

Jesse opened his mouth, then snapped it shut. "Just," he held up and hand, "give me a second to catch up and compose my thoughts."

"Of course."

He turned around and looked out the small window, unable to bear the looks of the others, shaking his head, he spun back. "No. No. There's no way it's one of them. Zain is committed for life. Tomas took his mother and sister before he could even shift—this has been his sole purpose in his adult life to do anything to bring Tomas down." He closed his eyes for a second, trying to process his chaotic thoughts into words, "Amari," he huffed out a breath, "she's freaking lethal. I've seen her cut down Tomas' people without a second of hesitation. She's from an Alpha family, she knows the lives that have been lost in this fight." Calum nodded; he'd worked with her. "And Foster," Jesse shook his head, "has lost so many in his life because of Aiden Tomas' father," he glared at the phone, "he's running himself into an early grave to help any affected."

"I don't know much about Deva, she's the newest on your team."

Jesse rubbed his hand across his forehead. "It's not Deva," Jesse smirked, "in fact if I were part of Tomas' crew, I'd be terrified of her ever crossing my path."

Calum grinned. "I can vouch for Miss Weller, Shep, she is solid."

"All right, what about the other two, Jesse?"

Jesse opened his mouth and then blew out a breath. "Webb is the biggest advocate of our kind for co-existing with the one-forms, sir, he'd cut off his left paw before he'd ever consider helping the vile acts Tomas has committed—and Asher, he's solid. I know he's a bit standoffish on the outside, but he has good reason, he's the last in his family. The rest of his family were slaughtered by Tomas' people, sir, he'd never help them."

"All right then. I will look at your team no further." Shep cleared his throat. "Devin and I are compiling a list of any that have access to information."

Jesse cut him off, regardless of his standing, "that's a huge list, sir. Every Alpha and second family in every clan can access information through contacts at the Alliance offices."

"Yes, it's not going to be an easy task."

"Do we bring Jesse's team in on this, Dad? They see a lot, communicate with all the clans face to face that we don't see."

"That's a good idea." His father answered. "Jesse, can I task you with that?"

Jesse shrugged, still shocked and annoyed he'd had to vouch for his team. "Yeah." He had no idea how he was going to even begin to explain it to them, did he tell them they'd been suspect?

"Good. Okay, I have a meeting to get to, so we'll leave off here." There was a pause. "Blair, I know you have a lot going on right now but keep an eye on the guards there."

Blair nodded, the look on his face was harder than Jesse had ever seen. "I trust Cale, I don't know the others well enough yet."

"Let me know if you have any doubts. Any suspected will be removed and placed in a menial position somewhere."

Jesse's head was spinning with the information. All their work, the hours of driving, and the months he'd spent on the road were being completely undermined by a traitor. What kind of shifter would do that to their own? Did they have any idea what their kind went through in Tomas' possession? He'd seen the victims with his own eyes, he knew how much they suffered. "Sir," he held his hand out toward the phone, "are there any we've recovered working in the Alliance offices?"

"There's a select number that has access, we're working out a plan to eliminate them from being suspected."

Jesse nodded, "of course, sorry, I'm still catching up here."

"It's understandable. I'm sorry we couldn't give you any warning, this was the only way."

Jess nodded. "I understand." He didn't completely though.

"We'll discuss the retrieval team in a few days. I've contacted the other two I'm adding, so we'll arrange a video call to introduce everyone."

Calum and Jesse looked at each other for a second. There were going to be more on the team they didn't know.

"I will talk to you all later," Shepard said and then the background went quiet.

"I'm going to go as well. Rayne needs me to go over some plans with her."

"Plans?"

"Yeah, she's working out some ideas for different safe houses."

"Keep us in the loop," Calum said quietly. "And send me the info on these others being added to the team."

"Will do. Stay safe people." The line clicked silent.

"Sorry." Calum looked at him. "We were told not to warn you."

"Fuck." Jesse put his hands on his hips and glared at him. "This is fucking insane. Not only do I have to watch over my shoulder now, but I have to watch the people around me too?"

"It's bullshit," Blair said in agreement. "I trust Cale though."

Jesse snorted, "yeah, that crazy son of a bitch would kill all of Tomas' people if given the opportunity." He looked at Shaelan to see her look shocked. "Sorry," He waved his hand around, "I'm still a little taken back by all this."

"It's fine." She gave him an understanding look, "I was, ah, quite upset when I found out too."

Kobie glanced at her and nodded her head quickly, "how do we know going to those addresses now will be a surprise."

Blair snarled, "we don't."

Calum took a deep breath and then exhaled, "Devin and I are working on that. Once numbers have been confirmed the observation teams will be replaced with one of ours we trust."

Jesse nodded. "Yeah. The fewer involved the better."

"Doesn't that make it more dangerous?" Shaelan asked.

Jesse shrugged one shoulder, then looked at her mate, "sometimes one or a few can get more done under the radar than a whole force."

Calum's mouth twitched like he wanted to smirk but didn't. Jesse knew the instances running through his mind were probably the same ones in his. Those times when it was just the two of them and a very few others rushing in with no plan to get their kind out.

Blowing out a breath, Jesse motioned to the phone, "well, this was fun." He turned to the door. "I need some air."

He got to the middle of the yard and then stopped and stood there looking at the earth in front of him. How the hell was he explaining all of this to the team? They were close— shared the mutual endless hours driving from one end of the continent to the other. He shook his head and pulled his phone out, there was no way he was telling them that they'd been suspected. None. He frowned for a second, wondering if at any point he'd been on that suspect list. Shaking his head, he brought up the group they had on an app. Calum would have shut that shit down fast if anyone had questioned Jesse's loyalty. They'd worked together too much for him to have doubts. Hell, he'd trekked up into that nightmare where Shaelan's clan was only because it was Calum needing assistance.

Typing with jerky movements, he tried to word it so they'd respond as soon as they could. *Need to have a quick informative group call. Soon. Let me know when is good for everyone.*

He didn't even exit the app before the first response appeared.

Anytime works for me. I'm on-site organizing a move. Webb had written.

Organizing a move meant he'd found some of a clan. *How many?*

20! Able bodied and all. Makes up for the ones that were gone. Jesse nodded as he answered. *I get that.*

The dots telling him someone else was typing appeared.

Give me a couple of hours and I'll be stopped for the night. I need downtime BAD I'm seeing things on the road that aren't there. Asher added to the chat.

Stop sooner if you need to Ash, we don't need a splattered kitty on the road. Foster of course would say something like that. Jesse smirked. *I'm stopping for some eats in about an hour, so I can talk then unless you all want to call and keep me company.*

Pass. Anytime is good for me, I'm meeting up with someone from one of the BC clans so they can help me check locations. Deva added a yawning emoji to that.

What is this informative group call about?? Zain typed. *BTW I'm unpacking new goodies for all of you poor saps on the road. Some interesting things in this one boys and girls. What have you all been up to that we need some of this? Aside from Jesse getting shot, I wasn't aware of anything serious happening.*

Jesse cringed, of course, Zain knew. Calum probably told Devin, who told his father…

You got shot, Jesse? Amari put in the group.

I'm fine. Wasn't serious. Some damn hunters I didn't pick up on until they were shooting.

Did you go back and eat them? Foster asked.

No. I had a, he paused for a second, not knowing what to say to describe Leah. He shrugged and kept typing, *real leopard with me and her owner to transport.*

What, a real real leopard?

No, a fake real one, Webb, that's why he wrote 'real'. Jesse cringed at the comment from Deva.

So two hours from now work for everyone? He typed quickly before those two started tearing each other apart in the chat—again. He watched as six thumbs up appeared beside his text. *I'll talk to you all then, and Ash, stop now before you wreck the van.*

Yes mother lol Asher responded.

Blowing out a breath, Jesse exited the app and put his phone in his pocket. Two hours. He had time to figure out how to explain to them that someone out there was undermining all the hours and sacrifices they'd made. Looking around, he wondered if Leah was still in the trailer writing in the journal. Starting that way, he decided they should both go for a run. He really needed more time with Minn, so he could pick up on her moods more easily. Then again, he still hadn't figured out half of Leah and Evanna's cues either, or triggers.

Rolling his shoulders, he tried to drop some of the tension from them. Complicated mating didn't even cover what was happening. And now a traitor. "Another fun-filled day in the life of me." He mumbled as he went to look for his mate.

Chapter Thirty-Two

"Are you serious?" Deva hissed out a long breath. "I heard about a breach at one of the safe houses I'd dropped some at, but had no idea it was because someone told that Tomas jerk."

Jesse glanced over to see Leah sitting with Daisie and looking at a book together. "I know. I just stood there with my mouth hanging open when I was told." Not a complete lie.

"So, are we out here chasing our tails or what?" Asher sounded groggy.

"I'm so mad," Amari growled in a low voice.

"Do they have any idea who?" Foster's usual jovial tone was gone.

"They don't." Jesse wanted to keep this as brief as possible. He still hadn't gotten to talk to Leah about her call with the doctor.

"What do we do now? Who do we report to?" Webb demanded.

"I guess me?" Zain offered. "I know before we brought in Alpha's and others, but maybe just me for now and I'll run things by the boss from now on."

Jesse nodded, "yeah find out what protocol we're to use and let us know."

"What about the teams we work with transporting and setting them up at new sites? Are they okay to call us in still?" Amari sounded calmer.

"Again, Zain will have to sus out the new protocols and send it to all of us." Jesse watched Leah laugh and wondered what had been so amusing.

"This sucks so bad," Asher mumbled.

"Yeah, it does." Jesse agreed quickly before anyone else could interrupt. "Devin and his dad want us to keep our eyes open and if we sense anyone that doesn't seem straight up to let them know."

"They want us to find the traitor?" Foster sounded annoyed.

"Not necessarily, just—because we're out there and see a lot of clans, they want us to keep our eyes open for anything odd."

"What would be considered odd?" Webb asked.

Jesse blew out a breath, "I don't know. Someone asking far too many questions? Or if someone that doesn't need to be in the know is too curious, I can't really say right now."

"This is crazy," Amari mumbled. "Because we don't have enough to do now."

Jesse shrugged, he agreed there. "I'm going to talk to Devin about adding more to our team. I think it's needed."

"Tell me about it. I don't even know where I am most of the day lately." Deva sounded tired.

"Where are you now, Jesse?" Webb wondered.

"I'm back at Blair's they have weapons training set up here." Jesse should have known this call wouldn't be short. They never were when all of them were on it.

"Who's training and for what? More guards?" Asher was sounding more awake now.

"No. A new retrieval team."

"Oh, that sounds promising and hopefully means they're going into more locations soon."

"Yeah, Ash, there's quite a few." He didn't want to go into too much detail, not because he didn't trust them, but because he didn't know how to explain his current situation.

"Anyone we know on it? Aside from you, I presume." Foster asked.

"Yeah, I'm part of it, ah, Calum—"

"Ha, they're toast." Foster laughed.

Jesse grinned, "Blair from Ed's clan…"

"Oh, damn this is a serious team. I ran against him a few years back." Foster made a gasping sound, "hardest run of my *life*."

"Are there any women on this team?" Amari of course would ask that.

Jesse smirked, "actually yes. Calum's mate is, she's a trained healer…"

"That's handy and much needed." Webb interrupted.

"Yeah. Also, Blair's mate is on it, and I'm a bit intimidated by her tracking skills. She's the one that figured out that tidbit I shared with the use of rubbing alcohol." He still couldn't believe something that simple erased any scent.

"That was brilliant." Foster said, "I tried it, and damn it does work."

"I'm impressed." Deva stated, "they're adding women to a team like that."

He glanced back over at Leah. "There may be more, I'm not sure just yet, there's a few more that have been added." He didn't want her to go, but if it was something she needed to do to heal, then he had no choice.

"Let us know if you need backup or pickup." Foster offered.

Jesse blew out a breath, "I came across a few addresses that have checked out, so I may need to call in some of you." He leaned against the side of the trailer and watched Leah. "I know you guys know how to get people out fast, without issue."

"You know you can always count on us, Jesse, especially if it's getting our kind away from that lunatic," Asher said in a cold tone.

"I know and thanks. I'll get in touch when I know more and

see who is where at that point."

"I will probably still be in the middle of nowhere," Deva said sounded bored, "I still have many to check at the top of the map."

Jesse smirked, she always said on the right of the map or lower left, or something like that. "Who are you meeting up with?" He felt so out of the loop, normally he knew where the rest of the team were and what they were doing.

"A few from Liz's clan to help scout the area."

"Oh, you get overwatch, excellent. I love when I have eyes in the sky." Foster chuckled.

Jesse ran through the clans in his head. Liz, if he wasn't mistaken was Alpha of the crowned eagle clan. "Watch your back up there." He cautioned, "it's a lot of open space."

"I will, Jesse."

"Set up check-in times with Zain before you set out." He made it sound like a suggestion, but he was technically in charge of this team.

"I'll send you call-in codes," Zain said quickly. "It's a new thing, so you automatically get patched through to me."

"Is this part of the containing information getting to the wrong people?" Asher asked.

"I had no idea, but now that I know what's going on, that would explain it."

"So, Jesse, where did you find a real leopard?" Webb asked with a quiet chuckle.

"Michigan." Jesse shrugged, "the woman, the last of her clan had rescued her from some zoo or animal park." He realized he'd never asked more about that. Deciding almost immediately that it might bring up the wrong memories and he'd better not.

"Kudos to her. I want to set them all free anytime I'm near one." Amari huffed out a breath.

"What's she like? The leopard." Webb asked.

Jesse looked to his left to where Thera was laying. "She's pretty cool, calm for the most part, I swear she understands every word I say."

"Leave it up to you to come across a real leopard."
Jesse grinned.
"You came across those minxes that time." Asher reminded him.
"Ugh, don't even go there. Those things were rabid and crazy."
Jesse laughed at Foster's tone. "Could have been worse. They could have followed you home."
"Shush." Foster hissed out an annoyed breath, "I have to get moving. I want to get a few more hours in before I crash for the night."
"Where are you headed?"
"Let's put it this way, if Deva runs into trouble at the *top* of the map, I'll be nearby." He didn't sound impressed.
"Sorry about that, Foster, I have to go with the transport of this group," Webb said.
"It's fine. It will be totally worth it if I find some clans along the way."
"Maybe a few more members in our little group would be good," Zain said. "Since I've been stuck here on office detail, you guys could need a few more out there."
"You were handpicked by the king to work at the Alliance headquarters with him." Asher said, "I don't see that as a hardship."
"Yeah. Still a few more out there helping would save you guys the crazy long drives."
Jesse nodded to Zain's words, "I'll talk to Devin, he'll probably have a few in mind."
"They just need to like being alone, but sociable and lethal," Deva said in a serious tone.
"You make us sound terrible," Asher complained.
"None of it is wrong though," Amari added.
"I need to drive, people, we can have one of our three-hour talks later." Foster sounded like he'd just yawned.
"Eyes open, Wile E," Amari said.
Jesse grinned at her nickname for him, "Be careful. All of

you." He looked toward the trailer. "I need to go now anyway." He literally couldn't stand being this far away from Leah any longer. He started walking in that direction.

"I'll be sending out emails with the list of new supplies. Let me know which drop site you want yours sent to." Zain said hurriedly.

"Yup," Webb said.

"Will do."

"Talk soon."

"Send me details of those rescue ops, Jesse."

He just kept nodding; it wasn't even registering who was speaking. Leah was watching him walk toward her and, at this moment, that smile on her face was all that mattered to him. The line went quiet and he realized everyone was gone. Hanging up, he stuffed the phone in his back pocket and headed toward his mate with longer strides.

Chapter Thirty-Three

Evanna looked to see the other bed empty. She sat up. How long had she been asleep? Leaning over, she moved the curtain and looked outside, it looked like early morning. That shift had been hard. Frowning, she looked around for the journal, she was sure it had been on the table between the beds.

Getting up, she stood there for a moment trying to assess how she felt. There were no sharp pains in her head. Those painkillers were something else. She started for the door and then glanced down to see she was wearing a pink shirt that went to her knees. Leah had been out. Deciding the pink would be acceptable until after she had coffee, she went out into the little kitchen area.

The coffee maker was nothing like her brewing it at home, this was faster, and the taste was more consistent. Home? Where was that now? She'd have to think about that. She was okay with being here, but it didn't feel like home.

The journal was sitting on the little table that was attached to the floor. Setting the cup beside the gurgling machine, she picked it up and opened it. Her eyes widened, for two days. She'd been gone two days.

She reached internally for Minn and was pleasantly

surprised that she was content. Hopefully, she stayed that way because she did not need another forced change if they were going to affect her for two days. What if Leah had needed her in that time? Then what? She silently chastised Minn, things like that wouldn't do.

The door opened and she spun around the see Jesse standing there grinning. He looked at her face for a moment. "Good morning, Evanna."

It pleased her more than she could express that he knew from a look which one of them was on the outside. "Hi." She swatted the hair out of her eyes, this shirt thing didn't have pockets, so she knew a hair tie wasn't going to be an option. "I guess that shift knocked me out for a few days."

"I was worried." He said quietly as he came all the way in.

"Was everything okay while I was gone?" She wanted to put her hands on her hips but didn't want to draw attention to what she was wearing.

"Minn behaved." He reached around her and poured her coffee and then held the cup out to her, "Leah had a few minor moments, but she's been working hard."

Evanna took a sip and savored it for a moment. "Working?" What was there for her to work at here?

"Yeah." He picked up his cup from the sink and rinsed it before pouring some coffee in. "She's been getting some training on how to communicate with Minn," he opened a container and added some to his coffee, "and she's talked to the doctor over the laptop twice now."

Evanna glanced at the journal, "that would explain why there are so many pages." She sat down, carefully so the shirt would come with her and cover everything. She stared at the book, seeing it, but not entirely. "I have a lot of gaps," she confessed quietly, "I'm not used to that."

Jesse sat down across from her. "If I ask anything you don't want to talk about, be brutally honest with me about it, okay? The more I understand, the more I can help you."

She smirked, "brutally honest is part of my charm." Evanna laughed, "that's what Aunt Tillie used to tell me."

"That's not a bad quality."

"You really want to help us." She blew on the hot liquid, "I still have trouble with that." She leaned forward, "not that I'm complaining, it's just—new."

"Many others want to help you too. You're not alone anymore, Evanna."

Sucking in a quick breath, she ignored the emotions trying to choke her. "I'm getting that."

Reaching across the table, he touched her hand, "why did you look so upset when I came in?"

She liked his hand on hers, it was comforting. She'd spent years comforting Leah and Minn, but no one did that for her. "I uh, was angry with myself."

"For what?"

She watched his eyes; she could tell every word he said was true when she did. "For being gone so long. If-if Leah had needed me..."

"Hey," he leaned further across the table, "she was never out of my sight the whole time you were gone, I watched over her and will always do that for you and Minn too."

Her chest felt like it was tightening, but not in a painful way, not really. "I, uh," she grinned, "I'm not used to that."

"I know."

She loved his voice, that soft tone he used, it felt like it vibrated right through her. "It's going to take some time to get that, you know what I'm saying?"

He didn't interrupt her, just nodded, while giving her his complete focus. This man was like nothing she could have ever pictured.

"I haven't read yet, but what if," she wasn't sure how to say it and didn't want to sound stupid or naive around him, "what if I'm not needed anymore with all this help and everything? What if I don't come out anymore."

He didn't laugh at her, and his eyes didn't falter from hers, "I don't know as much about this as I'd like to, but it is my understanding that there is no magic or cure for this, managing it isn't getting rid of it—getting rid of you or Minn, or even Leah."

"I need to know more." She looked at the cup because she wasn't sure what she was feeling. "I've always protected Leah, always and when I couldn't," she closed her eyes, "when I wasn't able to keep going to get Leah far from that place, Minn came out and ran for days at a time."

"I know," he reached across the table and lifted her chin gently so she'd look at him again, "I don't know the details, I hope someday I will, but I do know there's no Leah without you and no you without Leah. That's not going to change, the only change will be it won't be so hard on all of you, and I'm in the equation now."

"I can't believe you want to take this on, deal with us, it's not easy," she glanced away for a second because the tender look on his face was killing her slowly, "our own grandparents struggled with it."

"I'm sure there will be bad days, there are for all mates regardless of other circumstances, but," still holding her hand, he slid out from the table and came around to kneel in front of her, "know this, I am not going anywhere."

She couldn't have looked away from his eyes if she'd wanted to, it was as if she was frozen unable to lower her eyes away from his. When he leaned closer and she could feel his breath on her face, the air in her chest hitched. He brushed his lips over hers, once, twice. They were so warm. Releasing her chin, he kissed her again, a little harder this time and her stomach felt funny, but not in a bad way.

"I'll let you read and get caught up, I just have to go help Blair with a few things and then I'll be back. The doctor will be calling in a few hours, so you'll be able to speak to her yourself." He reached behind him and then set a phone on the table. "This is yours." Letting go of her hand, he turned it and tapped the screen, it changed. "That's how you turn it on." He pointed to this little symbol. "I made a shortcut to call me, just tap that." He did it and numbers came on the screen, then hit the green button and it will phone me. He looked back at her face, "call me if you need anything, okay?"

She nodded in a jerky motion. "Okay," she barely whispered.

He kissed her quickly again and stood up. Turning in the doorway, he tilted his head, "if me kissing you bothers you; you can tell me that too."

She blinked, "no. No," she shook her head, "it doesn't bother me." She felt her cheeks get hot.

He flashed her a quick grin. "Good."

Evanna sat there staring at the door long after he closed it. "Okay, that happened." Blowing out a loud, long breath, she smirked, "movies don't prepare you for *that*." Glancing down at the phone, she picked it up and turned it over in her hand. She had a phone. No cords, small enough to fit in her pocket, she looked down and then remembered she was in this pink thing. *Okay, clothes, coffee and read,* she got up, "maybe one of those bars too."

Evanna reread the first few pages. Leah had put a lot of information on those. If the rest had this much in it, she was going to get a headache processing it. She'd met several of the others, and while wasn't completely comfortable with them, she was able to stay present.

Leah had really liked two of them, Nichelle, a teen that hadn't been shifting long. Evanna felt hope when she said that she was having trouble with her cat. Jesse had been right, there may be ways to make things better for them.

The other female that Leah liked being around was Daisie. She grinned, having met the kid, she could see why. Evanna was sure she read the one paragraph ten times. It had been Daisie that had calmed Minn and enabled her to take control again. "Kid is some kind of magic." She whispered as she turned the page to read the next part.

I don't know why I can't feel you like I normally do, but it has me worried. I know there are times when I'm out for days, but you have always been close by watching. I hope you're all right, Evanna. I am keeping myself busy, trying to learn things that will help all of us. I'm still in shock that I'm able to feel Minn and to communicate with her. I'm not great at it, there are times when she just won't communicate at all, but it is nice feeling her contentment and not just rage. Franki and Kobie said they will work with you and Minn as well. I know you will master it much faster because you've always dealt with Minn and her moods.

Evanna sighed. Would that be possible? To control Minn without suffering for it later? She planned on finding out.

The next part was written in sloppier writing. Leah's only looked like that when she was emotional. Brows furrowed, she continued.

I spoke with Doctor Collins on a video call on Jesse's laptop today. She explained what was wrong with us, I didn't absorb as much of it as I'd like to have. (I saved the computer site pages she suggested on the laptop for you to read)

She looked around for the laptop and didn't see it. Snorting, she shook her head, not that she had the first clue how to work the thing. She'd wait and ask Jesse when he got back.

I'm going to try to tell you what I learned. Doctor Collins says with regular therapy (talking and things like that) it will be easier for us to not be triggered. I don't even know if you have a trigger, but we both know the list is long with things that cause me to recede (I think that's what it's called). When I am out it means I am 'fronting'. There is so much to learn Evanna, I don't know how to sort it all.

She also said medication can be effective in some cases, but usually, in her experience with shifters proper diet management and a few herbal brews or supplements can be as effective.

Minn is not one of the identities. As a shifter, she is just our cat, although she is somewhat out of control because our situation caused her to manifest sooner than she should have. Doctor Collins says she's like an adolescent cat that has tantrums. Now. She has tantrums now, when she first came out it was a fight or flight response. I don't remember much about that time, so I can't be sure.

Evanna set the journal down and went over and opened the fridge. She didn't like thinking about that time either. She hadn't been *fronting* when they got out of there, so she didn't have all the details, only knew that she was suddenly standing in the middle of an alley and had no idea where she was. She had read Leah's mother's letter to know what to do, then spent a day trying to figure out which direction was the right direction. Three days later, she was exhausted, couldn't sense Leah hardly at all and then Minn appeared. Of course, Minn had appeared to save her and if she hadn't, well, Evanna didn't want to think about what would have happened. The rest of the trip wasn't that clear, a few times of searching for clothes and not having to wear the see-through thin dress that had been stuffed into the bag they'd sent Leah out with was all she could really remember.

Grabbing a bottle of juice and an apple, she went and sat back down. Minn wasn't an identity. She snorted, try telling Minn that. Taking a sip, she flipped the journal back over and kept reading.

You are going to have to talk to her about when Minn came out that first time. I have so many memory gaps. I remember little things here and there, but as a whole I can't tell her everything that happened. The doctor says I have repressed those memories and you would have been fronting as soon as something happened I couldn't handle. Do you know about everything that happened? Do you remember what I don't? How are we going to figure this out?

Closing her eyes, she felt for Leah. She could feel the emotional turmoil just reading her words. Leah was there and safe, that was all that mattered. Opening her eyes, she took a bite and kept reading.

I can't write more about that right now. You will talk to the doctor probably tomorrow, I'm getting really cloudy and tired, so I know you'll be out then. I know you aren't big on feelings, Evanna, but we have to do this.

Evanna rolled her eyes, the way Leah used underlined words was like she'd have no choice because of a line.

Jesse has been so good to me. He makes sure I'm okay with everything, whether it's going for a walk, who wants to talk to me. I told Jesse you wanted me to stay away from that man Niles and he agreed, said he was so ugly on the inside that it festered to the outside. I'm not sure what that means, but I stayed away from him. Jesse also sat on the step outside the trailer when I talk to the doctor and told me if I get upset to just call him. He said if being here was too much for us we could go somewhere else. He has his own land, away from his clan. He looked happy when he talked about it. His house isn't finished, but there is a trailer there too. He said I could plant gardens and sunflowers.

Evanna grinned, sunflowers, how many failed attempts had she tried on the mountain. She'd lost count. Of course, sunflowers would be a positive point for Leah.

As much as it pleases me that he would take us there, I don't think it's right if he stops doing his job with the Alliance and his team. There are so many of our kind that need saving and Jesse is part of that team. Do you agree with that? It's hard for me to be near others, but what Jesse does is so important.

She took a bite of the apple and chewed it without tasting it. She had trouble thinking of the others that were being held in places like they had been. Jesse was like a hero in her eyes, he found those lost or taken. Yeah, she agreed with Leah, what he did was too important for them to prevent it. She looked at the apple and turned it slowly. Could they stay here without him? The idea bothered her, so she knew that Leah wouldn't be able to. First, she needed to find out more about that training that was going to take place. She knew she could do that, what she had to decide was if it was worth putting Leah through them helping the teams that went in because that part hadn't changed, she wanted to *do* something that mattered.

I will close this for now. The doctor is supposed to be calling soon and I have to go get Jesse to help me set up the laptop. Please write back.

L

Sipping the juice, she stared at the blank space under Leah's writing. She couldn't even remember half of what she was supposed to be replying to. Staring at the closed journal, she decided a short walk and then she's answer her.

Setting the pen down, she flipped back and page and started reading, hoping she covered everything that Leah needed to know.

First, don't expect a ten page reply. We both know that will <u>never</u> happen.

Evanna smirked at the underlined word, maybe Leah would see how ridiculous it was.

I can't believe I left you unprotected for two days, Leah. I am sorry. It's never happened before and I don't know why it happened.

I haven't talked to the doctor yet, but I will try to do what you want because I agree we both need it. I will definitely work with others to communicate with Minn because to be honest I have never felt her this calm and quiet, so something is working. If I never have to force her to shift back again, it will be like some kind of miracle. I won't miss the pain from it either, that's for sure.

Jesse is, I don't even know how to explain it. He just seems to understand us and that's so different I'm afraid to trust it, but I'm going to. He kissed me Leah. Like a real kiss and those movies Aunt Tillie used to watch were nothing like this. I want to talk to one of the women, I'm thinking Kobie (I can relate to her easily) and find out more about this mate stuff. I mean, he's ours so we need to know more about it.

As far as Jesse continuing to help the Alliance, I agree completely. He can't stop doing that. If any of our clan are left, I know he will find them. My chest gets tight when I think of seeing any of them again and I know it will be emotional soup if we do, but also I hope for their sake that we get that chance.

I talked to him about the training the others are taking to be on the team and I want to do it. Not just to be included with the team, but to better protect us. I failed to protect us on that trip and it's my fault that Minn was out early and so out of control. I know she got us home, but I'm going to make sure I have the ability to protect us in any situation from now on. This training is going to involve guns and knives and fighting, so if it upsets you I want you to go to your safe place and stay there while I do it. I don't know how Minn is going to react, so I'm going to talk to that Franki lady before it to help me keep Minn inside.

I can't believe I'm writing this much.

Jesse said that there is no you without me and no me without you and to be honest that made me feel better because I don't know what is going to happen from now on.

He gave me a phone. I can't believe we have our own phone that works. I don't know what I can do with it yet, but I plan on finding out because it seems like it's an important part of life in this world now, everyone is looking at theirs and tapping the screen all the time. I will make sure Jesse shows it to you, but I'm certain he will because he seems to understand us. When I woke up he took one look and knew I was me and not you, has that ever happened? I don't think so.

Okay. I have to go. Busy day ahead, Minn training, the doctor and weapons training.
Love E

It was probably the longest note she'd ever left Leah. Picking up the phone she looked at it and grinned. It had a clock. No winding it or anything, it just knew what time it was. Closing the journal, she got up and tucked the phone into her back pocket. With a grin, she pulled it back out and turned it on as Jesse had shown her. "He did say call." She smirked and tapped the green button, which really wasn't a button because it was flat.

"Evanna? Is everything okay?"

"Yeah, it really is." She held the phone away from her ear and looked at it. This was crazy. Putting it back to her ear, she nodded, "I wanted to talk to that lady, Franki, Leah says she can help me with Minn." She wasn't sure if she should wait for him to answer or what the proper way to talk on a phone was, so she kept going. "I think I should get in touch with Minn before that training?"

"I can find Franki for you, sure. Do you want to wait at the trailer?"

She looked at the door, "yeah I'll wait outside. I don't want people gawking at me while we do that." She didn't even know what 'that' was exactly."

"Okay. I'm in the house right now, do you want some sandwiches? Cortney made a ton of them."

"I could eat." She grinned.

"Okay, I'll be there in a few minutes."

"All right. I will be here." She laughed and held the phone away from her ear and tapped the red non-button thing. "That was kind of amazing." She mumbled and then tucked it back into her pocket.

Chapter Thirty-Four

Jesse leaned against the tree and watched Blair and Cale set up targets. Jake and Noah were setting up a few tables. He really wasn't needed for this part, but this was keeping him out of Evanna's face. He'd been surprised and very happy to see her this morning. He wanted her to read the journal from Leah, get time to get caught up, but he was also worried about her now after some of the things she said. He wanted to give her answers when she asked questions.

"I'll just be a few more moments, Jesse." Doctor Collins said softly into the phone.

"No problem, take your time." The line went quiet as she put him on hold again. He probably should have set up a time to talk to her and not called her out of the blue, but his brain and cat wouldn't shut up and he needed answers.

He looked back in the direction of the trailer, for what was probably the hundredth time since he'd walked out the door. He didn't see Franki or Evanna now. Hopefully, that was going okay. Why he couldn't explain to her how to reach Minn, he wasn't sure. He'd done it many times with young shifters but now when it mattered, he couldn't find the way to explain the path to the animal inside.

"Sorry about that, Jesse. There are so many little ones here, I'm trying to spend equal time with all of them."

"I understand. Is it going well?"

"If you mean have I found any that set off red flags, then no, I haven't so far."

He felt relief flood through him. "That's great."

"Yes. I haven't gotten to the older children yet, but so far so good." She paused for a moment, "I've been expecting you to call. Shaelan told me that you were mated to Leah and Evanna..."

"And Minn, her cat." He added, wanting to be clear.

"Of course, her animal as well, which makes sense. Her animal isn't another alter, it's just her animal side like you and I and our kind."

He blew out a breath.

"The reason her cat is thought of as an alter is because of her shifting so young, she's never had time to bond. Most, as you know do it before or shortly after their first shift, they didn't have the chance."

"Yeah, Minn is, ah, a hand full."

"I'm sure she is. Leah is afraid of her. I'm not sure about Evanna because we haven't met yet..."

"Evanna is fronting today, so you will get to."

"Ah, perfect, it's easier to see the whole picture once I've spoken to all the alters. Have you noticed any oddities in either of their behavior that would suggest there are more alters?"

Jesse shook his head, "No. It's fairly easy to tell who is fronting, and as far as I know, they know it's just the two of them." He was relieved to have confirmation that Minn was her animal side and not another alter. He thought of his own cat, and shrugged, he most definitely had his own personality, he couldn't imagine if they were out of synch and not able to convey thought to each other.

"Sorry, just making notes so I remember the pertinent facts later."

"No problem. Listen, I'm really out of my depth here, I

don't know what I should or shouldn't do. I want to help and have no idea how to."

"What you're feeling isn't uncommon. There's no definite answer to that. Each system is different."

"System?"

"Yes, that's what they are, a system or different alters sharing the one body."

"Okay." He was mated to a system. That didn't sound right to him.

"As far as what you should or shouldn't do, those answers you will have to get from Leah and Evanna."

"Okay, what—how do I ask them that?"

"Starting with asking about their triggers is the best route."

"Triggers, what makes the other one come out?"

"Yes, causing a switch can be very jarring and disorienting at the same time."

"I've noticed. I know of a few things, but won't asking them set them off or cause a," what has she said, "switch?"

"It could, but I'm sure the fact that you're interested in order to help them and making sure they feel safe will mean a lot to both of them."

"All right, I can do that." He cleared his throat. "Both have said they're interested in joining a team," he made sure not to give away too much, "part of it may involve weapons use and situations that could be dangerous." What was he trying to ask her again? "Should—is it smart to let them be exposed to that?"

"That is another question you need to ask them. They need to feel that they have control in their world, or it could cause more serious issues."

He nodded and decided he didn't want to ask about what more serious issues could be. "This is all," he glanced around, "hard. I don't know how it works as a mate in this situation."

"Again there is no one solution for that, each mated to a system has to work it out with them."

She made it sound cold, and clinical and it was starting to grate on his nerves. "So, talk to them?" He nodded before she could answer.

"The most important thing right now is they feel safe, are getting enough rest and proper diet is even more important to them than it is with other shifters."

"Yeah, I've been working on that. So how long..."

"Jesse, if you're about to ask me how long they will need therapy and other help, there is no answer. It could be forever."

"Right." He scowled at the ground, "and the best possible outcome is?"

"In this situation, I feel there is a more positive solution than in others. With two alters and," she made a soft chuffing noise, "an adolescent cat, the best outcome may actually happen."

He went over her words trying to figure out if she'd said what that was. "And that is?"

"Their alters would integrate into one personality."

He jolted as if she'd hit him. "One of them is gone?" His cat didn't like that idea any more than he did.

"No, more like both of them are still there in one personality."

"That's possible?"

"It's rare, but I always hope for the best."

He heaved a sigh. "Yeah, I do too, whatever works for them is what I want."

"I'm glad they have you. A supportive partner makes it one hundred percent easier for them to heal eventually."

"Eventually." That was a huge word in his mind. It could also mean never. "Thanks, Doctor Collins, I will probably call again later on with more questions, but right now it's all mixed in with everything going on."

"If you ever just need to talk, I'm here."

He cringed, "thanks. I'll let you go."

"All right. Tell Evanna I will be speaking to her in roughly an hour."

"I'll make sure she's set up for it."

"Thank you, Jesse."

He waited until he knew she hung up, before holding the phone out and glaring at it. None of that was very helpful at all. The only thing he got from all of it was it was better to talk to Leah and Evanna than it was to talk to someone about them

Chapter Thirty-Five

Jesse's cat was not happy with the man that had arrived with his female partner to help train the others. He'd expected the older man that had done the training before. He glanced at Gage, who had come over at Kelsey's insistence and the expression on his face was much the same as his own feelings. This Heath guy was smiling at Gage's mate as well. In fact, he kept sending that come hither smile to all the women.

Jesse knew Yasmin, she was always involved when there were women in on the training. After a git of cussing, he went over to her.

"Hey Jesse, how have you been?"

No flirty smiles, she kept her distance from all the males, as most shifters knew to do. "Not too bad, Yasmin." He glanced at her partner, "listen do you think you could tell your co-worker to tone down the million-dollar smile? He's making a lot of mates a little hostile."

She visibly sighed and looked over at Heath "Sorry about that, he's like that with everyone and it's a bit annoying."

Jesse crossed his arms and nodded.

"Oh, your mate is here?" She looked around at the others nearby. "Which one? Wait, tell me it's the lovely one sitting with that animal." She smiled, "I can't believe we have a real leopard among us. Will she be all right with the guns?"

"I'm going to test that out beforehand." He wasn't feeling positive about it either, but Evanna had assured him that as long as she or Thera weren't being threatened, she would be fine.

"I'll go talk to Heath and tell him to back off," you, she pointed to Thera, "go talk to your animal and make her promise not to take any chunks out of us."

He nodded and picked up one of the handguns. Turning it over, he checked the chamber and then grabbed a cartridge. Glancing at Calum, he wasn't surprised that he gave Jesse a slight nod as if to say he was ready if this went wrong. Jesse shook his head as he walked toward Evanna, only Calum would take on a real leopard if they got out of hand.

Thera sat up when he got closer, he could see her scenting the air. She knew full well what he held in his hand.

"I'm more worried about her reaction than ours," Evanna said getting to her knees beside her.

"Yeah, I'm the same." He squatted down beside Thera and ran his hand over her coat. She gave him a steady look when he stopped. Holding up the hand that held the gun and clip, he let her take her time checking it out. Her ears weren't upright completely. "It's okay, girl, it's not to be used on you or any of us." With careful movements, he held just the weapon out to Evanna, "let her see that you're okay with it."

Evanna nodded, a look of focus on her face. "Okay. It's not loaded right?" She smirked, "I don't want to shoot anyone by mistake."

As she took the gun, he showed her the clip. "No, it's not."

She didn't get up from beside Thera as she turned the gun over in her hand and examined it. Thera watched her carefully, scenting constantly to check Evanna's emotions. "It's pretty amazing, eh girl?" Evanna switched the gun into her other hand and then held her other hand out for the cat to sniff it.

"How's Leah doing with this?"

Evanna continued to pet the animal, "she's not too close, so I think she'll be okay. She knows this is important."

Jesse nodded and held his hand out for the gun again. When he put the clip in Thera jolted noticeably. "It's okay." He assured her. With a quick glance around to see where everyone was, he stood up. "Try not to react." He said quietly.

"I'm good."

Pointing it toward the sky, he flipped the safety and squeezed the trigger.

Thera jumped and looked up at him as if to say 'why did you do that?' He smiled down at her, "see, girl, not for us. You ready to try it?" He asked Evanna.

Without hesitation, she nodded and stood up.

"I'm excited." She told him.

"Just try not to flinch or send out the wrong vibes to her."

"Okay." She stood beside him and held out her hand.

"Safety is off, so don't point it toward anyone, point it into the air and squeeze the trigger once."

Evanna had a serious look on her face as she took it and pointed it in the air. "Now?"

"Whenever you're ready." He watched Thera as the shot rang out. She was not impressed but didn't go into protect mode. "Now hand it back to me and let her smell your hand."

"Okay." She kept the gun pointed to the ground and held it out to him. As soon as he took it she lowered her hand near Thera's face. She checked it out then snuffed out a breath, unimpressed with it completely. Getting up she walked toward the trees lay down in the shade of the closest ones and stared in their direction.

"I think she'll be okay."

Jesse nodded, "we'll just have to find entertainment for her when it comes to the close-up defense training."

"I don't know what that is."

Jesse took the clip out, checked the chamber, and then smirked at her. "Pretend to fight, but she may take it as a threat."

"Oh." Her eyes widened and she looked over at the cat, "we'll send her to keep Daisie company when that happens."

Jesse looked around at the others. There were a lot of people here. Aside from those here that were to have the training, Franki, Kelsey, Jake, and Gary wanted in on it. "Are you okay with this many around you?"

Evanna tucked her hands in her pockets and nodded. "I've met them all, so I think we'll be fine."

When he turned to walk back to the table, she put her hand on his arm and moved closer.

"Uh, Jesse?"

He looked down to see the worry in her eyes. "What is it?"

"The pretend fighting," she glanced at the ground, then back to him, "um, I can't stand the back of my neck touched." The worry turned to an anxious look. "Minn will come out." She whispered.

"It's a trigger for you."

She nodded, "I guess that's what it's called."

He ran his hand down her arm softly. "I'll let Yasmin know, she's the one that will be working with you."

She held his look for a moment and then blew out a breath. "Okay. I thought it was just guns and knives."

"It's okay." He leaned down and kissed her mouth softly, hoping it reassured her. Straightening, he smiled at her, "just so the charming one knows you are off-limits," he winked at her.

She smirked, "that guy? Not even Thera likes his smiles."

Jesse grinned. "Good." He checked to see if everyone was ready yet, seeing they weren't he leaned down and spoke softly. "I don't know if anyone ever told you, but our animals take it as a threat if the opposite gender is near our mates."

She gave him a shocked look. "No," She shook her head, "Aunt Tillie didn't cover that part," she shrugged, "that's okay though, the only male I'm comfortable around is you, so no problems with that."

Jesse's cat was thrilled to hear her say that. "Good." He kissed her again because it was better than the alternative of picking her up and taking her away from everyone, which is what he'd wanted to do since she had gotten here.

"Hey," she rubbed her hand on his chest, "thanks for this," she smiled up at him, "letting us do this because I know you're not comfortable with it."

"You can sense that?"

She shrugged, "I don't know if that's it but the cold looks you've been giving everyone here was almost as if you were shouting it out."

He rested his head on her forehead for a second. "I'll be honest, this whole mating thing, I have no idea what I'm doing either."

"Is that the truth?" She leaned back and looked at him.

"One hundred percent."

"Huh," she licked her lips, "that makes me feel a lot better," he cringed, "sorry, but we have no idea either."

Jesse straightened and put his hand behind her back to move them back toward the others, "I guess we'll muddle through this together then."

Evanna leaned into him, "that works for us."

Staying out of the way was hard, but he was determined not to interfere and let Evanna learn like the others were. It also allowed him to monitor her reactions and Thera's as well. They had gone through the safety talk with the weapons, loading, and unloading so far. Each person had the opportunity to fire it once, just to feel the recoil in their hands. Heath was now discussing aiming and the factors that affected it. Evanna's sole focus was on the instructor, which pleased him, but not his cat. After her confession to them, about her trigger, his cat was in protect mode. At least Heath was all business and no flitting looks now that he was discussing safety with them, it didn't calm his cat much, but he accepted it.

Yasmin moved over so she was across from a target and began her instruction.

Out of the corner of his eye, Jesse saw Thera stand up and scent the air. He inhaled slowly and then realized he wouldn't pick up what she was because of all the guns and bodies between them.

When she gave a low meow, Evanna turned and started in her direction with fast steps. When her shirt hit the ground, Jesse froze and looked at Calum. The shock was clear on his face too. Swearing under his breath he started to jog toward her.

He'd go over this in his mind for the rest of his life, but he'd never seen a shifter strip their clothes that fast. She was running, naked into the trees, and then midstride she was her Minn.

The shocked look on Blair and Calum's faces was clear as he ran and tossed his shirt to the ground. "Something's wrong." He told them and hoped he had back up. As he paused to get rid of his jeans and boots, he saw the instructors pick up guns load them and start looking all around them.

"Women to house." Blair barked loudly.

Jesse didn't wait to see who listened and who didn't, he shifted faster than he ever had and tore off into the bush after his mate. The sound of paws registered behind him, and he knew it would be Calum and Blair hot on his tail.

He was able to follow their scent without a problem and was stunned when he found the scent of another animal and not the wild variety. Slowing, he checked behind him to see Blair and Noah following. Calum was nowhere in sight, but he knew he'd be out here somewhere. When he turned back, he caught a glimpse of Thera's tail heading deeper into the growth and took off after her.

As he cleared the trees, he came to a skidding halt to see Minn with her jaws clamped around the neck of a jackal.

"We need him alive." Calum's said from somewhere in the trees.

Blair and Noah moved up beside him.

Minn gave a low warning growl as Thera paced in front of her, keeping her body between them and what she perceived as Minn's kill.

Jesse shifted so quickly he stumbled a few steps. "Minn, we need him alive. You have to let him shift back."

She growled low at him.

"We have no jackal clans in the Alliance," Calum said from the other side of Minn. Jesse still couldn't see him but knew he was purposely staying out of her sight.

"Babe," Jesse was a foot from her now, "we need him alive to question him."

Her eyes connected with him, and he could see it wasn't fully Minn in control.

"Evanna," he said softly, "release him, we need him alive to get information that could help others."

With a hesitant look, she dropped him to the ground and stepped back, but remained crouched and ready to spring if he did anything wrong.

Jesse looked at the animal lying there panting. "I suggest you change or she's going to get really upset."

He glanced to see Blair and Noah had escape routes covered that way. Calum came out from behind a tree, back in cat form, his ears flat. The growl he issued was going to be his only warning.

Thera added her opinion, which caused Minn to pace back and forth.

He looked back at the jackal and didn't have to tell him again as he lay there shifting back to skin. Jesse turned around and looked at Noah, "go grab him something, a blanket or whatever, we don't need Daisie seeing us drag a naked man back." He leaned down and looked at his neck, there were no visible marks to be seen. They must have got here just as she'd caught him. "Are there any others on this property? Or nearby?"

Minn shoved past Thera and got right in his face, the low roar she issued let him know he had one chance to get it right.

He shook his head and crawled backward on his hands to put some space between them.

Jesse went over and put his hand on her back. "Go back and get dressed, we'll be there shortly." She looked up at him and he could see the hesitant look in her eyes. He nodded, "you did amazing, now let us look like we did something useful." He smiled down at her. She nudged her shoulder against his bare leg and took off back in the direction they'd come. Jesse watched Thera give the man on the ground a quick once over and then bound after her. He didn't take his eyes off the shaggy-looking male specimen in front of him. He heard bones snapping to change form and figured it was Calum.

"Holy hell your girl can shift." Blair came up beside him. "I may have strained an eye when they popped out of my head, she was in mid-air when she did that."

Jesse grinned, "I can see you trying to jump and shift in mid-air now."

Blair snorted, "of course, I have to try it."

That was an image Jess didn't need, one of Blair naked jumping into the air trying to shift on the run.

"How did the leopard know and none of us sensed it?" Calum came up to stand with them.

"We were all pretty close to the guns," Blair crossed his arms over his chest and looked down at the man, "no jackals in the Alliance?"

Calum shook his head.

"One of them that took Daisie was a jackal."

"Interesting." Calum looked at Jesse for a moment, "I guess we need to get Devin looking into where they hail from."

A sound from behind them had all three tense and glance. It was Noah dragging back a blanket and a pair of jeans.

Calum went over and picked up the blanket and tossed it at the man. "Get up." He picked up the jeans and looked at them, then threw them at Blair. "I guess you get to drag him back."

Blair grinned, in an unpleasant way, "lucky me."

Chapter Thirty-Six

"Where is he now?" Devin asked.

Calum glanced over at the building. "He's in one of the small buildings. Cale is standing outside his door with a shotgun."

"We're able to talk freely?" The king asked.

Calum nodded, "yes, it's Jesse, Blair, Noah, and Evanna here with me."

"Calum sent me a message saying you'd killed a Jackal in the mountains, Blair."

"I did but I didn't know it was worth mentioning." Blair crossed his arms over his chest and looked at the phone Calum held.

"We've never had a Jackal clan in the Alliance." The King informed them.

Evanna looked from Calum to Jesse, she wasn't sure what that meant. She was still having trouble thinking past seeing Jesse completely naked. She knew she shouldn't have been thinking about that right now, or even pausing to look then, but she still was. If a male body could be beautiful, he was for sure.

"Where are there Jackal clans?" Jesse was scowling now.

Whatever was wrong, it wasn't good. It made her feel much happier about catching him.

"We're confirming that now," Devin answered.

What did that mean? She had to wonder.

"How did you know he was on the property?" He continued.

"The real leopard sensed him." Blair grinned at her, "Evanna hunted him down and had him before we could even react."

"On the mountain," she looked at Jesse wondering if she should speak, he nodded, so she finished, "we could scent anything that came up it, I guess that works for Thera anywhere."

"I can't tell you how happy we are you were there with your Thera," The king said quietly, "I'm arranging transport for your guest, I'll be back in a moment."

"Can we question him, Dev?" Calum asked.

Blair nodded his head briskly, "I need to know if it was him that poisoned Jake, how many others have been here…"

"Can you do that and keep him alive?"

She thought Devin was joking, but the expression on the men's face told her he wasn't.

"We can." Calum finally said after giving Blair and Jesse a look.

"Okay, see what you can find out. Did Noah recognize him?"

Noah hadn't spoken until now. "No. There were no jackal shifters in any of the places I was."

"So this may be fairly new." Devin mused. "Make sure he's able to talk when he's picked up, Cal, he holds a lot of information and doesn't even know he does."

"Will do."

"A helicopter will land at Ed's in two hours. No one else knows other than the two men transporting and the pilot." The king said in a low tone.

"I'll give Ed and Gage a heads up," Noah said.

"Thank you, Noah. I'm going to have to go now, arrange a few things. Thank you, Miss Cardenas, for what you did today and please give your leopard a big steak from me."

Evanna smiled, "I will—sir."

"Okay guys I'm going to go and help with some research," Devin huffed out a breath, "hopefully this ends people on your land, Blair."

Blair shrugged, "I'm not letting my guard down until all of Tomas' servants are dealt with."

"Probably a good idea." Devin cleared his throat, "I'll message when I know more. Oh, Zain has set up some joint email thing that will update all of you on the retrieval team at once, so we're always on the same page."

Jesse nodded, "we have that with the co-ordinators team too, makes things simple."

"Simple sounds good," Blair said as he looked over his shoulder. "I have to go. Jake is here and looks like he's determined to have a word with our unwelcome guest."

Calum turned and looked back at the building too. "Keep us informed, Dev."

"I will. Let me know if he tells you anything." The line went quiet.

"You want in on this?" Calum looked at Jesse.

Jesse turned to me, "I'll be there in a few minutes."

Evanna watched the three men walk away.

"Hey," she looked back at Jesse, "you're amazing." He smiled at her and made her whole body tingle, in a good way. "How's Minn and Leah after that?"

She didn't need to focus to know, "Leah hides whenever I'm in protect or hunting mode. Minn is fine too." She grinned up at him, "that was me running the cat, not Minn. If it were her, the guy would have been dead before you men got there."

His smile widened. Moving closer, he rested a hand on either of her hips and squeezed lightly. "I'm very glad you were in control then because apparently, we needed to catch us a jackal."

She put her hands on his chest, liking this closeness. "Do

you think he knows something important?" His eyes, she thought, she could stand here all day and look at just his eyes.

"Devin and his father seem to think it's an important find, so I'd say he can probably fill in a few blanks for us." He leaned down and rested his forehead against hers. "I'm so proud of the way you handled yourself, I didn't get a chance to tell you with everyone stuck to us."

As far as she could remember, she couldn't recall being told that by anyone. He was proud of her. "I didn't even think, I just reacted."

"Well, seeing you *react* makes me feel better about you coming to help." His eyes held her almost prisoner, she couldn't look away, "I've been worrying about it."

"I know. I have concerns too, but we won't know unless we try things." She didn't want to move away from him, "I have to talk to the doctor soon."

"Shit, I forgot about that." He made a low rumbling sound in his chest, and it sent heat through her. "Training is postponed until tomorrow now, so I'll get you set up on the laptop and then go give Calum and Blair a hand."

"Or make sure they behave?"

He smirked, "mostly that."

"You are such a good man, Jesse." She didn't know what possessed her to do it, but she stretched up and wanted to kiss his mouth but wasn't sure if she should.

When she went to move away, he touched the back of her head, avoiding touching anywhere near her neck, and kissed her again, longer, slowly, the softest of touches. Her head felt fuzzy when he stopped.

He made another quiet rumbling noise and straightened up. "I need to get you set up on the laptop and go do what I'm supposed to be doing." His grin said he wasn't as serious as his words.

"I like your kisses." She felt her face heat but didn't care. The truth was always the best way. Aunt Tillie had drilled that into her more than anything else.

"If we can ever find more than a minute that doesn't require us to be doing something else, we'll do a lot more of that."

He stepped back and then leaned forward again and dropped another kiss on her mouth. "And in case I forgot, thank you." He gave her an earnest look, "for sharing with me what can trigger you to switch."

She could only nod, it felt like there was something stuck in her throat.

"Come on, I'll give you a crash course on the laptop."

She cringed. She could barely manage the electronic things like the coffee maker. Stepping into the trailer, she watched him open it. "I'm not good with gadgets."

He glanced over at her, "we'll get it set up so all you have to do is hit a button, then when you're done, just close it."

"That's it, just close it?"

He nodded and motioned to the seat. "Call me if you need me, okay?"

Evanna took the phone out of her pocket and set it beside his laptop. She nodded and sat down. Her nerves were tense, she didn't know what to expect. She'd never imagined talking to someone about Leah and her, ever, never mind someone that knew why they were this way and how to help them.

"You'll be fine. I spoke to the doctor earlier today and she seems nice."

Evanna nodded, "I'm glad it's a woman, I don't know if I could talk to a man."

He smirked, "you talk to me."

She smirked right back at him, "I think you're the exception to many rules."

Jesse chuckled, "I'm very happy to hear that." The sound his phone made interrupted them. He pulled it out and looked at it. "I have to go; Calum wants me there now." He kissed her mouth so quickly; that she didn't have time to kiss him back. "Call if you need me." He backed to the door and then turned and went out it.

She looked at the screen. He didn't tell her what to hit. She looked down at it and read all the letters on the keys. They weren't even in order. That wasn't helpful at all. She'd watched him run his finger over the big square and touched it, then looked at the screen. "Oh." She smiled when she saw that when she did that a little arrow moved. "Okay, I can do this." It took her a minute to make the arrow go the way she wanted smoothly, but it wasn't too hard. She looked at the phone and decided keeping it within reach was a good plan.

She looked out the window again, Jesse still wasn't coming. It was dark now. The helicopter had left quite a while ago. It had been odd not having to hide from one flying overhead.

Kobie had brought her a plate earlier and said the men were still busy with that man and she didn't want to interrupt anything. Blowing out a breath, she looked at the journal. After talking to the doctor, she understood why Leah had been so confused, but excited. It was so strange to have someone know about how things were with them. She'd left Leah a short note about the jackal, the training, and the doctor, but she was hoping for the first time ever that she would be out tomorrow too.

Yawning, she decided to go lay down and wait for Jesse. This day had been exhausting but she wouldn't have missed any of it. She felt wanted, needed, and important for the first time in her life, aside from Leah and Minn of course. She didn't know what had brought a man like Jesse up their mountain, but she was really happy it had been him.

Laying down, she touched her mouth. She really did like it when Jesse kissed her. Tomorrow she was going to make sure she talked to Kobie or maybe Shaelan about mates, as much as she liked being around Jesse, she didn't know what was or wasn't expected of her.

Chapter Thirty-Seven

Jesse watched the chopper fly over his head. The last few hours had been trying. They had gotten some information, finally after the jackal shifter realized he wasn't going to be free again, ever. Jesse didn't ask what happened to him after the Alliance was done with him, that was just something he didn't need to know.

Calum and Cale had to remove Blair from the equation right around the time the man had said they were fed information and knew how many women were here. He didn't know how they got the numbers or who told them, he was low on the totem pole and just followed orders. Orders were given by Lindon, Blair's brother. That information had put Blair over the top as far as tolerating him went.

To know your own estranged brother was that deep inside Tomas' organization was something Jesse didn't know how Blair was managing to cope with. He didn't blame him at all for wanting to find his sibling and end him.

Calum walked by him talking low on his phone, no doubt telling Devin everything that they'd learned. Hopefully, the Alliance would be able to get addresses and locations from him.

Jesse gnawed on his cheek and stared at the ground. The jackal, he smirked, they should have gotten his name—his clan was from an entirely different continent. What did that mean exactly? Had they moved to North America or were they brought here to help Tomas? That was a question they really needed the answer to.

His phone buzzing in his pocket brought him back out of his head. It was Shepard. He could count on one hand the number of times the king had called him and not the other way around.

"Sir."

"Jesse. I just spoke to Ed, and he gave me a quick rundown."

"It went better than we planned."

"I'm glad my son gave you the go-ahead, if we'd waited, he may have had time to come up with stories."

Jesse grinned, "I'm pretty sure having Blair and Calum staring him down inspired him to share what he knew."

"That would help, yes. I'm calling you because in the past you have come up with some very creative distractions and I need some input on how we can lead them away from Blair's clan."

Jesse tried to hide his shock but failed when he blew out a long breath, "problem with that is before we weren't aware someone was sharing information. How do we know who to trust if we do something as a decoy?"

"We have been working hard on a select group that we know we can trust. What would you suggest we do to plant false information?"

Jesse rubbed the back of his neck, trying to relieve some of the tension in it. "Well, uh," nothing like being put on the spot, "I'd go about sending the information down the line the way we always have and say they're changing locations. Something wasn't working out here, space or whatever. Then actually send transports and have them drive to wherever the new location would be."

"Have an assault team waiting there?"

"I'd probably send some of them in the transports. Moving nine females was scary as hell the first time and I think the only reason we didn't run into problems was that Cal and I changed the plan at the last minute and didn't communicate that to anyone."

"It's a good plan. How would we know if they continued to watch Blair's land?"

"I'm not sure. Our jackal friend admitted he was the one watching the land and had been on it several times. His counterparts were only here the one time they tried to poison one of the women and ended up getting Jake instead."

"Do we know why it was only him?"

"The others were called back, something more important was happening."

"More important than nine females? That's fairly significant."

"That's our take too, sir. We're wondering if the information that we have those addresses has leaked back to them."

"I don't know if Calum told you, but I've put a temporary hold on hitting any of those addresses until we ferret out who we can trust or get enough in place that once you go in the backup is there when you get out."

"How long of a delay?" He thought of telling Evanna they'd have to wait to see if any of her clan survived this long.

"We're keeping someone at the locations, to monitor any movement if that's your concern. If ours are moved, we'll know. I understand you want to find your mate's clan members, but we have to protect the whole of the clans with the Alliance." He made a low growling sound, "all of this started during my grandfather and father's time and has been left to run rampant all this time, like a festering wound. We need to nail it down, now and put a stop to it."

"I understand." He did, mostly, the idea that so many things had been mishandled had to be weighing on the king heavily. Like clans such as Shaelan's falling off the radar for so long.

Entire clans vanishing was also a heavyweight on the king's back. "Sir, before I forget, I was talking to the clan co-ord team and we'd like to add a few to our roster. It's hard for so few of us to cover so much ground." He closed his eyes to try and think through everything else he had in his head, "my first thoughts of who would be a good fit are Gia Marin and Calla Hart."

"That's understandable, we need more now than ever. Marin? That's an Alpha family?"

"Yes, she is, but she's good and I doubt any weapons training would be required."

Shepard chuckled, "bored female children in Alpha families always tend to excel in all things combat."

Jesse smirked; he'd never thought of it but it was true.

"I will leave that up to you and Cal, who you want to bring into the fold. Both of you know many more of ours on a personal level than I do."

"Okay, I'll talk it over with Cal."

"Cal's mate sent us a new list of things the co-ord team should have, so all of that has been updated and is ready for pickup."

Jesse nodded, "Zain sent us the list, it's a lot more than we had, but after this last trip, I'm understanding the need for it."

"We do try to look after you." He sounded distracted for a second, "The weapons training is going to continue there, we're moving it over to Ed's because it's any easier location to monitor, especially now with us acting as if we're moving Blair's clan."

"That's a good idea, sir." At least the king trusted him enough to make the split decision to follow Jesses suggestion to pretend to relocate the clan.

"It will take a few days to get that in play, to bring in the assault team members we know we can trust, so I'm going to ask you something of a more personal nature now, Jesse."

He stared at the ground, not sure what it could be.

"Rayne shared with Irene the challenges ahead with your mate, although I'm extremely impressed that she and her leopard caught the jackal, I'm concerned for both of you that we're just tossing you into everything when she may require something else."

"How do you mean?"

"I'm not going to claim to be an expert on it, because I'm only going on what Rayne and Irene have told me, they've been talking to specialists and researching, but I understand it's going to be a long road ahead in her treatment."

"It could possibly be the rest of our lives, sir."

"I know you will find a way to cope with it, Jesse, you've shown me your logic and patience on many occasions. Here's what I'm proposing, just understand this is a suggestion, not an order."

Jesse cleared his throat, still not sure where this was going. "Okay."

"While we get things sorted and set up, would you like a week off to go home and spend it with your mate, get to know one another better, and get her started on the right path to healing? I'm sorry if I keep saying she, Irene told me I should say them or they, but I'm old, son, I don't quite grasp all of this."

"She is fine. They are both females, so it applies."

"Well, I suppose that's a good thing then."

Jesse glared at the ground. He didn't even want to think of what it would be like if there was a male alter. He realized the king was waiting for him to answer. "I, uh, yeah going home for some peace for a week would be helpful. I'd like Leah and Evanna to have some quiet space to learn how to communicate and control their cat."

"That's understandable, although after her being able to sense and track that jackal, maybe let's not put too tight of a leash on her, we need trackers like that."

"Oh, that was Evanna controlling Mi—her cat today."

"That's good to know. Are you considering her being on the retrieval team?"

Jesse snorted, "I don't think my thoughts weigh in much, sir, she—both of them have said they're on it."

Shepard chuckled, "I understand that completely. Which reminds me in your travels if you spot any plots of land and good defensible locations jot down the details for me."

Jesse frowned, "for?"

"Oh, *my* mate has decided we need to buy Devin and Rayne a nice private getaway spot where they can go to be alone now that the campground is filling up."

"Oh," Jesse smirked, "I can keep my eyes open for sure. There's a lot of land between here and my place."

"Irene says we'll never have grandchildren if Rayne is too busy being a mother to the entire Alliance."

Jesse chuckled, "well I can't help with grandchildren, but I will keep an eye out for land."

"Thank you. One more thing before I let you go, both Devin and Calum have mentioned they have two more members to add to the retrieval team, apparently, they have skill sets that will be helpful. I'd like your feedback too."

Jesse was a bit surprised the king was asking his opinion when Cal had already spoken to him about it. "Who do they have in mind?"

"Uh, one second, let me find it." He could hear papers rustling. "Here it is, the other two members are Creed and Bear."

Jesse grinned, "yeah, those two would be helpful. Creed is a flyer, so that would be very helpful, and Bear's strength is insane."

"I never considered a flyer, that's brilliant. And this Bear, I'm guessing he's from one of our bear clans?"

Jesse's grin grew wider, "no, he's not. I guess his parents just had a really good sense of humor."

"Oh. All right then. So, you agree with Devin and Calum's choice?"

"I do sir."

"Very well, I'm going to send them to Blair's for training this next week while your home dealing with things that need to be dealt with. I trust you can do the weapons training with your mate while you're there?"

Jesse smirked, "I can." He had no intentions of her ever being right in the mix and needed it, but he could still prepare her.

"Thank you once again, Jesse. I'll let you get back to things now."

"Anytime, sir." The line went quiet.

Staring at his phone, he blinked a few times. That was not the call he'd expected at all. Sighing, he glanced in the direction of the trailer. If he hurried, he might be able to get in a quick run before he checked on Evanna. He didn't want to bother her. She would have 'homework' after talking to the doctor and he wanted her to focus on the information she sent her to read through.

After a quick trip into the house to grab a beer, he sat in the open doors of his van. He made so many calls from here, the van was like his office. The first thing to get out of the way, he opened the chat room with the co-ord team and typed out a message telling him about his choices for two new members. He smirked as he took a drink, he already knew the reactions he was going to get.

Yes. We need more females on this team. Was Deva's reply.

I like Gia, she's really good. Amari wrote. *I don't know Calla personally but have heard good things about her.* Followed by a thumbs-up symbol.

Jesse, I thought you like us. Foster wrote. *Gia beat my ass the last time we were in the same events.*

Jesse set the beer down and replied, *you were 12, Foster, I'm sure she's forgotten your reaction.*

Reaction?? Oh I HAVE to hear this story. Webb put in the chat.

No you don't. Foster used a pouting emoji. *I agree to choices though, Calla is both charming and scary.*

I can't recall either, but if everyone agrees, I'm in. Asher wrote.

Okay, Zain, I leave it to you to contact them, give them my number if they have doubts or questions. They should probably ride with someone for at least one trip to get the feel. Jesse waited for the gripes to post.

I have no problem taking either of them along. To his surprise Amari replied.

Someone to talk to on a drive sounds great to me. Foster put down.

Zain, you set them up for a training round, then with whichever one of us are closest to their locations. He stared at the blinking cursor. *I'm going to be at home for the next week, but will still be in touch.* He took a drink and waited.

You're getting downtime? Now? Foster wrote.

I've been given a week off so I can show my mate my place and get some time with her. He wrote. Other explanations would come later. He glanced over at the trailer. He'd like to see her sometime tonight, so more information could wait.

Woe. Did not see that coming. Congrats! Foster put.

That's excellent, Jesse. Deva added.

I'm sure she's a kickass woman, Jesse. Amari put in.

You're still with the team, right? Asher wondered.

Yes. Nothing has changed there or with the retrieval team. I'd just like some time with her while I'm not running all over the map.

We'll try not to screw up for a week. Foster put in.

Like that's going to happen. Webb added. *Congrats, Jesse. Hope to meet her soon…if I'm ever home again.*

I have to go. Zain will keep everyone updated on the new members and pick up your new packs ASAP all of it will make our running around easier. Bye.

He watched for a moment to see thumbs up or smiley faces but there were no more comments. Closing it, he picked up the beer again.

"One thing off the list." He mumbled then took a drink.

"Hard day at the office?"

He startled. Calum and Shaelan standing *right* there. "No, just a long to-do list." He waved the beer bottle around, "I had a call from Shepard and now I have a to-do list."

Calum smirked, "that tends to happen. I have one too from his son."

Jesse grinned, "Shepard is sending me home with Evanna for a week," he shrugged, "some downtime so she can connect with the doctor and her cat…"

"Good." Calum hugged Shaelan against his side, "you look like shit."

Jesse rolled his eyes. "How do you guys do it? Running all over and you haven't been together that long?"

Shaelan smiled up at her mate for a moment, "it's easy, he has to travel, and I never have, so I'm all for new locations and road trips." She gave Jesse an understanding look, "I think Leah and Evanna will be for that too once they come to terms with a few things."

Jesse toasted her with the bottle, "I hope so." He cleared his throat, "I'm sure Dev told you about the training?" Calum nodded, "okay, well there's a new plan," he made quote marks in the air, "happening that's not *really* happening if you get my drift."

"I do," Calum said no more than that.

"All right, I'll leave you to that while I'm gone. Oh, and big thumbs up on the two new additions to the retrieval team, they'll be here this week for the training."

Calum grinned, "that should shake things up a bit and give us an advantage."

"New team members?" Shaelan looked from me to her mate.

"Yes, Creed and Bear will be joining us on our ventures." Calum glanced to Jesse briefly, "Creed is a flyer, so we'll literally have eyes in the sky."

"Oh, that will be handy."

He nodded his head slowly.

"And Bear is a bear shifter?" Shaelan asked.

Jesse grinned, then shook his head, "no he's actually a lion and stronger than anyone I've ever met."

"He's a lion shifter and his name is Bear?" She looked from one to the other, "is that a nickname?"

Calum was trying hard not to laugh, "No, that's his given name."

"That's interesting. Poor man." Shaelan said with a puzzled look on her face.

"Anything else before we go for a run?" Calum looked impatient now.

"Ah, we're adding two new members to the co-ord team as well, because let's face it, with Tomas' ramping up his shit, we need more on the road."

Calum glanced at his phone and then tucked it into his pocket. "Who are you adding?"

"Calla Hart and Gia Marin." Jesse lifted his phone, "the team just gave them a thumbs up."

"Those are good choices, both can be diplomatic, but know what they're doing when things get real."

"I'm not guessing their clan," Shaelan smirked.

"Lioness and fox," Jesse told her then took another small sip.

"I'll have to read up on their health info." Shaelan mused.

"Oh good, we need you to read and research more." Calum beamed down at her.

"Shush you. What I know comes in handy, like when your friends get shot." She looked at Jesse.

He laughed, "anything to put your knowledge to good use." He looked over at the trailer again.

"If that's it, we're going to go now." Calum said, "better call your folks and get them to clean up your trailer."

Jesse's eyes locked on him, "shit." He could hear Calum's chuckle as he hit the dial button. His trailer was a complete disaster. How could he forget about that?

"Jesse?"

Of course, he'd called his mother and not his father. "Hi. I have a huge, *huge* favor to ask of you and the girls."

"Oh?" She sounded amused.

"I need you to go clean up my trailer." He drank the rest of his beer.

"Right now?" She chuckled, "it's a bit late to go there with a shovel and garbage can."

He rolled his eyes. "No, not *right* now, but in the morning."

"I'm going to guess you're coming home and bringing your mate with you."

He got up and tried to figure out if he could arrange it by morning. Seven hours of travel time including the boat trip, at least it was still boat season and not a plane. "Yes. I've been given a week off so we can go spend some quiet time there, while she adjusts to therapy and other things."

"Have you marked her?"

Jesse shook his head, "no, we're not there yet, it's more complicated…"

"I know, dear, I've been reading everything I can about that disorder, and so have your sisters and dad."

Jesse wasn't sure if he was relieved now or anxious. "Oh. Okay, then you know this is not a simple bring-the-girl-home-to-meet-your-family thing."

His mother laughed again, "nothing with you has ever been the simple, easy way."

He grinned, "so will you go clean the place up, maybe open a window, change the bedding?" He frowned, "make up that little pull out too for me, I'll crash on that."

"The fencing hasn't been finished, Jesse, it's barely started."

He rubbed his hand over his forehead, "we should be okay for a week, Thera won't wander too far from Leah."

"Which reminds me what do we call her? I mean how do we know…"

"You'll understand when you meet her, but a really good indicator is Leah wears her hair down and dresses, and Evanna pulls hers up and likes jeans," he paused when it hit him what she'd told him about her neck and how she immediately pulled her hair up, "but you'll know, you have twins, you of all people will notice everything." Probably more than him, he thought.

"That's encouraging. When are you headed back?"

"I'm hoping by the morning. I still have to call Ezra and see when he can have the boat to the pickup point." He had no idea how Thera was going to react to a boat ride or Leah. Evanna he was pretty sure would be up for something new.

"Ezra has taken some time off, he and his mate are on some island. Kolten is running it right now."

Jesse frowned, "do I call him or the office?"

"The office."

"Okay."

"I'll have one of the clan drop off your jeep at the docks."

Jesse wondered if Thera would ride in the jeep. "Can you see if Dad can get someone to give him a hand putting the hardtop on it?"

"So you don't lose the leopard?"

He nodded, a big grin on his face. "Yes."

"Okay, honey, we'll get everything ready for you. Do you need groceries taken to the trailer or..."

"Please. At least the basics. Uh, a few herbal teas as well as coffee and protein bars, the caramel ones and vanilla."

"Since when do you like those?"

"I don't, both Leah and Evanna think they're the best thing ever."

"I like them."

He looked over to see the lights were off in the trailer. Now, he was really looking forward to this next week. "Thanks, and Mom, don't share that I'm coming home with anyone but Dad and the girls, okay? I'll explain why when I see you."

"Oh, okay."

"We should be there by dinner, I hope."

"Okay, we won't arrive unannounced, you let us know when it's a good time." She sounded emotional he thought, "I don't want to upset your mate in any way."

"I'm sure you'll be fine Mom."

"Okay, talk to you tomorrow."

"Thanks, Mom. I love you."

"I love you too, Jesse." She hung up.

Jesse glanced at the phone and then looked up at the darkening sky, hopefully, Kolten answered, the last thing he needed was a delay and wasting two of the days off on transport.

Chapter Thirty-Eight

Jesse glanced in the mirror to see Thera still giving him that look. She had not been fond of the boat ride *at all*. Kolten had been a little more than nervous with her behavior the whole trip. Evanna on the other hand was almost hanging out of the boat and asked so many questions that some of them even made him pause to think of the answer.

He glanced over at her, the trip had been more motion than she was used to, so she was sleeping now. Which wasn't surprising, she'd gotten so excited with the gift his mom had left for her. Leave it up to his mother to think of something like a warm jacket. He was so used to the cooler temperatures at home, he hadn't thought of it. The fact that she'd gotten Evanna a black jacket and Leah a white one told him that his mother understood their needs more than he did.

Thera moved forward and bumped his shoulder.

"Ten minutes, girl, and then I promise I won't stick you in a boat or car for a few days." She huffed out a breath against his neck, telling him she still wasn't impressed with this trip. "You'll like the land," he said quietly, "hills, lots of trees, and more rabbits than I can figure out what to do with." He grinned, knowing Thera would have a purpose for them.

"Are we there?"

He glanced over to see Evanna was wide awake again. "Soon."

"This jacket is so warm I think it made me pass out."

Jesse grinned, "you didn't have to zip it up to your neck."

"I have never seen a coat like this before, it's so puffy, but not heavy. I might never take it off."

"It's getting colder up here; we may even see some snow while we're here." That made him think of boots. "We'll have to get some winter boots for you too."

"I like these boots." She tapped her feet on the floor mat.

"They won't be very warm in the winter."

Evanna laughed quietly, "I had the same pair for five years, anything is warmer than that. Leah was going to figure out how to line them with fur this year."

He couldn't argue with that. "Now you have access to stores and won't have to make anything with furs if you don't want to."

"I guess we do. I still want to see inside a grocery store," she looked over at him and grinned, "Kobie told me about them."

Jesse laughed, "I don't know if taking you into one is a good idea. So far, you've liked everything you've eaten—we may end up with more than we have room for."

Her expression sobered, "then we give it to others that need it."

He didn't know what to say to that. It shouldn't surprise him that she'd think of others, it was part of who she was. He could only nod. Looking out the window, he pointed to the left, "my property starts here. "

"Where that fence is?"

"Uh, yeah." It shocked him to see a fence was already up along the border of his land. His father had worked some kind of magic making it happen so fast. It wasn't along the roadside yet, but still, he had no idea they'd started it. "It's not fenced in completely yet, so we'll have to keep an eye on Thera for now." On cue, she shoved between him and the door. "Hold on." He grinned and put the window down a few inches so she could scent the area.

Evanna put the window down on her side too and inhaled slowly. "It's so clean here." She sounded happy with that.

"I chose this location because it's not near any big towns, no manufacturing or anything to pollute the air."

After the coats and fence, he didn't know what to expect when they reached the trailer. He pointed, "there's a river just over that hill, it's not too deep for most of the property, but it's great for a swim in the summer."

"Are there fish? I love fish."

"Yeah, there's some when it's not running fast."

She nodded her head but didn't look away from the scenery.

"I had my dad get a crew here to work on fencing, but I can't decide if we need a gate at the entrance or leave it open and put one closer to the house." He smirked when there is a house.

"Papa Low said seeing the gate from the house was best." She still didn't look at him as he turned and went up the lane.

"The house is framed in, foundation poured, but there are no interior walls yet."

Now she turned and looked at him, "I can help, Papa Virgil taught me how to build, we fixed up all the houses, even the roofing."

"Another pair of hands would be great." He'd had Calum and Foster help him out with the framework and trusses, but their lives didn't allow for a lot of free time at the same time to finish it. "I might hire someone to get the rest of the outer walls up, to seal it up for the winter."

Her seatbelt was off now, so she could lean forward and look around. "Do you get a lot of time here?"

"Not lately. There's too many out there that we need to find."

She nodded, a somber expression on her face. "I'm good with traveling," she glanced at Thera, "I don't know about Thera and Leah though."

"How is Leah after the trip?"

She paused for a moment, staring upward, "she's quiet, in no hurry to come out." She blinked, "new things scare her a lot."

"I hope she'll be comfortable here. There's no one around for miles and with the placement of the house, or trailer, for now, you can scent anyone coming from any direction."

"That's good. You're a smart man, Jesse." She looked back out the window.

He didn't say anything as they crested the hill, and the skeleton of the house became visible. Every time he saw it, he pictured what it was going to look like when it was finished, now though he was glad it wasn't finished because he'd like Evanna and Leah to have some input on how the inside was done.

"It's going to be big." She said quietly.

"The interior design is just roughly figured out right now, I haven't decided if I want more rooms or more of an open concept."

"Can I see the plans?"

He nodded, "yeah if you ignore the bad drawings, I have all over them."

She chuckled, "I can't draw at all, so I won't judge."

He pulled the jeep up to the side of the house and motioned to the trailer. "It's not fancy, but it's a bit bigger than the one at Blair's."

"It's warm and dry, that's all that matters." She was out the door before he could put it in park. Thera was right behind her.

By the time he got out she was standing where he planned to put a big deck and looking down over the property.

"Jesse, this place is beautiful."

He went over and stood beside her and looked down at it. "This view right here is why I picked this land." He motioned to the house, "I'm thinking big bay window so I can sit there and watch the sun go down."

She nodded and then turned and looked at the house. "It's even bigger now that I'm standing beside it." Her brow creased, "were you planning for a big family?"

He shrugged, "I don't know, I just wanted options." He motioned to the trailer, "I spend so much time in a vehicle or motel, I just wanted space to roam when I'm home."

She walked beside him, "I get that. I don't mind being in the vehicle but getting out is always good too."

"I'll get the bags in a minute." He unlocked the door and opened it, motioning for her to go in. he followed her and held his breath. When he went up the steps, he didn't even recognize the inside. "I asked my mom and sister to come to clean it up and air it out." He looked around, wondering where they put all the papers that had covered the table.

Evanna slipped her boots off and went in further. "Oh look." She went over to the table leaned down and inhaled the scent of the flowers that were sitting there in a vase. She titled her head, and picked up a piece of paper beside them, "welcome to the family." Straightening she turned and looked at her, "you told your family we're mates?"

He nodded, "yeah, considering I've never brought another female here, I thought some explanation was needed."

She smiled. "I'm glad." She shrugged, "that you don't bring other females here." She tapped her chest, "I get, I'm not sure, not good feelings when I think about it."

Jesse grinned, "that would be your cat being territorial. I get the same every time another male so much as glances in your direction.

"Really?" She bit her lip, "I thought it was just me."

He shook his head, "no it's not." Kicking off his boots, he went over and opened the fridge. It was fuller than he'd ever seen it. Evanna came over and looked around him in it.

"Your mother is a good shopper."

Jesse grinned, "yeah her and my sisters."

Evanna moved by him and slid the door to look in the bedroom area. "There's one bed."

Closing the fridge, he rubbed his hand over his jaw, "the uh, couch pulls out, I'll crash there."

"Shouldn't it be me that sleeps there? This is your place."

He leaned back against the counter and shook his head, "no, this is our place," he smirked, "well, temporary place until the house is done."

"This is home?" Her voice was quiet, almost as soft as Leah's was.

"It is." He cleared his throat, "I'm not going to rush you or—or Leah, with marking you," he grimaced, "even my cat knows that, so you have lots of time to adjust. And," he was nervous now, "don't think I brought you here for that because I didn't. I just wanted to uh," his cat was oddly silent inside him as he bumbled his way through this, "for us to get to know each other, for, uh, you to have somewhere quiet to adjust..."

She spun around and launched herself at him. Grabbing him around the waist, she rested her face against his chest. "I love it here. I didn't think I needed to know where home was going to be, but I was wrong, and I did."

Wrapping his arms around her, he held her and closed his eyes. He'd wanted to hold her since the moment he'd laid eyes on her and this was the first real embrace between them. "I should have thought of that sooner, rather than dragging you all over the place."

She shook her head but didn't release him, "no, no. It was great at Blair's, we were okay there, I just thought Leah was the one needing home and permanence, but now that I'm here, I feel like I can breathe." She loosened her grip enough to look up at him, "thank you. I don't know how to be a mate, Jesse, I don't-I just don't, but we're going to try."

Touching the side of her face, he looked down into those deep dark eyes and his chest felt like it might burst with so many emotions. "I don't know either. It's just been me all this time. Finding my mate never even crossed my mind, so I guess we're going to have to muddle through this as best as we can."

The intense look in her eyes started to fade. "I'm glad you came up our mountain." She frowned,

"What is it?"

Her look changed to confusion, "It's Minn, she's being all," she gave her head a slight shake, strange. I've never felt her be like this."

Jesse chuckled softly, "oh that." His own cat felt like he was rubbing against him as if somehow, he could get closer to her cat. "Mine is too, being all-loving and gentle right now."

"What is that?" Her eyes were wide when she looked back up at him.

He squeezed her in his arms gently, "it's because we're this close, they like being close."

She leaned back and looked down between them, "if I suddenly get hairier it's because it feels like she going to push right through my skin."

Tipping her chin, up, he studied her face for a moment, "I think I know what will settle them down."

"You do?"

"Yeah," he lowered his head slowly, "this." He brushed his lips over hers gently, not wanting to kiss her the way he'd been wanting for days now. When she leaned into him more, he kissed her again, taking his time to slowly taste her. His cat was still now, waiting. He couldn't stop the low rumble in his chest as he lightly put his hand against the back of her head, making sure to avoid touching anywhere near her neck, and deepened the kiss. When she hesitantly touched her tongue against his, he thought he might lose his mind if she pulled away now.

Her taste burst through him, making his cat shudder. So sweet, a taste that was uniquely hers. He knew her scent had hints of something close to citrus in it, but he never imagined that he'd taste that.

When she reached up and grasped the back of his head, he had to fight to control the kiss and not take it too far. His cat cautioned him that they didn't know what would upset her and what wouldn't.

Tearing his mouth away, he sucked in oxygen and then had no choice but to kiss her some more. She had a tight hold on his head and breathing seemed to be the last thing she wanted. Without warning, the kiss changed and now he sensed a sweeter taste on his tongue, hers was still there, but more was added to it. The pressure of her grasp changed but only for a moment and then she moaned quietly, and his cat forced him to pull away. It was too soon. They had to be careful with her.

Resting his forehead against hers, he listened to their combined breathing as it filled the silence in the small space. "Is Leah close?" He needed to understand.

"Mmm, for a moment yeah." She dropped her head to press her ear against his chest, "we were, what does the doctor call it?" She rubbed her cheek over his chest, "co-conscious I think that's it." Lifting her face away, she looked up at him with alluring lust-filled eyes, "you sensed her?"

He had to fight not to pick her up and carry her into the bedroom with the look she was giving him, "yes, well, tasted her for a second."

"We have a taste?"

He growled playfully, "a taste, your own unique scents, both are driving me mad right now."

She slowly smiled at him, "your taste is better than anything I've had in my mouth—ever."

Just the image that popped into his head with her words made him startle. He gripped her shoulders and pushed her back a few inches. "We need to get out of this little space and run or something."

"Minn is good with being with your cat, but I almost want to just stay here with you, like this."

Jesse nodded and moved her back a little further. "I want to stay here like this too, but right now the reason isn't right—it's called lust and my whole system is drugged with it now." He leaned down and kissed her mouth hard for a second, "and if I don't get out of here, I'm going to end up rushing you and I don't want to do that."

She licked her lips and looked up at him. "I don't understand what that means, Jesse." She rolled her eyes, "I do, sort of, I've watched movies with Aunt Tillie, but I don't know what—how..."

"Hey," he leaned down so she would look at him instead of his chest, "there's no rush, we can take the time, go slow." If it kills me, he thought, and it just might.

She nodded, not looking at all assured by what he said. "I don't want to disappoint you. I-we've never cared about that before, what someone else thought of us, but with you it's..."

"You're not going to disappoint me." He offered her a playful look, "in fact my cat and I are very happy you have no experience with that."

She took a ragged breath, "yeah?"

"Yes. Just knowing I'll be the only man you'll ever be with makes the animal side of me very happy." That wasn't entirely the truth, as a man, he would enjoy killing anyone that even looked at her with sexual intent in their eyes. "So, no rush, we can take all the time you need." He really wanted to pull her into his arms again, to feel her against him, but even his cat was issuing warnings of how bad that will be.

"All the time in the world," she smiled, "Aunt Tillie used to say that."

"Yes, all the time in the world." He made a pouting face, "just maybe not years or anything, okay? I won't survive that."

She laughed and it hit him right in the gut. The sound vibrated through him. "Okay, run, then we'll get the stuff brought in." He stepped back as far as the small space would let him. "I want to show you the property."

With a smile on her face, she took off her jacket and lay it down carefully, smoothing it out on the couch before straightening. In that small movement, he realized she'd never really had anything new in her life and he wanted to give her the world, Leah as well.

Stripping her shirt off over her head and tossed it on top of the jacket. Jesse's breath got caught in his throat as she stood there topless in front of him. He'd seen her naked before, but not while lust was fueling his system. Clearing his throat, he stepped around her, trying to keep his eyes from staring at where his mouth wanted to be. "I'll be outside."

She nodded and undid her jeans, "it feels like rain, so I'll just leave my clothes here." She looked him up and down as if to say, 'why aren't you taking yours off?'

With jerky movements, he undid his boots and took them off. Pulling his shirt over his head, he tossed it in the direction of the sink. His hands went to the button on his jeans and then he paused. She stood in front of him now completely naked. As his gaze moved down over her, he realized she was tanned everywhere, with no strap lines anywhere. At that moment he decided the gate was being built away from the yard, so no one could see her if she chose to wander around without clothes. He'd never get any work done, but he didn't care.

"Are you all right?"

Blinking, he looked back at her face. "Yeah, uh, fine, just thinking."

She smiled, "about a run I hope," she motioned down her body that he didn't need attention brought back to, "I'm ready."

His mouth dried out. "Yeah," he croaked. He couldn't take his jeans off in front of her. Not only was the shift going to be uncomfortable, but he didn't want to scare her or have to explain why he was so hard it hurt.

"I'm so happy, Jesse." She gave him a big grin and then moved fast into his arms. "I liked it at Blair's, but it felt awkward, you know?" She pressed her cheek against his chest. "Sometimes no clothes rubbing all over you feels right." She looked up at him and then frowned. "What's wrong?"

"Not a damn thing." His voice was gravelly, lust was riding him hard right now. "I have, uh, no problem if you want to walk around naked—while we're here, but please don't do that around others, I'd have to claw their eyes from their skull."

She nodded, "no, I get that. It bothered me when you had no shirt on around Kobie and Shaelan." She leaned back and smoothed her hand slowly over his chest.

He couldn't stop the low growl as she touched him. Grasping her wrist, he stopped her from moving. "Okay, we have to go for a run now."

She looked confused, "did I do something wrong?"

He shook his head quickly, "no. No you didn't. I'm just," he moved his tongue around in his mouth to create saliva so he could speak, "very turned on right now." Her expression told him she didn't understand, "very excited to be this close to you."

She looked relieved, "is that it? I feel so..."

He put his finger over her lips, "don't say it. I'm really struggling right now." He didn't need her to tell him she was turned on as well, he could scent that. Grasping her shoulders lightly, he pushed her a foot away from him. "I need to go outside and shift." It was going to be painful in some areas and that's why he usually avoided it, but he needed his cat right now, his cat that would put a stop to doing something stupid that could scare her. His cat would stop this drive to sink his teeth into her neck and mark her, right here, right now.

"Okay," her tone cut through him like a blade. She didn't understand.

Still holding her shoulders, he made a point of looking down at the bulge in his jeans and then back to her face. She was looking at the front of his jeans now, and he honestly couldn't decipher what the expression in her eyes was. "As I said, very excited."

"I've never," she licked her lips and he had to bite his to not moan, "the movies didn't show me that."

"I know, that's why I just need a moment to shift."

"Are you okay? Shifting like that?" She reached a hand out to touch the bulge and he jumped back before she could.

"I'll be fine, I'm just really turned on right now."

"So you want me? Now?"

He clamped his teeth down on his tongue so he wouldn't answer and say what his lust-hazy brain was thinking. He tasted blood but kept his mouth shut and nodded.

She blushed a small smile on her mouth, "okay. Do you want me to wait here or do you need help?" She reached her hand out again.

Jesse stumbled past her to the door. "I'll be fine, just give me five minutes."

"Okay. Give a roar when I can come out."

He didn't reply. He almost fell down the step getting out of there. Closing the door, he leaned his head against it and then swallowed down the blood in his mouth. Closing his eyes, he reached for his cat, he needed him right now. His cat was there, a little stunned right now. Jesse didn't lose control, ever, he'd also never been tempted like he was right now. Pushing away from the trailer, he walked stiff legged to the end of it. Thera was there, she lifted her head and scented the air in his direction. "Don't even start with me." He told her and undid his jeans. Having a mate was going to test his control to its absolute limit he realized. Peeling his jeans off, he took a few deep breaths, this was going to be painful. He grit his teeth and focused to let his cat come to the surface. "Help me out." He whispered to the animal inside, "we have to handle this the right way."

Chapter Thirty-Nine

"Kobie? It's Evanna."

"Is everything all right?"

Evanna looked out across the land. "Yeah, yeah, no I'm fine. Jesse is fine. Sorry if I panicked you. Jesse gave me your number."

"I'm just a little surprised to hear from you is all."

"I didn't—I wasn't sure who to call."

"It's fine, Evanna, really."

"Is it a good time to talk?" She bit her lip and tried to think how to say what she needed to.

"Yes, it's fine. The guys are out checking the property right now, so I have time before training starts."

"How's that going?" She didn't want to blurt out what was on her mind."

"It's interesting." Kobie laughed, "learning how to throw Blair around has been fun."

"I'd like to see that."

"Jesse told Calum he was going to show you some moves too while you're there."

She glanced back at the trailer where Jesse was mumbling over his laptop. "I'll have to ask him."

"Is everything, uh, going well between you and Jesse?"

She looked at the grass beneath her feet, "I think so. Leah hasn't been out much, so I'm getting to spend a lot of time with him."

"That's a good thing, right?"

Evanna nodded, "yeah. It's different being alone with him—here. Which is why I'm calling you; I have questions."

"Oh, okay, I'll try to help."

She scowled at the ground, "I, uh, things are..." she blew out an abrupt breath, "I don't know how to say this. I know nothing about," she squeezed her eyes shut, "intimacy with mates and stuff."

"Oh. Oh, okay. What would you like to know?" Kobie made a strange noise, "I mean, obviously it's not your cycle or you wouldn't sound so calm."

"My cycle?" Evanna opened her eyes, "oh, that. Aunt Tillie explained *that*. I haven't had that yet."

"That's a small blessing." She cleared her throat, "so obviously if you were on a mountain alone, you've never been with..."

Evanna shook her head. "No. Haven't done that either." She glanced behind her to make sure Jesse was still in the trailer, not that she thought he'd listen, but some things she didn't know how to talk about with him—or if she should.

"Okay, so what part are you wondering about?"

"Uh, the um, mating stuff." All of this sounded better in her head, but now that her mouth was saying it, none of it was coming outright. "How does all that work? I mean, I haven't talked to Leah about it yet, but I know she agrees, and we don't have a problem with Jesse as our mate," she snorted, "We never imagined we would have a mate, you know because we're," she shrugged, "different. Jesse is one of the good ones, right? I know I don't know a lot about people overall, but I do know how bad they can be, we've lived that—" she trailed off for a moment, and had to focus hard to bring her mind back to the task, "we're lucky it's Jesse, aren't we?"

"I haven't known him that long, Evanna, but yes I believe

he's one of the good ones. Blair and Calum are always referring to him in good ways."

She nodded, "yeah, I sense he's a good person, and he's patient," she scowled, "which is why I needed to call you, he said there's no rush, we can take all the time we need, but he's so patient, it could take *years*."

"I know he's concerned about you and Leah and doesn't want to force anything before you're ready."

"Did he tell you that?" She jammed her hand in the pocket of her jacket and looked at the sky. Snow wasn't far off.

"No, he didn't tell me, but he did speak to Shaelan, who brought me into the circle. "

Evanna nodded, "did Shaelan tell him it would be bad for us to, uh, make it official?"

"Not that I know of."

"Okay."

"Evanna, tell me what you want to know."

She shook her head; she was sounding like an idiot to this woman. "What-what is the," she waved her hand around in the air, "order or-or the protocol of how that works? Like I know the sex part, well, not *know*—know it, but I know it happens." She closed her eyes, *get it together*. "Aunt Tillie told me once things were different with it than they had been long ago and she was glad for it—I don't know what that means."

"Yes, sex is involved."

Evanna nodded her head slowly, "so is there some sort of ritual or something?"

"Not really, oh, actually the female has to consent and mark her mate first before he can." She made another strange noise, almost like a giggle but not, "they're not allowed to touch you until you have accepted and marked them."

Turning, she looked at the trailer. "I just bite him?" She frowned, "with these teeth or Minn's?"

"I didn't have to shift," Kobie said quietly, "but my teeth somehow did, so it's a cat's teeth I marked Blair with."

"They just come out? Just teeth?" She blew out a breath,

she couldn't stand anything near her neck, especially the back of it. Biting her lip, she stood there, trying to figure out if she was going to be okay with him marking her neck. Minn stirred inside her. Taking a deep breath, she focused on settling her heartbeat, so the cat would stay calm.

"Is there anything else you needed to know?" Kobie asked her quietly.

"I don't know. I don't think so." She tried to sense if Leah was close, a prompt in the right direction would have been good. She knew from the journal entries she felt the same about Jesse and Evanna did, of course, she'd never say it straight out.

"I'm always here if you have more questions, Evanna. For Leah as well."

Evanna nodded, still trying to sense Leah, "I'll leave a note and tell her that." Blinking, she blew out a breath. "It sounds so simple, but it's not really, is it?"

"It changes everything," Kobie said in a soft voice.

"Changes how?"

"It's hard to explain," there was a short pause, "it's like, even though I thought I was happy with who I was and how I am, once Blair and I were mated, I felt," Evanna heard her sigh, "complete. Stronger in so many ways, in my mind and heart." She heard a small laugh, "it sounds silly, but there is no way to really explain it."

"Do you," she bit her lip for a second, "do you think it will help Leah and me, you know about what's going on with us."

"Oh, um, I don't know that much about it." Kobie made a soft noise like she was thinking, "I've been around both of you and you're both strong in different ways." She made a clicking noise with her tongue, "if anything—in my opinion, it might make you both feel more stable, less, I'm not sure how to word this, Evanna, bear with me a moment."

Evanna kicked at the ground with, "I can wait."

"I haven't noticed it much with you, maybe the odd thing, but with Leah, she's so unsure and hesitant many times, I think the mates' bond will help keep her steady, feel more secure in things, does that make sense?"

"I get what you mean. This mates bond, it does that?"

"Yes, Blair and I are more in tune with each other, our feelings and emotions, I can almost sense what's going on with him now, whereas before I had to keep guessing." She laughed abruptly, "this is so hard to put into words."

"Feelings and stuff always are."

"Yes, they are." Evanna heard Kobie sigh, "have I helped at all? I'm not really the person to talk to about most of this."

Evanna smirked, "I thought of Shaelan at first, but she gets all doctorly sometimes and loses me with what she's saying. I relate to you better."

"Thank you. I can see us working well together when we go with the team."

"Yeah, our cats ran well together, so it's a good sign we could also work together without problems." Taking a deep breath, she let it out slowly. "Thanks for answering my questions, Kobie, I feel better." She huffed out a breath, "I have a lot to think about, but knowing more will help."

"I'm happy to help. With all of your doubts, you could talk to Jesse, I'm sure he'd try to help as much as he could."

Evanna grinned, "it's hard to talk about the problem with the one that is the problem, know what I mean?"

Kobie chuckled, "I do. Blair had a lot of those moments before we were mated."

"He's very distracting."

"They are until you're mated, I found out. I think a lot of my issues were my cat distracting me and not my own mind."

Minn stirred again like she wanted Evanna to go to the trailer. "Yes, this needing to be near him and his cat constantly is a bit much at times."

"It can be."

Evanna heard the trailer door before she saw Jesse come around the corner. "I'll let you get back to it, Kobie. Thanks for the help."

"Anytime, Evanna, I'll see you next week."

Chapter Forty

Jesse watched her for a few minutes, something was off. Evanna wasn't this quiet, this long. Leah could be quiet for long periods, but not Evanna. "What's wrong?"

She glanced at him, taking the time to really look at him. "Just thinking."

He gave her a half-smirk, "about?"

"Which one do you prefer?"

He looked at the diagram and then at the laptop screen with the paint colors on it. He shrugged, "I don't have a preference," he grinned, "as long as it's not pink."

Evanna's brows drew together, "not the color, although, I agree. No pink." She motioned to herself, "us."

Jesse opened his mouth and then closed it again to sort through his words. "Are you asking me if I have like you or Leah better?"

She nodded, a serious look on her face.

He squatted down so he could see her face. "Why would you even be thinking about something like that?"

She glanced at the table, but he knew she wasn't really looking at it. "I was gone yesterday, and you didn't say a word when you saw it was me."

"I didn't know if I should." He felt his muscles tense, a reaction from his cat's response to this. "It seemed rude to say, 'hey welcome back.'

"I guess."

Jesse had no idea how to word this, how to explain his view on this. "You're not really gone when Leah is fronting," She looked at him now, a confused look on her face. "I see you in things she does or expressions, I know you're close, I know you watch over her all the time."

She gave a slight shrug. "I need to."

"I know, I understand that."

"This is stupid. I'm being stupid, aren't I?" She sighed.

"I don't think so. This is new territory for all of us." He tilted his head to the side, "most men have to worry about keeping a mate happy, I have to do that with both of you."

"What do you mean keeping a mate happy?"

"Well, it's like that's the most important thing, that my cat and I look after you and ensure you're happy, safe," he lifted his hand and pointed to himself, "it's a constant need to the point of distraction."

She shrugged, "I'm happy." Her expression said otherwise.

He grinned, "yeah, the huge smile on your face tells me that."

She glared at him, "maybe not this second, but my head," she tapped it, "is a mess right now. I feel like I'm jealous of Leah, that-that she was out and spent time with you, and it's time I lost."

It felt like his heart was being squeezed to hear that much angst in her voice. "We went over garden plans, where to plant her sunflowers..."

She motioned to the journal, "I know." Evanna looked down at her hands, "she said she likes kissing you..."

Jesse tried not to smile, "that's a good thing, isn't it?"

"Sure, I guess."

His cat was one step from having a meltdown, demanding

Jesse fix this. He had no idea how to. Dropping to his knees, he reached and turned her in the seat, so she was completely facing him. "You both kiss differently. You both taste differently. I can tell when it's both of you there and not. I have no preference for one or the other." He moved his head to follow when she dropped her gaze from his, "it's like," he sighed, "it's like you're each a part of a whole, does that make sense? I'm constantly scared I'll do something wrong with both of you, something that will trigger you or upset you, something that will hurt you and affect your whole system." He shook his head, "I don't want just one of you, I want all of you, Minn included, there is no choosing or preference at all." She finally looked right at him; he couldn't tell what she was thinking at all. Her breathing was a little faster than he'd liked and now he was worried he was going to trigger her by upsetting her. "Hey," he touched her chin lightly, so she'd completely focus on him and not the internal discussion she was having. "When I kiss you," he huffed out a breath, "hell, sometimes when I just look at you I want to pick you up and carry you to the bed and lay you down and not stop kissing you, not control myself." He paused to see if she understood what he was saying. "Every second of every day all I can think about is marking you as mine and binding us together forever. But I can't, I won't take a chance of doing that and causing something to go wrong with you, or Leah or your cat." He shrugged, then shook his head, "and I don't know what to do about it."

Evanna sat there, her breathing heavy, her dark eyes locked on his for what felt like an eternity. He searched, trying to find what else he could say to help her through this moment, and couldn't find anything he thought would be helpful.

"I didn't know," she finally said quietly. "So," she licked her lips, "how do I fix this?" She jerked her head to the side, "I can't say all of this in the journal, I'm not good with writing stuff. It's not like I can sit Leah down and talk to her the next time I see her." She frowned, "I've never seen her." She snorted softly, "and Minn, she's like pacing in a circle inside us, all the time now, like she's annoyed with me." She frowned, "I'm surprised Leah didn't lose control of her when she was out."

Jesse nodded his head slowly, "my cat is doing the same." Her eyes widened in surprise. "It's because they know we're mates and to them, they don't see the problem." He smirked, "mine is trying to understand, but in his opinion, I've found my mate, just mark her and let's lock this in."

"Is that what it is?"

He nodded, "more than likely." His phone vibrated in his pocket, but he ignored it. "I have an idea of how you can see Leah."

She quirked one eyebrow at him like he'd lost his mind.

"Grab your phone."

Leaning back, she reached over and picked it up, then held it out to him.

Taking it, he turned it around and opened the camera. "You can take pictures or make a video for her and then her for you."

"It's a camera too?" She frowned, "I didn't want to mess anything up, so I didn't touch anything but that button you showed me."

He clicked a few pictures of her and then turned it around and showed her. "A camera, a phone, a notepad, it's my lifeline." He grinned.

Taking the phone, she looked at the picture. "I can just talk to my phone, and she'll see it?"

Getting up, he leaned over and opened the camera again and his video, "just tap this, talk and when you're done, hit it again." He stopped it and then replayed him telling her what to do.

"Jesse this is amazing." She looked up at him and then back to the phone and played it again. "I won't have to write in the journal anymore."

He chuckled, "I don't know about that, it's a good way to have a record of things, and I know Leah loves that journal."

"Uh, too much. She loves writing on and on." She nodded,

okay, "this could work, we could talk and see each other."

Leaning down, he kissed the top of her head. "Good, now you two can get on the same page, hopefully."

Turning, she looked up at him and then smiled at him and stretched up to kiss his mouth lightly. It was the first time either of them had initiated a real kiss and his cat felt like it was doing flips inside him.

"You record a message for her, and I'll make sure she sees." She nodded. "I have to go see who keeps buzzing my phone and deal with that."

"Okay." She nodded and looked at the phone again. "Just touch that and talk?" She pointed to it.

"Yep, that's it."

"Okay. I'm going to have a chat with Leah." She sounded so excited.

Jesse went outside and exhaled a deep breath as he stared down the hill. He was going to lose his freaking mind if they didn't figure it out. Leah constantly asked about Evanna, then Evanna felt left out when Leah fronted. Minn, at least he was on level ground with her. As far as he and his cat could tell she just wanted the mating to happen so Jesse's cat was with hers and he was marked and taken.

Blowing out a breath, he pulled out his phone and looked at it. Calum, Zain, and his mother had all sent messages. He looked at them, trying to decide which one first. Zain, he could handle right now. Jesse was in charge of the clan co-ord team, so he didn't have to do anything to avoid or appease him. He hit tapped the message to open it.

Two new team members are on board and riding shotgun with the Deva and Amari. They're going to go over self-defence and weapons, although apparently Gia will not require such a thing according to Amari.

Jesse smirked; he knew she was very proficient in that area. Having four older brothers was good for something.

Calla is pretty good as well, Deva is going to run her through it until she can do it in her sleep. P.S. is it bad for me to admit I'm a little scared of the four kickass women we have working with us?

Jesse laughed, then replied. *Keep me posted on their progress, we're going to need all the help we can get when it comes to visiting those sites.* He added a winking emoji, so Zain understood what he was talking about. *Also it's not bad, it means you have a brain to fear our kickass team members.* Hitting send, he opened Cal's message next.

Training is going good. New members of the team are quick studies. We'll be ready to go by middle of next week. I won't ask how it's going. Let me know when you're heading back.

He read it again while trying to decide if it required a reply. "Shit." He hit call and started walking down the hill, Thera came running after him to accompany him on his stress walk.

"The fact that you're calling me tells me how well it's going."

Jesse sneered to the amused tone in Calum's voice. "Yeah, it's going."

"I don't envy you."

"Thanks, that's helpful, Cal."

"If I could be helpful, I would offer. Shae wants to know how Leah and Evanna are."

"They're more relaxed here. I have been stalling my family though." He paused while Cal relayed to his mate. "Does she have any words of wisdom for me?"

He listened as they talked but couldn't make out much of it.

"She says it always best to talk to them, ask them, include them in your thought process."

Jesse stood there for a moment so he wouldn't say the first thing that came to mind, which likely wasn't complimentary to Cal's mates' advice. "Thanks." That was what he settled on saying out loud.

"Okay, she's gone to check on Niles and Jay."

"Everything okay?"

"Yes, it's just Shae being herself and wanting to heal the

world."

Jesse grinned, "you sound edgy."

"Impatient."

"New recruits on my team will be up to speed and ready to help when they finally let you go be you."

"Are you coming back for that?"

Jesse turned and looked back up at the trailer. "Yeah, we'll be there."

"Will you be mated by then? Because I know how distracting it is when you're close, but not and we're going to need to be on the top of our game for this."

He nodded, even though he had no idea. "We're figuring it out."

"I don't know what that means."

"Neither do I." he grinned. "Bear and Creed fitting in good?"

"Yeah, that male instructor is going to be dead soon though if he doesn't back off on the flirty looks."

"I'm pretty sure Devin would get upset if you killed Heath."

Calum chuckled, "it's not me that wants to, well, not just me. Gage caught him ogling Kelsey this morning."

"Oh shit."

"Yeah. The sooner we're done with him the better."

Jesse cleared his throat, "did they get any more information from our visitor?"

"I'm told they have, but Devin wants to share in person."

"When?"

"He's coming with us next week, as a co-ordinator, so to speak."

"And his princess?"

"Oh, if I know Rayne, she'll be there with him and have the right boots to wear."

Jesse grinned, "I'm sure she will at that. It's risky though, her being back there."

"He's aware, and not at all happy about it."

"So, what you're saying is he'll be the most distracted."

"Yeah, that covers it."

"Okay." Jesse glanced down at Thera who was watching the trailer. "I have to go. I still need to talk to Mom."

"They're going to have to meet your family at some point, might as well do it sooner than later."

"I know. I'm just feeling my way along on this."

"Shae's advice wasn't all bad."

"No, it was good, just not easy."

Calum laughed that deep annoying laugh of his that always warned Jesse that he was going to say something cliché and yet true.

"Aren't you the one that told me easy was boring?"

"I was talking about an obstacle course during training."

"It still applies."

Thera started back up the hill. "I suppose. I'll let you know when we're heading back."

"Okay, you can probably buy an extra day if you just come to the location we will be at."

"I might, keep me informed."

"Will do." The line went quiet.

Jesse looked at his phone and opened his mother's message.

Your sisters want to meet your mate, they have something for her.

Dammit, she had to use the girls. That was cheating. He adored those two troublemakers, and she knew it. *Stop around after breakfast tomorrow. Just try to get the girls to keep it calm and not crowd her please. Love you.*

Tucking the phone back in his pocket, he started walking. He still needed to go over the basic defense with Evanna. Leah had looked like she was going to pass out when he'd tried talking to her about it, so he had to make sure Evanna was good with it. If she wasn't then he didn't know how she was going to be able to come with him. Which was a huge problem because he didn't know if he could leave her behind. Easy is boring. He snorted; he could stand a little bit of boredom right about now.

Chapter Forty-One

Jesse watched Evanna pace back and forth beside the jeep. Getting up off the step he went over to her. "It's just my family..."

She spun around and glared at him, "*just* your family?" She blinked at him, "only the most important people in your life."

Jesse smirked, then forced it from his mouth, "it's okay, you don't have to worry about them."

"I do." She crossed her arms over her chest, "they *matter*. What they think of me matters."

She looked like she was going to vibrate right out of her skin. "I'm not," her brows furrowed, "I probably don't make a very good first impression, you know, I'm rough around the edges," she cringed, "Aunt Tillie used to tell me that."

"Hey," he grasped her shoulders gently, "listen the only thing they're going to care about is if I'm happy— if you're happy." He followed the movement of her head with his own until she looked at him again, "they're not going to care if you are proper or rough around the edges," he offered her a smile, "when you meet my sisters, you'll get it. Trust me."

"They should meet Leah first," She whispered, then chewed on her lip.

"They'll meet her another time, it's fine." Leaning down, he kissed her mouth softly, so she'd stop abusing her own lip. "In case you didn't know, this mating thing is forever, there will be plenty of opportunities for them to spend time with both of you," he kissed her again because his cat was prodding him to be closer, to calm their mate, "even Minn, they'll get time with her too." Even though she nodded, her expression told him that she didn't agree with him. He pulled her into his arms and hugged her gently. "If you can't do this, it's okay."

"I'm sorry. I really want to meet them." She looked up at him, "I do." Stretching up, she kissed him quickly and then pulled out of his arms. She rushed over to the door.

"Where are you going?"

"To change. I need to convince Leah to come out. I can't do this."

He stared at the closed door. Shaking his head, he looked over at Thera, "she can chase down an intruder, but not meet my family." He blew out a breath, hopefully, Leah was okay with this. He knew his parents would understand, but Evanna was going to be hard on herself over this, he knew it.

The sound of a vehicle had him turn to watch the SUV come up the hill. Thera was up on her feet, beside him now. "It's okay, girl, they're friends." He brushed his hand over the back of her neck. "My sisters are going to love you." That was the only part of his job that he didn't like, having to spend long periods of time away from them. He'd been an only child for thirteen years and wanted a sibling, then he got two at one time. There had been a few years he wasn't sure he was going to survive them, but now that they were older, he wouldn't change a thing.

As soon as the wheels stopped moving the back doors opened and out jumped the teenagers. They both raced to the front of the vehicle and then stopped, their eyes on Thera. "Can we pet her?" Jaide asked, an excited look on her face.

Jesse looked down at Thera who was scenting the air, "that's up to her." He walked toward them, so they wouldn't rush at the cat.

Joslin squealed and jumped at him when he was a foot away. He caught her when she lunged at him and hugged her. "I missed you."

He grinned and then leaned back and looked at her. "You are getting tall."

She gave him a pleased grin. "I'm a quarter of an inch taller than Jaide."

"Your shoes had thicker souls when we measured." Jaide nudged her out of the way and hugged Jesse. She looked up at him, "I like the shaggy hair."

Jesse laughed, "I haven't had time for a haircut and now that winter is coming, I might as well leave it."

She pulled away and looked at Thera, "she's so pretty."

As if the compliment was acceptable, Thera came over and bumped her head against Jesse's leg. "She won't object to you petting her."

Both girls dropped down onto their knees and rubbed their hands along her coat.

"She's so soft. Oh," she looked at her twin, "go get what we brought her."

Jesse glanced over at his mother, "you brought Thera something?"

Joslin rolled her eyes, "of course we did. She's going to *love* us."

He smirked. "I'm sure she will."

Jaide jumped out, leaving the door open, and held up a bag.

Jesse didn't need to ask what it was, the bloody raw meat was easy enough for him to smell, even through the plastic. He looked down to see Thera knew what the offering they'd brought was as well. "Be polite." He told her.

"Girls, offer it to her, then leave her be while she eats it." His father warned.

Jesse heard the trailer door open and turned to see Leah standing in the doorway. He smiled at her and went over. Holding out his hand, he grasped hers firmly when she placed it in his. He could tell by the look on her face, she was still, foggy as Evanna explained it, and not entirely sure what had brought her out. He leaned down and kissed her cheek. "Evanna was afraid she was too rough around the edges to meet my family."

With a startled expression in her eyes, she looked up at him. "That explains it. Her forcing me out is *not* normal."

He grinned, "she was freaking out." Putting his arm around her, he glanced at his folks. The girls were standing with them now, looking like perfect children. He smirked, knowing that was a lie. "Come on."

After another unsure look up at him, she nodded her head slightly.

He stopped so there were five feet between them, trying not to make her too uncomfortable. He motioned to his sister's, "this is Joslin and Jaide."

Leah gave them a hesitant smile. "It's nice to meet you." She looked from one to the other, "you really are almost identical."

"See," Joslin looked at Jaide, "I told you there were differences."

"Girls now is not the time for *that* discussion." His mother issued them a warned look and then smiled at Leah. "I'm Jesse's mom, Joanie," she held out her hand.

Jesse moved with Leah, staying close to her side, so she'd know he was there if she needed him. She took his mother's hand and shook it slightly.

"It's lovely to meet you, Mrs. Pruitt."

"Oh, please, Joan or Joanie is fine."

"Jasper," His dad didn't hold out his hand or move toward her. "We're glad you're here."

"Thank you. It's nice to meet you." She leaned into Jesse's arm and wrapped her hand around it.

Jesse could feel the tension in her grip.

"Oh, we brought you something." Joslin spun around and went back to the open door.

"It's not new," Jaide explained, "but we don't need it

anymore because the Alliance gave us new laptops for our schooling."

Joslin came rushing back and held out a tablet. "The case was all covered in stickers, so we took that off." She looked at Jesse, "you can get her a new case, right?"

Jesse nodded.

Leah took the tablet and looked at it. "Thank you." Her voice was barely a whisper.

He leaned down, "it's a tablet, like my laptop, only no keyboard."

"Oh." She looked at it again, "Oh, thank you."

"We loaded it with movies, so you have something to do when Jesse is mumbling over his laptop with work stuff." Joslin grinned at him.

Leah smiled shyly, "thank you."

Jesse gave them a look then grinned at his mother.

"You will," Leah cleared her throat softly, "you will have to show me how to work it? So, I can watch the movies." She looked from Jaide to Joslin.

"Yeah." Joslin nodded, "sure."

"We can sit over here and do it." Jaide went over toward the foundation of the house.

"Okay." Leah looked up at him, he could see she was working hard to stay calm. He gave her a slight nod.

With slow steps, she clutched the tablet against her jacket and went over to where the girls already were.

"She'll be fine." His mother said softly.

Jesse moved, so he could keep an eye on Leah and talk to his parents at the same time.

"She's lovely." His mother smiled at him.

"Evanna thought you should meet Leah first." He told her in a hushed voice.

"Is that normal? To switch like that?"

He blew out a breath, "I have no idea." Jesse motioned to Thera, "how do you feel about cat sitting?"

His father gave him an astonished look.

"Leah, well Evanna really, will be going with me on some

retrieval runs and I don't think Thera will blend in while we're in the city."

"I suppose, if the creature agrees, we could." His father said with a smirk.

"I'm going to talk to Leah about it and see what she thinks. If she won't stay with you, I'm not sure what we're going to do with her."

"When?"

He looked at his mother, "the next few days. We have several locations now to go into."

His mother covered her mouth for a moment, then nodded, "we'll get something set up for her. It will give your sisters something to do, they miss school and their friends."

Jesse nodded slowly, "it's going to be that way for a while, Mom, no school."

"What's going on?" His dad crossed his arms over his chest, no longer in father mode, but in sub-leader frame of mind. "We've been getting calls from different divisions in the Alliance all of a sudden."

Jesse watched Leah for a moment, leaving it up to his sisters to have her feeling comfortable and smiling. He continued to watch while he spoke. "Someone in the Alliance or close enough ties to get information is feeding it to Aiden Tomas." His mother's gasp had him look back to his parents.

"That explains Deshon telling me to watch out for anyone acting out of character." His dad ran his hand along his jaw. "Do they have any idea who?"

"How do you know this?" His mother's eyes were filled with worry.

"We," he smirked, "actually, Thera and Evanna caught one of Tomas' shifters on Blair's land. A jackal," he looked at his father, "the Alliance doesn't have any clans of the type," his father tilted his head, giving Jesse his undivided attention, "we got the information out of him." He decided not to give details to protect everyone.

"I'm assuming we're not to share this information with

anyone."

He nodded, glancing briefly back to Leah, "I'm sure Shepard will share when the time is right."

"That makes what you're doing more dangerous." His mom touched his arm.

Jesse put his hand over hers, "we're adjusting plans and protocol to compensate for that, Mom. We've got a good team put together too," he smirked, "Calum is on it."

"Oh," she grinned, "well, I guess having him watch your back, is the best we could hope for."

Grinning, Jesse watched his sisters for a moment. "Leah's entire clan was gone, most Tomas took." He turned to his dad, "if we find some of them, I'm going to bring them to you."

The amused look faded on both his parent's faces. His father nodded, "we've been building a dorm building, in preparation since the Alliance sent out notices that many of our kind were being rescued."

Jesse nodded, "that's good." He paused, "also probably how the traitor got the information as well." He rolled his shoulders, trying to keep the rising tension from setting in, "some of them that we get out will never have even known clan life," he motioned to Leah, "she got out and back to find only a few elders left in hers, so she doesn't understand much of how a clan works."

His mother leaned against his shoulder, "we'll help, in any way we can."

"Now I know why you look like you haven't slept in weeks." His father now stood on the other side of him, "that's a lot to deal with and finding your mate as well."

"It's been eventful." Jesse mused quietly. "Blair, you remember him?" His father nodded, "he went in to transport remaining members of a clan, *nine* females," his father's eyes went wide, "one was his mate, he's the new Alpha of a clan now."

"Jesus." His father blew out a breath, "and I was complaining about having to rearrange the common house for this online schooling." He smirked at him, "I think you young guys have it a bit worse."

Jesse laughed, "maybe." Leah looked over at him, her look assessing all was well, she offered him a small smile and then looked back to what Joslin was saying.

"Are you able to," his mom glanced over at the girls for a second, before giving him a concerned look, "are you able to proceed with a normal mating?"

Jesse tried not to smirk at her and failed, he nodded slowly, "it's a little more complicated, but from what I've been told it will actually help her and Evanna stabilize a bit."

"Oh, that's good." She didn't look relieved, "I've been reading a lot about it," she lifted one shoulder in a slight shrug, "I suppose it's good that it's only two of them."

Jesse nodded, "yeah, the biggest struggle has been getting control of their cat." He glanced to his father, "she came out when they were sixteen," he turned to look back to Leah, "when they escaped from Tomas."

"Oh my goodness." His mother's eyes glistened with tears. "She's so strong," she whispered.

"Yeah, she is, but doesn't think so." He cleared his throat, "I'm hoping to find her mother at one of the locations, and her sister." He thought of the information Noah had told him regarding Ashtyn, "there's a lot of children involved too."

"Well," his mother's tone was harder now, "any you bring to us will be looked after, you know that."

"I know." He smiled down at her.

"Hug your boy, Mother, we'll drag the girls out of here so they can have some quiet." His father gripped Jesse's shoulder and gave it a squeeze. "You keep in touch when you can."

"You know I will." His mom leaned into him and wrapped her arms around him.

"You be careful, Jesse."

Dropping a kiss on the top of her head, he hugged her back. "I always am."

"Girls." His dad stepped back over to stand in front of their SUV, "we have to get going. You have classes soon."

Reluctantly, they got up and came back toward them. Leah followed and went straight to Jesse to stand beside him.

His mom gave her one of those caring, motherly looks. "It was lovely to meet you." She smiled, "you get my number from Jesse and if you have any questions about anything, you call me."

Leah nodded, her face a little flushed, "thank you."

Jesse could feel the anxiety pouring off her and put his arm around her and hugged her against him. "We'll see you in a few days."

They stood together and watched them go down the hill. "That wasn't too bad." Jesse looked down at her, she was hugging the tablet still.

"Your sisters are so," she smiled up at him, "energetic."

Jesse laughed, "that's one way to put it." He jerked his chin toward the tablet, "do I want to know what movies they loaded up for you?"

"Oh, they said you wouldn't enjoy them at all." She smiled, "they're *chic flicks*." She enunciated carefully.

He snorted, "Oh great, that's just what I need playing in the background." Pulling out his phone, he checked the time. "We have time for a run before the doctor's session."

"Oh," she nodded, "I'd enjoy that." She smiled, "I've never felt Minn this calm and wouldn't mind running when I'm not scared she'll take over."

Jesse hugged her and turned to walk them to the trailer, "you guys are doing great, learning to work with her."

"It's different." She said quietly. "So much is different."

When she looked up at him, he couldn't tell what she was thinking. There was something there though, the way she was looking at him had changed, she wasn't as apprehensive as she'd been before. Whatever they were doing with the doctor and communicating back and forth must be helping. He could only hope that the changes continued in a positive way. His cat reminded him he'd said run and was more than ready to go for one. "We'll talk about everything after a run." He glanced at the sky, "I think we're going to see snow by tonight, so I just want to go over where they marked the areas for the fence."

She stepped into the trailer, "there's probably already snow on the mountain."

He paused and looked at the forlorn expression on her face. "When things have settled down, and we know it's safe, we'll go back there and visit." He grimaced, "after winter, I don't even want to think about the trek up that mountain in the snow."

She grinned, "it's quite a chore."

"I have no doubt." He dropped a quick kiss on her mouth and then backed away. "I'm going out to shift, come out when you're ready." He turned and left quickly, knowing if she started stripping in front of him it was going to try his restraint. He didn't know if she was as comfortable with her body as Evanna was, but after the last painful shift, he wasn't sticking around to find out.

Chapter Forty-Two

Leah set the phone down and looked out the window. Everything is changing. She smiled Evanna was right about that. It was such a strange feeling to see her and hear her. She'd only ever heard her inside her head, she sounded so different on the outside. In all the years since Evanna had been around, she'd never known her to be like she had on the video. She'd sounded hesitant, almost insecure.

"Are you all right?" Jesse stood at the open door.

"I'm just," she pointed to the phone, "that was different, seeing her talking to me."

Jesse didn't move to come inside, "we thought it would be an easier way for her to communicate because she's not big on writing."

Leah smirked, "no she's not. I could write an entire book and she prefers five-word entries. The amused feeling faded. "She's worried about," she wasn't sure how to word it, "things." Turning in the seat, she clasped her hands in her lap and looked down at them, "about things with her and I and," she glanced at him quickly, then looked away, "and how things will work with us."

Closing the door, he sat on the step, he filled the small space and didn't seem to notice. "It's going to take a lot of communication with the three of us to make this work." He paused, making her look back at him, "I want this to work. I don't want either of you to feel any less than you are, because to me you're both important."

She nodded, more to tell him she understood what he was saying, she didn't know if she agreed, she was so unsure of everything. "How do we make it work?"

He studied her for a moment, taking his time answering. "I don't know, that's what we need to figure out." Sitting back against the corner of the cupboards that were beside the door, he brought one knee up and leaned on it. "Next week we're going to Chicago, with the retrieval team and we can't go there if we're not in synch," he shook his head, "it will be too distracting. You or Evanna will be clear of anything happening, but I might be in the mix of it with Calum, Blair, and the others so I need to be able to..."

"Focus and not be distracted by us." She finished quickly. He nodded his head slowly, "what do we need to do?"

"Well, first," he paused and looked at her, "we all need to be completely truthful with each other, if we aren't it will never work."

"I agree with that, no good can come out of any of us lying or hiding the truth." She chewed on her lip lightly, "Evanna said the doctor said the only way us being mated, completely," she couldn't stop the flush of her cheeks as she said it, "is if we agree with the new arrangement."

"New arrangement?"

She nodded, "yes, Doctor Collins and I spoke about it too, before on the mountain," she looked out the window for a second, happy that this area felt like home too, "I did the cooking and gardening," she looked back to see his entire focus was on her, "Evanna controlled Minn to hunt," she exhaled slowly, doing the focused breathing the doctor had taught her, "if I felt threatened or- or scared, Evanna was out."

"Okay, we'll need to figure that out now that things have

changed."

She nodded, "yes. Like," she licked her lips, having trouble concentrating with his pale eyes watching her so closely, "when you are with," she took a deep breath, trying to talk about it without feeling frightened, "your team, obviously Evanna will be the one fronting because I-I can't."

"And that's fine, if you are uncomfortable in any way at any time, I understand."

His tone was so soft, so gentle, it calmed the jitters and allowed her to continue. "I'm not sure what my part will be now." She touched the skirt material, "I don't need to sew, we can buy what we need," she looked over at the small kitchen space, "there's not much to cooking here with so many things already done," she turned back to him, "I don't know my part or what I'm to do."

He stood up slowly, always his moves were careful, so he didn't startle her, and she appreciated that he knew to do that. Holding out his hand, he motioned to the small sofa, that she still couldn't believe hid a bed inside it.

"Come sit here with me." He waited until she stood up and then took her hand and sat down. Sitting beside him, she turned so she was facing him and smoothed the material over her legs. He took her hand again, his eyes searching her face, the look in them made her feel adored, something she couldn't say she'd ever felt before.

"We don't have to carve it in stone," he shifted so he was facing her completely, "who is to do what and when," he lifted one shoulder then dropped it, "there will be bumps along the way, I'm sure, but we'll work together and figure it out."

"All right." She felt better with his words but still couldn't picture how that would work.

"Evanna is worried too," he told her, a serious look on his face, "she doesn't know what her part will be either now that things are changing, and you both are able to control your cat better."

"It is a strange feeling," she touched her chest with the palm of her hand, "to feel Minn so calm and settled. I won't miss that tense feeling all the time."

He nodded his head slowly, "she'll still have her moments, all of our animals do, but you'll be able to sense things better and keep a handle on her," he smirked, mostly.

"And you have this with your cat too."

He smirked, "all the time. What I want isn't always what he wants, but we work it out."

"Your cat," she looked at his chest like she'd be able to see him, "is he okay with all of this?" She hesitated for a second, "with us?"

"He is." He slumped his shoulders for a second, "he's perfectly fine with you as our mate, that includes Evanna and Minn, he's good with it." Leaning closer, he brushed the hair back from her face, the way his fingertips barely touched her cheek sent a small shiver through her. "If he had his way we'd already be completely mated."

Her face heated at his words. "I don't entirely know how that works," her face went hot, "I-I mean, I know um, that we," she bit her lip, not sure how to say it.

Jesse grinned, "yes, there's that, but there's more."

"More how?" She licked her dry lips again, trying to settle her nerves.

"We mark each other, you've seen those on other couples, haven't you?"

She nodded, touching the side of her neck, and running her fingertips over to her shoulder, "yes, the marks, I've seen them. Are those so others will see and know?"

There was amusement in his eyes, "that's not the sole purpose, but more of an added bonus." He cleared his throat, "if you want the technical explanation, I'm sure Shaelan could explain it to you, but," he gave her a soft look, "when we mark our mate, it combines our scents and that never fades," he paused and watched her for a moment, "that is how others in our world know who is mated and who isn't." He cringed, "maybe *I* should ask Shaelan about the technicalities of it." He grinned, "that was a pretty sad explanation."

She smiled back at him, "no, it was uh, helpful." She blew out a quick breath, "I never knew it did that. There's a lot I don't understand about my own kind."

"That's not your fault, your grandparents did right, keeping you hidden up on that mountain, I don't know if Tomas' people would have gone looking for you, but you staying up there kept you off their radar."

"I didn't think of that."

"Your safety is all I think about."

Those seven words were probably the most important thing he ever could have said to her, it made her steadier, just knowing that.

Evanna's video came to mind, she didn't have answers to everything she'd asked her, not until right now. Her heartbeat started beating a little faster, but not in a bad way for once. She bit her lip and looked at him.

"What?" He titled his head and gave her one of those half-smiles of his. She couldn't help but look at his mouth.

"Nothing, I was just thinking about Evanna's video to me. I should leave her one too." She bit her lip, "I have no idea how to do that."

"I can show you," he pulled out his phone and glanced at it. "You can do that while I talk to the contractor, he'll be here soon."

"Contractor?"

He put his phone back in his pocket reached across the table and picked up the one he'd given Evanna. "Yeah, I'm having him close in the outer walls, get some doors and windows in, so when we come back it's sealed up from the weather and we can start putting some rooms in it."

"Oh," she grimaced, "I hope you mean Evanna when you say we, I am not proficient with a hammer at all."

He grinned, "that's fine, Evanna said she was not wielding a paintbrush, so I guess you're the decorator."

"Oh yes, I love painting, pictures, walls, anything."

Jesse smiled at her, "just as long as there are no pink shades, we're good with whatever you choose."

She couldn't hide how excited she was about that. "I can't wait." She glanced at the phone he held. "How do I do a video?" He leaned closer and held the phone out to her, so many emotions and thoughts were going through her mind right now and for the first time ever, she wasn't afraid of any of them.

Chapter Forty-Three

Leah frowned at her image on the phone, "I hope I'm doing this right." She glanced at the little counter at the bottom of the screen, "it says I'm recording." She blinked and smiled at herself, "I love writing, you know that, but this is exciting, isn't it? Seeing each other? You are so pretty, Evanna and nothing like I pictured you. I've heard you in my head for so long, but to hear you is," she frowned, "it's strange? Considering we share the same body and features? I don't know, but it's the truth." She looked at the counter again, "I don't know how long this can record, so if it ends, I will start another one, okay?"

Leaning back, she cleared her throat and glanced out the window, "Jesse is outside with a contractor about getting the walls up on the house." She looked back to the screen, "I'm so excited about the house," she sobered, "I'm actually relieved that this will be home, are you? It's so peaceful here," she shrugged, "the mountain was too, but that felt secluded and limited, with all the trees," she smiled, "here it's so open and free feeling. Does that make sense?"

Rolling her eyes, she blew out a breath. "I met his family, although I'm still shocked you forced me to come out to do it.

His sisters are so cute and energetic. Oh," she picked up the tablet and awkwardly moved it around until it was in the picture, "they gave us this tablet, it's like Jesse's laptop only without a keyboard." She set it back down, "Jesse will show you how to use it. There are so many movies on it. They did that for us." She nodded. "His parents seem nice." She couldn't show her the phone, because she was on it, "his mother had Jesse put her phone number in our phone and said to call if we had any questions, I don't know if I could, but it was very nice of her to offer."

She took a deep breath and blew it out, "I had another session with the doctor today, I," she watched her reflection blush, "spoke to her about your video to me and she says if we are both in agreement it will only help make us stronger, to have that," she dropped her head down and grinned, "connection." She whispered before looking back to the screen. "She said being shifters makes it much easier to stabilize than if we were one-forms—normal people." She wasn't sure if Evanna knew what a one-form was, but she'd just learned about it today.

Sucking in a quick breath, she pushed it out, so it made a whooshing sound, "I agree with what you were saying, Evanna, all of it." She sat there staring at her image on the phone, "I don't think I can front during it if you know what I mean." She blushed again, "I can't say it out loud, I'm sorry.

She nodded her head slowly, composing her thoughts, "Jesse is a wonderful man and I truly believe he will protect us from anything. He told me our safety is all he thinks about. I had to work hard and not cry when he said that, Evanna, it's so important and I don't know if he realizes it. *And* it helps you to have someone else keeping a watch over me, you know I can crumble without warning." She sniffled, to keep the tears she felt just under the surface on the inside. "The doctor has more things for us to do, to help with that, my crumbling and she said that it's normal and, in most times, good that we don't know all the memories." She nodded, "um, that it's not healthy for us to know everything, that they are locked from us for a reason. She also said that flashbacks, if memories are forced, can be dangerous and shut down the whole system." She paused, staring into the phone. "I think having Jesse close to us will make a world of difference, he won't let anything happen."

She sucked in another breath, then shook her head, "I can barely breath when I think about this retrieval," she sighed, "missions or whatever they're called, but I know you and Minn can do it. I just know you are strong enough to do what it takes to help those people be free." She offered a slight smile, "so do that, Evanna. Help free our people."

Looking out the window, she saw Thera bounding across the field, "I think Jesse's family is going to watch Thera while we're away with that team, I think she'll be happy there." She looked back at the phone and chuckled, "being among a whole clan of leopards, she's going to be in her glory having so many others to run with." Her hand was starting to shake slightly, "it's going to be strange not having her with me, but it's the best thing to keep her safe. She hates cities," Leah took a ragged breath, "I hate cities, but I know you will be able to do this."

She sat there for a moment, "okay I'm going to go now." She smiled, "I think the best thing that has ever happened to us was Jesse coming up our mountain and even though I'm half scared out of my skin, I can't wait to see what the next chapter is in our life."

She stared at the phone and then reached over and tapped the button. Blowing out a breath, she debated on watching what she'd just done. Setting the phone down quickly, she shook her head, "I'd probably erase it."

Getting up, she went over and moved the curtain so she could see Jesse. Sitting on the couch, she leaned on the back of it and watched him. He was a lot larger than the man he was talking to, but he didn't flaunt the fact. They were both looking at the house and pointing to it every few moments. As the man wrote something in the notebook he held, Jesse turned and looked right at her. She blushed, not sure how he knew she was watching him. He didn't look mad, so she continued to do it.

When he held up his hand to tell the man to wait, she leaned back away from the window as he walked quickly toward the trailer.

She stood up, eyes wide when he stepped inside. Was he upset with her?

He smiled at her, "Quick question, do we want the bay windows to wind outward," he motioned with his hand, "or slide across?"

She blinked; she knew nothing about windows. "It's your..."

He was up the step and in front of her before she could finish, "it's our house or will be if it's ever finished, you have a say in it." He brushed the hair back from her face with a gentle touch.

That movement distracted her briefly, "okay. Uh, I looked at the diagrams, but they're very technical," she looked out the window at the frame that stood there. "What is going to be on the outside of it?"

"Stonework, Evanna and I both liked the look of that." He moved to stand beside her, their arms touching.

"I think windows that wind out would look good." she glanced up at him.

"Yeah. Do you have a door color preference?" He smirked, "I didn't even know that was an option."

"Oh," she looked back outside, trying to picture the stone walls, a window, "maybe a wooden framed one, if the window frames are a light wood shade, then I think the door should match. It will look more natural, not like some of those white slat houses we passed in that town."

Jesse made a low sound of amusement. "Yeah, I'm not a fan of siding either. Okay," he leaned down and kissed her mouth softly, "stone and wood." Straightening he smiled down at her, "you are going to make this place look so much better than I ever would."

She smiled up at him, "it's going to be our castle, like in the encyclopedia books I've read, only it's a house."

"Our house," he whispered and kissed her again. Clearing his throat, he backed away, "I'll go tell him what we want."

"Is it really going to have walls when we come back?"

He nodded, "it will, then we can start on the inside." He shrugged, "stonework won't be done until spring, but if we work hard, we won't have to stay in the trailer much longer."

She looked around the trailer, "I'm okay in here," she smiled, "but a big house," she bit her lip, "I have so many ideas."

He winked at her, "write them down because there's no way I can relay it all to Evanna and not screw it up."

She nodded and watched him go out the door. "Our house." She mused quietly, "with gardens and flowerbeds." Sucking in a breath, she went over and picked up the booklet Jesse wrote his lists in, "the next chapter," she said out loud. Squeezing her eyes, shut, she reached to see if Evanna was close, "we have so much to do." She whispered and hoped that Evanna was close enough to hear her.

Chapter Forty-Four

Evanna set the phone down like it was burning her fingers and then stared at it. She looked out the window to see Jesse was still talking on his phone. Getting up she paced the length of the trailer; Leah was nothing like she'd imagined. Her voice was so soft and gentle, the opposite of her own.

Turning she looked at herself in the small mirror in the bathroom, then stepped in and leaned closer. It was ridiculous, they had one body to share, one face, but Leah looked completely different. Her mouth formed a small smile that she watched in the reflection. It wasn't surprising now that Jesse could take a glance and know who was out. She stared at her own dark eyes and thought maybe Leah's were somehow a lighter shade. Would the memories they carried be the reason there was such a difference? Taking a deep breath, she held her reflection hostage for a moment and then turned and went back out.

Spotting the journal, she went to it and opened it, just to check if Leah had added more after the video. There was no entry. What she'd said in her message was her decision. Flipping the book shut, she held it down with her hand and looked out at Jesse again. Leah wanted to be mated to him as much as she did.

A nervous wave went through her stomach. It was great that they agreed, but now there was just one thing she had to figure out. How did she go about it? Did she tell Jesse straight out that they wanted his mark?

Straightening from the table, she put her hand against the side of her neck and moved it slowly down to where the muscle from her shoulder started. This is where his mark would be placed. Her stomach clenched, could she stand him touching her neck? She didn't know.

Dropping her hand away, she closed her eyes. The last thing she needed was to botch that up by being triggered. Taking a deep breath, she blew it out and reached for Minn, she was going to have to work with her to do this. It startled her to realize the cat was there, just beneath the surface, so close that she wasn't sure how she didn't sense her before now. "You're going to have to help me," she whispered, knowing the animal could hear. Opening her eyes, she looked down at the phone. She honestly hadn't expected Leah to agree immediately. Rolling her eyes, she smirked well, she knew how she felt about Jesse because it was the same as her own feelings.

Biting her lip, she sat down and picked up the phone, the doctor had told her it would help them? The connection to their mate would help them? She didn't know how that worked. How would she? Until recently she hadn't even been able to connect with her own animal side without expending every ounce of energy she had. Setting the phone back down, she got up grabbed her jacket, and slipped her feet into her boots. Putting it on quickly, she went outside and closed the door.

Jesse was still on the phone, his expression was hard, making her wonder who he was talking to. When he looked over at her, he smiled, wiping the serious look off his face. She did that for him, she thought. The smile changed as he tilted his head and sent her a concerned look.

She realized then she was standing here scowling at the man. She smirked and gave her head a shake, hoping to convey it had nothing to do with him, why she was looking at him that way. *Get it together.*

He spoke into the phone again, and then hung it up and tucked it into his pocket. With long strides, he came toward her. "Is everything okay?"

She blew out a breath, trying to rid herself of the tension that had settled in her guts. "Yeah, just," she waved her hand in front of her face, "stuck in my head."

"The video from Leah?" He stopped right in front of her.

Evanna cursed at herself for having a face that was so easy to read. "It wasn't bad, just," she gave him a wide-eyed look, "it was weird seeing her and hearing her *outside* my head." She inhaled and could only smell him. She loved his scent. "She, um, was talking about some things she and Doctor Collins talked about."

"Oh? Anything I can help with?"

The look of genuine concern filled his pale eyes, making her stomach knot up more. "I don't," she looked at his mouth, which was a mistake, *distracting*, "I'm not sure yet."

His gaze flicked to her mouth, then back to her eyes, "okay, well let me know if I can do anything to help." He gave her an easy smile, "Feel like going for a walk? The guys are coming to work on the fence, and I want to tell them to work away from the lane for now, until we're not here." He glanced at Thera, "or Thera's not here."

"Yeah, sure." She shrugged; it would give her more time to work out how she was going to do this.

He smiled at her and then looked down at her feet. By the time it dawned on her that he was telling her to tie her boots, he had already knelt and was doing them up. Evanna swallowed the strange feeling in her throat. How was it something so simple felt so endearing? She had to focus hard to mask the expression on her face as he stood up. She knew she failed when he pulled her jacket together and zipped it halfway up. There was no amusement in his eyes though when he leaned down and kissed her mouth softly. She could only stand there like a stunned idiot by his caring gestures.

Jesse took her hand and gave it a tug, so she started walking. She didn't know if it was natural or if he adjusted his stride, but they were walking in sync with each other as they headed down the lane.

She looked around to avoid staring at him. "This land is gorgeous, Jesse."

He smiled down at her. "First time I looked at it, I knew this was home." He squeezed her hand gently, "I walked to the top of the hill where the trailer is and just knew I had to buy it." He chuckled, "I wasn't even looking for land then. I was just out driving and saw it."

"It's perfect." She said quietly.

With a quick glance her way, he nodded.

"Are the people doing the fence our kind?"

"Yeah, I think they all are." He paused to watch Thera startle some birds and send them scattering in all directions. "There's some one-forms that know about us and are okay with it."

She watched as he spoke, drawn to the easy manner he talked about things.

"Most of them are second or third generation, so it's normal for them."

"I don't think it is that way for all one-forms."

His gaze connected with hers for a moment. "No, but some of ours even marry outside out clans, even to one-forms."

"Really?" She wondered how that worked.

Jesse grinned, "Yeah, Devin's sister is one of those."

"The king's daughter married a normal person."

He chucked, "who's to say what's normal?" He looked down at her, "I think shifters are normal."

She thought about that for a moment. "I guess you're right. So, a one-form is less offensive to use."

He nodded. "I think so."

"I have a lot to learn."

Tugging her hand, he pulled her closer. Lifting their clasped hands, he kissed the back of hers. "You don't have to do it all at once, there's a lot of time."

Who would have thought having her hand kissed would make her insides turn to mush? She cleared her throat, "just don't let me do anything stupid around others."

"Promise." He winked at her.

Her cat was working hard to convey something inside her and she couldn't figure out what. Glaring at the ground in front of them for a few steps, she mentally conveyed to the animal to back it down a bit, so she didn't have to concentrate so hard just to talk. "I guess necks are an important feature to our kind." She blurted out, then stared straight ahead, trying to figure out how she'd wanted to say it. She was afraid to see what his expression was after that.

"I've never thought of it that way," he said after what felt like an eternity. "But, yeah, they are very important."

"That figures," she snorted, "that I'm broken when it comes to my neck." She was messing this up so bad, that there was probably no way to save it.

Jesse stopped and stepped in front of her. "You are *not* broken. Everyone, shifter or not has some part of them they don't like touched." He moved his head in any direction she tried to look, so there was no way to avoid eye contact.

"Everyone?" She asked, there was no hiding the doubt in her tone, it was drenched with it.

"Yeah," his expression lightened, "everyone." With a simple shrug, he nodded, "I don't like—"

Her cat snarled inside her. "Wait." She put her hand over his mouth. "Don't say it if it has to do with your being with a woman." She frowned, "My cat just got all rage-y inside me."

Taking her hand away, he kissed it then grinned, "relax, tell her to take it down a notch. I was going to say I hate my sides being touched because I'm so ticklish." He gave her a wide-eyed stare, "my uncle used to tickle me to the point I couldn't breathe when I was little."

"Oh." She nodded her head slowly. "I'll try to remember that."

"A normal touch is okay, but no poking or you know, lingering touches."

She frowned, "I don't know what a lingering touch is exactly."

His gaze held her prisoner with an intense look. "Like this," he tilted her chin up with one hand, and slowly, barely touching her, he ran his fingertips from her jaw down her throat. "It took a long time before I could handle a normal touch on my sides, without tensing and freaking out." His voice was soothing, almost hypnotic, "but," he leaned down and pressed his lips against her jaw, "with practice," he kissed her again, just below her jaw, "anything," his mouth touched the pulse in her neck, "can be overcome." He kissed the side of her neck, and a shiver of awareness went through her whole body. There was no panic, only pleasure.

"Don't stop." She said so softly she wasn't sure if she'd said it out loud.

A low rumble came from him as he pulled her closer and kissed her neck again. When he licked over it, her cat went completely still inside her.

"Jesse," she gasped and what she wanted to say was forgotten when he crushed her mouth with his. She no longer cared what she thought she'd needed to say. Wrapping her arms around his neck, she grasped his hair, holding him so he couldn't pull away from her. *This*, her cat and mind echoed. *Just this*, was all she wanted. His mouth commanding hers. His taste flooded every pore of her body. His scent consumed her until she didn't know where she ended, and he started. *Just this. Just him.*

Jesse tore his mouth from hers, his darkened eyes held hers in a look that set her insides ablaze. "I should stop." He blew out a ragged breath.

Her tongue touched her sharper teeth that now filled her mouth. Her cat's not too subtle a hint of their objective today. "What if I don't want you to?" She whispered, stretching up so her lips brushed his as she spoke.

He lifted his head and searched her eyes. "What about..."

"She agrees." She said quickly. Evanna didn't know if he was going to say Leah or their cat or what exactly, she just knew that she needed him in a way she never thought possible, ever.

A low growl came from him as he boosted her up against his body. She wrapped her legs tight around him and clung to him. When he turned and started walking back up the lane, his mouth moved back to hers, devouring her slowly.

Before her mind was completely filled with him, it dawned on her how strong he was as he moved quickly toward the trailer—and yet he'd never shown her anything but tenderness. A low sound, almost a growl came from her throat, and she knew her cat was right there with her, guiding her along. She wanted her mate claimed and marked. Today.

Her back hit the trailer as he pinned her against it and opened the door. There was no way they'd fit through it like this, so he picked her up away from him and set her on the step.

She stumbled backward; his hands clamped on her hips guiding her. When she reached the top step, she unzipped the jacket and tossed it in the direction of the couch.

Jesse's followed hers. Dropping to his knee, he undid her boots and pulled them from her feet. She heard them clunk down the steps as he straightened and stood in front of her.

His cool hands ran up under her shirt over her ribs as his breath brushed over her mouth.

She felt her nipples tense and wanted the material gone from her body. With a jerky movement, she tore the shirt over her head. Before she could get her arms freed, his mouth closed over her breast, and she thought her knees were going to give out.

Shaking the shirt off her arm, she gripped his head and held it so he'd keep doing that. She felt him undo the button of her jeans and released his head to undo them and shove them down her hips.

Jesse switched to her other breast, she sucked in a breath from the intense feeling his mouth created. With a frantic movement, she jerked on his shirt, trying to pull it up his body, she wanted to touch him, to feel his skin.

He lifted his head and got rid of his shirt in a fast move. His eyes never left hers as he pulled her jeans down far enough that she could step out of them. When he stood up again, she ran her hands down his chest and felt the muscles clench beneath her fingers.

Leaning forward, she touched his skin with her tongue. His skin was hot, his flavor caused heat to rush between her legs. Jesse stood there, massaging her hips in his grip, allowing her to do what she wanted. She had no idea if it would affect him the same way, but she had to try it. Moving her lips over his skin, she placed her mouth over his nipple and sucked on it. His grip tightened and a deep rumble went through his chest. Spurred on by his reaction, she did it with the other one as she moved to undo his jeans.

Chapter Forty-Five

Jesse's hands stopped the movement. "In a minute." He whispered against her ear.

She looked up at him, his eyes were dark and heavy, the same way her own felt. She licked her lips, wanting his mouth on hers again. As if he'd read her mind, he kissed her. It was fast, frantic, his tongue stroking hers. She moaned, it felt so good.

He tore his mouth from hers and started backing her down the hallway.

She grabbed his jeans again, wanting to see him.

He grasped both her hands in one of his. "Not yet. I'm not a little man, babe, I need to get you ready." He stopped by the bathroom and turned her so she could see them in the mirror. He wrapped his hand around her waist and pulled her back against him. He watched her reflection. "Have you ever touched yourself? Made yourself feel good?"

She shook her head, watching his reaction as she did.

He made a low noise, that vibrated against her ear. She sucked in a breath as his hands ran over her breasts and cupped them. Releasing one, he covered her hand with his and slid it down her body. Nudging her legs apart with his knee, she let him guide her hand between her legs.

A low moan came from her throat as he moved her hand through the wetness. "Our bedroom," he whispered against her neck, "is going to have a full-length mirror, so I can see all of you."

She swallowed, trying to find the words to speak, and couldn't. Between his hand on her breast and the way he was moving hers, she couldn't think, couldn't focus.

His breathing was as rough as hers, pulling her hand up, he leaned around her and sucked on her fingers. He growled low and turned her, so her back was facing the mirror now. Dropping to his knees, he lifted her one leg and put her knee over his shoulder.

She gasped when he ran his tongue over where her fingers had been. She couldn't see, or hear anything, she was only aware of him and what he was doing to her. She was gasping and trying to hold herself up.

Without warning, he sucked on her hard and she cried out as her whole body erupted into waves of pleasure. She felt like she was floating up and falling at the same time.

Jesse stood up and held her against him, his hand still rubbing against her as his mouth swallowed her screams of pleasure. His kiss gentled as she felt like she was floating in his arms now. She could taste herself on his lips and found it an odd thing that she didn't mind at all.

"Catch your breath, we're not done." He said against her mouth. Picking her up, he turned to get them out of the small space and down the hall.

He lay her on the bed and then leaned down and licked one nipple. Ripples of pleasure shivered through her. He did the other one and more delight filled her, she sucked in a sharp breath.

"So fucking responsive." He rubbed his hand over the front of his jeans. "It's killing me."

As her mind cleared, it came back to her what her intentions had been. Still not able to breathe normally, she got to her knees and rubbed her palm over the bulge in his jeans.

Jesse hissed out a breath but didn't stop her. When her fingers fumbled, trying to undo the button, he made faster work of removing them.

Her breath caught in her throat as he revealed all of his body. She glanced up at him to see he was watching her carefully as if he was waiting for her to reject him. Lowering her gaze again, she ran her hand across his waist and then took him in her hand. He sucked in a breath. She felt like she had power over him and that pleased her more than she thought possible. She squeezed lightly and ran her hand down the length of him.

Jesse growled deep in his throat then put his hand over her, "not a good idea this time." He moved and then dropped down on the bed, taking her with him. "I want you too much right now and I don't want to hurt you." He brushed his lips over hers.

His kiss was slow as if he were tasting her and she felt her whole body respond. She wanted to devour him. At that thought, she became aware of her cat again, and there was no mistaking the message she was conveying. *Ours. Claim him.*

Pulling back from him, she put her hand on his shoulder to stop him from leaning in to kiss her again. His kisses made her forget things and she needed to focus right now. She needed to get this right.

"Jesse," she waited until his sexy eyes connected with hers, "I," no that wouldn't work, "we accept you." A surprised look appeared on his face, "we claim you as our mate."

He held her look for a few seconds and then leaned back until he was lying flat on the bed. When he moved his head to the side, baring his neck to her, she knew she'd said it right and he understood. He dropped his hands away from his body and lay there.

She had no idea what she was doing. She touched her teeth with her tongue, they were just regular teeth. *Now* her cat left her alone?

"Don't be nervous, babe, you don't even have to think about this, your cat knows what to do." He tilted his jaw, so he could look at her, "I'm not supposed to touch you, but if you were to hold my hand, I don't think that counts." He held up his hand.

Exactly that. She thought, is why he's our mate, why I want him so much. He just knew what she needed, what they needed, every time.

Taking his hand, she moved over, so she was leaning across him. Their eyes connected again.

"I love everything about you," he whispered, "all of you."

When he turned his head again giving her free access to his throat, her cat was there. Her mouth filled with sharp enough teeth to puncture his skin. Leaning down, she licked over his skin, not even second-guessing where she should mark. "You're ours, Jesse Pruitt." She hissed out in a vaguely human voice, then bit into him.

Her whole body was on fire again as she lifted her head and licked over the bloodied mark in his skin.

Jesse growled and flipped her to lay on her side, pulling her back into his hard body. "Vanna," he whispered close to her ear, "don't fight me, my cat," he nipped her jaw, "is too close."

She understood what he was saying and pressed back against him.

He leaned over and touched her jaw, so she'd turn her head. His mouth clashed with hers with such a force, that she tasted blood. She didn't know or care if it was her own or his. His hand moved down her hip and then lifted her leg, so he could place his between them. "I don't want to hurt you." He gasped against her mouth.

She could feel him shaking as he tried to control his movements. "Tell me," She hissed out a breath when he stroked between her legs, "what to do, Jesse."

He growled in response, then turned her to lay on her stomach.

Before she could figure out why that position, he reached under her hips and pulled her to her knees. He leaned over her, forcing her to bend closer to the mattress.

She felt him push into her, stretch her, and fill her and she thought she might die when he stopped. Her cat wanted this.

"Is that okay?" He was breathless.

"Don't stop," she managed to say.

He moved a little more then stopped, "my cat." He growled.

She didn't understand about sex or anything except her mate was distressed, and she needed something more. Before she could puzzle it out, her animal guided her movement to push back against him. There was a brief stabbing feeling, and then she realized how good it felt.

Jesse nipped her shoulder and started moving in and out of her. His hand moved down between her legs and held her still from there so he could move faster.

Her legs were shaking, her whole body was heating up fast. He grasped her hair and held her head exposing her neck. She expected the panic when his hot breath was against her neck, but her cat took over and made her submit to what he wanted.

Evanna thought she was going to explode when his teeth pierced her flesh. She cried out, her body convulsing and clamping around him sending waves of pleasure through her.

He didn't release his bite on her neck until she was moaning and unable to move.

Lifting his head, he licked over his mark and then thrust harder into her. She could hear their bodies slapping together and thought she'd never felt this good in her life.

With a sudden move, he pushed her legs further apart with his own and reached to rub between them. Her whole body clenched as he did that, she tried to move her head so she could look, but he stopped her and pushed it to the other side.

"Mine." He said against her ear then his teeth sunk into the other side of her neck.

She heard herself scream as the convulsing hit her again. She thought she might not survive it. Jesse stiffened over her, then released her neck and groaned against the back of it.

She wasn't sure how much time passed as she lay there trying to remember how to breathe.

His weight was crushing her, but she couldn't have cared less.

He moved her one leg, then the other, and rolled them onto their sides while he was still inside her. Her whole body was numb but throbbing at the same time.

"Did I hurt you?" He said between panting and trying to breathe.

She shook her head, "No." Was the only talking she could manage.

"My cat took over."

She smirked, "mine too." She felt his deep chuckle against her back.

"The two marks," he said quietly, "there's a reason for them."

"So that men know regardless of what side they see?"

He laughed, "no, but that works too." She felt his breath against the back of her neck, "so if I touch your neck, this happens." He licked over the one mark, and she clenched around him.

She gasped.

He did it again. "Instead of an awful memory, you'll want me inside you instead." He licked over it a third time and her inner muscles gripped him tight. She felt him harden again and was both shocked and excited. She had a lot to learn about this.

He pulled out and flipped her onto her back. With a playful grin, he pushed between her legs and nudged them apart. "Now that you're ready for me, I won't hurt you."

She moaned as he entered her again. Sure, she might not survive more, but she didn't care at all.

Chapter Forty-Six

Jesse pulled away from the docks. Evanna had been quiet since they'd dropped off Thera. "She'll be fine, the center of attention."

She nodded, "I think she will be."

He reached over and took her hand. "You did good, meeting everyone."

"I knew Leah couldn't walk away from Thera, she said as much in a video to me."

Jesse focused on the road, there were too many animals in this area. "I didn't even know she made you one."

"You were outside on the phone apologizing to the fence guys for Thera scaring them."

He cleared his throat, "that's your fault. I forgot all about them until he called last night." He glanced over quickly to see her blush. "Leah was okay in the video?"

Evanna snorted, "she was giddy. I didn't know she knew how to be giddy."

Jesse cleared his throat to avoid saying something male and in turn, stupid. "That's good, that she was happy. I was worried after the conversation about Thera."

"Yeah."

Her tone concerned him. "Are you happy with everything?" He lifted their hands and kissed hers.

"I am, I just," she shifted in the seat and looked at him.

Jesse didn't want to ignore her or hit any animals, so he slowed the van and pulled over. Putting it into park, he undid his seat belt and shifted so he was looking at her. "What is it?"

"My stupid brain." She said with a smirk.

"Okay, what's on your mind?" He watched the internal battle flash through her eyes.

"I'm not jealous." She blurted out quickly. "I just," she heaved a sigh, "are we different?"

Jesse knew his eyes widened for a second. He opened his mouth to answer and then closed it and nodded. It felt like a trap, that regardless of what he said it was going to be wrong.

"Okay." She nodded.

He thought for a second that was it, problem resolved, then her brows drew together.

"Are you," she locked eyes with him, "are you happier with one more than the other?"

"No." He answered before he remembered no words were better. "After you yesterday, and this morning and Leah last night, I'm so fucking *happy* I'm surprised I can walk." He cursed in his head, "you're so damn distracting, we almost missed the boat and were late dropping off Thera."

She blushed.

"Look," he grasped both her hands, "you're both different—I adore both of you, equally, but I can not, will *not* compare you to each other in any way—*ever*. I don't think of you as two different women. You're both parts of one woman. My mate. Understand?"

She looked at him for a moment, emotions going through her eyes, then she bit her lip and nodded.

"Damn, don't do that." He leaned over and kissed her mouth. "Every time you abuse that lip, I feel like I have to kiss it better."

She smiled, a real one, that he could see in her eyes.

He groaned, "we must go. I want to be out of the woods,"

he motioned out the window, "literally, before it gets too dark."

"Thank you." She said with another smile. "For understanding, this is all so new."

He turned and put his seatbelt back on. "I hope it never feels old between us. Now," he glanced at her, "try not to look so fucking sexy and don't give me those sweet looks, or else I'm going to end up driving off the road."

She laughed, "I will just sit here."

Jesse gave his head a shake, "that will probably still distract me."

He put the van back into drive and pulled out onto the narrow road.

"How long are we driving through this? I don't remember it on the other trip."

"That's because we didn't take it this way. I'm trying not to be predictable." He slowed down for another sharp turn, "forty-five minutes and we should be out of this area."

"Can I help? Watch for animals or something?"

"That would be good." He heard her roll down the window and knew she wasn't only going to look, but to use her sense of smell as well. "Have I told you how much I love your scent, now that it's blended with mine?"

"Not since we got off the boat." She said and he could tell she was smiling. "You smell pretty great too, now that you're mine." She told him quietly. "Now, stop distracting me so I can help you."

"Yes, 'mam." He grinned and gave the road his full attention.

Jesse glanced over after he turned the corner. Evanna was sleeping soundly. It was no wonder, he thought, switching as much as they had in the past few days was exhausting, not to mention him keeping her occupied all day yesterday. His cat rolled against him inside, as if to say, 'focus on what you're doing and not on our gorgeous mate.' He glanced in the mirror and saw lights coming around the corner.

This route wasn't used much because it wasn't paved. He tried to recall if there were any homes nearby. There were none he could think of. Leaning forward he tapped the GPS and then again so it would light up and he could see the screen.

His gut was suddenly tense, and he never ignored that feeling. "Shit." There was only one road he could turn off on. He checked the mirror again; the car wasn't moving any closer. He still didn't like it.

"Evanna, wake up."

She stirred in the seat, "are we there?"

"Not yet. I need you to wake up."

She inhaled a sharp breath. "What's wrong?"

"There's a car following us." He leaned forward again and slid the map screen over so he could see what his options were. The one turn split into four corners a mile after it. He knew the one direction was a dead end and there were no homes on it because he'd run it with Foster on one of their long drives.

"Undo your seatbelt. Under my seat is a case with a handgun in it. Get it, load the clip, and put the other one in your pocket."

She moved to do what he said without comment.

Jesse turned the corner without signaling or warning the car behind them. He'd told Devin they needed to get rid of the white vans and switch up the colors. Driving these were like huge beacons. The car followed him around the corner. He glanced at Evanna to see her zipping the spare clip into her pocket. "Safety on?"

She checked, "yes."

There was no panic or fear in her voice. He reached over and grabbed her empty hand and gave it a squeeze. "We're going to be fine."

She nodded, "They're not if they don't drive away." She said in a quiet voice.

He grinned and kissed her hand before releasing it. Reaching over, he brought up his dial pad on his phone and hit six, so it would call Zain.

"Jesse?" He answered on the first ring.

"Is that tracking app up and running now?"

"Yeah, I got everyone's numbers loaded into it yesterday."

"Start tracking mine." He slowed so he didn't go right past the turn-off.

"Shit. You in trouble?" He could hear Zain running.

"We have a tail and in about a minute I'll know for sure."

"Okay, it's loading now. Shit, you're in the middle of nowhere."

"Yeah. I took a different route, but it still lands on the main road to head to Ed's." He saw the faded road sign ahead. "I'm about to drive up into a dead end, then we're going to run into the bush and hide."

"Shit."

Jesse turned and then watched in his mirror.

Evanna shifted in her seat to look out the window. "They're going slower."

When the lights hit the van, Jesse stepped on the gas. "Zain, send help. Evanna grab my phone and our packs."

"Yeah." She turned in the seat to get them.

"I'm calling Devin, he's at Blair's with the chopper."

"Okay, hang up now."

"Run like the wind," Zain told him.

"Get the phone and put it in my pack."

Evanna hurried to do what he said.

"When I stop, get out and run straight ahead. The lights will stay on for about forty-five seconds. We must be out of sight by then."

"Okay." She shifted closer to the door.

Jesse was pissed that his mate had to go through this. "Don't shift until we're in the cover of the trees." He undid his seatbelt.

"I'm ready."

He slowed slightly and then hit the brakes. Turning it off, he grabbed the keys and jumped out. He turned to check how close they were. "Shit." They were close.

Evanna was almost to the thicker growth. Jesse cursed again and went after her. If it had been just him, he would have waited until they were close enough and shot them. But he wasn't alone.

He jumped across the trickling stream and slid a few feet on the wet ground. He didn't hear them following but wasn't about to waste precious seconds turning around and looing.

Something stung his thigh as he ran. What the hell, there wasn't even any growth here. Reaching down, he felt something sticking out of his leg, he grabbed it. "Shit." He'd been shot with a dart.

Growling, he reached for his cat. He had to get to Evanna before this affected him. As he hit the trees, he stumbled.

"Jesse." Evanna was suddenly right before him.

"Tranq dart." He held it up and he stumbled again. She caught him and dragged him over to lean against a tree. "Stay down out of sight..." He was having trouble seeing. "Shoot anything," he gave his head a shake, "that moves."

"I will." She moved over so he could feel her right against him.

"If—" he tried to get his mouth to move.

"No ifs. I will protect us." She said right in his face.

Jesse tried to turn his head to see if they were well hidden, but everything was fading. He thought he heard gunfire and then everything went quiet.

Chapter Forty-Seven

His head was pounding as he tried to open his eyes. He was laying down and moving in a vehicle. Inhaling he tried to scent who was with him, but couldn't smell anything, his face felt numb. Jesse's whole skull felt like it was pulsing.

"Jesse," he felt a gentle touch on his face.

He forced his eyes to open and saw Evanna's worried eyes a few inches from his own. "Are you okay?" He tried to sit up and got his head a few inches from the floor before he had to hold his forehead before it imploded.

"I'm okay."

He leaned down and put his hand on her leg. "Who's driving?"

"I am."

He heard Devin answer.

"What?" He lifted his head again. "You shouldn't be here."

"Relax," Calum's voice came from the passenger seat. "I'm here too."

Jesse slumped back into Evanna's lap.

"The chopper is circling around looking for that car."

"They got away?"

"One of them didn't," Calum told him, "Your mate shot

him right in the heart."

He felt a moment of pride before the throbbing overrode it.

"We tossed him in the chopper and sent it to find the car."

"Your mate almost shot me." Devin didn't sound happy.

"I told you not to go charging into the bush until I called him." Calum sounded entertained.

"They fucking tranq'd me." Jesse blew out a breath.

"How's the head?" Calum must have turned in the seat because it sounded like he was yelling in his ear now. "That's one thing I'll never forget, the headache after the darts."

"I've never been followed before," Jesse moved his tongue around trying to create some saliva, "they knew I have Evanna with me."

"That's what we figure." Calum's voice was at half volume now.

"How the fuck did they know?" Jesse growled, "only my folks and—" he hissed out a breath, "we dropped Thera off at my clan before heading to the boat."

"Dad is talking to Deshon now, to see if there were any visitors around when you did. We're going to the campground, in the chopper tonight. Your mate's location will be a guessing game from now on until we take down Tomas."

Jesse opened his eyes and looked up at Evanna. This wasn't what he wanted for her. This meant they were going to have to keep moving around, stay off the grid, and never tell anyone where they were. He'd promised her a home, stability—safety. This was not even close to that.

"You have to stop getting shot, Jesse. It upsets us *a lot*." She enunciated slowly.

He studied her for a moment. She didn't look angry or freaked out. She looked steady and calm. He smiled at her slowly, "I'll do what I can, babe, but apparently I'm *really* easy to shoot."

He could hear Calum's chuckle as he closed his eyes and wished for the pain to stop. Someone was going to pay for his mate going through this. He inhaled slow, someone was definitely going to pay, just as soon as this pain eased.

"You ready to get back to it?" He heard Cal but wasn't going to try to lift his head to look at him.

"Yeah."

"No time for drug-induced naps, Jesse." Devin sounded amused. He was going to hear about this forever. That time he got tranq'd and his mate saved his ass. *Forever.*

Opening his eyes, he looked up at Evanna's looking down at him. The concern on her face made a lump form in his throat. Lifting his hand, he touched her cheek softly. He didn't know how he was going to do his job and keep her safe, not after what had just happened. He also knew there was no way he could leave her behind. She smirked like she was reading his mind and then leaned down and kissed his mouth softly.

"Stop thinking and rest." She held his look for a moment and then glanced over her shoulder and looked at the men in the seats. "They will watch over us and shoot anyone that comes close."

Jesse smiled and then closed his eyes again. He was so glad he had gone up that mountain and found her.

KEEP READING FOR AN EXCERPT OF

Faith

Animal Senses Series Book 6

By Jacqueline Paige

Chapter One

She *never* should have stopped back home. Gia cursed at herself, "what possessed you to do that?" She did not have a choice if she wanted more of her belongings. After spending the last week and a half with Amari, she realized this job, the new world that the Clan co-ordinator job showed her that was it for her, she wasn't turning back.

Smirking, she looked around the van. "I guess this is home now." Things had not gone well with her parents, at all. They hadn't told her not to come back, well, not outright, but it had been implied that she either straightened up and worked *with* them and their ideals of what the daughter of an Alpha was or not being part of the family.

Closing the tote, she assessed if she'd done everything Amari had suggested. All personal 'shit' in a small tote, with a lock, backpack with a change of clothes, hygiene items, and your run pack. All of the rest of the gear was secured under the two bench seats that ran along the sides of the van. Shutting the door, she turned around and looked down the road. Freedom. This was new and something she'd wanted for most of her twenty-four years of life.

Riding with Amari Hughes had both been educational and enlightening. She was also the daughter of an Alpha, they'd connected on so many levels, and Gia was still shocked by it. Her entire life she'd thought she was alone and it was just her that wasn't all gaga with being part of the Alpha family, Amari set that straight right off.

"Okay," she patted the side of the van and then went and got in the driver's seat. "I'm going to nail this first assignment and show them all that this is what I am meant to do." Pulling out of the parking lot, she tapped the GPS to double-check her own route. She had a day of driving ahead of her before she reached this 'safe house' many of them were going to be at. The details of what they were all doing were sketchy, but according to Amari that was for her own safety. Gia didn't care about the details right now. She was just happy to be on the road and driving in the opposite direction of her family.

Her phone lit up and started playing circus music. Her favorite of her four brothers. She grinned and answered the phone. "Hey, bro."

"Sister, my heart." Walker chuckled.

She glanced at the time on the radio's clock. "I expected you to call a few hours ago."

"I had to get out of the house before I could call, you know that." She heard a door close and knew he was probably hiding in his office at the clan's community building. "I can't believe you did that."

"You heard?"

Walker snorted, "the whole clan probably heard."

She blew out a breath, "I just couldn't…"

"I know, I know. I'm not saying you were wrong, just— you've got balls, Gia, to go toe to toe with Dad like that."

Gia searched inside to see if she felt bad for yelling at their father, when she couldn't find a trace of remorse, she shrugged. "I have no purpose there. None. Why can't he see that?"

"I know, babes, Mom does too, but she'd never speak out against him, you know that." There was a quiet pause, "you will come back sometimes though, right?"

"I don't know, Walker, I don't know right now. The Co-ord team doesn't get a lot of downtime lately…"

"Which is fucking amazing if you ask me, that the Alliance is finally closing in on that Tomas dick and getting our kind out of there."

Gia nodded, "and I get to be a part of it. I have purpose and I am going to nail this job and make Dad see."

"Well, don't hold your breath there. Shit, I better go, Vance and Nash are coming this way and they have that look."

"What look?"

"Oh, the one that says, what-the-hell-did-our-sister-do-this-time, look."

She grinned, "good luck with that. Tell them I'm on my way to meet a team on the other side of the border."

"Shh, no discussing things over open lines, Dad drilled that into all of us before you made him go red in the face."

"I know. Love you bro."

"Be careful, babes."

The line clicked and then was silent. She blew out a breath, feeling bad that Walker was going to have to go face to face with two of their brothers. Brothers. She had more than enough of those. Gia was the youngest and only female of five children. Worse than that, she was a surprise and born later than the 'planned' Alpha family. She always figured it couldn't have been too much of a surprise, as shifters knew when they could or couldn't conceive. It made her feel better most times, that her mother had wanted her. It also proved her father was clueless about some things. So her birth was a win-win. She felt like a heel though, that she couldn't be the perfect only daughter to an Alpha wife.

Picturing Walker and his wordiness all up in Nash and Vance's faces made her grin. Nash was the oldest sibling and very much fit the Alpha expectations of the son to take over, Vance was the third son and almost a carbon copy of him. They both had perfect little petite, complacent mates, and she was sure would soon have perfectly behaved Alpha family children. "You've got this, bro." Walker was the only brother she got along with, the only one that silently backed her up. He would never say so in front of their father, but they'd spent many hours hidden somewhere talking about everything. His support, regardless of whether it was masked most of the time, meant everything to her.

Gia pictured her second oldest brother's reaction if he'd been at the house. Nox wouldn't have quietly stood on the sidelines. He never did. He wasn't training for Alpha leadership, but he was a big *macho man* on the incursion team. Gia had every confidence that he was good at his job, he was great with hand to hand and weapons, it was his personality that she found so flawed she would leave the room anytime he visited. She didn't know the first thing about what he did. She imagined his whole team was comprised of large, opinionated he-man types though.

Life with four older brothers was not something she would wish on anyone. Your every waking moment, every decision, and every step you took was overridden by their opinion of what they thought you *should* be doing.

Her shoulders tensed, just thinking about her brothers did that to her. Except for Walker, she really did adore him. If it hadn't been for him setting her up for secret self-defense training, she would have died a slow and boring death as she grinned and bowed her head as the Alpha's 'showpiece' daughter. Of course, she could never tell anyone else in her family he'd done that, or he'd be an outcast too. She'd excelled at the training and kept going with as much as she could come up with excuses as to what she told others she was doing.

Her phone lit up with a text message, she tapped it to read. It was from her brother Nox, *Keep your head on a swivel.*

She looked back at the road, what did that even mean? With her teeth clenched in a huge fake smile, she tapped it and sent him back a thumb's up emoji.

"Head on a swivel." She snorted, "what am I, an owl?" Picking up her worn baseball cap off the dash, she jammed it on her head. If she'd been born a male, none of this would have been a problem. Turning up the radio, she settled back and focused on the road.

~

Gia was impressed with how far she'd gotten so far. Traffic had been good, but then again, she was doing what Amari suggested and always taking the less obvious route. Amari had told her in confidence what was going on inside the Alliance and Gia had been shocked by it. What kind of shifter would rat out their own kind to someone like Aiden Tomas or any of his associates? It had cemented things in her mind, she was going to do this job and help as many as she could.

Her phone lit up and she was startled to see it was Jesse, the leader of the co-ord team. Muting the music, she hit speaker on the phone. "Jesse, hi."

"Gia, how are you doing?"

"I'm making good time. I crossed the," she stopped, not sure what she should or shouldn't say over the phone.

"All the team phones are secure." He said quietly.

"Okay, uh, I crossed the border about twenty minutes ago. The location Amari said she used."

"Good. Several of ours work at that location."

She pushed her hat up, a little surprised by that. She was learning so much about the Alliance, things she could never have dreamed.

"Listen, I wanted to give you a heads up, your father called the Alliance."

Gia's heart stuttered. Was this where he told her she was off the team and being sent back home? "Oh."

"Too bad the king was busy, and the call was sent to his son, Devin."

She watched the road, afraid to look at the phone. "I'm sorry if my dad…"

"Devin told him that you were an integral part of the co-ord team." He sounded like he was grinning.

"Oh." She didn't know what else to say.

"What was he going to do, argue with the prince?"

The prince had stood up for her with her father for her to

stay on the team? "I don't know what to say."

"Hey, you're now one of us and the king is behind my decision to have you on the team, so Alpha or not, your father is just going to have to accept that."

"Thank you. Uh, I don't even know if I'm allowed to go home again."

"You're going to be on the road a lot for the next while, so we'll deal with that later, okay?"

She nodded, feeling weepy and grateful. "Yes."

"The reason I called is, a decision was just made to change things up a bit, after some recent events, it's for everyone's safety."

She sat straighter, "Okay."

"From now on when you're transporting or heading into unknown clan territory a member of the incursion team will be traveling with you."

"Oh." Her heart felt like it was running out of steam as it slowed in her chest. "Um, do we get to pick or…"

"It was going to be randomly assigned by who is closest and if any ops are running, why?"

She cleared her throat. "My brother, Nox, is part of that team."

Jesse sounded like he laughed, "you'd prefer not to have him ride with you?"

"If at all possible, yes." She said quietly, afraid to breathe.

"Okay, I'll tell Zain of your wishes." This time he did chuckle.

"Thank you." The breath she hadn't realized she was holding whooshed out of her lungs.

"When you're closer to Chicago, shoot Zain a text and he'll give you the exact location. We're not sending anything out in advance from now on."

"Okay, I can do that."

"And Gia?"

"Yes?"

"Welcome to the team. I'll see you when you reach the safe house."

She smiled. "Thank you, Jesse."

Gia swatted at the tear rolling down her cheek. Now was not the time to turn all 'sappy female'. Sucking in a deep breath, she blew it out. She had the prince and the King of the Alliance backing her up, that kind of support she could get used to.

About Jacqueline Paige

I am a multi-published author of 'all things paranormal'. My book list proves this is my niche with my stories of witches, ghosts, psychics, shifters, and more now on the shelves. My current genres are paranormal romance, paranormal fantasy, and paranormal romantic suspense.
My books are available in many formats around the globe, including book/reading apps. Since adding them during the pandemic, my books have had over a million reads and my 'to be written' list is growing longer each day. I can't write fast enough.

I began my writing career in 2006 (as a joke) and my first book was published in 2009. I haven't stopped since then. I am an avid reader and will read 'anything with words', whether it's a novel, article, or even every sign I pass.

I live in Ontario, Canada in a small town that's part of the popular Georgian Triangle area. Even though I can see the mountains, I do not ski.

When I'm not in one of my writing worlds, I spend time with my grand-monsters.   I have nine of them (so far) and I look forward to corrupting them in the years to come.
Jacqueline also writes under the pseudonym of J. Risk

Jacqueline loves to hear from her readers, you can find her at

http://jacquelinepaige.com/

www.ingramcontent.com/pod-product-compliance
Lightning Source LLC
Chambersburg PA
CBHW032146050726
47591CB00001B/105